A Heron Books Collection

CREATURES OF CIRCUMSTANCE

W. SOMERSET MAUGHAM

CREATURES OF CIRCUMSTANCE

with Original Illustrations by
Pauline Ellison

HERON BOOKS, LONDON

Published by arrangement with
William Heinemann Ltd., London

CONTENTS

The Author Excuses Himself

I OWE my readers an apology for the publication of this volume. At the beginning of the war I brought out a collection of short stories which I called *The Mixture As Before* and for which I wrote a short preface. I was occupied then with work that took all my time and so asked my friend Edward Marsh if he would correct the proofs. He wrote and told me that he was sorry to see by my preface that I had decided to write no more stories. I did not know what he meant, but was too busy to inquire. I saw no reviews and a copy of the book only when I returned to England some months later. Then I found out. I had written: "I shall not write many more stories," and either the typist or the type-setter, thinking perhaps that I had written quite enough stories, had left out an *m,* so that the line ran: "I shall not write any more stories." I have looked at my manuscript and I had in fact, as I intended, written *many.*

I had several stories written for which I could not find a place in *The Mixture As Before* and several in mind, and it was my plan even then in due course to publish a further volume. So my readers must not think that I wilfully misled them. I dare not even now promise them that I shall write no more; no writer can be sure that an idea will not one day occur to him that takes his fancy so that he is in the end driven to write it.

Some of these stories were written long ago, but I have left them as they were, for I did not think I could make them more readable by bringing them up to date; nor have I thought it necessary in one story, *Winter Cruise,* to change the nationality of various characters that take part in it to avoid affronting those who are persuaded that all the nationals of a country with which we have been at war are equally hateful; one story was written during the war and others since its close. They have all been published in magazines.

I know that in admitting this I lay myself open to critical depreciation, for to describe a story as a magazine story is to dismiss it with contumely. But when the critics do this they show less acumen than may reasonably be expected of them. Nor do they show much knowledge of literary history. For ever since magazines became a popular form of publication authors have found them a useful medium to put their work before readers. All the greatest short story writers have published their stories in magazines, Balzac, Flaubert and Maupassant; Chekov, Henry James, Rudyard Kipling. I do not think it is rash to say that the only short stories that have not been published in a magazine are the stories that no editor would accept. So to damn a story because it is a magazine story is absurd. The magazines doubtless publish a great many bad stories, but then more bad stories are written than good ones, and an editor, even of a magazine with literary pretensions, is often obliged to print a story of which he doesn't think highly because he can get nothing better. Some editors of popular magazines think their readers demand a certain type of story and will take nothing else; and they manage to find writers who can turn out the sort of thing they want and often make a very good job of it. This is the machine-made article that has given the magazine story a bad name. But after all no one is obliged to read it. It gives satisfaction to many people since it allows them for a brief period to experience in fancy the romance and adventure which in the monotony of their lives they crave for.

But if I may judge from the reviews I have read of the volumes of short stories that are frequently published, where the critics to my mind err is when they dismiss stories as magazine stories because they are well constructed, dramatic and have a surprise ending. There is nothing to be condemned in a surprise ending if it is the natural end of a story. On the contrary it is an excellence. It is only bad when, as in some of O. Henry's stories, it is dragged in without reason to give the reader a kick. Nor is a story any the worse for being neatly built with a beginning, a middle and an end. All good story writers have done their best to achieve this. It is the fashion of today for writers, under the influence of an inadequate acquaintance with Chekov, to write stories that begin anywhere and end inconclusively. They think it enough if they have described a mood, or given an impression, or drawn a character. That is all very well, but it is not a story, and I do not think it satisfies the reader. He does not like to be left wondering. He wants to have his questions answered. There is also today a fear of incident. The result is a spate of drab stories in which nothing happens. I think Chekov is perhaps responsible for this too; on one occasion he wrote: "People do not go to the North Pole and fall off icebergs; they go to offices, quarrel with their wives and eat cabbage soup." But people *do* go to the North Pole, and if they don't fall off icebergs they undergo experiences as perilous; and there is no reason in the world why the writer shouldn't write as good stories about them as about people who eat cabbage soup. But obviously it is not enough that they should go to offices, quarrel with their wives and eat cabbage soup. Chekov certainly never thought it was. In order to make a story at all they must steal the petty cash at the office, murder or leave their wives, and when they eat their cabbage soup it must be with emotion or significance. Cabbage soup then becomes a symbol of the satisfaction of a domestic life or of the anguish of a frustrated one. To eat it may thus be as catastrophic as falling off an iceberg. But it is just as unusual. The simple fact is that Chekov believed what writers, being human, are very apt to believe, namely that what he was best able to do was the best thing to do.

I read some time ago an article on how to write a short story. Certain points the author made were useful, but to

3

my mind the central thesis was wrong. She stated that the "focal point" of a short story should be the building of character and that the incidents should be invented solely to "liven" personality. Oddly enough she remarked earlier in her article that the parables are the best short stories that have ever been written. I think it would be difficult to describe the characters of the Prodigal Son and his brother or of the Good Samaritan and the Man who fell among thieves. They are in fact purely conventional types and we have to guess what sort of people they were, for we are only told about them the essential facts necessary for the pointing of the moral. And that is about all the short story writer can do. He has not room to describe and develop a character; he can only give the salient traits that bring the character to life and so make the story he has to tell plausible. Since the beginning of history men have gathered round the camp fire or in a group in the market place to listen to the telling of stories. The desire to listen to them appears to be as deeply rooted in the human animal as the sense of property. I have never pretended to be anything but a story teller. It has amused me to tell stories and I have told a great many. It is a misfortune for me that the telling of a story just for the sake of the story is not an activity that is in favour with the intelligentsia. I endeavour to bear my misfortunes with fortitude.

THE
COLONEL'S
LADY

ALL this happened two or three years before the outbreak of the war.

The Peregrines were having breakfast. Though they were alone and the table was long they sat at opposite ends of it. From the walls George Peregrine's ancestors, painted by the fashionable painters of the day, looked down upon them. The butler brought in the morning post. There were several letters for the colonel, business letters, *The Times* and a small parcel for his wife Evie. He looked at his letters and then, opening *The Times,* began to read it. They finished breakfast and rose from the table. He noticed that his wife hadn't opened the parcel.

"What's that?" he asked.

"Only some books."

"Shall I open it for you?"

"If you like."

He hated to cut string and so with some difficulty untied the knots.

"But they're all the same," he said when he had unwrapped the parcel. "What on earth d'you want six copies of the same book for?" He opened one of them. "Poetry." Then he looked at the title page. *When Pyramids Decay,* he read, by E. K. Hamilton. Eva Katherine Hamilton: that was his wife's maiden name. He looked at her with smiling surprise. "Have you written a book, Evie? You are a slyboots."

"I didn't think it would interest you very much. Would you like a copy?"

"Well, you know poetry isn't much in my line, but—yes, I'd like a copy; I'll read it. I'll take it along to my study. I've got a lot to do this morning."

5

He gathered up *The Times,* his letters and the book, and went out. His study was a large and comfortable room, with a big desk, leather arm-chairs and what he called "trophies of the chase" on the walls. On the bookshelves were works of reference, books on farming, gardening, fishing and shooting, and books on the last war, in which he had won an M.C. and a D.S.O. For before his marriage he had been in the Welsh Guards. At the end of the war he retired and settled down to the life of a country gentleman in the spacious house, some twenty miles from Sheffield, which one of his forebears had built in the reign of George III. George Peregrine had an estate of some fifteen hundred acres which he managed with ability; he was a Justice of the Peace and performed his duties conscientiously. During the season he rode to hounds two days a week. He was a good shot, a golfer, and though now a little over fifty could still play a hard game of tennis. He could describe himself with propriety as an all-round sportsman.

He had been putting on weight lately, but was still a fine figure of a man; tall, with grey curly hair, only just beginning to grow thin on the crown, frank blue eyes, good features and a high colour. He was a public-spirited man, chairman of any number of local organisations and, as became his class and station, a loyal member of the Conservative Party. He looked upon it as his duty to see to the welfare of the people on his estate and it was a satisfaction to him to know that Evie could be trusted to tend the sick and succour the poor. He had built a cottage hospital on the outskirts of the village and paid the wages of a nurse out of his own pocket. All he asked of the recipients of his bounty was that at elections, county or general, they should vote for his candidate. He was a friendly man, affable to his inferiors, considerate with his tenants and popular with the neighbouring gentry. He would have been pleased and at the same time slightly embarrassed if someone had told him he was a jolly good fellow. That was what he wanted to be. He desired no higher praise.

It was hard luck that he had no children. He would have

6

been an excellent father, kindly but strict, and would have brought up his sons as gentlemen's sons should be brought up, sent them to Eton, you know, taught them to fish, shoot and ride. As it was, his heir was a nephew, son of his brother killed in a motor accident, not a bad boy, but not a chip off the old block, no, sir, far from it; and would you believe it, his fool of a mother was sending him to a co-educational school. Evie had been a sad disappointment to him. Of course she was a lady, and she had a bit of money of her own; she managed the house uncommonly well and she was a good hostess. The village people adored her. She had been a pretty little thing when he married her, with a creamy skin, light brown hair and a trim figure, healthy too and not a bad tennis player; he couldn't understand why she'd had no children; of course she was faded now, she must be getting on for five and forty; her skin was drab, her hair had lost its sheen and she was as thin as a rail. She was always neat and suitably dressed, but she didn't seem to bother how she looked, she wore no make-up and didn't even use lipstick; sometimes at night when she dolled herself up for a party you could tell that once she'd been quite attractive, but ordinarily she was— well, the sort of woman you simply didn't notice. A nice woman, of course, a good wife, and it wasn't her fault if she was barren, but it was tough on a fellow who wanted an heir of his own loins; she hadn't any vitality, that's what was the matter with her. He supposed he'd been in love with her when he asked her to marry him, at least sufficiently in love for a man who wanted to marry and settle down, but with time he discovered that they had nothing much in common. She didn't care about hunting, and fishing bored her. Naturally they'd drifted apart. He had to do her the justice to admit that she'd never bothered him. There'd been no scenes. They had no quarrels. She seemed to take it for granted that he should go his own way. When he went up to London now and then she never wanted to come with him. He had a girl there, well, she wasn't exactly a girl, she was thirty-five if she was a day, but she was blonde and luscious and he only had to wire ahead of time and they'd dine, do a show and spend the night together. Well, a man, a healthy normal man had to have some fun in his life. The thought crossed his mind that if Evie hadn't been such a good woman she'd have been a better wife; but it was not the sort of thought that he welcomed and he put it away from him.

George Peregrine finished his *Times* and being a considerate fellow rang the bell and told the butler to take it to Evie. Then he looked at his watch. It was half-past ten and at eleven he had an appointment with one of his tenants. He had half an hour to spare.

"I'd better have a look at Evie's book," he said to himself.

He took it up with a smile. Evie had a lot of highbrow books in her sitting-room, not the sort of books that interested him, but if they amused her he had no objection to her reading them. He noticed that the volume he now held in his hand contained no more than ninety pages. That was all to the good. He shared Edgar Allan Poe's opinion that poems should be short. But as he turned the pages he noticed that several of Evie's had long lines of irregular length and didn't rhyme. He didn't like that. At his first school, when he was a little boy, he remembered learning a poem that began: *The boy stood on the burning deck,* and later, at Eton, one that started: *Ruin seize thee, ruthless king;* and then there was Henry V; they'd had to take that, one half. He stared at Evie's pages with consternation.

"That's not what I call poetry," he said.

Fortunately it wasn't all like that. Interspersed with the pieces that looked so odd, lines of three or four words and then a line of ten or fifteen, there were little poems, quite short, that rhymed, thank God, with the lines all the same length. Several of the pages were just headed with the word *Sonnet,* and out of curiosity he counted the lines; there were fourteen of them. He read them. They seemed all right, but he didn't quite know what they were all about. He repeated to himself: *Ruin seize thee, ruthless king.*

"Poor Evie," he sighed.

At that moment the farmer he was expecting was ushered into the study, and putting the book down he made him welcome. They embarked on their business.

"I read your book, Evie," he said as they sat down to lunch. "Jolly good. Did it cost you a packet to have it printed?"

"No, I was lucky. I sent it to a publisher and he took it."

"Not much money in poetry, my dear," he said in his good-natured, hearty way.

"No, I don't suppose there is. What did Bannock want to see you about this morning?"

Bannock was the tenant who had interrupted his reading of Evie's poems.

"He's asked me to advance the money for a pedigree bull he wants to buy. He's a good man and I've half a mind to do it."

George Peregrine saw that Evie didn't want to talk about her book and he was not sorry to change the subject. He was glad she had used her maiden name on the title page; he didn't suppose anyone would ever hear about the book, but he was proud of his own unusual name and he wouldn't have liked it if some damned penny-a-liner had made fun of Evie's effort in one of the papers.

During the few weeks that followed he thought it tactful not to ask Evie any questions about her venture into verse, and she never referred to it. It might have been a discreditable incident that they had silently agreed not to mention. But then a strange thing happened. He had to go to London on business and he took Daphne out to dinner. That was the name of the girl with whom he was in the habit of passing a few agreeable hours whenever he went to town.

"Oh, George," she said, "is that your wife who's written a book they're all talking about?"

9

"What on earth d'you mean?"

"Well, there's a fellow I know who's a critic. He took me out to dinner the other night and he had a book with him. 'Got anything for me to read?' I said. 'What's that?' 'Oh, I don't think that's your cup of tea,' he said. 'It's poetry. I've just been reviewing it.' 'No poetry for me,' I said. 'It's about the hottest stuff I ever read,' he said. 'Selling like hot cakes. And it's damned good.' "

"Who's the book by?" asked George.

"A woman called Hamilton. My friend told me that wasn't her real name. He said her real name was Peregrine. 'Funny,' I said, 'I know a fellow called Peregrine.' 'Colonel in the army,' he said. 'Lives near Sheffield.' "

"I'd just as soon you didn't talk about me to your friends," said George with a frown of vexation.

"Keep your shirt on, dearie. Who d'you take me for? I just said: 'It's not the same one.' " Daphne giggled. "My friend said: 'They say he's a regular Colonel Blimp.' "

George had a keen sense of humour.

"You could tell them better than that," he laughed. "If my wife had written a book I'd be the first to know about it, wouldn't I?"

"I suppose you would."

Anyhow the matter didn't interest her and when the colonel began to talk of other things she forgot about it. He put it out of his mind too. There was nothing to it, he decided, and that silly fool of a critic had just been pulling Daphne's leg. He was amused at the thought of her tackling that book because she had been told it was hot stuff and then finding it just a lot of bosh cut up into unequal lines.

He was a member of several clubs and next day he thought he'd lunch at one in St. James's Street. He was catching a train back to Sheffield early in the afternoon. He was sitting in a comfortable arm-chair having a glass of sherry before going into the dining-room when an old friend came up to him.

10

THE COLONEL'S LADY

"Well, old boy, how's life?" he said. "How d'you like being the husband of a celebrity?"

George Peregrine looked at his friend. He thought he saw an amused twinkle in his eyes.

"I don't know what you're talking about," he answered.

"Come off it, George. Everyone knows E. K. Hamilton is your wife. Not often a book of verse has a success like that. Look here, Henry Dashwood is lunching with me. He'd like to meet you."

"Who the devil is Henry Dashwood and why should he want to meet me?"

"Oh, my dear fellow, what do you do with yourself all the time in the country? Henry's about the best critic we've got. He wrote a wonderful review of Evie's book. D'you mean to say she didn't show it you?"

Before George could answer his friend had called a man over. A tall, thin man, with a high forehead, a beard, a long nose and a stoop, just the sort of man whom George was prepared to dislike at first sight. Introductions were effected. Henry Dashwood sat down.

"Is Mrs. Peregrine in London by any chance? I should very much like to meet her," he said.

"No, my wife doesn't like London. She prefers the country," said George stiffly.

"She wrote me a very nice letter about my review. I was pleased. You know, we critics get more kicks than halfpence. I was simply bowled over by her book. It's so fresh and original, very modern without being obscure. She seems to be as much at her ease in free verse as in the classical metres." Then because he was a critic he thought he should criticise. "Sometimes her ear is a trifle at fault, but you can say the same of Emily Dickinson. There are several of those short lyrics of hers that might have been written by Landor."

All this was gibberish to George Peregrine. The man was nothing but a disgusting highbrow. But the colonel had good manners and he answered with proper civility: Henry

11

Dashwood went on as though he hadn't spoken.

"But what makes the book so outstanding is the passion that throbs in every line. So many of these young poets are so anæmic, cold, bloodless, dully intellectual, but here you have real naked, earthy passion; of course deep, sincere emotion like that is tragic—ah, my dear Colonel, how right Heine was when he said that the poet makes little songs out of his great sorrows. You know, now and then, as I read and re-read those heart-rending pages I thought of Sappho."

This was too much for George Peregrine and he got up.

"Well, it's jolly nice of you to say such nice things about my wife's little book. I'm sure she'll be delighted. But I must bolt, I've got to catch a train and I want to get a bite of lunch."

"Damned fool," he said irritably to himself as he walked upstairs to the dining-room.

He got home in time for dinner and after Evie had gone to bed he went into his study and looked for her book. He thought he'd just glance through it again to see for himself what they were making such a fuss about, but he couldn't find it. Evie must have taken it away.

"Silly," he muttered.

He'd told her he thought it jolly good. What more could a fellow be expected to say? Well, it didn't matter. He lit his pipe and read the *Field* till he felt sleepy. But a week or so later it happened that he had to go into Sheffield for the day. He lunched there at his club. He had nearly finished when the Duke of Haverel came in. This was the great local magnate and of course the colonel knew him, but only to say how d'you do to; and he was surprised when the Duke stopped at his table.

"We're so sorry your wife couldn't come to us for the week-end," he said, with a sort of shy cordiality. "We're expecting rather a nice lot of people."

George was taken aback. He guessed that the Haverels had

asked him and Evie over for the week-end and Evie, without saying a word to him about it, had refused. He had the presence of mind to say he was sorry too.

"Better luck next time," said the Duke pleasantly and moved on.

Colonel Peregrine was very angry and when he got home he said to his wife:

"Look here, what's this about our being asked over to Haverel? Why on earth did you say we couldn't go? We've never been asked before and it's the best shooting in the county."

"I didn't think of that. I thought it would only bore you."

"Damn it all, you might at least have asked me if I wanted to go."

"I'm sorry."

He looked at her closely. There was something in her expression that he didn't quite understand. He frowned.

"I suppose *I* was asked?" he barked.

Evie flushed a little.

"Well, in point of fact you weren't."

"I call it damned rude of them to ask you without asking me."

"I suppose they thought it wasn't your sort of party. The Duchess is rather fond of writers and people like that, you know. She's having Henry Dashwood, the critic, and for some reason he wants to meet me."

"It was damned nice of you to refuse, Evie."

"It's the least I could do," she smiled. She hesitated a moment. "George, my publishers want to give a little dinner party for me one day towards the end of the month and of course they want you to come too."

"Oh, I don't think that's quite my mark. I'll come up to London with you if you like. I'll find someone to dine with."

Daphne.

"I expect it'll be very dull, but they're making rather a point of it. And the day after, the American publisher who's taken

13

CREATURES OF CIRCUMSTANCE

my book is giving a cocktail party at Claridge's. I'd like you to come to that if you wouldn't mind."

"Sounds like a crashing bore, but if you really want me to come I'll come."

"It would be sweet of you."

George Peregrine was dazed by the cocktail party. There were a lot of people. Some of them didn't look so bad, a few of the women were decently turned out, but the men seemed to him pretty awful. He was introduced to everyone as Colonel Peregrine, E. K. Hamilton's husband, you know. The men didn't seem to have anything to say to him, but the women gushed.

"You *must* be proud of your wife. Isn't it *wonderful?* You know, I read it right through at a sitting, I simply couldn't put it down, and when I'd finished, I started again at the beginning and read it right through a second time. I was simply *thrilled."*

The English publisher said to him:

"We've not had a success like this with a book of verse for twenty years. I've never seen such reviews."

The American publisher said to him:

"It's swell. It'll be a smash hit in America. You wait and see."

The American publisher had sent Evie a great spray of orchids. Damned ridiculous, thought George. As they came in, people were taken up to Evie, and it was evident that they said flattering things to her, which she took with a pleasant smile and a word of two of thanks. She was a trifle flushed with the excitement, but seemed quite at ease. Though he thought the whole thing a lot of stuff and nonsense George noted with approval that his wife was carrying it off in just the right way.

"Well, there's one thing," he said to himself, "you can see she's a lady and that's a damned sight more than you can say of anyone else here."

He drank a good many cocktails. But there was one thing

that bothered him. He had a notion that some of the people he was introduced to looked at him in rather a funny sort of way, he couldn't quite make out what it meant, and once when he strolled by two women who were sitting together on a sofa he had the impression that they were talking about him and after he passed he was almost certain they tittered. He was very glad when the party came to an end.

In the taxi on their way back to their hotel Evie said to him:

"You were wonderful, dear. You made quite a hit. The girls simply raved about you; they thought you so handsome."

"Girls," he said bitterly. "Old hags."

"Were you bored, dear?"

"Stiff."

She pressed his hand in a gesture of sympathy.

"I hope you won't mind if we wait and go down by the afternoon train. I've got some things to do in the morning."

"No, that's all right. Shopping?"

"I do want to buy one or two things, but I've got to go and be photographed. I hate the idea, but they think I ought to be. For America, you know."

He said nothing. But he thought. He thought it would be a shock to the American public when they saw the portrait of the homely, desiccated little woman who was his wife. He'd always been under the impression that they liked glamour in America.

He went on thinking, and next morning when Evie had gone out he went to his club and up to the library. There he looked up recent numbers of *The Times Literary Supplement*, *The New Statesman* and *The Spectator*. Presently he found reviews of Evie's book. He didn't read them very carefully, but enough to see that they were extremely favourable. Then he went to the bookseller's in Piccadilly where he occasionally bought books. He'd made up his mind that he had to read this damned thing of Evie's properly, but he didn't want to ask her what she'd done with the copy she'd given him. He'd buy one for himself. Before going in he looked in the window and the first thing he saw was a display of *When Pyramids Decay*. Damned silly title! He went in. A young man came forward and asked if he could help him.

"No, I'm just having a look round." It embarrassed him to ask for Evie's book and he thought he'd find it for himself and then take it to the salesman. But he couldn't see it anywhere and at last, finding the young man near him, he said in a carefully casual tone: "By the way, have you got a book called *When Pyramids Decay?*"

"The new edition came in this morning. I'll get a copy."

In a moment the young man returned with it. He was a short, rather stout young man, with a shock of untidy carroty hair and spectacles. George Peregrine, tall, upstanding, very military, towered over him.

"Is this a new edition then?" he asked.

"Yes, sir. The fifth. It might be a novel the way it's selling."

George Peregrine hesitated a moment.

"Why d'you suppose it's such a success? I've always been told no one reads poetry."

"Well, it's good, you know. I've read it meself." The young man, though obviously cultured, had a slight Cockney accent, and George quite instinctively adopted a patronising attitude. "It's the story they like. Sexy, you know, but tragic.

George frowned a little. He was coming to the conclusion that the young man was rather impertinent. No one had told him anything about there being a story in the damned book and he had not gathered that from reading the reviews. The young man went on:

"Of course it's only a flash in the pan, if you know what I mean. The way I look at it, she was sort of inspired like by a personal experience, like Housman was with *The Shropshire Lad*. She'll never write anything else."

"How much is the book?" said George coldly to stop his chatter. "You needn't wrap it up, I'll just slip it into my pocket."

16

THE COLONEL'S LADY

The November morning was raw and he was wearing a greatcoat.

At the station he bought the evening papers and magazines and he and Evie settled themselves comfortably in opposite corners of a first-class carriage and read. At five o'clock they went along to the restaurant car to have tea and chatted a little. They arrived. They drove home in the car which was waiting for them. They bathed, dressed for dinner, and after dinner Evie, saying she was tired out, went to bed. She kissed him, as was her habit, on the forehead. Then he went into the hall, took Evie's book out of his greatcoat pocket and going into the study began to read it. He didn't read verse very easily and though he read with attention, every word of it, the impression he received was far from clear. Then he began at the beginning again and read it a second time. He read with increasing malaise, but he was not a stupid man and when he had finished he had a distinct understanding of what it was all about. Part of the book was in free verse, part in conventional metres, but the story it related was coherent and plain to the meanest intelligence. It was the story of a passionate love affair between an older woman, married, and a young man. George Peregrine made out the steps of it as easily as if he had been doing a sum in simple addition.

Written in the first person, it began with the tremulous surprise of the woman, past her youth, when it dawned upon her that the young man was in love with her. She hesitated to believe it. She thought she must be deceiving herself. And she was terrified when on a sudden she discovered that she was passionately in love with him. She told herself it was absurd; with the disparity of age between them nothing but unhappiness could come to her if she yielded to her emotion. She tried to prevent him from speaking, but the day came when he told her that he loved her and forced her to tell him that she loved him too. He begged her to run away with him. She couldn't leave her husband, her home; and what life could they look forward to, she an ageing woman, he so young?

17

How could she expect his love to last? She begged him to have mercy on her. But his love was impetuous. He wanted her, he wanted her with all his heart, and at last trembling, afraid, desirous, she yielded to him. Then there was a period of ecstatic happiness. The world, the dull, humdrum world of every day, blazed with glory. Love songs flowed from her pen. The woman worshipped the young, virile body of her lover. George flushed darkly when she praised his broad chest and slim flanks, the beauty of his legs and the flatness of his belly.

Hot stuff, Daphne's friend had said. It was that all right. Disgusting.

There were sad little pieces in which she lamented the emptiness of her life when as must happen he left her, but they ended with a cry that all she had to suffer would be worth it for the bliss that for a while had been hers. She wrote of the long, tremulous nights they passed together and the languor that lulled them to sleep in one another's arms. She wrote of the rapture of brief stolen moments when, braving all danger, their passion overwhelmed them and they surrendered to its call.

She thought it would be an affair of a few weeks, but miraculously it lasted. One of the poems referred to three years having gone by without lessening the love that filled their hearts. It looked as though he continued to press her to go away with him, far away, to a hill town in Italy, a Greek island, a walled city in Tunisia, so that they could be together always, for in another of the poems she besought him to let things be as they were. Their happiness was precarious. Perhaps it was owing to the difficulties they had to encounter and the rarity of their meetings that their love had retained for so long its first enchanting ardour. Then on a sudden the young man died. How, when or where George could not discover. There followed a long, heartbroken cry of bitter grief, grief she could not indulge in, grief that had to be hidden. She had to be cheerful, give dinner-parties and go out to dinner, behave as she had always behaved, though the light had gone out of her life and she was bowed down with anguish. The last poem of all was a set of four short stanzas in which the writer, sadly resigned to her loss, thanked the dark powers that rule man's destiny that she had been privileged at least for a while to enjoy the greatest happiness that we poor human beings can ever hope to know.

It was three oclock in the morning when George Peregrine finally put the book down. It had seemed to him that he heard Evie's voice in every line, over and over again he came upon turns of phrase he had heard her use, there were details that were as familiar to him as to her; there was no doubt about it; it was her own story she had told, and it was as plain as anything could be that she had had a lover and her lover had died. It was not anger so much that he felt, nor horror or dismay, though he was dismayed and he was horrified, but amazement. It was as inconceivable that Evie should have had a love affair, and a wildly passionate one at that, as that the trout in a glass case over the chimney piece in his study, the finest he had ever caught, should suddenly wag its tail. He understood now the meaning of the amused look he had seen in the eyes of that man he had spoken to at the club, he understood why Daphne when she was talking about the book had seemed to be enjoying a private joke, and why those two women at the cocktail party had tittered when he strolled past them.

He broke out into a sweat. Then on a sudden he was seized with fury and he jumped up to go and awake Evie and ask her sternly for an explanation. But he stopped at the door. After all what proof had he? A book. He remembered that he'd told Evie he thought it jolly good. True, he hadn't read it, but he'd pretended he had. He would look a perfect fool if he had to admit that.

"I must watch my step," he muttered.

He made up his mind to wait for two or three days and think it all over. Then he'd decide what to do. He went to bed, but he couldn't sleep for a long time.

"Evie," he kept on saying to himself. "Evie, of all people."

They met at breakfast next morning as usual. Evie was as she always was, quiet, demure and self-possessed, a middle-aged woman who made no effort to look younger than she was, a woman who had nothing of what he still called It. He looked at her as he hadn't looked at her for years. She had her usual placid serenity. Her pale blue eyes were untroubled. There was no sign of guilt on her candid brow. She made the same little casual remarks she always made.

"It's nice to get back to the country again after those two hectic days in London. What are you going to do this morning?"

It was incomprehensible.

Three days later he went to see his solicitor. Henry Blane was an old friend of George's as well as his lawyer. He had a place not far from Peregrine's and for years they had shot over one another's preserves. For two days a week he was a country gentleman and for the other five a busy lawyer in Sheffield. He was a tall, robust fellow, with a boisterous manner and a jovial laugh, which suggested that he liked to be looked upon essentially as a sportsman and a good fellow and only incidentally as a lawyer. But he was shrewd and worldly-wise.

"Well, George, what's brought you here today?" he boomed as the colonel was shown into his office. "Have a good time in London? I'm taking my missus up for a few days next week. How's Evie?"

"It's about Evie I've come to see you," said Peregrine, giving him a suspicious look. "Have you read her book?"

His sensitivity had been sharpened during those last days of troubled thought and he was conscious of a faint change in the lawyer's expression. It was as though he were suddenly on his guard.

"Yes, I've read it. Great success, isn't it? Fancy Evie breaking out into poetry. Wonders will never cease."

George Peregrine was inclined to lose his temper.

"It's made me look a perfect damned fool."

20

"Oh, what nonsense, George! There's no harm in Evie's writing a book. You ought to be jolly proud of her."

"Don't talk such rot. It's her own story. You know it and everyone else knows it. I suppose I'm the only one who doesn't know who her lover was."

"There is such a thing as imagination, old boy. There's no reason to suppose the whole thing isn't just made up."

"Look here, Henry, we've known one another all our lives. We've had all sorts of good times together. Be honest with me. Can you look me in the face and tell me you believe it's a made-up story?"

Harry Blane moved uneasily in his chair. He was disturbed by the distress in old George's voice.

"You've got no right to ask me a question like that. Ask Evie."

"I daren't," George answered after an anguished pause. "I'm afraid she'd tell me the truth."

There was an uncomfortable silence.

"Who was the chap?"

Harry Blane looked at him straight in the eye.

"I don't know, and if I did, I wouldn't tell you."

"You swine. Don't you see what a position I'm in? Do you think it's very pleasant to be made absolutely ridiculous?"

The lawyer lit a cigarette and for some moments silently puffed it.

"I don't see what I can do for you," he said at last.

"You've got private detectives you employ, I suppose. I want you to put them on the job and let them find everything out."

"It's not very pretty to put detectives on one's wife, old boy; and besides, taking for granted for a moment that Evie had an affair, it was a good many years ago and I don't suppose it would be possible to find out a thing. They seem to have covered their tracks pretty carefully."

"I don't care. You put the detectives on. I want to know the truth."

"I won't, George. If you're determined to do that you'd better

21

consult someone else. And look here, even if you got evidence that Evie had been unfaithful to you what would you do with it? You'd look rather silly divorcing your wife because she'd committed adultery ten years ago."

"At all events I could have it out with her."

"You can do that now, but you know just as well as I do that if you do she'll leave you. D'you want her to do that?"

George gave him an unhappy look.

"I don't know. I always thought she'd been a damned good wife to me. She runs the house perfectly, we never have any servant trouble; she's done wonders with the garden and she's splendid with all the village people. But damn it, I have my self-respect to think of. How can I go on living with her when I know that she was grossly unfaithful to me?"

"Have you always been faithful to her?"

"More or less, you know. After all, we've been married for nearly twenty-four years and Evie was never much for bed."

The solicitor slightly raised his eyebrows, but George was too intent on what he was saying to notice.

"I don't deny that I've had a bit of fun now and then. A man wants it. Women are different."

"We only have men's word for that," said Harry Blane, with a faint smile.

"Evie's absolutely the last woman I'd have suspected of kicking over the traces. I mean, she's a very fastidious, reticent woman. What on earth made her write the damned book?"

"I suppose it was a very poignant experience and perhaps it was a relief to her to get it off her chest like that."

"Well, if she had to write it why the devil didn't she write it under an assumed name?"

"She used her maiden name. I suppose she thought that was enough, and it would have been if the book hadn't had this amazing boom."

George Peregrine and the lawyer were sitting opposite one another with a desk between them. George, his elbow on the desk, his cheek resting on his hand, frowned at his thought.

22

"It's so rotten not to know what sort of a chap he was. One can't even tell if he was by way of being a gentleman. I mean, for all I know he may have been a farm-hand or a clerk in a lawyer's office."

Harry Blane did not permit himself to smile and when he answered there was in his eyes a kindly, tolerant look.

"Knowing Evie so well I think the probabilities are that he was all right. Anyhow I'm sure he wasn't a clerk in my office."

"It's been such a shock to me," the colonel sighed. "I thought she was fond of me. She couldn't have written that book unless she hated me."

"Oh, I don't believe that. I don't think she's capable of hatred."

"You're not going to pretend that she loves me."

"No."

"Well, what does she feel for me?"

Harry Blane leaned back in his swivel chair and looked at George reflectively.

"Indifference, I should say."

The colonel gave a little shudder and reddened.

"After all, you're not in love with her, are you?"

George Peregrine did not answer directly.

"It's been a great blow to me not to have any children, but I've never let her see that I think she's let me down. I've always been kind to her. Within reasonable limits I've tried to do my duty by her."

The lawyer passed a large hand over his mouth to conceal the smile that trembled on his lips.

"It's been such an awful shock to me," Peregrine went on. "Damn it all, even ten years ago Evie was no chicken and God knows, she wasn't much to look at. It's so ugly." He sighed deeply. "What would *you* do in my place?"

"Nothing."

George Peregrine drew himself bolt upright in his chair and he looked at Harry with his stern set face that he must have worn when he inspected his regiment.

"I can't overlook a thing like this. I've been made a laughing-stock. I can never hold up my head again."

"Nonsense," said the lawyer sharply, and then in a pleasant, kindly manner. "Listen, old boy: the man's dead; it all happened a long while back. Forget it. Talk to people about Evie's book, rave about it, tell 'em how proud you are of her. Behave as though you had so much confidence in her, you *knew* she could never have been unfaithful to you. The world moves so quickly and people's memories are so short. They'll forget."

"I shan't forget."

"You're both middle-aged people. She probably does a great deal more for you than you think and you'd be awfully lonely without her. I don't think it matters if you don't forget. It'll be all to the good if you can get it into that thick head of yours that there's a lot more in Evie than you ever had the gumption to see."

"Damn it all, you talk as if *I* were to blame."

"No, I don't think you were to blame, but I'm not so sure that Evie was either. I don't suppose she wanted to fall in love with this boy. D'you remember those verses right at the end? The impression they gave me was that though she was shattered by his death, in a strange sort of way she welcomed it. All through she'd been aware of the fragility of the tie that bound them. He died in the full flush of his first love and had never known that love so seldom endures; he'd only known its bliss and beauty. In her own bitter grief she found solace in the thought that he'd been spared all sorrow."

"All that's a bit above my head, old boy. I see more or less what you mean."

George Peregrine stared unhappily at the inkstand on the desk. He was silent and the lawyer looked at him with curious, yet sympathetic, eyes.

"Do you realise what courage she must have had never by a sign to show how dreadfully unhappy she was?" he said gently.

Colonel Peregrine sighed.

24

"I'm broken. I suppose you're right; it's no good crying over spilt milk and it would only make things worse if I made a fuss."

"Well?"

George Peregrine gave a pitiful little smile.

"I'll take your advice. I'll do nothing. Let them think me a damned fool and to hell with them. The truth is, I don't know what I'd do without Evie. But I'll tell you what, there's one thing I shall never understand till my dying day: What in the name of heaven did the fellow ever see in her?"

FLOTSAM AND
JETSAM

NORMAN GRANGE was a rubber-planter. He was up before day-
break to take the roll-call of his labour and then walked over
the estate to see that the tapping was properly done. This duty
performed, he came home, bathed and changed, and now with
his wife opposite him he was eating the substantial meal, half
breakfast and half luncheon, which in Borneo is called brunch.
He read as he ate. The dining-room was dingy. The worn
electro-plate, the shabby cruet, the chipped dishes betokened
poverty, but a poverty accepted with apathy. A few flowers
would have brightened the table, but there was apparently
no one to care how things looked. When Grange had finished
he belched, filled his pipe and lit it, rose from the table and
went out on to the veranda. He took no more notice of his wife
than if she had not been there. He lay down in a long rattan
chair and went on reading. Mrs. Grange reached over for a
tin of cigarettes and smoked while she sipped her tea. Suddenly
she looked out, for the house boy came up the steps and
accompanied by two men went up to her husband. One was a
Dyak and the other Chinese. Strangers seldom came and she
could not imagine what they wanted. She got up and went to
the door to listen. Though she had lived in Borneo for so
many years she knew no more Malay than was necessary to
get along with the boys, and she only vaguely understood
what was said. She gathered from her husband's tone that
something had happened to annoy him. He seemed to be
asking questions first of the Chink and then of the Dyak; it
looked as though they were pressing him to do something he
didn't want to do; at length, however, with a frown on his face
he raised himself from his chair and followed by the men
walked down the steps. Curious to see where he was going

she slipped out on to the veranda. He had taken the path that led down to the river. She shrugged her thin shoulders and went to her room. Presently she gave a violent start, for she heard her husband call her.

"Vesta."

She came out.

"Get a bed ready. There's a white man in a prahu at the landing-stage. He's damned ill."

"Who is he?"

"How the hell should I know? They're just bringing him up."

"We can't have anyone to stay here."

"Shut up and do as I tell you."

He left her on that and again went down to the river. Mrs. Grange called the boy and told him to put sheets on the bed in the spare room. Then she stood at the top of the steps and waited. In a little while she saw her husband coming back and behind him a huddle of Dyaks carrying a man on a mattress. She stood aside to let them pass and caught a glimpse of a white face.

"What shall I do?" she asked her husband.

"Get out and keep quiet."

"Polite, aren't you?"

The sick man was taken into the room, and in two or three minutes the Dyaks and Grange came out.

"I'm going to see about his kit. I'll have it brought up. His boy's looking after him and there's no cause for you to butt in!"

"What's the matter with him?"

"Malaria. His boatmen are afraid he's going to die and won't take him on. His name's Skelton."

"He isn't going to die, is he?"

"If he does we'll bury him."

But Skelton didn't die. He woke next morning to find himself in a room, in bed and under a mosquito-net. He couldn't think where he was. It was a cheap iron bed and the mattress

27

was hard, but to lie on it was a relief after the discomfort of the prahu. He could see nothing of the room but a chest of drawers, roughly made by a native carpenter, and a wooden chair. Opposite was a doorway, with a blind down, and this he guessed led on to a veranda.

"Kong," he called.

The blind was drawn aside and his boy came in. The Chinaman's face broke into a grin when he saw that his master was free from fever.

"You more better, Tuan. Velly glad."

"Where the devil am I?"

Kong explained.

"Luggage all right?" asked Skelton.

"Yes, him all right."

"What's the name of this fellow—the tuan whose house this is?"

"Mr. Norman Glange."

To confirm what he said he showed Skelton a little book in which the owner's name was written. It was Grange. Skelton noticed that the book was Bacon's *Essays*. It was curious to find it in a planter's house away up a river in Borneo.

"Tell him I'll be glad to see him."

"Tuan out. Him come presently."

"What about my having a wash? And by God, I want a shave."

He tried to get out of bed, but his head swam and with a bewildered cry he sank back. But Kong shaved and washed him, and changed the shorts and singlet in which he had been lying ever since he fell ill for a sarong and a baju. After that he was glad to lie still. But presently Kong came in and said that the tuan of the house was back. There was a knock on the door and a large stoutish man stepped in.

"I hear you're better," he said.

"Oh, much. It's terribly kind of you to have taken me in like this. It seems awful, planting myself on you."

28

Grange answered a trifle harshly.

"That's all right. You were pretty bad, you know. No wonder those Dyaks wanted to get rid of you."

"I don't want to impose myself on you longer than I need. If I could hire a launch here, or a prahu, I could get off this afternoon."

"There's no launch to hire. You'd better stay a bit. You must be as weak as a rat."

"I'm afraid I shall be a frightful bother."

"I don't see why. You've got your own boy and he'll look after you."

Grange had just come in from his round of the estate and wore dirty shorts, a khaki shirt open at the neck and an old, battered terai hat. He looked as shabby as a beachcomber. He took off his hat to wipe his sweating brow; he had close-cropped grey hair; his face was red, a broad, fleshy face, with a large mouth under a stubble of grey moustache, a short, pugnacious nose and small, mean eyes.

"I wonder if you could let me have something to read," said Skelton.

"What sort of thing?"

"I don't mind so long as it's lightish."

"I'm not much of a novel reader myself, but I'll send you in two or three books. My wife can provide you with novels. They'll be trash, because that's all she reads. But it may suit you."

With a nod he withdrew. Not a very likeable man. But he was obviously very poor, the room in which Skelton lay, something in Grange's appearance, indicated that; he was probably manager of an estate on a cut salary, and it was not unlikely that the expense of a guest and his servant was unwelcome. Living in that remote spot, and so seeing white men but seldom, it might be that he was ill at ease with strangers. Some people improve unbelievably on acquaintance. But his hard, shifty little eyes were disconcerting; they gave the lie to the red face and the massive frame which otherwise might have persuaded

29

you that this was a jolly sort of fellow with whom you could quickly make friends.

After a while the house boy came in with a parcel of books. There were half a dozen novels by authors he had never heard of, and a glance told him they were slop; these must be Mrs. Grange's; and then there was a Boswell's *Johnson*, Borrow's *Lavengro* and Lamb's *Essays*. It was an odd choice. They were not the books you would have expected to find in a planter's house. In most planter's houses there is not more than a shelf or two of books and for the most part they're detective stories. Skelton had a disinterested curiosity in human creatures, and he amused himself now by trying to make out from the books Norman Grange had sent, from the look of him and from the few words they had exchanged, what sort of a man he could be. Skelton was a little surprised that his host did not come to see him again that day; it looked as though he were going to content himself with giving his uninvited guest board and lodging, but were not sufficiently interested in him to seek his company. Next morning he felt well enough to get up, and with Kong's help settled himself in a long chair on the veranda. It badly needed a coat of paint. The bungalow stood on the brow of a hill, about fifty yards from the river; and on the opposite bank, looking very small across that great stretch of water, you could see native houses on piles nestling among the greenery. Skelton had not yet the activity of mind to read steadily, and after a page or two, his thoughts wandering, he found himself content to watch idly the sluggish flow of the turbid stream. Suddenly he heard a step. He saw a little elderly woman come towards him, and knowing that this must be Mrs. Grange tried to get up.

"Don't move," she said. "I only came to see if you had everything you wanted."

She wore a blue cotton dress, simple enough, but more suited to a young girl than to a woman of her age; her short hair was tousled, as though on getting out of bed she had scarcely troubled to pass a comb through it, and dyed a vivid yellow, but

30

badly, and the roots showed white. Her skin was raddled and dry, and there was a great dab of rouge on each cheekbone, put on however so clumsily that you could not for a moment take it for a natural colour, and a smear of lipstick on her mouth. But the strangest thing about her was a tic she had that made her jerk her head as though she were beckoning you to an inner room. It seemed to come at regular intervals, perhaps three times a minute, and her left hand was in almost constant movement; it was not quite a tremble, it was a rapid twirl as though she wanted to draw your attention to something behind her back. Skelton was startled by her appearance and embarrassed by her tic.

"I hope I'm not making myself too great a nuisance," he said. "I think I shall be well enough to make a move tomorrow or the day after."

"It's not often we see anybody in a place like this, you know. It's a treat to have someone to talk to."

"Won't you sit down? I'll tell my boy to bring you a chair."

"Norman said I was to leave you alone."

"I haven't spoken to a white person for two years. I've been longing for a good old talk."

Her head twitched violently, more quickly than usual, and her hand gave that queer spasmodic gesture.

"He won't be back for another hour. I'll get a chair."

Skelton told her who he was and what he had been doing, but he discovered that she had questioned his boy and already knew all about him.

"You must be crazy to get back to England?" she asked.

"I shan't be sorry."

Suddenly Mrs. Grange seemed to be attacked by what one could only describe as a nerve storm. Her head twitched so madly, her hand shook with such fury, that it was disconcerting. You could only look away.

"I haven't been to England for sixteen years," she said.

"You don't mean that? Why, I thought all you planters went home every five years at the longest."

"We can't afford it; we're broke to the wide. Norman put all the money he had into this plantation, and it hasn't really paid for years. It only just brings in enough to keep us from starvation. Of course it doesn't matter to Norman. He isn't English really."

"He looks English enough."

"He was born in Sarawak. His father was in the government service. If he's anything he's a native of Borneo."

Then, without warning, she began to cry. It was horribly painful to see the tears running down the raddled, painted cheeks of that woman with the constant tic. Skelton knew neither what to say nor what to do. He did what was probably the best thing, he kept silent. She dried her eyes.

"You must think me a silly old fool. I sometimes wonder that after all these years I can still cry. I suppose it's in my nature. I always could cry very easy when I was on the stage."

"Oh, were you on the stage?"

"Yes, before I married. That's how I met Norman. We were playing in Singapore and he was there on holiday. I don't suppose I shall ever see England any more. I shall stay here till I die and every day of my life I shall look at that beastly river. I shall never get away now. Never."

"How did you happen to find yourself in Singapore?"

"Well, it was soon after the war, I couldn't get anything to suit me in London, I'd been on the stage a good many years and I was fed up with playing small parts; the agents told me a fellow called Victor Palace was taking a company out East. His wife was playing lead, but I could play seconds. They'd got half a dozen plays, comedies, you know, and farces. The salary wasn't much, but they were going to Egypt and India, the Malay States and China and then down to Australia. It was a chance to see the world and I accepted. We didn't do badly in Cairo and I think we made money in India, but Burma wasn't much good, and Siam was worse; Penang was a disaster and so were the rest of the Malay States. Well, one day Victor called us together and said he was bust, he hadn't got the money for our fares on to Hong Kong, and the tour was a wash-out and he was very sorry but we'd have to get back home as best we could. Of course we told him he couldn't do that to us. You never heard such a row. Well, the long and short of it was that he said we could have the scenery and the props if we thought they was any good to us, but as to money it was no use asking for it because he damned well hadn't got it. And next day we found out that him and his wife, without saying a word to anybody, had got on a French boat and skipped. I was in a rare state, I can tell you. I had a few pounds I'd saved out of me salary, and that was all; somebody told me if we was absolutely stranded the government would have to send us home, but only steerage, and I didn't much fancy that. We got the Press to put our plight before the public and someone came along with the proposition that we should give a benefit performance. Well, we did, but it wasn't much without Victor or his wife, and by the time we'd paid the expenses we weren't any better off than we'd been before. I was at my wits' end, I don't mind telling you. It was then that Norman proposed to me. The funny thing is that I hardly knew him. He'd taken me for a drive round the island and we'd had tea two or three times at the Europe and danced. Men don't often do things for you without wanting something in return, and I thought he expected to get a little bit of fun, but I'd had a good deal of experience and I thought he'd be clever if he got round me. But when he asked me to marry him, well, I was so surprised, I couldn't hardly believe me own ears. He said he'd got his own estate in Borneo and it only wanted a little patience and he'd make a packet. And it was on the banks of a fine river and all round was the jungle. He made it sound very romantic. I was getting on, you know, I was thirty, it wasn't going to be any easier to get work as time went on, and it was tempting to have a house of me own and all that. Never to have to hang around agents' offices no more. Never to have to lay awake no more and wonder how you was going to pay next week's rent. He wasn't a bad-looking

33

chap in those days, brown and big and virile. No one could say I was willing to marry anybody just to . . ." Suddenly she stopped. "There he is. Don't say you've seen me."

She picked up the chair she had been sitting in and quickly slipped away with it into the house. Skelton was bewildered. Her grotesque appearance, the painful tears, her story told with that incessant twitching; and then her obvious fear when she heard her husband's voice in the compound, and her hurried escape; he could make nothing of it.

In a few minutes Norman Grange stumped along the veranda.

"I hear you're better," he said.

"Much, thanks."

"If you care to join us at brunch I'll have a place laid for you."

"I'd like it very much."

"All right. I'm just going to have a bath and a change."

He walked away. Presently a boy came along and told Skelton his tuan was waiting for him. Skelton followed him into a small sitting-room, with the jalousies drawn to keep out the heat, an uncomfortable, overcrowded room with a medley of furniture, English and Chinese, and occasional tables littered with worthless junk. It was neither cosy nor cool. Grange had changed into a sarong and baju and in the native dress looked coarse but powerful. He introduced Skelton to his wife. She shook hands with him as though she had never seen him before and uttered a few polite words of greeting. The boy announced that their meal was ready and they went into the dining-room.

"I hear that you've been in this bloody country for some time," said Grange.

"Two years. I'm an anthropologist, and I wanted to study the manners and customs of tribes that haven't had any contact with civilisation."

Skelton felt that he should tell his host how it had come about that he had been forced to accept a hospitality which he

34

could not but feel was grudgingly offered. After leaving the village that had been his headquarters he had journeyed by land for ten days till he reached the river. There he had engaged a couple of prahus, one for himself and his luggage and the other for Kong, his Chinese servant, and the camp equipment, to take him to the coast. The long trek across country had been hard going and he found it very comfortable to lie on a mattress under an awning of rattan matting and take his ease. All the time he had been away Skelton had been in perfect health, and as he travelled down the river he could not but think that he was very lucky; but even as the thought passed through his mind, it occurred to him that if he happened just then to congratulate himself on his good fortune in this respect, it was because he did not feel quite so well as usual. It was true that he had been forced to drink a great deal of arak the night before at the long-house where he had put up, but he was used to it and that hardly accounted for his headache. He had a general sense of malaise. He was wearing nothing but shorts and a singlet, and he felt chilly; it was curious because the sun was shining fiercely and when he put his head on the gunwale of the prahu the heat was hardly bearable. If he had had a coat handy he would have put it on. He grew colder and colder and presently his teeth began to chatter; he huddled up on his mattress, shivering all over in a desperate effort to get warm. He could not fail to guess what was the matter.

"Christ," he groaned. "Malaria."

He called the headman, who was steering the prahu.

"Get Kong."

The headman shouted to the second prahu and ordered his own paddlers to stop. In a moment the two boats were side by side and Kong stepped in.

"I've got fever, Kong," gasped Skelton. "Get me the medicine chest and, for God's sake, blankets. I'm freezing to death."

Kong gave his master a big dose of quinine and piled on him what coverings they had. They started off again.

Skelton was too ill to be taken ashore when they tied up for

35

the night and so passed it in the prahu. All next day and the day after he was very ill. Sometimes one or other of the crew came and looked at him, and often the headman stayed for quite a long while staring at him thoughtfully.

"How many days to the coast?" Skelton asked the boy.

"Four, five." He paused for a minute. "Headman, he no go coast. He say, he wantchee go home."

"Tell him to go to hell."

"Headman say, you velly sick, you die. If you die and he go coast he catchee trouble."

"I'm not thinking of dying," said Skelton. "I shall be all right. It's just an ordinary go of malaria."

Kong did not answer. The silence irritated Skelton. He knew that the Chinese had something in mind that he did not like to say.

"Spit it out, you fool," he cried.

Skelton's heart sank when Kong told him the truth. When they reached their resting-place that night the headman was going to demand his money and slip away with the two prahus before dawn. He was too frightened to carry a dying man farther. Skelton had no strength to take the determined attitude that might have availed him; he could only hope by the offer of more money to persuade the headman to carry out his agreement. The day passed in long arguments between Kong and the headman, but when they tied up for the night the headman came to Skelton and told him sulkily that he would go no farther. There was a long-house nearby where he might get lodging till he grew better. He began to unload the baggage. Skelton refused to move. He got Kong to give him his revolver and swore to shoot anyone who came near him.

Kong, the crew and the headman went up to the long-house and Skelton was left alone. Hour after hour he lay there, the fever burning his body and his mouth parched, while muddled thoughts hammered away in his brain. Then there were lights and the sound of men talking. The Chinese boy came with the headman and another man, whom Skelton had not yet seen, from the neighbouring long-house. He did his best to under- stand what Kong was telling him. It appeared that a few hours down-stream there lived a white man, and to his house, if that would satisfy Skelton, the headman was willing to take him.

"More better you say yes," said Kong. "Maybe white man has launch, then we go down to coast chop-chop."

"Who is he?"

"Planter," said Kong. "This fellow say, him have rubber estate."

Skelton was too tired to argue further. All he wanted just then was to sleep. He accepted the compromise.

"To tell you the truth," he finished, "I don't remember much more till I woke up yesterday morning to find myself an un- invited guest in your house."

"I don't blame those Dyaks, you know," said Grange. "When I came down to the prahu and saw you, I thought you were for it."

Mrs. Grange sat silent while Skelton told his story, her head and her hand twitching regularly, as though by the action of some invisible clockwork, but when her husband addressed her, asking for the Worcester Sauce, and that was the only time he spoke to her, she was seized with such a paroxysm of involuntary movement that it was horrible to see. She passed him what he asked for without a word. Skelton got an uncom- fortable impression that she was terrified of Grange. It was odd, because to all appearance he was not a bad sort. He was knowledgeable and far from stupid; and though you could not have said that his manner was cordial, it was plain that he was ready to be of what service he could.

They finished their meal and separated to rest through the heat of the day.

"See you again at six for a sun-downer," said Grange.

When Skelton had had a good sleep, a bath and a read, he went out on to the veranda. Mrs. Grange came up to him. It looked as though she had been waiting.

37

"He's back from the office. Don't think it's funny if I don't speak to you. If he thought I liked having you here he'd turn you out tomorrow."

She said these words in a whisper and slipped back into the house. Skelton was startled. It was a strange house he had come into in a strange manner. He went into the overcrowded sitting-room and there found his host. He had been worried by the evident poverty of the establishment and he felt that the Granges could ill afford even the small expense he must be putting them to. But he had already formed the impression that Grange was a quick-tempered, susceptible man and he did not know how he would take an offer to help. He made up his mind to risk it.

"Look here," he said to him, "it looks as though I might have to inflict myself on you for several days, I'd be so much more comfortable if you'd let me pay for my board and lodging."

"Oh, that's all right, your lodging costs nothing, the house belongs to the mortgagees, and your board doesn't come to much."

"Well, there are drinks anyway and I've had to come down on your stores of tobacco and cigarettes."

"It's not more than once a year that anyone comes up here, and then it's only the D.O. or someone like that—besides, when one's as broke as I am nothing matters much."

"Well, then, will you take my camp equipment? I shan't be wanting it any more, and if you'd like one of my guns, I'd be only too glad to leave it with you."

Grange hesitated. There was a glimmer of cupidity in those small, cunning eyes of his.

"If you'd let me have one of your guns you'd pay for your board and lodging over and over again."

"That's settled, then."

They began to talk over the whisky and sparkler with which, following the Eastern habit, they celebrated the setting of the sun. Discovering that they both played chess they had a game.

38

Mrs. Grange did not join them till dinner. The meal was dull. An insipid soup, a tasteless river fish, a tough piece of steak and a caramel pudding. Norman Grange and Skelton drank beer; Mrs. Grange water. She never of her own will uttered a word. Skelton had again the uncomfortable impression that she was scared to death of her husband. Once or twice, Skelton from common politeness sought to bring her into the conversation, addressing himself to her, telling her a story or asking her a question, but it evidently distressed her so much, her head twitched so violently, her hand was agitated by gestures so spasmodic that he thought it kinder not to insist. When the meal was over she got up.

"I'll leave you gentlemen to your port," she said.

Both the men got up as she left the room. It was rather absurd, and somehow sinister, to see this social pretence in those poverty-stricken surroundings on a Borneo river.

"I may add that there is no port. There might be a little Benedictine left."

"Oh, don't bother."

They talked for a while and Grange began to yawn. He got up every morning before sunrise and by nine o'clock at night could hardly keep his eyes open.

"Well, I'm going to turn in," he said.

He nodded to Skelton and without further ceremony left him. Skelton went to bed, but he could not sleep. Though the heat was oppressive, it was not the heat that kept him awake. There was something horrible about that house and those two people who lived in it. He didn't know what it was that affected him with this peculiar uneasiness, but this he knew, that he would be heartily thankful to be out of it and away from them. Grange had talked a good deal about himself, but he knew no more of him than he had learned at the first glance. To all appearances he was just the commonplace planter who had fallen upon evil days. He had bought his land immediately after the war and had planted trees; but by the time they were bearing the slump had come and since then

39

it had been a constant struggle to keep going. The estate and the house were heavily mortgaged, and now that rubber was once more selling profitably all he made went to the mortgagees. That was an old story in Malaya. What made Grange somewhat unusual was that he was a man without a country. Born in Borneo, he had lived there with his parents till he was old enough to go to school in England; at seventeen he had come back and had never left it since except to go to Mesopotamia during the war. England meant nothing to him. He had neither relations nor friends there. Most planters, like civil servants, have come from England, go back on leave now and then, and look forward to settling down there when they retire. But what had England to offer Norman Grange?

"I was born here," he said, "and I shall die here. I'm a stranger in England. I don't like their ways over there and I don't understand the things they talk about. And yet I'm a stranger here too. To the Malays and the Chinese I'm a white man, though I speak Malay as well as they do, and a white man I shall always be." Then he said a significant thing. "Of course if I'd had any sense I'd have married a Malay girl and had half a dozen half-caste kids. That's the only solution really for us chaps who were born and bred here."

Grange's bitterness was greater than could be explained by his financial embarrassment. He had little good to say of any of the white men in the colony. He seemed to think that they despised him because he was native-born. He was a sour, disappointed fellow, and a conceited one. He had shown Skelton his books. There were not many of them, but they were the best on the whole that English literature can show; he had read them over and over again; but it looked as though he had learnt from them neither charity nor loving-kindness, it looked as though their beauty had left him unmoved; and to know them so well had only made him self-complacent. His exterior, which was so hearty and English, seemed to have little relation to the man within; you could not resist the suspicion that it masked a very sinister being.

P Ellison

FLOTSAM AND JETSAM

Early next morning, to enjoy the cool of the day, Skelton, with his pipe and a book, was sitting on the veranda outside his room. He was still very weak, but felt much better. In a little while Mrs. Grange joined him. She held in her hand a large album.

"I thought I'd like to show you some of me old photos and me notices. You mustn't think I always looked like what I do now. He's off on his round and he won't be back for two or three hours yet."

Mrs. Grange, in the same blue dress she had worn the day before, her hair as untidy, appeared strangely excited.

"It's all I have to remind me of the past. Sometimes when I can't bear life any more I look at my album."

She sat by Skelton's side as he turned the pages. The notices were from provincial papers, and the references to Mrs. Grange, whose stage name had been apparently Vesta Blaise, were carefully underlined. From the photographs you could see that she had been pretty enough in an undistinguished way. She had acted in musical comedy and revue, in farce and comedy, and taking the photographs and the notices together it was easy to tell that here had been the common, dreary, rather vulgar career of the girl with no particular talent who has taken to the stage on the strength of a pretty face and a good figure. Her head twitching, her hand shaking, Mrs. Grange looked at the photographs and read the notices with as much interest as if she had never seen them before.

"You've got to have influence on the stage, and I never had any," she said. "If I'd only had my chance I know I'd have made good. I had bad luck, there's no doubt about that."

It was all sordid and somewhat pathetic.

"I daresay you're better off as you are," said Skelton.

She snatched the book from him and shut it with a bang. She had a paroxysm so violent that it was really frightening to look at her.

"What d'you mean by that? What d'you know about the life I lead here? I'd have killed myself years ago only I know

41

he wants me to die. That's the only way I can get back on him, by living, and I'm going to live; I'm going to live as long as he does. Oh, I hate him. I've often thought I'd poison him, but I was afraid. I didn't know how to do it really, and if he died the Chinks would foreclose and I'd be turned out. And where should I go then? I haven't a friend in the world."

Skelton was aghast. It flashed through his mind that she was crazy. He hadn't a notion what to say. She gave him a keen look.

"I suppose it surprises you to hear me talk like that. I mean it, you know, every word of it. He'd like to kill me too, but he daren't either. And he knows how to do it all right. He knows how the Malays kill people. He was born here. There's nothing he doesn't know about the country."

Skelton forced himself to speak.

"You know, Mrs. Grange, I'm a total stranger. Don't you think it's rather unwise to tell me all sorts of things there's no need for me to know? After all, you live a very solitary life. I daresay you get on one another's nerves. Now that things are looking up perhaps you'll be able to take a trip to England."

"I don't want to go to England. I'd be ashamed to let them see me like I am now. D'you know how old I am? Forty-six. I look sixty and I know it. That's why I showed you those photos, so as you might see I wasn't always like what I am now. Oh, my God, how I've wasted my life! They talk of the romance of the East. They can have it. I'd rather be a dresser in a provincial theatre, I'd rather be one of the sweepers that keep it clean, than what I am now. Until I came here I'd never been alone in me life, I'd always lived in a crowd; you don't know what it is to have nobody to talk to from year's end to year's end. To have to keep it all bottled up. How would you like to see no one, week in and week out, day after day for sixteen years, except the man you hate most in the world? How would you like to live for sixteen years with a man who hates you so he can't bear to look at you?"

42

"Oh come, it can't be as bad as that."

"I'm telling you the truth. Why should I tell you a lie? I shall never see you again; what do I care what you think of me? And if you tell them what I've said when you get down to the coast, what's the odds? They'll say: 'God, you don't mean to say you stayed with those people? I pity you. He's an outsider and she's crazy; got a tic; they say it looks as if she was always trying to wipe the blood off her dress. They were mixed up in a damned funny business, but no one ever really knew the ins and outs of it; it all happened a long time ago and the country was pretty wild in those days.' A damned funny business and no mistake. I'd tell you for two pins. That would be a bit of dirt for them at the club. You wouldn't have to pay for a drink for days. Damn them. Oh, Christ, how I hate this country. I hate that river. I hate this house. I hate that damned rubber. I loathe the filthy natives. And that's all I've got to look forward to till I die—till I die without a doctor to take care of me, without a friend to hold me hand."

She began to cry hysterically. Mrs. Grange had spoken with a dramatic intensity of which Skelton would never have thought her capable. Her coarse irony was as painful as her anguish. Skelton was young, he was not yet thirty, and he did not know how to deal with the difficult situation. But he could not keep silent.

"I'm terribly sorry, Mrs. Grange. I wish I could do something to help you."

"I'm not asking for your help. No one can help me."

Skelton was distressed. From what she said he could not but suspect that she had been concerned in a mysterious and perhaps dreadful occurrence, and it might be that to tell him about it without fear of the consequences was just the relief she needed.

"I don't want to butt into what's no business of mine, but, Mrs. Grange, if you think it would ease your mind to tell me— what you were referring to just now, I mean what you said was a damned funny business, I promise you on my word of honour that I'll never repeat it to a living soul."

She stopped crying quite suddenly and gave him a long, intent look. She hesitated. He had an impression that the desire to speak was almost irresistible. But she shook her head and sighed.

"It wouldn't do any good. Nothing can do me any good."

She got up and abruptly left him.

The two men sat down to brunch by themselves.

"My wife asks you to excuse her," said Grange. "She's got one of her sick headaches and she's staying in bed today."

"Oh, I'm sorry."

Skelton had a notion that in the searching look that Grange gave him was mistrust and animosity. It flashed through his mind that somehow he had discovered that Mrs. Grange had been talking to him, and perhaps had said things that should have been left unsaid. Skelton made an effort at conversation, but his host was taciturn, and they ended the meal in a silence that was only broken by Grange when he got up.

"You seem pretty fit today and I don't suppose you want to stay in this God-forsaken place longer than you must. I've sent over the river to arrange for a couple of prahus to take you down to the coast. They'll be here at six tomorrow morning."

Skelton felt sure then that he was right; Grange knew or guessed that his wife had spoken too freely, and he wanted to be rid as soon as possible of the dangerous visitor.

"That's terribly kind of you," Skelton answered, smiling. "I'm as fit as a fiddle."

But in Grange's eyes was no answering smile. They were coldly hostile.

"We might have another game of chess later on," said he.

"All right. When d'you get back from your office?"

"I haven't got much to do there today. I shall be about the house."

Skelton wondered if it were only his fancy that there was something very like a threat in the tone in which Grange uttered these words. It looked as though he were going to make sure that his wife and Skelton should not again be left alone.

Mrs. Grange did not come to dinner. They drank their coffee and smoked their cheroots. Then Grange, pushing back his chair, said:

"You've got to make an early start tomorrow. I daresay you'd like to turn in. I shall have started out on my round by the time you go, so I'll say good-bye to you now."

"Let me get my guns. I want you to take the one you like best."

"I'll tell the boy to fetch them."

The guns were brought and Grange made his choice. He gave no sign that he was pleased with the handsome gift.

"You quite understand that this gun's worth a damned sight more than what your food and drink and smoke have run me into?" he said.

"For all I know you saved my life. I don't think an old gun is an over-generous return for that."

"Oh, well, if you like to look at it that way, I suppose it's your own business. Thank you very much all the same."

They shook hands and parted.

Next morning, while the baggage was being stowed away in the prahus, Skelton asked the house boy whether, before starting, he could say good-bye to Mrs. Grange. The house boy said he would go and see. He waited a little while. Mrs. Grange came out of her room on to the veranda. She was wearing a pink dressing-gown, shabby, rumpled and none too clean, of Japanese silk, heavily trimmed with cheap lace. The powder was thick on her face, her cheeks were rouged and her lips scarlet with lipstick. Her head seemed to twitch more violently than usual and her hand was agitated by that strange gesture. When first Skelton saw it he had thought that it suggested a wish to call attention to something behind her back, but now, after what she had told him yesterday, it did indeed look as though she were constantly trying to brush something off her dress. Blood, she had said.

"I didn't want to go without thanking you for all your kindness to me," he said.

"Oh, that's all right."

"Well, good-bye."

"I'll walk down with you to the landing-stage."

They hadn't far to go. The boatmen were still arranging the luggage. Skelton looked across the river where you could see some native houses.

"I suppose these men come from over there. It looks quite a village."

"No, only those few houses. There used to be a rubber estate there, but the company went broke and it was abandoned."

"D'you ever go over there?"

"Me?" cried Mrs. Grange. Her voice rose shrill and her head, her hand, were on a sudden convulsed by a paroxysm of involuntary movement. "No. Why should I?"

Skelton could not imagine why that simple question, asked merely for something to say, should so greatly upset her. But by now all was in order and he shook hands with her. He stepped into the boat and comfortably settled down. They pushed off. He waved to Mrs. Grange. As the boat slid into the current she cried out with a harsh, strident scream:

"Give my regards to Leicester Square."

Skelton heaved a great sigh of relief as with their powerful strokes the paddlers took him farther and farther away from that dreadful house and from those two unhappy and yet repellent people. He was glad now that Mrs. Grange had not told him the story that was on the tip of her tongue to tell. He did not want some tragic tale of sin or folly to connect him with them in a recollection that he could not escape. He wanted to forget them as one forgets a bad dream.

But Mrs. Grange watched the two prahus till a bend of the river took them out of sight. She walked slowly up to the house and went into her bedroom. The light was dim because the blinds were drawn to keep out the heat, but she sat down at her dressing-table and stared at herself in the glass. Norman had had the dressing-table made for her soon after they were

46

married. It had been made by a native carpenter, of course, and they had had the mirror sent from Singapore, but it was made to her own design, of the exact size and shape she wanted, with plenty of room for all her toilet things and her make-up. It was the dressing-table she had hankered after for donkey's years and had never had. She remembered still how pleased she was when first she had it. She threw her arms round her husband's neck and kissed him.

"Oh, Norman, you are good to me," she said. "I'm a lucky little girl to have caught a chap like you, aren't I?"

But then everything delighted her. She was amused by the river life and the life of the jungle, the teeming growth of the forest, the birds with their gay plumage and the brilliant butterflies. She set about giving the house a woman's touch; she put out all her own photographs and she got vases to put flowers in; she routed around and got a lot of knick-knacks to place here and there. "They make a room look homey," she said. She wasn't in love with Norman, but she liked him all right; and it was lovely to be married; it was lovely to have nothing to do from morning till night, except play the gramophone, or patience, and read novels. It was lovely to think one hadn't got to bother about one's future. Of course it was a bit lonely sometimes, but Norman said she'd get used to that, and he'd promised that in a year, or two at the outside, he'd take her to England for three months. It would be a lark to show him off to her friends. She felt that what had caught him was the glamour of the stage and she'd made herself out a good deal more successful than she really had been. She wanted him to realise that she'd made a sacrifice when she'd thrown up her career to become a planter's wife. She'd claimed acquaintance with a good many stars that in point of fact she'd never even spoken to. That would need a bit of handling when they went home, but she'd manage it; after all, poor Norman knew no more about the stage than a babe unborn, if she couldn't cod a simple fellow like that, after twelve years on the stage, well, she'd wasted her time, that's all she could say.

CREATURES OF CIRCUMSTANCE

Things went all right the first year. At one moment she thought
she was going to have a baby. They were both disappointed
when it turned out not to be true. Then she began to grow
bored. It seemed to her that she'd done the same damned
thing day after day for ever and it frightened her to think that
she'd have to go on doing the same damned thing day after day
for ever more. Norman said he couldn't leave the plantation
that year. They had a bit of a scene. It was then that he'd said
something that scared her.

"I hate England," he said. "If I had my way I'd never set
foot in the damned country again."

Living this lonely life Mrs. Grange got into the habit of
talking out loud to herself. Shut up in her room she could be
heard chattering away hour after hour; and now, dipping the
puff in her powder and plastering her face with it, she addressed
her reflection in the mirror exactly as though she were talking
to another person.

"That ought to have warned me. I should have insisted on
going by myself, and who knows, I might have got a job when
I got to London. With all the experience I had and everything.
Then I'd have written to him and said I wasn't coming back."
Her thoughts turned to Skelton. "Pity I didn't tell him," she
continued. "I had half a mind to. P'raps he was right, p'raps
it would have eased me mind. I wonder what he'd have said."
She imitated his Oxford accent. "I'm so terribly sorry, Mrs.
Grange. I wish I could help you." She gave a chuckle which
was almost a sob. "I'd have liked to tell him about Jack. Oh,
Jack."

It was when they had been married for two years that they
got a neighbour. The price of rubber at that time was so high
that new estates were being put under cultivation and one of
the big companies had bought a great tract of land on the
opposite bank of the river. It was a rich company and everything was done on a lavish scale. The manager they had put
in had a launch at his disposal so that it was no trouble for him
to pop over and have a drink whenever he felt inclined. Jack

48

FLOTSAM AND JETSAM

Carr his name was. He was quite a different sort of chap from Norman; for one thing he was a gentleman, he'd been to a public school and a university; he was about thirty-five, tall, not beefy like Norman, but slight, he had the sort of figure that looked lovely in evening dress; and he had crisply curling hair and a laughing look in his eyes. Just her type. She took to him at once. It was a treat, having someone you could talk about London to, and the theatre. He was gay and easy. He made the sort of jokes you could understand. In a week or two she felt more at home with him than she did with her husband after two years. There had always been something about Norman that she hadn't quite been able to get to the bottom of. He was crazy about her, of course, and he'd told her a lot about himself, but she had a funny feeling that there was something he kept from her, not because he wanted to, but—well, you couldn't hardly explain it, because it was so alien, you might say, that he couldn't put it into words. Later, when she knew Jack better, she mentioned it to him, and Jack said it was because he was country-born; even though he hadn't a drop of native blood in his veins, something of the country had gone to the making of him so that he wasn't white really; he had an Eastern streak in him. However hard he tried he could never be quite English.

She chattered away aloud, in that empty house, for the two boys, the cook and the house boy, were in their own quarters, and the sound of her voice, ringing along the wooden floors, piercing the wooden walls, was like the uncanny, unhuman gibber of new wine fermenting in a vat. She spoke just as though Skelton were there, but so incoherently that if he had been, he would have had difficulty in following the story she told. It did not take her long to discover that Jack Carr wanted her. She was excited. She'd never been promiscuous, but in all those years she'd been on the stage naturally there'd been episodes. You couldn't hardly have put up with being on tour month after month if you didn't have a bit of fun sometimes. Of course now she wasn't going to give in too easily, she didn't

49

want to make herself cheap, but what with the life she led, she'd be a fool if she missed the chance; and as far as Norman was concerned, well, what the eye didn't see the heart didn't grieve over. They understood one another all right, Jack and her; they knew it was bound to happen sooner or later, it was only a matter of waiting for the opportunity; and the opportunity came. But then something happened that they hadn't bargained for: they fell madly in love with one another. If Mrs. Grange really had been telling the story to Skelton it might have seemed as unlikely to him as it did to them. They were two very ordinary people, he a jolly, good-natured, commonplace planter, and she a small-part actress far from clever, not even very young, with nothing to recommend her but a neat figure and a prettyish face. What started as a casual affair turned without warning into a devastating passion, and neither of them was of a texture to sustain its exorbitant compulsion. They longed to be with one another; they were restless and miserable apart. She'd been finding Norman a bore for some time, but she'd put up with him because he was her husband; now he irritated her to frenzy because he stood between her and Jack. There was no question of their going off together, Jack Carr had nothing but his salary, and he couldn't throw up a job he'd been only too glad to get. It was difficult for them to meet. They had to run awful risks. Perhaps the chances they had to take, the obstacles they had to surmount, were fuel to their love; a year passed and it was as overwhelming as at the beginning; it was a year of agony and bliss, of fear and thrill. Then she discovered that she was pregnant. She had no doubt that Jack Carr was the father and she was wildly happy. It was true life was difficult, so difficult sometimes that she felt she just couldn't cope with it, but there'd be a baby, his baby; and that would make everything easy. She was going to Kuching for her confinement. It happened about then that Jack Carr had to go to Singapore on business and was to be away for several weeks; but he promised to get back before she left and he said he'd send word by a native the moment he arrived. When at last the message came she felt sick with the anguish of her joy. She had never wanted him so badly.

"I hear that Jack is back," she told her husband at dinner. "I shall go over tomorrow morning and get the things he promised to bring me."

"I wouldn't do that. He's pretty sure to drop in towards sundown and he'll bring them himself."

"I can't wait. I'm crazy to have them."

"All right. Have it your own way."

She couldn't help talking about him. For some time now they had seemed to have little to say to one another, Norman and she, but that night, in high spirits, she chattered away as she had done during the first months of their marriage. She always rose early, at six, and next morning she went down to the river and had a bathe. There was a little dent in the bank just there, with a tiny sandy beach, and it was delicious to splash about in the cool, transparent water. A kingfisher stood on the branch of a tree overhanging the pool and its reflection was brilliantly blue in the water. Lovely. She had a cup of tea and then stepped into a dug-out. A boy paddled her across the river. It took a good half-hour. As they got near she scanned the bank; Jack knew she would come at the earliest opportunity; he must be on the look-out. Ah, there he was. The delicious pain in her heart was almost unbearable. He came down to the landing-stage and helped her to get out of the boat. They walked hand in hand up the pathway and when they were out of sight of the boy who had paddled her over and of prying eyes from the house, they stopped. He put his arms round her and she yielded with ecstasy to his embrace. She clung to him. His mouth sought hers. In that kiss was all the agony of their separation and all the bliss of their reunion. The miracle of love transfused them so that they were unconscious of time and place. They were not human any more, but two spirits united by a divine fire. No thought passed through their minds. No words issued from their lips. Suddenly there was a brutal shock, like a blow, and immediately, almost simultaneously, a deafening noise. Horrified, not understanding, she clung to Jack more tightly and his grip on her was spasmodic, so that she gasped; then she felt that he was bearing her over.

"Jack."

She tried to hold him up. His weight was too great for her and as he fell to the ground she fell with him. Then she gave a great cry, for she felt a gush of heat, and his blood sputtered over her. She began to scream. A rough hand seized her and dragged her to her feet. It was Norman. She was distraught. She could not understand.

"Norman, what have you done?"

"I've killed him."

She stared at him stupidly. She pushed him aside.

"Jack. Jack."

"Shut up. I'll go and get help. It was an accident."

He walked quickly up the pathway. She fell to her knees and took Jack's head in her arms.

"Darling," she moaned. "Oh, my darling."

Norman came back with some coolies and they carried him up to the house. That night she had a miscarriage and was so ill that for days it looked as if she would die. When she recovered she had the nervous tic that she'd had ever since. She expected that Norman would send her away; but he didn't, he had to keep her to allay suspicion. There was some talk among the natives, and after a while the District Officer came up and asked a lot of questions; but the natives were frightened of Norman, and the D.O. could get nothing out of them. The Dyak boy who paddled her over had vanished. Norman said something had gone wrong with his gun and Jack was looking at it to see what was the matter and it went off. They bury people quickly in that country and by the time they might have dug him up there wouldn't have been much left to show that Norman's story wasn't true. The D.O. hadn't been satisfied.

"It all looks damned fishy to me," he said, "but in the absence of any evidence, I suppose I must accept your version."

FLOTSAM AND JETSAM

She would have given anything to get away, but with that nervous affliction she had no ghost of a chance any longer of earning a living. She had to stay—or starve; and Norman had to keep her—or hang. Nothing had happened since then and now nothing ever would happen. The endless years one after another dragged out their weary length.

Mrs. Grange on a sudden stopped talking. Her sharp ears had caught the sound of a footstep on the path and she knew that Norman was back from his round. Her head twitching furiously, her hand agitated by that sinister, uncontrollable gesture, she looked in the untidy mess of her dressing-table for her precious lipstick. She smeared it on her lips, and then, she didn't know why, on a freakish impulse daubed it all over her nose till she looked like a red-nose comedian in a music-hall. She looked at herself in the glass and burst out laughing.

"To hell with life!" she shouted.

APPEARANCE
AND REALITY

I DO not vouch for the truth of this story, but it was told me
by a professor of French literature at an English university,
and he was a man of too high a character, I think, to have told
it to me unless it were true. His practice was to draw the attention of his students to three French writers who in his opinion
combined the qualities that are the mainsprings of the French
character. By reading them, he said, you could learn so much
about the French people that, if he had the power, he would
not trust such of our rulers as have to deal with the French
nation to enter upon their offices till they had passed a pretty
stiff examination on their works. They are Rabelais, with his
gauloiserie, which may be described as the ribaldry that likes
to call a spade something more than a bloody shovel; La
Fontaine, with his *bon sens,* which is just horse sense; and
finally Corneille, with his *panache.* This is translated in the
dictionaries as the plume, the plume the knight at arms wore
on his helmet, but metaphorically it seems to signify dignity
and bravado, display and heroism, vainglory and pride. It was
le panache that made the French gentlemen at Fontenoy say
to the officers of King George II, fire first, gentlemen; it was
le panache that wrung from Cambronne's bawdy lips at
Waterloo the phrase: the guard dies but never surrenders; and it
is *le panache* that urges an indigent French poet, awarded the
Nobel prize, with a splendid gesture to give it all away. My
professor was not a frivolous man and to his mind the story
I am about to tell brought out so distinctly the three master
qualities of the French that it had a high educational value.

I have called it Appearance and Reality. This is the title of
what I suppose may be looked upon as the most important
philosophical work that my country (right or wrong) produced

in the nineteenth century. It is stiff, but stimulating reading.
It is written in excellent English, with considerable humour,
and even though the lay reader is unlikely to follow with understanding some of its very subtle arguments he has nevertheless
the thrilling sensation of walking a spiritual tight-rope over a
metaphysical abyss, and he ends the book with a comfortable
feeling that nothing matters a hang anyway. There is no excuse
for my making use of the title of so celebrated a book except
that it so admirably suits my story. Though Lisette was a
philosopher only in the sense in which we are all philosophers,
and she exercised thought in dealing with the problems of
existence, her feeling for reality was so strong and her sympathy
for appearance so genuine that she might almost claim to have
established that reconciliation of irreconcilables at which the
philosophers have for so many centuries been aiming. Lisette
was French, and she passed several hours of every working
day dressing and undressing herself at one of the most expensive
and fashionable establishments in Paris. A pleasant occupation
for a young woman who was well aware that she had a lovely
figure. She was in short a mannequin. She was tall enough
to be able to wear a train with elegance and her hips were so slim
that in sports clothes she could bring the scent of heather to
your nostrils. Her long legs enabled her to wear pyjamas with
distinction, and her slim waist, her little breasts, made the
simplest bathing dress a ravishment. She could wear anything.
She had a way of huddling herself in a chinchilla coat that
made the most sensible persons admit that chinchilla was worth
all the money it cost. Fat women, gross women, stumpy women,
bony women, shapeless women, old women, plain women, sat
in the spacious armchairs and because Lisette looked so
sweet bought the clothes that so admirably suited her. She had
large brown eyes, a large red mouth and a very clear but slightly
freckled skin. It was difficult for her to preserve that haughty,
sullen and coldly indifferent demeanour that appears to be
essential to the mannequin as she sails in with deliberate steps,
turns round slowly and, with an air of contempt for the universe

55

equalled only by the camel's, sails out. There was the suspicion of a twinkle in Lisette's large brown eyes and her red lips seem to tremble as though on the smallest provocation they would break into a smile. It was the twinkle that attracted the attention of Monsieur Raymond Le Sueur.

He was sitting in a spurious Louis XVI chair by the side of his wife (in another) who had induced him to come with her to see the private view of the spring fashions. This was a proof of Monsieur Le Sueur's amiable disposition, for he was an extremely busy man who, one would have thought, had many more important things to do than to sit for an hour and watch a dozen beautiful young women parade themselves in a bewildering variety of costumes. He could not have thought that any of them could possibly make his wife other than she was, and she was a tall, angular woman of fifty, with features considerably larger than life-size. He had not indeed married her for her looks, and she had never, even in the first delirious days of their honeymoon, imagined that he had. He had married her in order to combine the flourishing steel works of which she was the heiress with his equally flourishing manufactory of locomotives. The marriage had been a success. She had provided him with a son who could play tennis nearly as well as a professional, dance quite as well as a gigolo, and hold his own at bridge with any of the experts; and a daughter whom he had been able to dower sufficiently to marry a very nearly authentic prince. He had reason to be proud of his children. By perseverance and a reasonable integrity he had prospered sufficiently to gain the controlling interest in a sugar refinery, a movie company, a firm that built motor-cars and a newspaper; and finally he had been able to spend enough money to persuade the free and independent electorate of a certain district to send him to the Senate. He was a man of a dignified presence, a pleasing corpulence and a sanguine complexion, with a neat grey beard cut square, a bald head and a roll of fat at the back of his neck. You had no need to look at the red button that adorned his black coat to surmise that he was a person of consequence.

He was a man who made up his mind quickly and when his wife left the dressmaker's to go and play bridge he parted from her, saying that for the sake of exercise he would walk to the Senate, where his duty to his country called him. He did not however go as far as this, but contented himself with taking his exercise up and down a back street into which he rightly surmised the young ladies of the dressmaker's establishment would emerge at the close of business hours. He had barely waited for a quarter of an hour when the appearance of a number of women in groups, some young and pretty, some not so young and far from pretty, apprised him that the moment for which he had been waiting was come, and in two or three minutes Lisette tripped into the street. The Senator was well aware that his appearance and his age made it unlikely that young women would find him attractive at first sight, but he had found that his wealth and his position counterbalanced these disadvantages. Lisette had a companion with her, which would possibly have embarrassed a man of less importance, but did not cause the Senator to hesitate for an instant; he went up to her, raising his hat politely but not so much as to show how bald he was, and bade her good evening.

"*Bon soir, Mademoiselle,*" he said with an ingratiating smile.

She gave him the shortest possible look and, her full red lips just trembling with a smile, stiffened; she turned her head away and breaking into conversation with her friend, walked on with a very good assumption of supreme indifference. Far from disconcerted, the Senator turned round and followed the two girls at a distance of a few yards. They walked along the little back street, turned into the boulevard and at the Place de la Madeleine took a bus. The Senator was well satisfied. He had drawn a number of correct conclusions. The fact that she was obviously going home with a girl friend proved that she had no accredited admirer. The fact that she had turned away when he had accosted her showed that she was discreet and modest and well behaved, which he liked young women to be when they were pretty; and her coat and skirt, the plain black hat and the rayon stockings proclaimed that she was poor and therefore virtuous. In those clothes she looked just as attractive as in the splendid garments he had seen her wearing before. He had a funny little feeling in his heart. He had not had that peculiar sensation, pleasurable and yet oddly painful, for several years, but he recognised it at once.

"It's love, by blue," he muttered.

He had never expected to feel it again, and squaring his shoulders he walked on with a confident step. He walked to the offices of a private detective and there left instructions that inquiries should be made about a young person called Lisette, who worked as a mannequin at such and such an address; and then, remembering that at the Senate they were discussing the American Debt, took a cab to the impressive building, entered the library, where there was an armchair he very much liked, and had a pleasant nap. The information he had asked for reached him three days later. It was cheap at the price. Mademoiselle Lisette Larion lived with a widowed aunt in a two-room apartment in the district of Paris known as the Batignolles. Her father, a wounded hero of the great war, had a *bureau de tabac* in a small country town in the south-west of France. The rent of the flat was two thousand francs. She led a regular life, but was fond of going to the pictures, was not known to have a lover, and was nineteen years old. She was well spoken of by the concierge of the apartments and well liked by her companions at the shop. Obviously she was a very respectable young woman and the Senator could not but think that she was eminently suited to solace the leisure moments of a man who wanted relaxation from the cares of state and the exacting pressure of Big Business.

It is unnecessary to relate in detail the steps that Monsieur Le Sueur took to achieve the end he had in view. He was too important and too busy to occupy himself with the matter personally, but he had a confidential secretary who was very clever at dealing with electors who had not made up their minds how to vote, and who certainly knew how to put before a young woman who was honest but poor the advantages that might ensue if she were lucky enough to secure the friendship of such a man as his employer. The confidential secretary paid the widowed aunt, Madame Saladin by name, a visit and told her that Monsieur Le Sueur, always abreast of the time, had lately begun to take an interest in films and was indeed about to engage in the production of a picture. (This shows how much a clever brain can make use of a fact that an ordinary person would have passed over as insignificant.) Monsieur Le Sueur had been struck by the appearance of Mademoiselle Lisette at the dressmaker's and the brilliant way she wore her clothes, and it had occurred to him that she might very well suit a part he had it in mind for her to play. (Like all intelligent people the Senator always stuck as close to the truth as he could.) The confidential secretary then invited Madame Saladin and her niece to a dinner where they could make one another's further acquaintance and the Senator could judge whether Mademoiselle Lisette had the aptitude for the screen that he suspected. Madame Saladin said she would ask her niece, but for her part seemed to think the suggestion quite reasonable.

When Madame Saladin put the proposition before Lisette and explained the rank, dignity and importance of their generous host, that young person shrugged her pretty shoulders disdainfully.

"*Cette vieille carpe,*" she said, of which the not quite literal translation is: that old trout.

"What does it matter if he's an old trout if he gives you a part?" said Madame Saladin.

"*Et ta sœur,*" said Lisette.

This phrase, which of course means: and your sister, and sounds harmless enough, and even pointless, is a trifle vulgar and is used by well-brought-up young women, I think, only if they want to shock. It expressed the most forcible unbelief, and the only correct translation into the vernacular is too coarse for my chaste pen.

59

"Anyhow we should get a slap-up dinner," said Madame Saladin. "After all, you're not a child any more."

"Where did he say we should dine?"

"The Château de Madrid. Everyone knows it's the most expensive restaurant in the world."

There is no reason why it should not be. The food is very good, the cellar is famous, and its situation makes it on a fine evening of early summer an enchanting place to eat at. A very pretty dimple appeared on Lisette's cheek and a smile on her large red mouth. She had perfect teeth.

"I can borrow a dress from the shop," she murmured.

A few days later the Senator's confidential secretary fetched them in a taxi and drove Madame Saladin and her engaging niece to the Bois de Boulogne. Lisette looked ravishing in one of the firm's most successful models and Madame Saladin extremely respectable in her own black satin and a hat that Lisette had made for the occasion. The secretary introduced the ladies to Monsieur Le Sueur, who greeted them with the benign dignity of the politician who is behaving graciously to the wife and daughter of a valued constituent; and this is exactly what in his astute way he thought people at adjacent tables who knew him would imagine his guests to be. The dinner passed off very agreeably, and less than a month later Lisette moved into a charming little flat at a convenient distance both from her place of business and from the Senate. It was decorated in the modern style by a fashionable upholsterer. Monsieur Le Sueur wished Lisette to continue to work. It suited him very well that she should have something to do during the hours that he was obliged to devote to affairs, for it would keep her out of mischief, and he very well knew that a woman who has nothing to do all day spends much more money than one who has an occupation. An intelligent man thinks of these things.

But extravagance was a vice to which Lisette was strange. The Senator was fond and generous. It was a source of satisfaction to him that Lisette began very soon to save money. She ran

60

her apartment with thrift and bought her clothes at trade prices, and every month sent a certain sum home to her heroic father, who purchased little plots of land with it. She continued to lead a quiet and modest life and Monsieur Le Sueur was pleased to learn from the concierge, who had a son she wanted to place in a government office, that Lisette's only visitors were her aunt and one or two girls from the shop.

The Senator had never been happier in his life. It was very satisfactory to him to think that even in this world a good action had its reward, for was it not from pure kindness that he had accompanied his wife to the dressmaker's on that afternoon when they were discussing the American Debt at the Senate and thus seen for the first time the charming Lisette? The more he knew her the more he doted on her. She was a delightful companion. She was gay and debonair. Her intelligence was respectable and she could listen cleverly when he discussed business matters or affairs of state with her. She rested him when he was weary and cheered him when he was depressed. She was glad to see him when he came, and he came frequently, generally from five till seven, and sorry when he went away. She gave him the impression that he was not only her lover but her friend. Sometimes they dined together in her apartment, and the well-appointed meal, the genial comfort, gave him a keen appreciation of the charm of domesticity. His friends told the Senator he looked twenty years younger. He felt it. He was conscious of his good fortune. He could not but feel, however, that after a life of honest toil and public service it was only his due.

It was thus a shock to him, after things had been proceeding so happily for nearly two years, on coming back to Paris early one Sunday morning unexpectedly after a visit to his constituency which was to last over the week-end, when he let himself into the apartment with his latchkey, thinking since it was the day of rest to find Lisette in bed, to discover her having breakfast in her bedroom *tête-à-tête* with a young gentleman he had never seen before who was wearing his (the Senator's)

61

brand new pyjamas. Lisette was surprised to see him. Indeed she gave a distinct start.

"*Tiens*," she said. "Where have you sprung from? I didn't expect you till tomorrow."

"The Ministry has fallen," he answered mechanically. "I have been sent for. I am to be offered the Ministry of the Interior." But that was not what he wanted to say at all. He gave the gentleman who was wearing his pyjamas a furious look. "Who is that young man?" he cried.

Lisette's large red mouth broke into a most alluring smile.

"My lover," she answered.

"Do you think I'm a fool?" shouted the Senator. "I know he's your lover."

"Why do you ask then?"

Monsieur Le Sueur was a man of action. He went straight up to Lisette and smacked her hard on her right cheek with his left hand and then smacked her hard on the left cheek with his right hand.

"Brute," screamed Lisette.

He turned to the young man, who had watched this scene of violence with some embarrassment, and, drawing himself to his full height, flung out his arm and with a dramatic finger pointed to the door.

"Get out," he cried. "Get out."

One would have thought, such was the commanding aspect of a man who was accustomed to sway a crowd of angry tax-payers and who could dominate with his frown an annual meeting of disappointed shareholders, that the young man would have made a bolt for the door; but he stood his ground, irresolutely it is true, but he stood his ground; he gave Lisette an appealing look and slightly shrugged his shoulders.

"What are you waiting for?" shouted the Senator. "Do you want me to use force?"

"He can't go out in his pyjamas," said Lisette.

"They're not his pyjamas, they're my pyjamas."

"He's waiting for his clothes."

Monsieur Le Sueur looked round and on the chair behind him, flung down in a disorderly fashion, was a variety of masculine garments. The Senator gave the young man a look of contempt.

"You may take your clothes, Monsieur," he said with cold disdain.

The young man picked them up in his arms, gathered up the shoes that were lying about the floor, and quickly left the room. Monsieur Le Sueur had a considerable gift of oratory. Never had he made better use of it than now. He told Lisette what he thought of her. It was not flattering. He painted her ingratitude in the blackest colours. He ransacked an extensive vocabulary in order to find opprobrious names to call her. He called all the powers of heaven to witness that never had a woman repaid with such gross decepion an honest man's belief in her. In short he said everything that anger, wounded vanity and disappointment suggested to him. Lisette did not seek to defend herself. She listened in silence, looking down and mechanically crumbling the roll which the Senator's appearance had prevented her from finishing. He flung an irritated glance at her plate.

"I was so anxious that you should be the first to hear my great news that I came straight here from the station. I was expecting to have my *petit déjeuner* with you, sitting at the end of your bed."

"My poor dear, haven't you had your breakfast? I'll order some for you at once."

"I don't want any."

"Nonsense. With the great responsibility you are about to assume you must keep up your strength."

She rang and when the maid came told her to bring in hot coffee. It was brought and Lisette poured it out. He would not touch it. She buttered a roll. He shrugged his shoulders and began to eat. Meanwhile he uttered a few remarks on the perfidy of women. She remained silent.

"At all events it is something," he said, "that you have not the effrontery to attempt to excuse yourself. You know that I am not a man who can be ill-used with impunity. The soul of generosity when people behave well to me I am pitiless when they behave badly. The very moment I have drunk my coffee I shall leave this apartment for ever."

Lisette sighed.

"I will tell you now that I had prepared a surprise for you. I had made up my mind to celebrate the second anniversary of our union by settling a sum of money on you sufficient to give you a modest independence if anything happened to me."

"How much?" asked Lisette sombrely.

"A million francs."

She sighed again. Suddenly something soft hit the Senator on the back of the head and he gave a start.

"What is that?" he cried.

"He's returning your pyjamas."

The young man had opened the door, flung the pyjamas at the Senator's head, and quickly closed it again. The Senator disengaged himself from the silk trousers that clung round his neck.

"What a way to return them! It is obvious that your friend has no education."

"Of course he has not your distinction," murmured Lisette.

"And has he my intelligence?"

"Oh, no."

"Is he rich?"

"Penniless."

"Then, name of a name, what is it you see in him?"

"He's young," smiled Lisette.

The Senator looked down at his plate and a tear rose in his eyes and rolled down his cheek into the coffee. Lisette gave him a kindly look.

"My poor friend, one can't have everything in this life," she said.

"I knew I was not young. But my situation, my fortune, my

64

vitality. I thought it made up. There are women who only like men of a certain age. There are celebrated actresses who look upon it as an honour to be the little friend of a Minister. I am too well brought up to throw your origins in your face, but the fact remains that you are a mannequin and I took you out of an apartment of which the rent is only two thousand francs a year. It was a step up for you."

"The daughter of poor but honest parents, I have no reason to be ashamed of my origins, and it is not because I have earned my living in a humble sphere that you have the right to reproach me."

"Do you love this boy?"

"Yes."

"And not me?"

"You too. I love you both, but I love you differently. I love you because you are so distinguished and your conversation is instructive and interesting. I love you because you are kind and generous. I love him because his eyes are so big and his hair waves and he dances divinely. It's very natural."

"You know that in my position I cannot take you to places where they dance and I daresay when he's as old as I am he'll have no more hair than I have."

"That may well be true," Lisette agreed, but she did not think it much mattered.

"What will your aunt, the respectable Madame Saladin, say to you when she hears what you have done?"

"It will not be exactly a surprise to her."

"Do you mean to say that worthy woman countenances your conduct? *O tempora, o mores!* How long then has this been going on?"

"Since I first went to the shop. He travels for a big silk firm in Lyons. He came in one day with his samples. We liked the look of one another."

"But your aunt was there to defend you from the temptations to which a young girl is exposed in Paris. She should never have allowed you to have anything to do with this young man."

"I did not ask her permission."

"It is enough to bring the grey hairs of your poor father to the grave. Had you no thought of that wounded hero whose services to his country have been rewarded with a licence to sell tobacco? Do you forget that as Minister of the Interior the department is under my control? I should be within my rights if I revoked the licence on account of your flagrant immorality."

"I know you are too great a gentleman to do a dastardly thing like that."

He waved his hand in an impressive, though perhaps too dramatic a manner.

"Don't be afraid, I will never stoop so low as to revenge myself on one who has deserved well of his country for the mis-deeds of a creature my sense of dignity forces me to despise."

He went on with his interrupted breakfast. Lisette did not speak and there was silence between them. But his appetite satisfied, his mood changed; he began to feel sorry for himself rather than angry with her, and with a strange ignorance of woman's heart he thought to arouse Lisette's remorse by exhibiting himself as an object of pity.

"It is hard to break a habit to which one has grown accustomed. It was a relief and a solace to me to come here when I could snatch a moment from my many occupations. Will you regret me a little, Lisette?"

"Of course."

He gave a deep sigh.

"I should never have thought you capable of so much deception."

"It is the deception that rankles." she murmured thoughtfully. "Men are funny in that way. They cannot forgive being made fools of. It is because they are so vain. They attach importance to things that are of no consequence."

"Do you call it a matter of no consequence that I should

66

find you having breakfast with a young man wearing my pyjamas?"

"If he were my husband and you were my lover you would think it perfectly natural."

"Obviously. For then I should be deceiving him and my honour would be secure."

"In short, I have only to marry him to make the situation perfectly regular."

For a moment he did not understand. Then her meaning flashed across his clever brain and he gave her a quick look. Her lovely eyes had the twinkle he always found so alluring and on her large red mouth was the suspicion of a roguish smile.

"Do not forget that as a member of the Senate I am by all the traditions of the Republic the authorised mainstay of morality and good behaviour."

"Does that weigh very heavily with you?"

He stroked his handsome square beard with a composed and dignified gesture.

"Not a row of beans," he replied, but the expression he used had a Gallic breadth that would perhaps have given his more conservative supporters something of a shock.

"Would he marry you?" he asked.

"He adores me. Of course he would marry me. If I told him I had a *dot* of a million francs he would ask nothing better."

Monsieur Le Sueur gave her another look. When in a moment of anger he told her it had been his intention to settle a million francs on her he had exaggerated a good deal in the desire to make her see how much her treachery was costing her. But he was not the man to draw back when his dignity was concerned.

"It is much more than a young man in his position of life could aspire to. But if he adores you he would be always at your side."

"Didn't I tell you that he was a commercial traveller? He can only come to Paris for the week-end."

"That of course is a horse of another colour," said the Senator. "It would naturally be a satisfaction to him to know that during his absence I should be there to keep an eye on you."

"A considerable satisfaction," said Lisette.

To facilitate the conversation she rose from her seat and made herself comfortable on the Senator's knee. He pressed her hand tenderly.

"I am very fond of you, Lisette," he said. "I should not like you to make a mistake. Are you sure he will make you happy."

"I think so."

"I will have proper enquiries made. I would never consent to your marrying anyone not of exemplary character and unimpeachable morality. For all our sakes we must make quite sure about this young man whom we are preparing to bring into our lives."

Lisette raised no objection. She was aware that the Senator liked to do things with order and method. He now prepared to leave her. He wanted to break his important news to Madame Le Sueur, and he had to get in touch with various persons in the parliamentary group to which he belonged.

"There is only one more thing," he said, as he bade Lisette an affectionate farewell, "if you marry I must insist on your giving up your work. The place of a wife is the home, and it is against all my principles that a married woman should take the bread out of a man's mouth."

Lisette reflected that a strapping young man would look rather funny walking round the room, with his hips swaying, to show off the latest models, but she respected the Senator's principles.

"It shall be as you wish, darling," she said.

The enquiries he made were satisfactory and the marriage took place on a Saturday morning as soon as the legal formalities were completed. Monsieur Le Sueur, Minister of the Interior, and Madame Saladin were witnesses. The bridegroom was a slim young man with a straight nose, fine eyes and black waving hair brushed straight back from his forehead. He looked more like a tennis-player than a traveller in silk. The Mayor, impressed by the august presence of the Minister of the Interior, made according to French practice a speech which he sought to render eloquent. He began by telling the married couple what presumably they knew already. He informed the bridegroom that he was the son of worthy parents and was engaged in an honourable profession. He congratulated him on entering the bonds of matrimony at an age when many young men thought only of their pleasures. He reminded the bride that her father was a hero of the great war, whose glorious wounds had been rewarded by a concession to sell tobacco, and he told her that she had earned a decent living since her arrival in Paris in an establishment that was one of the glories of French taste and luxury. The Mayor was of a literary turn and he briefly mentioned various celebrated lovers of fiction, Romeo and Juliet whose short but legitimate union had been interrupted by a regrettable misunderstanding, Paul and Virginia who had met her death at sea rather than sacrifice her modesty by taking off her clothes, and finally Daphnis and Chloe who had not consummated their marriage till it was sanctioned by the legitimate authority. He was so moving that Lisette shed a few tears. He paid a compliment to Madame Saladin whose example and precept had preserved her young and beautiful niece from the dangers that are likely to befall a young girl alone in a great city, and finally he congratulated the happy pair on the honour that the Minister of the Interior had done them in consenting to be a witness at the ceremony. It was a testimony to their own probity that this captain of industry and eminent statesman should find time to perform a humble office to persons in their modest sphere, and it proved not only the excellence of his heart but his lively sense of duty. His action showed that he appreciated the importance of early marriage, affirmed the security of the family and emphasised the desirability of producing offspring to increase the power, influence and consequence of the fair land of France. A very good speech indeed.

The wedding breakfast was held at the Château de Madrid which had sentimental associations for Monsieur Le Sueur. It has been mentioned already that among his many interests the Minister (as we must now call him) was interested in a firm of motor-cars. His wedding present to the bridegroom was a very nice two-seater of his own manufacture, and in this, when lunch was over, the young couple started off for their honeymoon. This could only last over the week-end since the young man had to get back to his work, which would take him to Marseilles, Toulon and Nice. Lisette kissed her aunt and she kissed Monsieur Le Sueur.

"I shall expect you at five on Monday," she whispered to him.

"I shall be there," he answered.

They drove away and for a moment Monsieur Le Sueur and Madame Saladin looked at the smart yellow roadster.

"As long as he makes her happy," sighed Madame Saladin, who was not used to champagne at lunch and felt unreasonably melancholy.

"If he does not make her happy he will have me to count with," said Monsieur Le Sueur impressively.

His car drove up.

"*Au revoir, chère Madame.* You will get a bus at the Avenue de Neuilly."

He stepped into his car and as he thought of the affairs of state that awaited his attention he sighed with content. It was evidently much more fitting to his situation that his mistress should be, not just a little mannequin in a dressmaker's shop, but a respectable married woman.

THE
MOTHER

Two or three people, hearing sounds of a quarrel in the patio,
came out of their rooms and listened.

"It's the new lodger," said a woman. "She's having a row
with the porter who brought her things."

It was a tenement house of two storeys, built round a patio,
in a back street of La Macarena, which is the roughest quarter
in Seville. The rooms were let to working men and the small
functionaries with whom Spain is overrun, postmen, policemen,
or tram-conductors, and the place swarmed with children.
There were twenty families there. They squabbled and made
it up; they chattered their heads off; they helped one another
when help was needed; for the Andalusians are good-natured
people, and on the whole they got on well enough together.
One room had been for some time unlet. A woman had taken
't that morning, and an hour later had brought her bits and
pieces, carrying as much as she could herself, a *gallego*—the
Galicians are the general porters of Spain—laden with the
rest.

But the quarrel was growing more violent, and the two
women above, on the first floor, anxious not to miss a word,
eant over the balcony.

They heard the newcomer's shrill voice raised in a torrent
f abuse and the man's sullen interjections. The two women
udged one another.

"I shan't go till you pay me," he kept on saying.

"But I've paid you already. You said you'd do it for three
reales."

"Never! You promised me four."

They were haggling over rather less than twopence
alfpenny.

71

"Four reales for moving those few things? You're crazy."
She tried to push him away.

"I shan't go till you pay me," he repeated.

"I'll give you a penny more."

"I won't take it."

The dispute grew more and more noisy. The woman screamed at the porter and cursed him. She shook her fist in his face. At last he lost patience.

"Oh, all right, give me the penny and I'll go. I'm not going to waste time on a slut like you."

She paid him, and the man, throwing down her mattress, left her. She flung a filthy word at him as he went. She came out of the room to drag the things in, and the two women in the balcony saw her face.

"*Carai*, what an evil face! She looks like a murderess."

A girl came up the stairs at that moment, and her mother called out: "Did you see her, Rosalia?"

"I asked the *gallego* where she came from, he says he brought the things from Triana. She promised him four reales and then wouldn't pay."

"Did he tell you her name?"

"He didn't know. But in Triana they called her La Cachirra."

The vixen appeared again to fetch a bundle she had forgotten. She glanced at the women in the balcony watching her unconcernedly, but said nothing. Rosalia shuddered.

"She frightens me."

La Cachirra was forty, haggard and very thin, with bony hands and fingers like a vulture's claws. Her cheeks were sunken and her skin wrinkled and yellow. When she opened her mouth, with its pale, heavy lips, she showed teeth that were pointed like those of a beast of prey. Her hair was black and coarse; she wore it in a clumsy knot, which seemed on the point of falling over her shoulders, and in front of each ear fell a straight wisp. Her eyes, deep-set in their sockets, large and black, shone fiercely. Her face bore an expression of such

72

ferocity that no one dared come near to speak with her. She kept entirely to herself. The curiosity of the neighbours was aroused. They knew she was very poor, for her clothes were wretched. She went out every morning at six and did not return till night; but they could not even find out how she earned her living. They urged a policeman who lived in the house to make inquiries.

"As long as she doesn't break the peace, I have nothing to do with her," said he.

But in Seville scandal travels quickly and in a few days a mason who lived in an upper room brought the news that a friend in Triana knew her story. La Cachirra had only come out of prison one month before, and she had spent seven years there—for murder. She had lodged in a house in Triana, but the children, finding out what had happened, threw stones at her and called her names; and she, turning upon them with foul words and with blows, had filled the whole place with such tumult that the landlord gave her notice. Cursing him and all who had turned her out, La Cachirra one morning suddenly disappeared.

"And whom did she murder?" asked Rosalia.

"They say it was her lover," replied the mason.

"She can never have had one," said Rosalia, with a laugh of scorn.

"Santa Maria!" cried Pilar, her mother, "I hope she won't kill any of us. I said she looked like a murderess!"

Rosalia, shivering, crossed herself. At that moment La Cachirra came in from her day's work and a sudden oppression fell upon the talkers. They made a movement as if to huddle together and looked nervously at the wild-eyed woman. She seemed to see something ominous in their silence and gave them a rapid, suspicious glance. The policeman, to make conversation, bade her good-evening.

"*Buena sera,*" she replied, with a scowl, and, passing quickly into her room, slammed the door.

They heard her lock it. The evil, sullen eyes had cast a

gloom over them and they talked in whispers as if under a mischievous spell.

"She has the devil in her," said Rosalia.

"I'm glad you're here to protect us, Manuel," added her mother to the policeman.

But La Cachirra seemed indisposed to give trouble. She went her way, unbending, never addressing so much as a word to anyone, and brusquely cut short every attempt at friendliness. She felt that the neighbours had discovered her secret, the homicide and the long years of imprisonment; and the lines in her face grew sterner, the expression of her deep-set eyes more inhuman. But gradually the anxiety she had caused was dispelled. Even the garrulous Pilar ceased to pay attention to the silent gaunt figure who occasionally passed through the group sitting in the patio.

"I dare say the prison has sent her mad, they say it often does."

But one day an event occurred to revive the gossip. A youth came to the *reja*—the wrought-iron gate that serves as front door to the Sevillan house—and asked for Antonia Sanchez. Pilar, who was mending a skirt in the patio, looked up at her daughter and shrugged her shoulders.

"No one of that name lives here," she said.

"Yes, she does," the young man answered; then, after a pause: "They call her La Cachirra."

"Ah!" Rosalia opened the gate and pointed to the door. "She's in there."

"Thank you."

The youth gave her a smile. She was a pretty girl, with a high colour and fine bold eyes. A red carnation threw up the glossy blackness of her hair. Her breasts were full and the nipples were prominent under her blouse.

"Blessed be the mother that bore you," he said, using a hackneyed phrase.

"*Vaya Usted con Dios,* go you with God," answered Pilar.

74

He passed on and knocked at the door. The two women looked after him curiously.

"Who can he be?" asked Pilar. "La Cachirra's never had a visitor before."

There was no reply to his knocking, and he knocked again. They heard La Cachirra's rasping voice ask who was there.

"Madre!" he cried. "Mother."

There was a shriek. The door was burst open.

"Currito!"

The woman threw her arms round his neck and kissed him passionately. She fondled him and with a loving gesture stroked his face with both her hands. The girl and her mother who watched would never have thought her capable of such tenderness. At last, with little sobs of joy, she dragged him into her room.

"He's her son," said Rosalia, with surprise. "Who'd have thought it! And a fine fellow like that."

Currito had a lean face and white, even teeth; his hair was cut very close, shaved on the temples, and set on the scalp with a truly Andalusian perfection. The shadow of his precocious beard showed blue beneath his brown skin. And of course he was a dandy. He had the national love of fine clothes and his trousers were skin-tight; his short jacket and his frilled shirt were as new as new could be. He wore a broad-brimmed hat.

At last the door of La Cachirra's room was opened and she appeared, hanging on her son's arm.

"You'll come again next Sunday?" she asked.

"If nothing stops me."

He glanced at Rosalia and, having bidden his mother good night, nodded to her also.

"Vaya Usted con Dios!" said she.

She gave him a smile and a flash of her dark eyes. La Cachirra intercepted the look; and the sullenness which her intense joy had driven away suddenly darkened her face like a thundercloud. She scowled fiercely at the handsome girl.

"Is that your son?" asked Pilar, when the youth was gone.

"Yes, he's my son," answered La Cachirra gruffly, going back to her room.

Nothing could soften her, and even when her heart was brimming over with happiness she repelled the overtures of friendship.

"He's a good-looking fellow," said Rosalia; and she thought of him more than once during the next few days.

It was a terrible love that La Cachirra had for her son. He was all she had in the world and she adored him with a fiery, jealous passion that demanded in return impossible devotion. She wished to be all in all to him. On account of his work they could not live together and it tortured her to imagine what he did when he was away from her. She could not bear him to look at a woman and she writhed at the bare idea that he might pay court to some girl. No amusement is more common in Seville than the long flirtation in which the maid sits at her window half the night long, guarded by iron bars, or stands at the gate, while her lover in the street pours his rapture into her willing ear. La Cachirra asked the boy if he had a *novia,* a sweetheart, aware that so attractive a youth must enjoy the smiles of women, and she knew he lied when he swore he spent his evenings at work. But his denials gave her a fierce delight.

When she saw Rosalia's provoking glance and Currito's answering smile, rage leapt to her throat. She had hated her neighbours before, because they were happy and she was wretched, because they knew her terrible secret; but now she hated them more, already fancying, half crazily, that they were conspiring to rob her of her son. On the following Sunday, in the afternoon, La Cachirra came out of her room, crossed the patio and stood at the gate. This was a proceeding so unusual that the neighbours commented upon it.

"Don't you know why she's there?" said Rosalia, with a stifled laugh. "Her precious son is coming, and she doesn't want us to see him."

"Does she think we'll eat him?"

76

Currito arrived and his mother took him quickly to her room. "She's as jealous of him as if he was her lover," said Pilar.

Rosalia looked at the closed door, laughing again, and her shining eyes were filled with mischief. It occurred to her that it would be very amusing to have a word with Currito. Rosalia's white teeth gleamed at the thought of La Cachirra's anger. She stationed herself at the gate, so that the pair, when they came out, could not help crossing her; but La Cachirra, seeing the girl, moved to the other side of her son so that not even a glance should pass between them. Rosalia shrugged her shoulders.

"You won't beat me so easily as that," she thought.

The Sunday after, when La Cachirra took up her place at the gate, Rosalia went out into the street and strolled along in the direction from which she guessed he would come. In a minute she saw Currito, and walked on, elaborately ignoring him.

"Hola!" said he, stopping.

"Is it you? I thought you were afraid to speak to me."

"I'm afraid of nothing," he answered boastingly.

"Except mamma!"

She walked on, as if she wanted him to leave her; but she knew very well he would do no such thing.

"Where are you going?" he asked.

"What has that to do with you, Currito? Go to your mother, my son, or she'll beat you. You're afraid to look at me when she's with you."

"What nonsense."

"Well, *vaya Usted con Dios!* I have commissions."

He went off rather sheepishly, and Rosalia laughed to herself. She was in the court-yard once more when he passed through with La Cachirra on his way out; and this time, shamed into courage, he stopped and said good night. La Cachirra turned red with anger.

"Come, Currito," she cried, with a rasping voice, "what are you waiting for?"

He went away, and the woman stopped a moment in front of Rosalia as if she were going to speak, but, with a visible effort, she restrained herself, and went back to her dark, silent room.

A few days later was the feast of San Isidoro, the patron saint of Seville, and to celebrate the holiday the mason and one or two others had put a string of Chinese lanterns in the patio. They glowed warmly in the clear summer night. The sky was soft against the shining stars. The people of the house were gathered in the middle of the patio, sitting on chairs; and the women, some with babies at their breasts, fanned themselves with little paper fans, interrupting their ceaseless chattering to fling a word of abuse at some older child who was making a nuisance of himself. The cool air was very pleasant after the day's breathless heat. Those who had been to the bull-fight were telling the less fortunate all about it. They described with precise detail a wonderful feat that Belmonte, the famous matador, had performed. With their vivid imaginations, the particulars gained every minute in variety and colour, so that it appeared that never in the history of Seville had there been a more excellent *corrida*. Everyone was present but La Cachirra, and in her room they saw the light of a solitary candle.

"And her son?"

"He's in there," answered Pilar. "I saw him pass an hour ago."

"He must be amusing himself," said Rosalia, with a laugh.

"Oh, don't bother about La Cachirra," said another. "Give us a dance, Rosalia."

"Yes, yes," they cried. "Go on, my girl. You dance."

In Spain they love dancing and they love to look at dancing. Years and years ago it was said that there was never a Spanish woman that was not born to dance.

The chairs were quickly set in a ring. The mason and the tram conductor fetched their guitars. Rosalia got her castanets, and stepping forward with another girl, began.

Currito, in the poky room, pricked up his ears when he heard the music.

"They're dancing," he said, and an itching shot down his limbs.

He looked through the curtain and saw the group in the mellow light of the Chinese lanterns. He saw the two girls dancing. Rosalia wore her Sunday clothes, and, as is customary, she was heavily powdered. A splendid carnation gleamed in her hair. Currito's heart beat quickly. Love in Spain grows fast, and he had thought often of the handsome girl since that day on which he first spoke to her. He moved towards the door.

"What are you doing?" asked La Cachirra.

"I'm going to look at them dance. You never wish me to amuse myself."

"It's Rosalia you want to see."

He pushed her away as she tried to stop him, and joined the group that watched the dancers. La Cachirra followed a step or two, and then stood, half hidden by the gloom, with fury gnawing at her heart. Rosalia saw him.

"Aren't you frightened to look at me?" she whispered, as she passed him.

The dancing had made her light-headed and she felt no fear of La Cachirra. When the measure ended and her partner sank into a chair, Rosalia marched up to Currito and stood in front of him, upright, with her head thrown back and her breast heaving with the rapid motion.

"Of course, you don't know how to dance," she said.

"Yes, I do."

"Well, come then."

She smiled provokingly, but he hesitated. He looked over his shoulder at his mother, whom he divined, rather than saw, in the darkness. Rosalia caught the glance and its meaning.

"Are you afraid?"

"What should I be afraid of?" he asked, with a shrug of the shoulders.

He stepped into the ring. The guitarists strummed

away and the onlookers rhythmically clapped their hands, punctuating the time with an occasional cry of Olé. A girl gave Currito a pair of castanets and the pair began to dance. They heard a little hiss, as of a serpent in the darkness, and Rosalia, quite reckless now, looked with a laugh at the face, ghastly white, that gleamed from the shadows. La Cachirra did not move. She watched the movements of the dance, the swaying of the bodies, the intricate steps; she saw Rosalia lean back with a graceful gesture and smile in Currito's face as he wound about her, clapping his castanets. Her eyes glowed like coals of fire and she felt them burning in the sockets; but no one noticed her, and she gave a groan of rage. The dance came to an end, and Rosalia, smiling with pleasure at the applause, told Currito she did not know he could dance so well.

La Cachirra flung herself into her room and bolted the door. She gave no answer when Currito came and bade her open.

"Well, I shall go home," he said.

Her heart bled with pain, but she would not speak. He was all she had, all she loved in the world; and yet she hated him. She could not sleep that night, but lay thinking, half-madly, that they were robbing her of her son. In the morning she did not go to work, but lay in wait for Rosalia. The girl came out at last, rather bedraggled after the night's festivities, and she started when La Cachirra suddenly faced her.

"What do you want with my son?"

"What do you mean?" replied Rosalia, assuming an expression of surprise.

La Cachirra quivered with passion and she bit her hand to keep herself quiet.

"Oh, you know what I mean. You're stealing him from me."

"Do you think I want your son? Keep him away from me. I can't help it if he runs after me wherever I go."

"That's a lie!"

"Ask him!" And now Rosalia's voice was so scornful that La Cachirra could hardly contain herself. "He waits an hour in the street to see me. Why don't you keep him to yourself?"

P.Alix

"You lie, you lie! You throw yourself in his way."

"If I wanted lovers I could get them without asking. I don't want the son of a murderess."

Then everything grew confused to La Cachirra; the blood leaped to her head and choked her eyes. She sprang at Rosalia and tore her hair. The girl gave a shrill cry and sought to defend herself, but immediately a passer-by wrenched them apart.

"If you don't leave Currito alone, I'll kill you!" cried La Cachirra.

"Do you think I'm frightened? Keep him from me if you can. You fool, don't you see that he loves me better than his eyes?"

"Now then, go away," said the man. "Don't answer her, Rosalia."

La Cachirra gave a little roar of passion, like a wild beast baulked of its prey, and pushed past into the street.

But the dance had left Currito madly in love with Rosalia, and all next day he thought of her red lips; the light of her eyes shone in his heart and filled him with enchantment. He passionately desired her. At nightfall he wandered towards the Macarena and presently found himself at her house. He waited in the darkness of the porch till he saw her in the patio. At the other end burned his mother's lonely light.

"Rosalia," he called in a low voice.

She turned, stifling a cry of surprise.

"Why are you here to-day?" she whispered, going towards him.

"I couldn't keep away from you."

"Why?" she smiled.

"Because I love you."

"Do you know your mother nearly killed me this morning?"

And with the embellishments necessary to the Andalusian temperament, she related the occurrence, omitting, however, the final taunt which had enraged La Cachirra beyond endurance.

"She's got the temper of the devil," said Currito; and then, with bravado: "I shall tell her that you're my sweetheart."

"She will be pleased," said Rosalia ironically.

"Will you come to the *reja* tomorrow?"

"Perhaps," she answered.

He gave a little chuckle, for he knew by her tone that she would. He swaggered even more than usual when he walked through the Sierpes on his way home. She was waiting for him when he came next day and, as is the way with lovers in Seville, they talked for hours under their breath, with the iron gate between them, and it never even occurred to Currito that it was a needless impediment. When he asked Rosalia if she loved him she answered with a little amorous sigh. They tried to see the passion that burnt hotly in one another's eyes. Then he went every night.

But fearing that his mother knew of his visits, Currito did not go to see her on the following Sunday. The wretched woman waited for him with an aching heart. She was ready to fall on her knees and beg him to forgive her, but then, when he did not come, she hated him; she would have liked to see him dead at her feet. Her heart sank when she thought that another week must pass before she could even hope to see him.

The week passed and still he did not come. She could not bear it. Anguish, anguish! She loved him as no sweetheart could ever love him. She told herself that this was Rosalia's doing and when she thought of her, rage filled her heart. At last Currito plucked up his courage and went to see his mother; but she had waited too long. It seemed as though her love was dead. She pushed him away when he wanted to kiss her.

"Why haven't you come before?"

"You locked the door on me. I thought you didn't want me!"

"Was it only that? Had you no other reason?"

"I've been busy," he said, shrugging his shoulders.

"Busy? An idle loafer like you. What have you been doing? You wouldn't have been too busy to come and see Rosalia."

"Why did you hit her?"

"How do you know I hit her? Have you seen her?" La

82

Cachirra strode up to her son; her eyes flashed. "She called me a murderess."

"Well, what of it?"

"What of it?" she screamed, so that they heard her in the patio. "And if I am a murderess—it was for you. Yes, I killed Pepe Santi; but it was because he was beating you. It was for your sake that I lay in prison for seven years—for seven years. Oh, you fool, you think she cares for you, and every night she spends hours at the gate."

"I know," Currito answered with a grin.

La Cachirra started violently. She shot a puzzled look at him and then she understood. She gasped with pain and wrath; she clutched at her heart as though the agony were too intense to bear.

"You've been coming every night to the *reja* and you never came near me? Oh, how cruel! I've done everything in the world for you. Do you think I loved Pepe Santi? I endured his blows so that I could give you bread; and I killed him when he beat you. Oh, God, I only lived for you. But for the thought of you I would have died rather than suffer those years of prison."

"Come, woman, be reasonable. I'm twenty. What d'you expect? If it wasn't Rosalia it would be another."

"You beast. I hate you. Get out."

She pushed him violently to the door. Currito shrugged his shoulders.

"You needn't think I want to stay."

He walked jauntily through the patio and slammed the iron gate behind him. La Cachirra stalked to and fro in her tiny room. The hours passed slowly. For a long while she remained at the window, watching with the horrible steadfastness of a savage beast ready to spring. She stood motionless, repressing the convulsive restlessness that tore at her heart-strings. There was a clapping of hands at the *reja* as a signal that someone was without, and she peered forward with panting mouth, her fiery eyes almost starting from her head. But it was only the mason. She waited longer, and Pilar, Rosalia's mother, came in and walked slowly up the stairs to her room. La Cachirra clutched at her throat to relieve the intolerable oppression of her breath. Still she waited. Now and then an extraordinary quiver travelled through all her limbs.

At last! There was a clap of light hands at the gate, and a voice above called out: "Who is it?"

"Peace!"

La Cachirra recognised Rosalia's voice. She gave a gasp of triumph. The door was opened from above, and Rosalia, entering, crossed the court-yard with a buoyant and easy step. The joy of life was in her every motion. She was about to put her foot on the stair when La Cachirra sprang forward and stopped her. She caught hold of her arm and the girl could not shake herself free.

"What do you want?" said Rosalia. "Let me pass."

"What have you been doing with my son?"

"Let me pass, or I shall call out."

"Is it true that you meet at the *reja* every night?"

"Mother, help! Antonio!" Rosalia cried out shrilly.

"Answer me."

"Well, if you want the truth, you can have it. He's going to marry me. He loves me, and I—I love him with all my heart." She turned on La Cachirra, trying to free herself from the vicious grip. "D'you think you can prevent us? D'you think he's frightened of you? He hates you, he told me so. He wishes you'd never come out of prison."

"He told you that?'

La Cachirra shrank back. Rosalia pursued the advantage.

"Yes, he told me that; and he told me much more. He told me that you murdered Pepe Santi; and that you were in prison for seven years; and he wished you were dead."

Rosalia hissed the words venomously, laughing with shrill voice when she saw the wretched woman shrink as though struck by palpable blows.

"And you ought to be proud that I don't refuse to marry the son of a murderess."

Then, giving La Cachirra a push, she leapt to the stairs; but the movement revived the woman, stunned by the horrible taunts, and with a cry of brutal rage she sprang upon Rosalia and caught her by the shoulders and dragged her down. Rosalia turned and hit her in the face. La Cachirra drew a knife from her bosom, and with an oath buried it in the girl's neck. Rosalia shrieked.

"Mother, she's killed me."

She fell to the bottom of the stairs and lay huddled up on the stones. Blood made a little pool on the ground.

Half a dozen doors were flung open at the despairing cry, and people rushed to seize La Cachirra; but she backed against the wall and faced them, with an expression of such ferocity on her face that no one dared approach her. The hesitation was momentary, but Pilar ran from the balcony shrieking, and the common attention for an instant was distracted. La Cachirra saw the opportunity and ran forward. She reached her room and locked and bolted the door behind her.

Suddenly the court was filled with people. Pilar with loud dreadful cries flung herself down on her daughter and would not let herself be dragged away. Someone rushed for a doctor and someone else went for the police. The crowd surged in from the street and collected round the door. The doctor hurried in with a black bag in his hand. When the police came a dozen people at once excitedly explained what had happened. They pointed to the door of La Cachirra's room, and the police broke in. There was a scuffle and they came out with La Cachirra handcuffed. The mob rushed forward, but the police surrounded her and with their scabbards beat the people off; but they shook their fists and hurled curses at her. She looked at them scornfully. She deigned to make no answer. Her eyes shone with triumph. The policemen led her through the patio and they passed by the body of Rosalia.

"Is she dead?" asked La Cachirra.

"Yes," the doctor answered gravely.

"Thanks be to God!" she said.

SANATORIUM

FOR the first six weeks that Ashenden was at the sanatorium he stayed in bed. He saw nobody but the doctor who visited him morning and evening, the nurses who looked after him and the maid who brought him his meals. He had contracted tuberculosis of the lungs and since at the time there were reasons that made it difficult for him to go to Switzerland the specialist he saw in London had sent him up to a sanatorium in the north of Scotland. At last the day came that he had been patiently looking forward to when the doctor told him he could get up; and in the afternoon his nurse, having helped him to dress, took him down to the veranda, placed cushions behind him, wrapped him up in rugs and left him to enjoy the sun that was streaming down from a cloudless sky. It was mid-winter. The sanatorium stood on the top of a hill and from it you had a spacious view of the snow-clad country. There were people lying all along the veranda in deck-chairs, some chatting with their neighbours and some reading. Every now and then one would have a fit of coughing and you noticed that at the end of it he looked anxiously at his handkerchief. Before the nurse left Ashenden she turned with a kind of professional briskness to the man who was lying in the next chair.

"I want to introduce Mr. Ashenden to you," she said. And then to Ashenden: "This is Mr. McLeod. He and Mr. Campbell have been here longer than anyone else."

On the other side of Ashenden was lying a pretty girl, with red hair and bright blue eyes; she had on no make-up, but her lips were very red and the colour on her cheeks was high. It emphasised the astonishing whiteness of her skin. It was lovely even when you realised that its delicate texture was due to illness. She wore a fur coat and was wrapped up in rugs, so that

86

you could see nothing of her body, but her face was extremely thin, so thin that it made her nose, which wasn't really large, look a trifle prominent. She gave Ashenden a friendly look, but did not speak, and Ashenden, feeling rather shy among all those strange people, waited to be spoken to.

"First time they've let you get up, is it?" said McLeod.

"Yes."

"Where's your room?"

Ashenden told him.

"Small. I know every room in the place. I've been here for seventeen years. I've got the best room here and so I damned well ought to have. Campbell's been trying to get me out of it, he wants it himself, but I'm not going to budge; I've got a right to it, I came here six months before he did."

McLeod, lying there, gave you the impression that he was immensely tall; his skin was stretched tight over his bones, his cheeks and temples hollow, so that you could see the formation of his skull under it; and in that emaciated face, with its great bony nose, the eyes were preternaturally large.

"Seventeen years is a long time," said Ashenden, because he could think of nothing else to say.

"Time passes very quickly. I like it here. At first, after a year or two, I went away in the summer, but I don't any more. It's my home now. I've got a brother and two sisters; but they're married and now they've got families; they don't want me. When you've been here a few years and you go back to ordinary life, you feel a bit out of it, you know. Your pals have gone their own ways and you've got nothing in common with them any more. It all seems an awful rush. Much ado about nothing, that's what it is. It's noisy and stuffy. No, one's better off here. I shan't stir again till they carry me out feet first in my coffin."

The specialist had told Ashenden that if he took care of himself for a reasonable time he would get well, and he looked at McLeod with curiosity.

"What do you do with yourself all day long?" he asked.

87

"Do? Having T.B. is a whole time job, my boy. There's my temperature to take and then I weigh myself. I don't hurry over my dressing. I have breakfast, I read the papers and go for a walk. Then I have my rest. I lunch and play bridge. I have another rest and then I dine. I play a bit more bridge and I go to bed. They've got quite a decent library here, we get all the new books, but I don't really have much time for reading. I talk to people. You meet all sorts here, you know. They come and they go. Sometimes they go because they think they're cured, but a lot of them come back, and sometimes they go because they die. I've seen a lot of people out and before I go I expect to see a lot more."

The girl sitting on Ashenden's other side suddenly spoke.

"I should tell you that few persons can get a heartier laugh out of a hearse than Mr. McLeod," she said.

McLeod chuckled.

"I don't know about that, but it wouldn't be human nature if I didn't say to myself: Well, I'm just as glad it's him and not me they're taking for a ride."

It occurred to him that Ashenden didn't know the pretty girl, so he introduced him.

"By the way, I don't think you've met Mr. Ashenden—Miss Bishop. She's English, but not a bad girl."

"How long have you been here?" asked Ashenden.

"Only two years. This is my last winter. Dr. Lennox says I shall be all right in a few months and there's no reason why I shouldn't go home."

"Silly, I call it," said McLeod. "Stay where you're well off, that's what I say."

At that moment a man, leaning on a stick, came walking slowly along the veranda.

"Oh, look, there's Major Templeton," said Miss Bishop, a smile lighting up her blue eyes; and then, as he came up: "I'm glad to see you up again."

"Oh, it was nothing. Only a bit of a cold. I'm quite all right now."

88

The words were hardly out of his mouth when he began to cough. He leaned heavily on his stick. But when the attack was over he smiled gaily.

"Can't get rid of this damned cough," he said. "Smoking too much. Dr. Lennox says I ought to give it up, but it's no good—I can't."

He was a tall fellow, good-looking in a slightly theatrical way, with a dusky, sallow face, fine very dark eyes and a neat black moustache. He was wearing a fur coat with an Astrakhan collar. His appearance was smart and perhaps a trifle showy. Miss Bishop made Ashenden known to him. Major Templeton said a few civil words in an easy, cordial way, and then asked the girl to go for a stroll with him; he had been ordered to walk to a certain place in the wood behind the sanatorium and back again. McLeod watched them as they sauntered off.

"I wonder if there's anything between those two," he said. "They do say Templeton was a devil with the girls before he got ill."

"He doesn't look up to much in that line just now," said Ashenden.

"You never can tell. I've seen a lot of rum things here in my day. I could tell you no end of stories if I wanted to."

"You evidently do, so why don't you?"

McLeod grinned.

"Well, I'll tell you one. Three or four years ago there was a woman here who was pretty hot stuff. Her husband used to come and see her every other week-end, he was crazy about her, used to fly up from London; but Dr. Lennox was pretty sure she was carrying on with somebody here, but he couldn't find out who. So one night when we'd all gone to bed he had a thin coat of paint put down just outside her room and next day he had everyone's slippers examined. Neat, wasn't it? The fellow whose slippers had paint on them got the push. Dr. Lennox has to be particular, you know. He doesn't want the place to get a bad name."

"How long has Templeton been here?"

"Three or four months. He's been in bed most of the time. He's for it all right. Ivy Bishop'll be a damned fool if she gets stuck on him. She's got a good chance of getting well. I've seen so many of them, you know, I can tell. When I look at a fellow I make up my mind at once whether he'll get well or whether he won't, and if he won't I can make a pretty shrewd guess how long he'll last. I'm very seldom mistaken. I give Templeton about two years myself."

McLeod gave Ashenden a speculative look and Ashenden, knowing what he was thinking, though he tried to be amused, could not help feeling somewhat concerned. There was a twinkle in McLeod's eyes. He plainly knew what was passing through Ashenden's mind.

"You'll get all right. I wouldn't have mentioned it if I hadn't been pretty sure of that. I don't want Dr. Lennox to hoof me out for putting the fear of God into his bloody patients."

Then Ashenden's nurse came to take him back to bed. Even though he had only sat out for an hour, he was tired, and was glad to find himself once more between the sheets. Dr. Lennox came in to see him in the course of the evening. He looked at his temperature chart.

"That's not so bad," he said.

Dr. Lennox was small, brisk and genial. He was a good enough doctor, an excellent business man, and an enthusiastic fisherman. When the fishing season began he was inclined to leave the care of his patients to his assistants; the patients grumbled a little, but were glad enough to eat the young salmon he brought back to vary their meals. He was fond of talking, and now, standing at the end of Ashenden's bed, he asked him, in his broad Scots, whether he had got into conversation with any of the patients that afternoon. Ashenden told him the nurse had introduced him to McLeod. Dr. Lennox laughed.

"The oldest living inhabitant. He knows more about the sanatorium and its inmates than I do. How he gets his information I haven't an idea, but there's not a thing about the private lives of anyone under this roof that he doesn't know. There's not an old maid in the place with a keener nose for a bit of scandal. Did he tell you about Campbell?"

"He mentioned him."

"He hates Campbell, and Campbell hates him. Funny, when you come to think of it, those two men, they've been here for seventeen years and they've got about one sound lung between them. They loathe the sight of one another. I've had to refuse to listen to the complaints about one another that they come to me with. Campbell's room is just below McLeod's and Campbell plays the fiddle. It drives McLeod wild. He says he's been listening to the same tunes for fifteen years, but Campbell says McLeod doesn't know one tune from another. McLeod wants me to stop Campbell playing, but I can't do that, he's got a perfect right to play so long as he doesn't play in the silence hours. I've offered to change McLeod's room, but he won't do that. He says Campbell only plays to drive him out of the room because it's the best in the house, and he's damned if he's going to have it. It's queer, isn't it, that two middle-aged men should think it worth while to make life hell for one another. Neither can leave the other alone. They have their meals at the same table, they play bridge together; and not a day passes without a row. Sometimes I've threatened to turn them both out if they don't behave like sensible fellows. That keeps them quiet for a bit. They don't want to go. They've been here so long, they've got no one any more who gives a damn for them, and they can't cope with the world outside. Campbell went away for a couple of months' holiday some years ago. He came back after a week; he said he couldn't stand the racket, and the sight of so many people in the streets scared him."

It was a strange world into which Ashenden found himself thrown when, his health gradually improving, he was able to mix with his fellow patients. One morning Dr. Lennox told him he could thenceforward lunch in the dining-room. This was a large, low room, with great window space; the windows were always wide open and on fine days the sun streamed in.

CREATURES OF CIRCUMSTANCE

There seemed to be a great many people and it took him some time to sort them out. They were of all kinds, young, middle-aged and old. There were some, like McLeod and Campbell, who had been at the sanatorium for years and expected to die there. Others had only been there for a few months. There was one middle-aged spinster called Miss Atkin who had been coming every winter for a long time and in the summer went to stay with friends and relations. She had nothing much the matter with her any more, and might just as well have stayed away altogether, but she liked the life. Her long residence had given her a sort of position, she was honorary librarian and hand in glove with the matron. She was always ready to gossip with you, but you were soon warned that everything you said was passed on. It was useful to Dr. Lennox to know that his patients were getting on well together and were happy, that they did nothing imprudent and followed his instructions. Little escaped Miss Atkin's sharp eyes, and from her it went to the matron and so to Dr. Lennox. Because she had been coming for so many years, she sat at the same table as McLeod and Campbell, together with an old general who had been put there on account of his rank. The table was in no way different from any other, and it was not more advantageously placed, but because the oldest residents sat there it was looked upon as the most desirable place to sit, and several elderly women were bitterly resentful because Miss Atkin, who went away for four or five months every summer, should be given a place there while they who spent the whole year in the sanatorium sat at other tables. There was an old Indian Civilian who had been at the sanatorium longer than anyone but McLeod and Campbell; he was a man who in his day had ruled a province, and he was waiting irascibly for either McLeod or Campbell to die so that he might take his place at the first table. Ashenden made the acquaintance of Campbell. He was a long, big-boned fellow with a bald head, so thin that you wondered how his limbs held together; and when he sat crumpled in an arm-chair he gave you the uncanny impression of a mannikin in a puppet-show. He was brusque, touchy and bad-tempered. The first thing he asked Ashenden was:

"Are you fond of music?"

"Yes."

"No one here cares a damn for it. I play the violin. But if you like it, come to my room one day and I'll play to you."

"Don't you go," said McLeod, who heard him. "It's torture."

"How can you be so rude?" cried Miss Atkin. "Mr. Campbell plays very nicely."

"There's no one in this beastly place that knows one note from another," said Campbell.

With a derisive chuckle McLeod walked off. Miss Atkin tried to smooth things down.

"You mustn't mind what Mr. McLeod said."

"Oh, I don't. I'll get back on him all right."

He played the same tune over and over again all that afternoon. McLeod banged on the floor, but Campbell went on. He sent a message by a maid to say that he had a headache and would Mr. Campbell mind not playing; Campbell replied that he had a perfect right to play and if Mr. McLeod didn't like it he could lump it. When next they met high words passed.

Ashenden was put at a table with the pretty Miss Bishop, with Templeton, and with a London man, an accountant, called Henry Chester. He was a stocky, broad-shouldered, wiry little fellow, and the last person you would ever have thought would be attacked by T.B. It had come upon him as a sudden and unexpected blow. He was a perfectly ordinary man, somewhere between thirty and forty, married, with two children. He lived in a decent suburb. He went up to the City every morning and read the morning paper; he came down from the City every evening and read the evening paper. He had no interests except his business and his family. He liked his work; he made enough money to live in comfort, he put by a reasonable sum every year, he played golf on Saturday afternoon and on Sunday, he went every August for a three weeks' holiday to the same place on the east coast; his children would grow up

93

and marry, then he would turn his business over to his son and retire with his wife to a little house in the country where he could potter about till death claimed him at a ripe old age. He asked nothing more from life than that, and it was a life that thousands upon thousands of his fellow-men lived with satisfaction. He was the average citizen. Then this thing happened. He had caught cold playing golf, it had gone to his chest, and he had had a cough that he couldn't shake off. He had always been strong and healthy, and had no opinion of doctors; but at last at his wife's persuasion he had consented to see one. It was a shock to him, a fearful shock, to learn that there was tubercle in both his lungs and that his only chance of life was to go immediately to a sanatorium. The specialist he saw then told him that he might be able to go back to work in a couple of years, but two years had passed and Dr. Lennox advised him not to think of it for at least a year more. He showed him the bacilli in his sputum, and in an X-ray photograph the actively-diseased patches in his lungs. He lost heart. It seemed to him a cruel and unjust trick that fate had played upon him. He could have understood it if he had led a wild life, if he had drunk too much, played around with women or kept late hours. He would have deserved it then. But he had done none of these things. It was monstrously unfair. Having no resources in himself, no interest in books, he had nothing to do but think of his health. It became an obsession. He watched his symptoms anxiously. They had to deprive him of a thermometer because he took his temperature a dozen times a day. He got it into his head that the doctors were taking his case too indifferently, and in order to force their attention used every method he could devise to make the thermometer register a temperature that would alarm; and when his tricks were foiled he grew sulky and querulous. But he was by nature a jovial, friendly creature, and when he forgot himself he talked and laughed gaily; then on a sudden he remembered that he was a sick man and you would see in his eyes the fear of death.

At the end of every month his wife came up to spend a day

or two in a lodging-house near-by. Dr. Lennox did not much like the visits that relatives paid the patients, it excited and unsettled them. It was moving to see the eagerness with which Henry Chester looked forward to his wife's arrival; but it was strange to notice that once she had come he seemed less pleased than one would have expected. Mrs. Chester was a pleasant, cheerful little woman, not pretty, but neat, as commonplace as her husband, and you only had to look at her to know that she was a good wife and mother, a careful housekeeper, a nice, quiet body who did her duty and interfered with nobody. She had been quite happy in the dull, domestic life they had led for so many years, her only dissipation a visit to the pictures, her great thrill the sales in the big London shops; and it had never occurred to her that it was monotonous. It completely satisfied her. Ashenden liked her. He listened with interest while she prattled about her children and her house in the suburbs, her neighbours and her trivial occupations. On one occasion he met her in the road. Chester for some reason connected with his treatment had stayed in and she was alone. Ashenden suggested that they should walk together. They talked for a little of indifferent things. Then she suddenly asked him how he thought her husband was.

"I think he seems to be getting on all right."

"I'm so terribly worried."

"You must remember it's a slow, long business. One has to have patience."

They walked on a little and then he saw she was crying.

"You mustn't be unhappy about him," said Ashenden gently.

"Oh, you don't know what I have to put up with when I come here. I know I ought not to speak about it, but I must. I can trust you, can't I?"

"Of course."

"I love him. I'm devoted to him. I'd do anything in the world I could for him. We've never quarrelled, we've never even differed about a single thing. He's beginning to hate me and it breaks my heart."

"Oh, I can't believe that. Why, when you're not here he talks of you all the time. He couldn't talk more nicely. He's devoted to you."

"Yes, that's when I'm not here. It's when I'm here, when he sees me well and strong, that it comes over him. You see, he resents it so terribly that he's ill and I'm well. He's afraid he's going to die and he hates me because I'm going to live. I have to be on my guard all the time; almost everything I say, if I speak of the children, if I speak of the future, exasperates him, and he says bitter, wounding things. When I speak of something I've had to do to the house or a servant I've had to change it irritates him beyond endurance. He complains that I treat him as if he didn't count any more. We used to be so united, and now I feel there's a great wall of antagonism between us. I know I shouldn't blame him, I know it's only his illness, he's a dear good man really, and kindness itself, normally he's the easiest man in the world to get on with; and now I simply dread coming here and I go with relief. He'd be terribly sorry if I had T.B. but I know that in his heart of hearts it would be a relief. He could forgive me, he could forgive fate, if he thought I was going to die too. Sometimes he tortures me by talking about what I shall do when he's dead, and when I get hysterical and cry out to him to stop, he says I needn't grudge him a little pleasure when he'll be dead so soon and I can go on living for years and years and have a good time. Oh, it's so frightful to think that this love we've had for one another all these years should die in this sordid, miserable way."

Mrs. Chester sat down on a stone by the roadside and gave way to passionate weeping. Ashenden looked at her with pity, but could find nothing to say that might comfort her. What she had told him did not come quite as a surprise.

"Give me a cigarette," she said at last. "I mustn't let my eyes get all red and swollen, or Henry'll know I've been crying and he'll think I've had bad news about him. Is death so horrible? Do we all fear death like that?"

96

"I don't know," said Ashenden.

"When my mother was dying she didn't seem to mind a bit. She knew it was coming and she even made little jokes about it. But she was an old woman."

Mrs. Chester pulled herself together and they set off again. They walked for a while in silence.

"You won't think any the worse of Henry for what I've told you?" she said at last.

"Of course not."

"He's been a good husband and a good father. I've never known a better man in my life. Until this illness I don't think an unkind or ungenerous thought ever passed through his head."

The conversation left Ashenden pensive. People often said he had a low opinion of human nature. It was because he did not always judge his fellows by the usual standards. He accepted, with a smile, a tear or a shrug of the shoulders, much that filled others with dismay. It was true that you would never have expected that good-natured, commonplace little chap to harbour such bitter and unworthy thought; but who has ever been able to tell to what depths man may fall or to what heights rise? The fault lay in the poverty of his ideals. Henry Chester was born and bred to lead an average life, exposed to the normal vicissitudes of existence, and when an unforeseeable accident befell him he had no means of coping with it. He was like a brick made to take its place with a million others in a huge factory, but by chance with a flaw in it so that it is inadequate to its purpose. And the brick too, if it had a mind, might cry: What have I done that I cannot fulfil my modest end, but must be taken away from all these other bricks that support me and thrown on the dust-heap? It was no fault of Henry Chester's that he was incapable of the conceptions that might have enabled him to bear his calamity with resignation. It is not everyone who can find solace in art or thought. It is the tragedy of our day that these humble souls have lost their faith in God, in whom lay hope, and their belief in a resurrec-

97

tion that might bring them the happiness that has been denied them on earth; and have found nothing to put in their place.

There are people who say that suffering ennobles. It is not true. As a general rule it makes man petty, querulous and selfish; but here in this sanatorium there was not much suffering. In certain stages of tuberculosis the slight fever that accompanies it excites rather than depresses, so that the patient feels alert and, upborne by hope, faces the future blithely; but for all that the idea of death haunts the subconscious. It is a sardonic theme song that runs through a sprightly operetta. Now and again the gay, melodious arias, the dance measures, deviate strangely into tragic strains that throb menacingly down the nerves; the petty interests of every day, the small jealousies and trivial concerns are as nothing; pity and terror make the heart on a sudden stand still and the awfulness of death broods as the silence that precedes a tropical storm broods over the tropical jungle. After Ashenden had been for some time at the sanatorium there came a boy of twenty. He was in the navy, a sub-lieutenant in a submarine, and he had what they used to call in novels galloping consumption. He was a tall, good-looking youth, with curly brown hair, blue eyes and a very sweet smile. Ashenden saw him two or three times lying on the terrace in the sun and passed the time of day with him. He was a cheerful lad. He talked of musical shows and film stars; and he read the paper for the football results and the boxing news. Then he was put to bed and Ashenden saw him no more. His relations were sent for and in two months he was dead. He died uncomplaining. He understood what was happening to him as little as an animal. For a day or two there was the same malaise in the sanatorium as there is in a prison when a man has been hanged; and then as though by universal consent, in obedience to an instinct of self-preservation, the boy was put out of mind: life, with it three meals a day, its golf on the miniature course, its regulated exercise, its prescribed rests, its quarrels and jealousies its scandal-mongering and petty vexations, went on as before

Campbell, to the exasperation of McLeod, continued to play the prize-song and "Annie Laurie" on his fiddle. McLeod continued to boast of his bridge and gossip about other people's health and morals. Miss Atkin continued to backbite. Henry Chester continued to complain that the doctors gave him insufficient attention and railed against fate because, after the model life he had led, it had played him such a dirty trick. Ashenden continued to read, and with amused tolerance to watch the vagaries of his fellow-creatures.

He became intimate with Major Templeton. Templeton was perhaps a little more than forty years of age. He had been in the Grenadier Guards, but had resigned his commission after the war. A man of ample means, he had since then devoted himself entirely to pleasure. He raced in the racing season, shot in the shooting season and hunted in the hunting season. When this was over he went to Monte Carlo. He told Ashenden of the large sums he had made and lost at baccarat. He was very fond of women and if his stories could be believed they were very fond of him. He loved good food and good drink. He knew by their first names the head waiters of every restaurant in London where you ate well. He belonged to half a dozen clubs. He had led for years a useless, selfish, worthless life, the sort of life which maybe it will be impossible for anyone to live in the future, but he had lived it without misgiving and had enjoyed it. Ashenden asked him once what he would do if he had his time over again and he answered that he would do exactly what he had done. He was an amusing talker, gay and pleasantly ironic, and he dealt with the surface of things, which was all he knew, with a light, easy and assured touch. He always had a pleasant word for the dowdy spinsters in the sanatorium and a joking one for the peppery old gentlemen, for he combined good manners with a natural kindliness. He knew his way about the superficial world of the people who have more money than they know what to do with as well as he knew his way about Mayfair. He was the kind of man who would always have been willing to take a bet, to help a friend and to give a tenner to a rogue. If he had never done much good in the world he had never done much harm. He amounted to nothing. But he was a more agreeable companion than many of more sterling character and of more admirable qualities. He was very ill now. He was dying and he knew it. He took it with the same easy, laughing nonchalance as he had taken all the rest. He'd had a thundering good time, he regretted nothing, it was rotten tough luck getting T.B., but to hell with it, no one can live for ever, and when you came to think of it, he might have been killed in the war or broken his bloody neck in a point-to-point. His principle all through life had been, when you've made a bad bet, pay up and forget about it. He'd had a good run for his money and he was ready to call it a day. It had been a damned good party while it lasted, but every party's got to come to an end, and next day it doesn't matter much if you went home with the milk or if you left while the fun was in full swing.

Of all those people in the sanatorium he was probably from the moral standpoint the least worthy, but he was the only one who genuinely accepted the inevitable with unconcern. He snapped his fingers in the face of death, and you could choose whether to call his levity unbecoming or his insouciance gallant.

The last thing that ever occurred to him when he came to the sanatorium was that he might fall more deeply in love there than he had ever done before. His amours had been numerous, but they had been light; he had been content with the politely mercenary love of chorus girls and with ephemeral unions with women of easy virtue whom he met at house parties. He had always taken care to avoid any attachment that might endanger his freedom. His only aim in life had been to get as much fun out of it as possible, and where sex was concerned he found every advantage and no inconvenience in ceaseless variety. But he liked women. Even when they were quite old he could not talk to them without a caress in

100

his eyes and a tenderness in his voice. He was prepared to do anything to please them. They were conscious of his interest in them and were agreeably flattered, and they felt, quite mistakenly, that they could trust him never to let them down. He once said a thing that Ashenden thought showed insight:

"You know, any man can get any woman he wants if he tries hard enough, there's nothing in that, but once he's got her, only a man who thinks the world of women can get rid of her without humiliating her."

It was simply from habit that he began to make love to Ivy Bishop. She was the prettiest and the youngest girl in the sanatorium. She was in point of fact not so young as Ashenden had first thought her, she was twenty-nine, but for the last eight years she had been wandering from one sanatorium to another, in Switzerland, England and Scotland, and the sheltered invalid life had preserved her youthful appearance so that you might easily have taken her for twenty. All she knew of the world she had learnt in these establishments, so that she combined rather curiously extreme innocence with extreme sophistication. She had seen a number of love affairs run their course. A good many men, of various nationalities, had made love to her; she accepted their attentions with self-possession and humour, but she had at her disposal plenty of firmness when they showed an inclination to go too far. She had a force of character unexpected in anyone who looked so flower-like and when it came to a show-down knew how to express her meaning in plain, cool and decisive words. She was quite ready to have a flirtation with George Templeton. It was a game she understood, and though always charming to him, it was with a bantering lightness that showed quite clearly that she had summed him up and had no mind to take the affair more seriously than he did. Like Ashenden, Templeton went to bed every evening at six and dined in his room, so that he saw Ivy only by day. They went for little walks together, but otherwise were seldom alone. At lunch the conversation between the four of them, Ivy, Templeton, Henry Chester and Ashenden, was general, but it was obvious that it was for neither of the two men that Templeton took so much trouble to be entertaining. It seemed to Ashenden that he was ceasing to flirt with Ivy to pass the time, and that his feeling for her was growing deeper and more sincere; but he could not tell whether she was conscious of it nor whether it meant anything to her. Whenever Templeton hazarded a remark that was more intimate than the occasion warranted she countered it with an ironic one that made them all laugh. But Templeton's laugh was rueful. He was no longer content to have her take him as a play-boy. The more Ashenden knew Ivy Bishop the more he liked her. There was something pathetic in her sick beauty, with that lovely transparent skin, the thin face in which the eyes were so large and so wonderfully blue; and there was something pathetic in her plight, for like so many others in the sanatorium she seemed to be alone in the world. Her mother led a busy social life, her sisters were married; they took but a perfunctory interest in the young woman from whom they had been separated now for eight years. They corresponded, they came to see her occasionally, but there was no longer very much between them. She accepted the situation without bitterness. She was friendly with everyone and prepared always to listen with sympathy to the complaints and the distress of all and sundry. She went out of her way to be nice to Henry Chester and did what she could to cheer him.

"Well, Mr. Chester," she said to him one day at lunch, "it' the end of the month, your wife will be coming tomorrow That's something to look forward to."

"No, she's not coming this month," he said quietly, looking down at his plate.

"Oh, I am sorry. Why not? The children are all right, aren' they?"

"Dr. Lennox thinks it's better for me that she shouldn' come."

There was a silence. Ivy looked at him with troubled eyes

102

"That's tough luck, old man," said Templeton in his hearty way. "Why didn't you tell Lennox to go to hell?"

"He must know best," said Chester.

Ivy gave him another look and began to talk of something else.

Looking back, Ashenden realised that she had at once suspected the truth. For next day he happened to walk with Chester.

"I'm awfully sorry your wife isn't coming," he said. "You'll miss her visit dreadfully."

"Dreadfully."

He gave Ashenden a sidelong glance. Ashenden felt that he had something he wanted to say, but could not bring himself to say it. He gave his shoulders an angry shrug.

"It's my fault if she's not coming. I asked Lennox to write and tell her not to. I couldn't stick it any more. I spend the whole month looking forward to her coming and then when she's here I hate her. You see, I resent so awfully having this filthy disease. She's strong and well and full of beans. It maddens me when I see the pain in her eyes. What does it matter to her really? Who cares if you're ill? They pretend to care, but they're jolly glad it's you and not them. I'm a swine, aren't I?"

Ashenden remembered how Mrs. Chester had sat on a stone by the side of the road and wept.

"Aren't you afraid you'll make her very unhappy, not letting her come?"

"She must put up with that. I've got enough with my own unhappiness without bothering with hers."

Ashenden did not know what to say and they talked on in silence. Suddenly Chester broke out irritably.

"It's all very well for you to be disinterested and unselfish, you're going to live. I'm going to die, and God damn it, I don't want to die. Why should I? It's not fair."

Time passed. In a place like the sanatorium where there was little to occupy the mind it was inevitable that soon everyone should know that George Templeton was in love with Ivy Bishop. But it was not so easy to tell what her feelings were. It was plain that she liked his company, but she did not seek it, and indeed it looked as though she took pains not to be alone with him. One or two of the middle-aged ladies tried to trap her into some compromising admission, but ingenuous as she was, she was easily a match for them. She ignored their hints and met their straight questions with incredulous laughter. She succeeded in exasperating them.

"She can't be so stupid as not to see that he's mad about her."

"She has no right to play with him like that."

"I believe she's just as much in love with him as he is with her."

"Dr. Lennox ought to tell her mother."

No one was more incensed than McLeod.

"Too ridiculous. After all, nothing can come of it. He's riddled with T.B. and she's not much better."

Campbell on the other hand was sardonic and gross.

"I'm all for their having a good time while they can. I bet there's a bit of hanky-panky going on if one only knew, and I don't blame 'em."

"You cad," said McLeod.

"Oh, come off it. Templeton isn't the sort of chap to play bumble-puppy bridge with a girl like that unless he's getting something out of it, and she knows a thing or two, I bet."

Ashenden, who saw most of them, knew them better than any of the others. Templeton at last had taken him into his confidence. He was rather amused at himself.

"Rum thing at my time of life, falling in love with a decent girl. Last thing I'd ever expected of myself. And it's no good denying it, I'm in it up to the neck; if I were a well man I'd ask her to marry me tomorrow. I never knew a girl could be as nice as that. I've always thought girls, decent girls, I mean damned bores. But she isn't a bore, she's as clever as she can stick. And pretty too. My God, what a skin! And that hair but it isn't any of that that's bowled me over like a row o

104

ninepins. D'you know what's got me? Damned ridiculous when you come to think of it. An old rip like me. Virtue. Makes me laugh like a hyena. Last thing I've ever wanted in a woman, but there it is, no getting away from it, she's good, and it makes me feel like a worm. Surprises you, I suppose?"

"Not a bit," said Ashenden. "You're not the first rake who's fallen to innocence. It's merely the sentimentality of middle age."

"Dirty dog," laughed Templeton.

"What does she say to it?"

"Good God, you don't suppose I've told her. I've never said a word to her that I wouldn't have said before anyone else. I may be dead in six months, and besides, what have I got to offer a girl like that?"

Ashenden by now was pretty sure that she was just as much in love with Templeton as he was with her. He had seen the flush that coloured her cheeks when Templeton came into the dining-room and he had noticed the soft glance she gave him now and then when he was not looking at her. There was a peculiar sweetness in her smile when she listened to him telling some of his old experiences. Ashenden had the impression that she basked comfortably in his love as the patients on the terrace, facing the snow, basked in the hot sunshine; but it might very well be that she was content to leave it at that, and it was certainly no business of his to tell Templeton what perhaps she had no wish that he should know.

Then an incident occurred to disurb the monotony of life. Though McLeod and Campbell were always at odds they played bridge together because, till Templeton came, they were the best players in the sanatorium. They bickered incessantly, their post-mortems were endless, but after so many years each knew the other's game perfectly and they took a keen delight in scoring off one another. As a rule Templeton refused to play with them; though a fine player he preferred to play with Ivy Bishop, and McLeod and Campbell were agreed on this, that she ruined the game. She was the kind of player who, having made a mistake that lost the rubber, would laugh and say: Well, it only made the difference of a trick. But one afternoon, since Ivy was staying in her room with a headache, Templeton consented to play with Campbell and McLeod. Ashenden was the fourth. Though it was the end of March there had been heavy snow for several days, and they played, in a veranda open on three sides to the wintry air, in fur coats and caps, with mittens on their heads. The stakes were too small for a gambler like Templeton to take the game seriously and his bidding was overbold, but he played so much better than the other three that he generally managed to make his contract or at least to come near it. But there was much doubling and redoubling. The cards ran high, so that an inordinate number of small slams were bid; it was a tempestuous game, and McLeod and Campbell lashed one another with their tongues. Half-past five arrived and the last rubber was started, for at six the bell rang to send everyone to rest. It was a hard-fought rubber, with sets on both sides, for McLeod and Campbell were opponents and each was determined that the other should not win. At ten minutes to six it was game all and the last hand was dealt. Templeton was McLeod's partner and Ashenden Campbell's. The bidding started with two clubs from McLeod; Ashenden said nothing; Templeton showed that he had substantial help, and finally McLeod called a grand slam. Campbell doubled and McLeod redoubled. Hearing this, the players at other tables who had broken off gathered round and the hands were played in deadly silence to a little crowd of onlookers. McLeod's face was white with excitement and there were beads of sweat on his brow. His hands trembled. Campbell was very grim. McLeod had to take two finesses and they both came off. He finished with a squeeze and got the last of the thirteen tricks. There was a burst of applause from the onlookers. McLeod, arrogant in victory, sprang to his feet. He shook his clenched fist at Campbell.

"Play that off on your blasted fiddle," he shouted. "Grand

106

slam doubled and redoubled. I've wanted to get it all my life and now I've got it. By God. By God."

He gasped. He staggered forward and fell across the table. A stream of blood poured from his mouth. The doctor was sent for. Attendants came. He was dead.

He was buried two days later, early in the morning so that the patients should not be disturbed by the sight of a funeral. A relation in black came from Glasgow to attend it. No one had liked him. No one regretted him. At the end of a week so far as one could tell, he was forgotten. The Indian Civilian took his place at the principal table and Campbell moved into the room he had so long wanted.

"Now we shall have peace," said Dr. Lennox to Ashenden. "When you think that I've had put up with the quarrels and complaints of those two men for years and years . . . Believe me, one has to have patience to run a sanatorium. And to think that after all the trouble he's given me he had to end up like that and scare all those people out of their wits."

"It was a bit of a shock, you know," said Ashenden.

"He was a worthless fellow and yet some of the women have been quite upset about it. Poor little Miss Bishop cried her eyes out."

"I suspect that she was the only one who cried for him and not for herself."

But presently it appeared that there was one person who had not forgotten him. Campbell went about like a lost dog. He wouldn't play bridge. He wouldn't talk. There was no doubt about it, he was moping for McLeod. For several days he remained in his room, having his meals brought to him, and then went to Dr. Lennox and said he didn't like it as well as his old one and wanted to be moved back. Dr. Lennox lost his temper, which he rarely did, and told him he had been pestering him to give him that room for years and now he could stay there or get out of the sanatorium. He returned to it and sat gloomily brooding.

"Why don't you play your violin?" the matron asked him

at length. "I haven't heard you play for a fortnight."

"I haven't."

"Why not?"

"It's no fun any more. I used to get a kick out of playing because I knew it maddened McLeod. But now nobody cares if I play or not. I shall never play again."

Nor did he for all the rest of the time that Ashenden was at the sanatorium. It was strange, now that McLeod was dead life had lost its savour for him. With no one to quarrel with, no one to infuriate, he had lost his incentive and it was plain that it would not be long before he followed his enemy to the grave.

But on Templeton McLeod's death had another effect, and one which was soon to have unexpected consequences. He talked to Ashenden about it in his cool, detached way.

"Grand, passing out like that in his moment of triumph. I can't make out why everyone got in such a state about it. He'd been here for years, hadn't he?"

"Eighteen, I believe."

"I wonder if it's worth it. I wonder if it's not better to have one's fling and take the consequences."

"I suppose it depends on how much you value life."

"But is this life?"

Ashenden had no answer. In a few months he could count on being well, but you only had to look at Templeton to know that he was not going to recover. The death-look was on his face.

"D'you know what I've done?" asked Templeton. "I've asked Ivy to marry me."

Ashenden was startled.

"What did she say?"

"Bless her little heart, she said it was the most ridiculous idea she'd ever heard in her life and I was crazy to think of such a thing."

"You must admit she was right."

"Quite. But she's going to marry me."

"It's madness."

"I dare say it is; but anyhow, we're going to see Lennox and ask him what he thinks about it."

The winter had broken at last; there was still snow on the hills, but in the valleys it was melted and on the lower slopes the birch-trees were in bud all ready to burst into delicate leaf. The enchantment of spring was in the air. The sun was hot. Everyone felt alert and some felt happy. The old stagers who came only for the winter were making their plans to go south. Templeton and Ivy went to see Dr. Lennox together. They told him what they had in mind. He examined them; they were X-rayed and various tests were taken. Dr. Lennox fixed a day when he would tell them the results and in the light of this discuss their proposal. Ashenden saw them just before they went to keep the appointment. They were anxious, but did their best to make a joke of it. Dr. Lennox showed them the results of his examinations and explained to them in plain language what their condition was.

"All that's very fine and large," said Templeton then, "but what we want to know is whether we can get married."

"It would be highly imprudent."

"We know that, but does it matter?"

"And criminal if you had a child."

"We weren't thinking of having one," said Ivy.

"Well, then I'll tell you in a very few words how the matter stands. Then you must decide for yourselves."

Templeton gave Ivy a little smile and took her hand. The doctor went on.

"I don't think Miss Bishop will ever be strong enough to lead a normal life, but if she continues to live as she has been doing for the last eight years . . ."

"In sanatoriums?"

"Yes. There's no reason why she shouldn't live very comfortably, if not to a ripe old age, as long as any sensible person wants to live. The disease it quiescent. If she marries, if she attempts to live an ordinary life, the foci of infection may

very well light up again, and what the results of that may be
no one can foretell. So far as you are concerned, Templeton,
I can put it even more shortly. You've seen the X-ray photos
yourself. Your lungs are riddled with tubercle. If you marry
you'll be dead in six months."

"And if I don't how long can I live?"

The doctor hesitated.

"Don't be afraid. You can tell me the truth."

"Two or three years."

"Thank you, that's all we wanted to know."

They went as they had come, hand in hand; Ivy was crying
softly. No one knew what they said to one another; but when
they came into luncheon they were radiant. They told
Ashenden and Chester that they were going to be married as
soon as they could get a licence. Then Ivy turned to Chester.

"I should so much like your wife to come up for my wedding.
D'you think she would?"

"You're not going to be married here?"

"Yes. Our respective relations will only disapprove, so we're
not going to tell them until it's all over. We shall ask Dr.
Lennox to give me away."

She looked mildly at Chester, waiting for him to speak, for
he had not answered her. The other two men watched him.
His voice shook a little when he spoke.

"It's very kind of you to want her. I'll write and ask her."

When the news spread among the patients, though everyone
congratulated them, most of them privately told one another
that it was very injudicious; but when they learnt, as sooner
or later everything that happened in the sanatorium was learnt,
that Dr. Lennox had told Templeton that if he married he
would be dead in six months, they were awed to silence. Even
the dullest were moved at the thought of these two persons who
loved one another so much that they were prepared to sacrifice
their lives. A spirit of kindliness and good will descended on
the sanatorium: people who hadn't been speaking spoke to one
another again; others forgot for a brief space their own

anxieties. Everyone seemed to share in the happiness of the happy pair. And it was not only the spring that filled those sick hearts with new hope, the great love that had taken possession of the man and the girl seemed to spread its effulgence on all that came near them. Ivy was quietly blissful; the excitement became her and she looked younger and prettier. Templeton seemed to walk on air. He laughed and joked as if he hadn't a care in the world. You would have said that he looked forward to long years of uninterrupted felicity. But one day he confided in Ashenden.

"This isn't a bad place, you know," he said. "Ivy's promised me that when I hand in my checks she'll come back here. She knows the people and she won't be so lonely."

"Doctors are often mistaken," said Ashenden. "If you live reasonably I don't see why you shouldn't go on for a long time yet."

"I'm only asking for three months. If I can only have that it'll be worth it."

Mrs. Chester came up two days before the wedding. She had not seen her husband for several months and they were shy with one another. It was easy to guess that when they were alone they felt awkward and constrained. Yet Chester did his best to shake off the depression that was now habitual and at all events at meal-times showed himself the jolly, hearty little fellow that he must have been before he fell ill. On the eve of the wedding day they all dined together, Templeton and Ashenden both sitting up for dinner; they drank champagne and stayed up till ten joking, laughing and enjoying themselves. The wedding took place next morning in the kirk. Ashenden was best man. Everyone in the sanatorium who could stand on his feet attended it. The newly married couple were setting out by car immediately after lunch. Patients, doctors and nurses assembled to see them off. Someone had tied an old shoe on the back of the car, and as Templeton and his wife came out of the door of the sanatorium rice was flung over them. A cheer was raised as they drove away, as they drove away to love and death. The crowd separated slowly. Chester and his wife went silently side by side. After they had gone a little way he shyly took her hand. Her heart seemed to miss a beat. With a sidelong glance she saw that his eyes were wet with tears.

"Forgive me, dear," he said. "I've been very unkind to you."

"I knew you didn't mean it," she faltered.

"Yes, I did. I wanted you to suffer because I was suffering. But not any more. All this about Templeton and Ivy Bishop— I don't know how to put it, it's made me see everything differently. I don't mind dying any more. I don't think death's very important, not so important as love. And I want you to live and be happy. I don't grudge you anything any more and I don't resent anything. I'm glad now it's me that must die and not you. I wish for you everything that's good in the world. I love you."

A WOMAN
OF FIFTY

My friend Wyman Holt is a professor of English Literature in one of the smaller universities of the Middle West, and hearing that I was speaking in a near-by city—near-by as distances go in the vastness of America—he wrote to ask me if I would come and give a talk to his class. He suggested that I should stay with him for a few days so that he could show me something of the surrounding country. I accepted the invitation, but told him that my engagements would prevent me from spending more than a couple of nights with him. He met me at the station, drove me to his house and after we had had a drink we walked over to the campus. I was somewhat taken aback to find so many people in the hall in which I was to speak, for I had not expected more than twenty at the outside and I was not prepared to give a solemn lecture, but only an informal chat. I was more than a little intimidated to see a number of middle-aged and elderly persons, some of whom I suspected were members of the faculty, and I was afraid they would find what I had to say very superficial. However, there was nothing to do but to start and, after Wyman had introduced me to the audience in a manner that I very well knew I couldn't live up to, that is what I did. I said my say, I answered as best I could a number of questions, and then I retired with Wyman into a little room at the back of the stage from which I had spoken.

Several people came in. They said the usual kindly things to me that are said on these occasions, and I made the usual polite replies. I was thirsting for a drink. Then a woman came in and held out her hand to me.

"How very nice it is to see you again," she said. "It's years since we last met."

To the best of my belief I'd never set eyes on her before. I forced a cordial smile to my tired, stiff lips, shook her proffered hand effusively and wondered who the devil she was. My professor must have seen from my face that I was trying to place her, for he said:

"Mrs. Greene is married to a member of our faculty and she gives a course on the Renaissance and Italian literature."

"Really," I said. "Interesting."

I was no wiser than before.

"Has Wyman told you that you're dining with us to-morrow night?"

"I'm very glad," I said.

"It's not a party. Only my husband, his brother and sister-in-law. I suppose Florence has changed a lot since then."

"Florence?" I said to myself. "Florence?"

That was evidently where I'd known her. She was a woman of about fifty with grey hair simply done and marcelled without exaggeration. She was a trifle too stout and she was dressed neatly enough, but without distinction, in a dress that I guessed had been bought ready-made at the local branch of a big store. She had rather large eyes of a pale blue and a poor complexion; she wore no rouge and had used a lipstick but sparingly. She seemed a nice creature. There was something maternal in her demeanour, something placid and fulfilled, which I found appealing. I supposed that I had run across her on one of my frequent visits to Florence and because it was perhaps the only time she had been there our meeting made more of an impression on her than on me. I must confess that my acquaintance with the wives of members of a faculty is very limited, but she was just the sort of person I should have expected the wife of a professor to be, and picturing her life, useful but uneventful, on scanty means, with its little social gatherings, its bickerings, its gossip, its busy dullness, I could easily imagine that her trip to Florence must linger with her as a thrilling and unforgettable experience.

On the way back to his house Wyman said to me:

114

"You'll like Jasper Greene. He's clever."

"What's he a professor of?"

"He's not a professor; he's an instructor. A fine scholar. He's her second husband. She was married to an Italian before."

"Oh?" That didn't chime in with my ideas at all. "What was her name?"

"I haven't a notion. I don't believe it was a great success." Wyman chuckled. "That's only a deduction I draw from the fact that she hasn't a single thing in the house to suggest that she ever spent any time in Italy. I should have expected her to have at least a refectory table, an old chest or two and an embroidered cope hanging on the wall."

I laughed. I knew those rather dreary pieces that people buy when they're in Italy, the gilt wooden candlesticks, the Venetian glass mirrors and the high-backed, comfortless chairs. They look well enough when you see them in the crowded shops of the dealers in antiques, but when you bring them to another country they're too often a sad disappointment. Even if they're genuine, which they seldom are, they look ill-at-ease and out of place.

"Laura has money," Wyman went on. "When they married she furnished the house from cellar to attic in Chicago. It's quite a show place; it's a little masterpiece of hideousness and vulgarity. I never go into the living-room without marvelling at the unerring taste with which she picked out exactly what you'd expect to find in the bridal suite of a second-class hotel in Atlantic City."

To explain this irony I should state that Wyman's living-room was all chromium and glass, rough modern fabrics, with a boldly Cubist rug on the floor, and on the walls Picasso prints and drawings by Tchelicheff. However, he gave me a very good dinner. We spent the evening chatting pleasantly about things that mutually interested us and finished it with a couple of bottles of beer. I went to bed in a room of somewhat aggressive modernity. I read for a while and then putting out the light composed myself to sleep.

115

CREATURES OF CIRCUMSTANCE

"Laura?" I said to myself. "Laura what?"

I tried to think back. I thought of all the people I knew in Florence, hoping that by association I might recall when and where I had come in contact with Mrs. Greene. Since I was going to dine with her I wanted to recall something that would prove that I had not forgotten her. People look upon it as a slight if you don't remember them. I suppose we all attach a sort of importance to ourselves, and it is humiliating to realise that we have left no impression at all upon the persons we have associated with. I dozed off, but before I fell into the blessedness of deep sleep, my subconscious, released from the effort of striving at recollection, I suppose, grew active and I was suddenly wide awake, for I remembered who Laura Greene was. It was no wonder that I had forgotten her, for it was twenty-five years since I had seen her, and then only haphazardly during a month I spent in Florence.

It was just after the First World War. She had been engaged to a man who was killed in it and she and her mother had managed to get over to France to see his grave. They were San Francisco people. After doing their sad errand they had come down to Italy and were spending the winter in Florence. At that time there was quite a large colony of English and Americans. I had some American friends, a Colonel Harding and his wife, colonel because he had occupied an important position in the Red Cross, who had a handsome villa in the Via Bolognese, and they asked me to stay with them. I spent most of my mornings sightseeing and met my friends at Doney's in the Via Tornabuoni round about noon to drink a cocktail. Doney's was the gathering-place of everybody one knew, Americans, English and such of the Italians as frequented their society. There you heard all the gossip of the town. There was generally a lunch-party either at a restaurant or at one or other of the villas with their fine old gardens a mile or two from the centre of the city. I had been given a card to the Florence Club, and in the afternoon Charley Harding and I used to go there to play bridge or a dangerous game of poker

116

with a pack of thirty-two cards. In the evening there would be a dinner-party with more bridge perhaps and often dancing. One met the same people all the time, but the group was large enough, the people sufficiently various, to prevent it from being tedious. Everyone was more or less interested in the arts, as was only right and proper in Florence, so that, idle as life seemed, it was not entirely frivolous.

Laura and her mother, Mrs. Clayton, a widow, lived in one of the better boarding-houses. They appeared to be comfortably off. They had come to Florence with letters of introduction and soon made many friends. Laura's story appealed to the sympathies, and people were glad on that account to do what they could for the two women, but they were in themselves nice and quickly became liked for themselves. They were hospitable and gave frequent lunches at one or other of the restaurants where one ate macaroni and the inevitable scaloppini, and drank Chianti. Mrs. Clayton was perhaps a little lost in this cosmopolitan society, where matters that were strange to her were seriously or gaily talked about, but Laura took to it as though it were her native element. She engaged an Italian woman to teach her the language and soon was reading the *Inferno* with her; she devoured books on the art of the Renaissance and on Florentine history, and I sometimes came across her, Baedeker in hand, at the Uffizzi or in some church studiously examining works of art.

She was twenty-four or twenty-five then and I was well over forty, so that though we often met we became cordially acquainted rather than intimate. She was by no means beautiful, but she was comely in rather an unusual way; she had an oval face with bright blue eyes and very dark hair which she wore very simply, parted in the middle, drawn over her ears and tied in a chignon low on the nape of her neck. She had a good skin and a naturally high colour; her features were good without being remarkable and her teeth were even, small and white; but her chief asset was her easy grace of movement, and I was not surprised when they told me that she danced "divinely".

Her figure was very good, somewhat fuller than was the fashion of the moment; and I think what made her attractive was the odd mingling in her appearance of the Madonna in an altar-piece by one of the later Italian painters and a suggestion of sensuality. It certainly made her very alluring to the Italians who gathered at Doney's in the morning or were occasionally invited to lunch or dinner in the American or English villas. She was evidently accustomed to dealing with amorous young men, for though she was charming, gracious and friendly with them she kept them at their distance. She quickly discovered that they were all looking for an American heiress who would restore the family fortunes, and with a demure amusement which I found admirable made them delicately understand that she was far from rich. They sighed a little and turned their attentions at Doney's, which was their happy hunting-ground, to more likely objects. They continued to dance with her, and to keep their hand in flirted with her, but their aspirations ceased to be matrimonial.

But there was one young man who persisted. I knew him slightly because he was one of the regular poker-players at the club. I played occasionally. It was impossible to win and the disgruntled foreigners used sometimes to say that the Italians ganged up on us, but it may be only that they knew the particular game they played better than we did. Laura's admirer, Tito di San Pietro, was a bold and even reckless player and would often lose sums he could ill afford. (That was not his real name, but I call him that since his own is famous in Florentine history.) He was a good-looking youth, neither short nor tall, with fine black eyes, thick black hair brushed back from his forehead and shining with oil, an olive skin, and features of classical regularity. He was poor and he had some vague occupation, which did not seem to interfere with his amusements, but he was always beautifully dressed. No one quite knew where he lived, in a furnished room perhaps or in the attic of some relation; and all that remained of his ancestors' great possessions was a cinquecento villa about thirty miles from

118

the city. I never saw it, but I was told that it was of amazing beauty, with a great neglected garden of cypresses and live oaks, overgrown borders of box, terraces, artificial grottoes and crumbling statues. His widowed father, the count, lived there alone and subsisted on the wine he made from the vines of the small property he still owned and the oil from his olive trees. He seldom came to Florence, so I never met him, but Charley Harding knew him fairly well.

"He's a perfect specimen of the Tuscan nobleman of the old school," he said. "He was in the diplomatic service in his youth and he knows the world. He has beautiful manners and such an air, you almost feel he's doing you a favour when he says how d'you do to you. He's a brilliant talker. Of course he hasn't a penny, he squandered the little he inherited on gambling and women, but he bears his poverty with great dignity. He acts as though money were something beneath his notice."

"What sort of age is he?" I asked.

"Fifty, I should say, but he's still the handsomest man I've ever seen in my life."

"Oh?"

"You describe him, Bessie. When he first came here he made a pass at Bessie. I've never been quite sure how far it went."

"Don't be a fool, Charley," Mrs. Harding laughed.

She gave him the sort of look a woman gives her husband when she has been married to him many years and is quite satisfied with him.

"He's very attractive to women and he knows it," she said. "When he talks to you he gives you the impression that you're the only woman in the world and of course it's flattering. But it's only a game and a woman would have to be a perfect fool to take him seriously. He *is* very handsome. Tall and spare and he holds himself well. He has great dark liquid eyes, like the boy's; his hair is snow-white, but very thick still, and the contrast with his bronzed, young face is really breathtaking. He has a ravaged, rather battered look, but at the same time a look of such distinction, it's really quite incredibly romantic."

"He also has his great dark liquid eyes on the main chance," said Charley Harding drily. "And he'll never let Tito marry a girl who has no more money than Laura."

"She has about five thousand dollars a year of her own," said Bessie. "And she'll get that much more when her mother dies."

"Her mother can live for another thirty years, and five thousand a year won't go far to keep a husband, a father and two or three children, and restore a ruined villa with practically not a stick of furniture in it."

"I think the boy's desperately in love with her."

"How old is he?" I asked.

"Twenty-six."

A few days after this Charley, on coming back to lunch, since for once we were lunching by ourselves, told me that he had run across Mrs. Clayton in the Via Tornabuoni and she had said that she and Laura were driving out that afternoon with Tito to meet his father and see the villa.

"What d'you suppose that means?" asked Bessie.

"My guess is that Tito is taking Laura to be inspected by his old man, and if he approves he's going to ask her to marry him."

"And will he approve?"

"Not on your life."

But Charley was wrong. After the two women had been shown over the house they were taken for a walk round the garden. Without exactly knowing how it had happened Mrs. Clayton found herself alone in an alley with the old count. She spoke no Italian, but he had been an attaché in London and his English was tolerable.

"Your daughter is charming, Mrs. Clayton," he said. "I am not surprised that my Tito has fallen in love with her."

Mrs. Clayton was no fool and it may be that she too had

guessed why the young man had asked them to go and see the ancestral villa.

"Young Italians are very impressionable. Laura is sensible enough not to take their attentions too seriously."

"I was hoping she was not quite indifferent to the boy."

"I have no reason to believe that she likes him any more than any other of the young men who dance with her," Mrs. Clayton answered somewhat coldly. "I think I should tell you at once that my daughter has a very moderate income and she will have no more till I die."

"I will be frank with you. I have nothing in the world but this house and the few acres that surround it. My son could not afford to marry a penniless girl, but he is not a fortune-hunter and he loves your daughter."

The count had not only the grand manner, but a great deal of charm and Mrs. Clayton was not insensible to it. She softened a little.

"All that is neither here nor there. We don't arrange our children's marriages in America. If Tito wants to marry her, let him ask her, and if she's prepared to marry him she'll presumably say so."

"Unless I am greatly mistaken that is just what he is doing now. I hope with all my heart that he will be successful."

They strolled on and presently saw walking towards them the two young people hand in hand. It was not difficult to guess what had passed. Tito kissed Mrs. Clayton's hand and his father on both cheeks.

"Mrs. Clayton, Papa, Laura has consented to be my wife."

The engagement made something of a stir in Florentine society and a number of parties were given for the young couple. It was quite evident that Tito was very much in love, but less so that Laura was. He was good-looking, adoring, high-spirited and gay; it was likely enough that she loved him; but she was a girl who did not display emotion and she remained what she had always been, somewhat placid, amiable, serious but friendly, and easy to talk to. I wondered to what extent she had been influenced to accept Tito's offer by his great name, with its historical associations, and the sight of that beautiful house with its lovely view and the romantic garden.

"Anyhow there's no doubt about its being a love match on his side," said Bessie Harding, when we were talking it over. "Mrs. Clayton tells me that neither Tito nor his father has shown any desire to know how much Laura has."

"I'd bet a million dollars that they know to the last cent what she's got and they've calculated exactly how much it comes to in *lire*," said Harding with a grunt.

"You're a beastly old man, darling," she answered.

He gave another grunt.

Shortly after that I left Florence. The marriage took place from the Hardings' house and a vast crowd came to it, ate their food and drank their champagne. Tito and his wife took an apartment on the Lungarno and the old count returned to his lonely villa in the hills. I did not go to Florence again for three years and then only for a week. I was staying once more with the Hardings. I asked about my old friends and then remembered Laura and her mother.

"Mrs. Clayton went back to San Francisco," said Bessie, "and Laura and Tito live at the villa with the count. They're very happy."

"Any babies?"

"No."

"Go on," said Harding.

Bessie gave her husband a look.

"I cannot imagine why I've lived thirty years with a man I dislike so much," she said. "They gave up the apartment on the Lungarno. Laura spent a good deal of money doing things to the villa, there wasn't a bathroom in it, she put in central heating, and she had to buy a lot of furniture to make it habitable, and then Tito lost a small fortune playing poker and poor Laura had to pay up."

"Hadn't he got a job?"

"It didn't amount to anything and it came to an end."

"What Bessie means by that is that he was fired," Harding put in.

"Well, to cut a long story short, they thought it would be more economical to live at the villa and Laura had the idea that it would keep Tito out of mischief. She loves the garden and she's made it lovely. Tito simply worships her and the old count's taken quite a fancy to her. So really it's all turned out very well."

"It may interest you to know that Tito was in last Thursday," said Harding. "He played like a madman and I don't know how much he lost."

"Oh, Charley. He promised Laura he'd never play again."

"As if a gambler ever kept a promise like that. It'll be like last time. He'll burst into tears and say he loves her and it's a debt of honour and unless he can get the money he'll blow his brains out. And Laura will pay as she paid before."

"He's weak, poor dear, but that's his only fault. Unlike most Italian husbands he's absolutely faithful to her and he's kindness itself." She looked at Harding with a sort of humorous grimness. "I've yet to find a husband who was perfect."

"You'd better start looking around pretty soon, dear, or it'll be too late," he retorted with a grin.

I left the Hardings and returned to London. Charley Harding and I corresponded in a desultory sort of way, and about a year later I got a letter from him. He told me as usual what he had been doing in the interval, and mentioned that he had been to Montecatini for the baths and had gone with Bessie to visit friends in Rome; he spoke of the various people I knew in Florence, So and So had just bought a Bellini and Mrs. Such and Such had gone to America to divorce her husband. Then he went on: "I suppose you've heard about the San Pietros. It's shaken us all and we can talk of nothing else. Laura's terribly upset, poor thing, and she's going to have a baby. The police keep on questioning her and that doesn't make it any easier for her. Of course we brought her to stay here. Tito comes up for trial in another month."

I hadn't the faintest notion what all this was about. So I wrote at once to Harding asking him what it meant. He answered with a long letter. What he had to tell me was terrible. I will relate the bare and brutal facts as shortly as I can. I learned them partly from Harding's letter and partly from what he and Bessie told me when two years later I was with them once more.

The count and Laura took to one another at once and Tito was pleased to see how quickly they had formed an affectionate friendship for he was as devoted to his father as he was in love with his wife. He was glad that the count began to come more often to Florence than he had been used to. They had a spare room in the apartment and on occasion he spent two or three nights with them. He and Laura would go bargain-hunting in the antique shops and buy old pieces to put in the villa. He had tact and knowledge and little by little the house, with its spacious rooms and marble floors, lost its forlorn air and became a friendly place to live in. Laura had a passion for gardening and she and the count spent long hours together planning and then supervising the workmen who were restoring the gardens to their ancient, rather stately, beauty.

Laura made light of it when Tito's financial difficulties forced them to give up the apartment in Florence; she had had enough of Florentine society by then and was not displeased to live altogether in the grand house that had belonged to his ancestors. Tito liked city life and the prospect dismayed him, but he could not complain since it was his own folly that had made it necessary for them to cut down expenses. They still had the car and he amused himself by taking long drives while his father and Laura were busy, and if they knew that now and then he went into Florence to have a flutter at the club they shut their eyes to it. So a year passed. Then, he hardly knew why, he was seized with vague misgiving. He couldn't put his finger on anything; he had an uneasy feeling that perhaps Laura didn't care for him so much as she had at first: sometimes it seemed to him that his father was inclined to be impatient with him; they appeared to have a great deal to say to one another, but he got the impression that he was being edged out of their conversation, as though he were a child who was expected to sit still and not interrupt while his elders talked of things over his head; he had a notion that often his presence was unwelcome to them and that they were more at their ease when he was not there. He knew his father, and his reputation, but the suspicion that arose in him was so horrible that he refused to entertain it. And yet sometimes he caught a look passing between them that disconcerted him, there was a tender possessiveness in his father's eyes, a sensual complacency in Laura's, which, if he had seen it in others, would have convinced him that they were lovers. But he couldn't, he wouldn't believe that there was anything between them. The count couldn't help make love to a woman and it was likely enough that Laura felt his extraordinary fascination, but it was shameful to suppose for a moment that they, these two people he loved, had formed a criminal, almost an incestuous, connection. He was sure that Laura had no idea that there was anything more in her feeling than the natural affection of a young, happily-married woman for her father-in-law. Notwithstanding he thought it better that she should not remain in everyday contact with his father, and one day he suggested that they should go back to live in Florence. Laura and the count were astonished that he should propose such a thing and would not hear of it. Laura said that, having spent so much money on the villa, she couldn't afford to set up another establishment, and the count that it was absurd to leave it, now that Laura had made it so comfortable, to live in a wretched apartment in the city. An argument started and Tito got rather excited. He took some remark of Laura's to mean that if she lived at the villa it was to keep him out of temptation. This reference to his losses at the poker-table angered him.

"You always throw your money in my face," he said passionately. "If I'd wanted to marry money I'd have had the sense to marry someone who had a great deal more than you."

Laura went very pale and glanced at the count.

"You have no right to speak to Laura like that," he said. "You are an ill-mannered oaf."

"I shall speak to my wife exactly as I choose."

"You are mistaken. So long as you are in my house you will treat her with the respect which is her right and your duty."

"When I want lessons in behaviour from you, Father, I will let you know."

"You are very impertinent, Tito. You will kindly leave the room."

He looked very stern and dignified and Tito, furious and yet slightly intimidated, leapt to his feet and stalked out slamming the door behind him. He took the car and drove into Florence. He won quite a lot of money that day (lucky at cards, unlucky in love) and to celebrate his winnings got more than a little drunk. He did not go back to the villa till the following morning. Laura was as friendly and placid as ever, but his father was somewhat cool. No reference was made to the scene. But from then on things went from bad to worse. Tito was sullen and moody, the count critical, and on occasion sharp words passed between them. Laura did not interfere, but Tito gained the impression that after a dispute that had been more than acrimonious Laura interceded with his father, for the count thenceforward, refusing to be annoyed, began to treat him with the tolerant patience with which you would treat a wayward child. He convinced himself that they were acting in concert and his suspicions grew formidable. They even increased when Laura in her good-natured way, saying that it must be very dull for him to remain so much in the country, encouraged him to go more often to Florence to see his friends. He jumped to the conclusion that she said this only to be rid of him. He began to watch them. He would enter suddenly a room in which he knew they were, expecting to catch them in a compromising position, or silently follow them to a secluded part of the garden. They were chatting uncon-

126

cernedly of trivial things. Laura greeted him with a pleasant smile. He could put his finger on nothing to confirm his torturing suspicions. He started to drink. He grew nervous and irritable. He had no proof, no proof whatever, that there was anything between them, and yet in his bones he was certain that they were grossly, shockingly deceiving him. He brooded till he felt he was going mad. A dark aching fire within him consumed his being. On one of his visits to Florence he bought a pistol. He made up his mind that if he could only have proof of what in his heart he was certain of, he would kill them both.

I don't know what brought on the final catastrophe. All that came out at the trial was that, driven beyond endurance, Tito had gone one night to his father's room to have it out with him. His father mocked and laughed at him. They had a furious quarrel and Tito took out his pistol and shot the count dead. Then he collapsed and fell, weeping hysterically, on his father's body; the repeated shots brought Laura and the servants rushing in. He jumped up and grabbed the pistol, to shoot himself he said afterwards, but he hesitated or they were too quick for him, and they snatched it out of his hand. The police were sent for. He spent most of his time in prison weeping; he would not eat and had to be forcibly fed; he told the examining magistrate that he had killed his father because he was his wife's lover. Laura, examined and examined again, swore that there had never been anything between the count and herself but a natural affection. The murder filled the Florentine public with horror. The Italians were convinced of her guilt, but her friends, English and American, felt that she was incapable of the crime of which she was accused. They went about saying that Tito was neurotic and insanely jealous and in his stupid way had mistaken her American freedom of behaviour for a criminal passion. On the face of it Tito's charge was absurd. Carlo di San Pietro was nearly thirty years older than she, an elderly man with white hair; who could suppose that there would have been anything between her and her father-in-law, when her husband was young, handsome and in love with her?

It was in Harding's presence that she saw the examining magistrate and the lawyers who had been engaged to defend Tito. They had decided to plead insanity. Experts for the defence examined him and decided that he was insane, experts for the prosecution examined him and decided that he was sane. The fact that he had bought a pistol three months before he committed the dreadful crime went to prove that it was premeditated. It was discovered that he was deeply in debt and his creditors were pressing him; the only means he had of settling with them was by selling the villa, and his father's death put him in possession of it. There is no capital punishment in Italy, but murder with premeditation is punished by solitary confinement for life. On the approach of the trial the lawyers came to Laura and told her that the only way in which Tito could be saved from this was for her to admit in court that the count had been her lover. Laura went very pale. Harding protested violently. He said they had no right to ask her to perjure herself and ruin her reputation to save that shiftless, drunken gambler whom she had been so unfortunate as to marry. Laura remained silent for a while.

"Very well," she said at last, "if that's the only way to save him I'll do it."

Harding tried to dissuade her, but she was decided.

"I should never have a moments' peace if I knew that Tito had to spend the rest of his life alone in a prison cell."

And that is what happened. The trial opened. She was called and under oath stated that for more than a year her father-in-law had been her lover. Tito was declared insane and sent to an asylum. Laura wanted to leave Florence at once, but in Italy the preliminaries to a trial are endless and by then she was near her time. The Hardings insisted on her remaining with them till she was confined. She had a child, a boy, but it only lived twenty-four hours. Her plan was to go back to San Francisco and live with her mother till she could find a job, for Tito's extravagance, the money she had spent on the villa, and then the cost of the trial had seriously impoverished her.

It was Harding who told me most of this; but one day when he was at the club and I was having a cup of tea with Bessie and we were again talking over these tragic happenings she said to me:

"You know, Charley hasn't told you the whole story because he doesn't know it. I never told him. Men are funny in some ways; they're much more easily shocked than women."

I raised my eyebrows, but said nothing.

"Just before Laura went away we had a talk. She was very low and I thought she was grieving over the loss of her baby. I wanted to say something to help her. 'You musn't take the baby's death too hardly,' I said. 'As things are, perhaps it's better it died.' 'Why?' she said. 'Think what the poor little thing's future would have been with a murderer for his father.' She looked at me for a moment in that strange quiet way of hers. And then what d'you think she said?"

"I haven't a notion," said I.

"She said: 'What makes you think his father was a murderer?' I felt myself grow as red as a turkey-cock. I could hardly believe my ears. 'Laura, what *do* you mean?' I said. 'You were in court,' she said. 'You heard me say Carlo was my lover.'"

Bessie Harding stared at me as she must have stared at Laura.

"What did you say then?" I asked.

"What was there for me to say? I said nothing. I wasn't so much horrified, I was bewildered. Laura looked at me and, believe it or not, I'm convinced there was a twinkle in her eyes. I felt a perfect fool."

"Poor Bessie," I smiled.

Poor Bessie, I repeated to myself now as I thought of this strange story. She and Charley were long since dead and by their death I had lost good friends. I went to sleep then, and next day Wyman Holt took me for a long drive.

We were to dine with the Greenes at seven and we reached

their house on the dot. Now that I had remembered who Laura was I was filled with an immense curiosity to see her again. Wyman had exaggerated nothing. The living-room into which we went was the quintessence of commonplace. It was comfortable enough, but there was not a trace of personality in it. It might have been furnished *en bloc* by a mail-order house. It had the bleakness of a government office. I was introduced first to my host Jasper Greene and then to his brother Emery and to his brother's wife Fanny. Jasper Greene was a large, plump man with a moon face and a shock of black, coarse, unkempt hair. He wore large cellulose-rimmed spectacles. I was staggered by his youth. He could not have been much over thirty and was therefore nearly twenty years younger than Laura. His brother, Emery, a composer and teacher in a New York school of music, might have been seven or eight and twenty. His wife, a pretty little thing, was an actress for the moment out of a job. Jasper Greene mixed us some very adequate cocktails but for a trifle too much vermouth, and we sat down to dinner. The conversation was gay and even boisterous. Jasper and his brother were loud-voiced and all three of them, Jasper, Emery and Emery's wife, were loquacious talkers. They chaffed one another, they joked and laughed; they discussed art, literature, music and the theatre. Wyman and I joined in when we had a chance, which was not often; Laura did not try to. She sat at the head of the table, serene, with an amused, indulgent smile on her lips as she listened to their scatter-brained nonsense; it was not stupid nonsense, mind you, it was intelligent and modern, but it was nonsense all the same. There was something maternal in her attitude, and I was reminded oddly of a sleek dachshund lying quietly in the sun while she looks lazily, and yet watchfully, at her litter of puppies romping round her. I wondered whether it crossed her mind that all this chatter about art didn't amount to much when compared with those incidents of blood and passion that she remembered. But did she remember? It had all happened a long time ago and perhaps it seemed no more than a bad dream.

Perhaps these commonplace surroundings were part of her deliberate effort to forget, and to be among these young people was restful to her spirit. Perhaps Jasper's clever stupidity was a comfort. After that searing tragedy it might be that she wanted nothing but the security of the humdrum.

Possibly because Wyman was an authority on the Elizabethan drama the conversation at one moment touched on that. I had already discovered that Jasper Greene was prepared to lay down the law on subjects all and sundry, and now he delivered himself as follows:

"Our theatre has gone all to pot because the dramatists of our day are afraid to deal with the violent emotions which are the proper subject matter of tragedy," he boomed. "In the sixteenth century they had a wealth of melodramatic and bloody themes to suit their purpose and so they produced great plays. But where can our playwrights look for themes? Our Anglo-Saxon blood is too phlegmatic, too supine, to provide them with material they can make anything of, and so they are condemned to occupy themselves with the trivialities of social intercourse."

I wondered what Laura thought of this, but I took care not to catch her eye. She could have told them a story of illicit love, jealousy and parricide which would have been meat to one of Shakespeare's successors, but had he treated it, I suppose he would have felt bound to finish it with at least one more corpse strewn about the stage. The end of her story, as I knew it now, was unexpected certainly, but sadly prosaic and a trifle grotesque. Real life more often ends things with a whimper than with a bang. I wondered too why she had gone out of her way to renew our old acquaintance. Of course she had no reason to suppose that I knew as much as I did; perhaps with a true instinct she was confident that I would not give her away; perhaps she didn't care if I did. I stole a glance at her now and then while she was quietly listening to the excited babbling of the three young people, but her friendly, pleasant face told me nothing. If I hadn't known otherwise I would

131

have sworn that no untoward circumstance had ever troubled the course of her uneventful life.

The evening came to an end and this is the end of my story, but for the fun of it I am going to relate a small incident that happened when Wyman and I got back to his house. We decided to have a bottle of beer before going to bed and went into the kitchen to fetch it. The clock in the hall struck eleven and at that moment the phone rang. Wyman went to answer it and when he came back was quietly chortling to himself.

"What's the joke?" I asked.

"It was one of my students. They're not supposed to call members of the faculty after ten-thirty, but he was all hot and bothered. He asked me how evil had come into the world."

"And did you tell him?"

"I told him that St. Thomas Aquinas had got hot and bothered too about that very question and he'd better worry it out for himself. I said that when he found the solution he was to call me, no matter what time it was. Two o'clock in the morning if he liked."

"I think you're pretty safe not to be disturbed for many a long night," I said.

"I won't conceal from you that I have formed pretty much the same impression myself," he grinned.

THE
ROMANTIC
YOUNG LADY

One of the many inconveniences of real life is that it seldom gives you a complete story. Some incident has excited your interest, the people who are concerned in it are in the devil's own muddle, and you wonder what on earth will happen next. Well, generally nothing happens. The inevitable catastrophe you foresaw wasn't inevitable after all, and high tragedy, without any regard to artistic decency, dwindles into drawing-room comedy. Now, growing old has many disadvantages, but it has this compensation (among, let us admit, not a few others), that sometimes it gives you the opportunity of seeing what was the outcome of certain events you had witnessed long ago. You had given up the hope of ever knowing what was the end of the story, and then, when you least expected it, it is handed to you on a platter.

These reflections occurred to me when, having escorted the Marquesa de San Esteban to her car, I went back into the hotel and sat down again in the lounge. I ordered a cocktail, lit a cigarette and composed myself to order my recollections. The hotel was new and splendid, it was like every other first-class hotel in Europe, and I had been regretting that for the sake of its modern plumbing I had deserted the old-fashioned, picturesque Hotel de Madrid to which I generally went when I stayed in Seville. It was true that from my hotel I had a view of the noble river, the Guadalquivir, but that did not make up for the *thés dansants* that filled the bar-lounge two or three days a week with a fashionable crowd whose exuberant conversation almost drowned the strident din of a jazz orchestra.

I had been out all the afternoon, and coming in found myself in the midst of a seething mob. I went to the desk and asked for my key so that I might go straight up to my room. But the porter, handing it to me, said that a lady had been asking for me.

"For me?"

"She wants to see you very much. It's the Marquesa de San Esteban."

I knew no one of that name.

"It must be some mistake."

As I said the words, looking rather vaguely around, a lady came up to me with outstretched hands and a bright smile on her lips. To the best of my knowledge I had never seen her before in my life. She seized my hands, both of them, and shook them warmly. She spoke in fluent French.

"How very nice to see you again after all these years. I saw by the paper that you were staying here and I said to myself: I must look him up. How many years is it since we danced together? I daren't think. Do you still dance? I do. And I'm a grandmother. I'm fat of course, I don't care, and it keeps me from getting fatter."

She talked with such a rush that it took my breath away to listen to her. She was a stout, more than middle-aged woman, very much made up, with dark red hair, obviously dyed, cut short; and she was dressed in the height of Parisian fashion, which never suits Spanish women very well. But she had a gay, fruity laugh that made you feel you wanted to laugh too. It was quite obvious that she thoroughly enjoyed life. She was a fine figure of a woman and I could well believe that in youth she had been beautiful. But I could not place her.

"Come and drink a glass of champagne with me and we will talk of old times. Or will you have a cocktail? Our dear old Seville has changed, you see. *Thés dansants* and cocktails. It's just like Paris and London now. We've caught up. We're a civilised people."

She led me to a table near the space where they were dancing and we sat down. I could not go on pretending I was at ease; I thought I should only get into a fearful mess.

134

"It's terribly stupid of me, I'm afraid," I said, "but I don't seem to be able to remember ever having known anyone of your name in the old days in Seville."

"San Esteban?" she interrupted before I could go on. "Naturally. My husband came from Salamanca. He was in the diplomatic service. I'm a widow. You knew me as Pilar Carreon. Of course having my hair red changes me a little, but otherwise I don't think I've altered much."

"Not at all," I said quickly. "It was only the name that bothered me."

Of course now I remembered her, but I was concerned at the moment only with the effort to conceal from her the mingled consternation and amusement that filled me as I realised that the Pilar Carreon I had danced with at the Countess de Marbella's parties and at the Fair had turned into this stout, flaunting dowager. I could not get over it. But I had to watch my step. I wondered if she knew how well I recollected the story that had shaken Seville to its foundations, and I was glad when after she had finally bidden me an effusive farewell I was able to recall it at ease.

In those days, forty years ago, Seville had not become a prosperous commercial city. It had quiet, white streets, paved with cobbles, with a multitude of churches on the belfries of which storks built their nests. Bull-fighters, students and loungers sauntered in the Sierpes all day long. Life was easy. This of course, was before the time of motor-cars, and the Sevillan would live in penury, practising every possible economy, in order to have a carriage. For this luxury he was willing to sacrifice the necessities of life. Everyone who had any claim to gentility drove up and down the Delicias, the park-like gardens by the Guadalquivir, every blessed afternoon from five to seven. You saw carriages of all sorts, from fashionable London victorias to old broken-down shays that seemed as though they would fall to pieces, magnificent horses and wretched hacks whose tragic end in the bull-ring was near at hand. But there was one equipage that could not fail to

135

attract the stranger's attention. It was a victoria, very smart and new, drawn by two beautiful mules; and the coachman and the footman wore the national costume of Andalusia in pale grey. It was the most splendid turn-out Seville had ever known, and it belonged to the Countess de Marbella. She was a Frenchwoman married to a Spaniard, who had enthusiastically adopted the manners and customs of her husband's country, but with a Parisian elegance that gave them a peculiar distinction. The rest of the carriages went at a snail's pace so that their occupants could see and be seen, but the countess, behind her mules, dashed up between the two crawling lines at a fast trot, went to the end of the Delicias and back twice and then drove away. The proceeding savoured somewhat of royalty. When you looked at her gracefully seated in that swift victoria, her head handsomely poised, her hair of too brilliant a gold to be natural, you did not wonder that her French vivacity and determination had given her the position she held. She made the fashion. Her decrees were law. But the countess had too many adorers not to have as many enemies, and the most determined of these was the widowed Duchess de Dos Palos, whose birth and social consequence made her claim as a right the first place in Society which the Frenchwoman had won by grace, wit and character.

Now the duchess had an only daughter. This was Doña Pilar. She was twenty when I first knew her and she was very beautiful. She had magnificent eyes and a skin that, however hard you tried to find a less hackneyed way to describe it, you could only call peach-like. She was very slim, rather tall for a Spanish girl, with a red mouth and dazzlingly white teeth. She wore her abundant, shining black hair dressed very elaborately in the Spanish style of the period. She was infinitely alluring. The fire in her black eyes, the warmth of her smile, the seductiveness of her movements suggested so much passion that it really wasn't quite fair. She belonged to the generation which was straining to break the old conventions that had kept

136

the Spanish girl of good family hidden away till it was time for her to be married. I often played tennis with her and I used to dance with her at the Countess de Marbella's parties. The duchess considered the Frenchwoman's parties, with champagne and a sit-down supper, ostentatious, and when she opened her own great house to Society, which was only twice a year, it was to give them lemonade and biscuits. But she bred fighting-bulls, as her husband had done, and on the occasions when the young bulls were tried out, she gave picnic luncheons to which her friends were asked, very gay and informal, but with a sort of feudal state which fascinated my romantic imagination. Once, when the duchess's bulls were to fight at a *corrida* in Seville, I rode in with them at night as one of the men escorting Doña Pilar, dressed in a costume that reminded one of a picture by Goya, who headed the cavalcade. It was a charming experience to ride through the night, on those prancing Andalusian horses, with the six bulls, surrounded by oxen, thundering along behind.

A good many men, rich or noble and sometimes both, had asked Doña Pilar's hand in marriage, but, notwithstanding her mother's remonstrances, she had refused them. The duchess had been married at fifteen and it seemed to her really indecent that her daughter at twenty should be still single. The duchess asked her what she was waiting for; it was absurd to be too difficult. It was her duty to marry. But Pilar was stubborn. She found reasons to reject every one of her suitors.

Then the truth came out.

During the daily drives in the Delicias which the duchess, accompanied by her daughter, took in a great old-fashioned landau, they passed the countess as she was twice swiftly driven up and down the promenade. The ladies were on such bad terms that they pretended not to see one another, but Pilar could not keep her eyes off the smart carriage and the two beautiful grey mules and, not wishing to catch the countess's somewhat ironic glance, her own fell on the coachman who drove her. He was the handsomest man in Seville and in his beautiful uniform he was a sight to see. Of course no one knew exactly what happened, but apparently the more Pilar looked at the coachman the more she liked the look of him, and somehow or other, for all this part of the story remained a mystery, the pair met. In Spain the classes are strangely mingled and the butler may have in his veins much nobler blood than the master. Pilar learnt, not I think without satisfaction, that the coachman belonged to the ancient family of Leon, than which there is none in Andalusia more distinguished; and really so far as birth went there was little to choose between them. Only her life had been passed in a ducal mansion, while fate had forced him to earn his living on the box of a victoria. Neither could regret this, since only in that exalted place could he have attracted the attention of the most difficult young woman in Seville. They fell madly in love with one another. It so happened that just then a young man called the Marques de San Esteban, whom they had met at San Sebastian the summer before, wrote to the duchess and asked for Pilar's hand in marriage. He was extremely eligible and the two families had formed alliances from time to time ever since the reign of Philip II. The duchess was determined not to stand any more nonsense, and when she told Pilar of the proposal added that she had shilly-shallied long enough. She must either marry him or she should go into a convent.

"I'm not going to do either the one or the other," said Pilar.

"What are you going to do then? I have given you a home long enough."

"I'm going to marry José Leon."

"Who is he?"

Pilar hesitated for a moment and it may be, it is indeed to be hoped, that she blushed a little.

"He's the countess's coachman."

"What countess?"

"The Countess de Marbella."

I remembered the duchess well and I am sure that when roused she stuck at little. She raged, she implored, she cried, she argued! There was a terrific scene. People said that she slapped her daughter and pulled her hair, but I have an impression that Pilar in such a pass was capable of hitting back. She repeated that she loved José Leon and he loved her. She was determined to marry him. The duchess called a family council. The matter was put before them and it was decided that to save them all from disgrace Pilar should be taken away to the country and kept there till she had recovered from her infatuation. Pilar got wind of the scheme and put a stop to it by slipping out of the window of her room one night when everyone was asleep and going to live with her lover's parents. They were respectable persons who inhabited a small apartment on the unfashionable side of the Guadalquivir, in the quarter called Triana.

After that no concealment was possible. The fat was in the fire and the clubs along the Sierpes buzzed with the scandal. Waiters were kept busy bringing trays of little glasses of Manzanilla to the members from the neighbouring wine-shops. They gossiped and laughed over the scandal and Pilar's rejected suitors were the recipients of many congratulations. What an escape! The duchess was in despair. She could think of nothing better to do than go to the Archbishop, her trusted friend and former confessor, and beg him himself to reason with the infatuated girl. Pilar was summoned to the episcopal palace, and the good old man, used to intervening in family quarrels, did his utmost to show her the folly of her course. But she would not be persuaded. Nothing that anyone could say would induce her to forsake the man she loved. The duchess, waiting in an adjoining room, was sent for and made a final appeal to her daughter. In vain. Pilar returned to her humble lodging and the duchess in tears was left alone with the Archbishop. The Archbishop was no less astute than he was pious, and when he saw that the distracted woman was in a fit state to listen to him, he advised her as a last resource to go to the Countess de Marbella. She was the cleverest woman in Seville and it might be that she could do something.

At first the duchess indignantly refused. She would never suffer the humiliation of appealing to her greatest enemy. Sooner might the ancient house of Dos Palos fall in ruin. The Archbishop was accustomed to dealing with tiresome women. He set himself with gentle cunning to induce her to change her mind and presently she consented to throw herself on the Frenchwoman's mercy. With rage in her heart she sent a message asking if she might see her, and that afternoon was ushered into her drawing-room. The countess of course had been one of the first to hear the story, but she listened to the unhappy mother as though she had not known a thing about it. She relished the situation enormously. It was the crowning triumph to have the vindictive duchess on her knees before her. But she was at heart a good-natured woman and she had a sense of humour.

"It's a most unfortunate situation," she said. "And I'm sorry that one of my servants should be the occasion of it. But I don't exactly see what I can do."

The duchess would have liked to slap her painted face and her voice trembled a little with the effort she made to control her anger.

"It is not for my own sake I'm asking you to help. It's for Pilar's. I know, we all know, that you are the cleverest woman in the city. It seemed to me, it seemed to the Archbishop, that if there was a way out, your quick wit would find it."

The countess knew she was being grossly flattered. She did not mind. She liked it.

"You must let me think."

"Of course, if he'd been a gentleman I could have sent for my son and he would have killed him, but the Duke of Dos Palos cannot fight a duel with the Countess de Marbella's coachman."

"Perhaps not."

"In the old days it would have been so simple. I should merely have hired a couple of ruffians and had the brute's throat cut one night in the street. But with all these laws they have nowadays decent people have no way of protecting themselves from insult."

"I should deplore any method of settling the difficulty that deprived me of the services of an excellent coachman," murmured the countess.

"But if he marries my daughter he cannot continue to be your coachman," cried the duchess indignantly.

"Are you going to give Pilar an income for them to live on?"

"Me? Not a peseta. I told Pilar at once that she should get nothing from me. They can starve for all I care."

"Well, I should think rather than that he will prefer to stay on as my coachman. There are very nice rooms over my stables."

The duchess went pale. The duchess went red.

"Forget all that has passed between us. Let us be friends. You can't expose me to such a humiliation. If I've ever done things to affront you I ask you on my knees to forgive me."

The duchess cried.

"Dry your eyes, Duchess," the Frenchwoman said at last. "I will do what I can."

"Is there anything you can do?"

"Perhaps. Is it true that Pilar has and will have no money of her own?"

"Not a penny if she marries without my consent."

The countess gave one of her brightest smiles.

"There is a common impression that southern people are romantic and northern people matter-of-fact. The reverse is true. It is the northerners who are incurably romantic. I have lived long enough among you Spaniards to know that you are nothing if not practical."

The duchess was too broken to resent openly these unpleasant remarks, but, oh, how she hated the woman! The Countess de Marbella rose to her feet.

"You shall hear from me in the course of the day."

She firmly dismissed her visitor.

The carriage was ordered for five o'clock and at ten minutes to, the countess, dressed for her drive, sent for José. When he came into the drawing-room, wearing his pale grey livery with such an air, she could not deny that he was very good to look upon. If he had not been her own coachman—well, it was not the moment for ideas of that sort. He stood before her, holding himself easily, but with a gallant swagger. There was nothing servile in his bearing.

"A Greek god," the countess murmured to herself. "It is only Andalusia that can produce such types." And then aloud: "I hear that you are going to marry the daughter of the Duchess of Dos Palos."

"If the countess does not object."

She shrugged her shoulders.

"Whoever you marry is a matter of complete indifference to me. You know of course that Doña Pilar will have no fortune."

"Yes, madam. I have a good place and I can keep my wife. I love her."

"I can't blame you for that. She is a beautiful girl. But I think it only right to tell you that I have a rooted objection to married coachmen. On your wedding-day you leave my service. That is all I had to say to you. You can go."

She began to look at the daily paper that had just arrived from Paris, but José, as she expected, did not stir. He stared down at the floor. Presently the countess looked up.

"What are you waiting for?"

"I never knew madam would send me away," he answered in a troubled tone.

"I have no doubt you'll find another place."

"Yes, but . . ."

"Well, what is it?" she asked sharply.

He sighed miserably.

"There's not a pair of mules in the whole of Spain to come up to ours. They're almost human beings. They understand every word I say to them."

The countess gave him a smile that would have turned the

head of anyone who was not madly in love already.

"I'm afraid you must choose between me and your betrothed."

He shifted from one foot to the other. He put his hand to his pocket to get himself a cigarette, but then, remembering where he was, restrained the gesture. He glanced at the countess and that peculiar shrewd smile came over his face which those who have lived in Andalusia know so well.

"In that case, I can't hesitate. Pilar must see that this alters my position entirely. One can get a wife any day of the week, but a place like this is found only once in a lifetime. I should be a fool to throw it up for a woman."

That was the end of the adventure. José Leon continued to drive the Countess de Marbella, but she noticed when they sped up and down the Delicias that thenceforward as many eyes were turned on her handsome coachman as on her latest hat; and a year later Pilar married the Marques de San Esteban.

A CASUAL
AFFAIR

I AM telling this story in the first person, though I am in no way connected with it, because I do not want to pretend to the reader that I know more about it than I really do. The facts are as I state them, but the reasons for them I can only guess, and it may be that when the reader has read them he will think me wrong. No one can know for certain. But if you are interested in human nature there are few things more diverting than to consider the motives that have resulted in certain actions. It was only by chance that I heard anything of the unhappy circumstances at all. I was spending two or three days on an island on the north coast of Borneo and the District Officer had very kindly offered to put me up. I had been roughing it for some time and I was glad enough to have a rest. The island had been at one time a place of some consequence, with a Governor of its own, but was so no longer; and now there was nothing much to be seen of its former importance except the imposing stone house in which the Governor had once lived and which now the District Officer, grumblingly because of its unnecessary size, inhabited. But it was a comfortable house to stay in, with an immense drawing-room, a dining-room large enough to seat forty people, and lofty, spacious bedrooms. It was shabby, because the government at Singapore very wisely spent as little money on it as possible; but I rather liked this, and the heavy official furniture gave it a sort of dull stateliness that was amusing. The garden was too large for the District Officer to keep up and it was a wild tangle of tropical vegetation. His name was Arthur Low; he was a quiet, smallish man in the later thirties, married, with two young children. The Lows had not tried to make themselves at home in this great place, but camped there, like

144

refugees from a stricken area, and looked forward to the time when they would be moved to some other post where they could settle down in surroundings more familiar to them.

I took a fancy to them at once. The D.O. had an easy manner and a humorous way with him. I am sure he performed his various duties admirably, but he did everything he could to avoid the official demeanour. He was slangy of speech and pleasantly caustic. It was charming to see him play with the two children. It was quite obvious that he had found marriage a very satisfactory state. Mrs. Low was an extremely nice little woman, plump, with dark eyes under fine eyebrows, not very pretty, but certainly attractive. She looked healthy and she had high spirits. They chaffed one another continually and each one seemed to look upon the other as immensely comic. Their jokes were neither very good nor very new, but they thought them so killing that you were obliged to laugh with them.

I think they were glad to see me, especially Mrs. Low, for with nothing much to do but keep an eye on the house and the children, she was thrown very much on her own resources. There were so few white people on the island that the social life was soon exhausted; and before I had been there twenty-four hours she pressed me to stay a week, a month or a year. On the evening of my arrival they gave a dinner-party to which the official population, the government surveyor, the doctor, the schoolmaster, the chief of constabulary, were invited, but on the following evening the three of us dined by ourselves. At the dinner-party the guests had brought their house-boys to help, but that night we were waited on by the Lows' one boy and my travelling servant. They brought in the coffee and left us to ourselves. Low and I lit cheroots.

"You know that I've seen you before," said Mrs. Low.

"Where?" I asked.

"In London. At a party. I heard someone point you out to somebody else. In Carlton House Terrace at Lady Kastellan's."

"Oh? When was that?"

145

"Last time we were home on leave. There were Russian dancers."

"I remember. About two or three years ago. Fancy you being there!"

"That's exactly what we said to one another at the time," said Low, with his slow, engaging smile. "We'd never been at such a party in our lives."

"It made a great splash, you know," I said. "It was *the* party of the season. Did you enjoy it?"

"I hated every minute of it," said Mrs. Low.

"Don't let's overlook the fact that you insisted on going, Bee," said Low. "I knew we'd be out of it among all those swells. My dress clothes were the same I'd had at Cambridge and they'd never been much of a fit."

"I bought a frock specially at Peter Robinson's. It looked lovely in the shop. I wished I hadn't wasted so much money when I got there; I never felt so dowdy in my life."

"Well, it didn't much matter. We weren't introduced to anybody."

I remembered the party quite well. The magnificent rooms in Carlton House Terrace had been decorated with great festoons of yellow roses and at one end of the vast drawing-room a stage had been erected. Special costumes of the Regency period had been designed for the dancers and a modern composer had written the music for the two charming ballets they danced. It was hard to look at it all and not allow the vulgar thought to cross one's mind that the affair must have cost an enormous amount of money. Lady Kastellan was a beautiful woman and a great hostess, but I do not think anyone would have ascribed to her any vast amount of kindliness, she knew too many people to care much for any one in particular, and I couldn't help wondering why she had asked to such a grand party two obscure and quite unimportant little persons from a distant colony.

"Had you known Lady Kastellan long?" I asked.

"We didn't know her at all. She sent us a card and we

went because I wanted to see what she was like," said Mrs. Low.

"She's a very able woman," I said.

"I dare say she is. She hadn't an idea who we were when the butler man announced us, but she remembered at once. 'Oh, yes,' she said, 'you're poor Jack's friends. Do go and find yourselves seats where you can see. You'll adore Lifar, he's too marvellous.' And then she turned to say how d'you do to the next people. But she gave me a look. She wondered how much I knew and she saw at once that I knew everything."

"Don't talk such nonsense, darling," said Low. "How could she know all you think she did by just looking at you, and how could you tell what she was thinking?"

"It's true, I tell you. We said everything in that one look, and unless I'm very much mistaken I spoilt her party for her."

Low laughed and I smiled, for Mrs. Low spoke in a tone of triumphant vindictiveness.

"You are terribly indiscreet, Bee."

"Is she a great friend of yours?" Mrs. Low asked me.

"Hardly. I've met her here and there for fifteen years. I've been to a good many parties at her house. She gives very good parties and she always asks you to meet people you want to see."

"What d'you think of her?"

"She's by way of being a considerable figure in London. She's amusing to talk to and she's nice to look at. She does a lot for art and music. What do *you* think of her?"

"I think she's a bitch," said Mrs. Low, with cheerful but decided frankness.

"That settles her," I said.

"Tell him, Arthur."

Low hesitated for a moment.

"I don't know that I ought to."

"If you don't, I shall."

"Bee's got her knife into her all right," he smiled. "It was rather a bad business really."

He made a perfect smoke-ring and watched it with absorption.

"Go on, Arthur," said Mrs. Low.

"Oh, well. It was before we went home last time. I was D.O. in Selangor and one day they came and told me that a white man was dead in a small town a couple of hours up the river. I didn't know there was a white man living there. I thought I'd better go and see about it, so I got in the launch and went up. I made inquiries when I got there. The police didn't know anything about him except that he'd been living there for a couple of years with a Chinese woman in the bazaar. It was rather a picturesque bazaar, tall houses on each side, with a board-walk in between, built on piles on the river-bank, and there were awnings above to keep out the sun. I took a couple of policemen with me and they led me to the house. They sold brass-ware in the shop below and the rooms above were let out. The master of the shop took me up two flights of dark, rickety stairs, foul with every kind of Chinese stench, and called out when we got to the top. The door was opened by a middle-aged Chinese woman and I saw that her face was all bloated with weeping. She didn't say anything, but made way for us to pass. It wasn't much more than a cubby-hole under the roof; there was a small window that looked on the street, but the awning that stretched across it dimmed the light. There wasn't any furniture except a deal table and a kitchen chair with a broken back. On a mat against the wall a dead man was lying. The first thing I did was to have the window opened. The room was so frowsty that I retched, and the strongest smell was the smell of opium. There was a small oil-lamp on the table and a long needle, and of course I knew what they were there for. The pipe had been hidden. The dead man lay on his back with nothing on but a sarong and a dirty singlet. He had long brown hair, going grey, and a short beard. He was a white man all right. I examined him as best I could. I had to judge whether death was due to natural causes. There were no signs of violence.

148

He was nothing but skin and bone. It looked to me as though he might very likely have died of starvation. I asked the man of the shop and the woman a number of questions. The policeman corroborated their statements. It appeared that the man coughed a great deal and brought up blood now and then, and his appearance suggested that he might very well have had T.B. The Chinaman said he'd been a confirmed opium smoker. It all seemed pretty obvious. Fortunately cases of that sort are rare, but they're not unheard-of—the white man who goes under and gradually sinks to the last stage of degradation. It appeared that the Chinese woman had been fond of him. She'd kept him on her own miserable earnings for the last two years. I gave the necessary instructions. Of course I wanted to know who he was. I supposed he'd been a clerk in some English firm or an assistant in an English store at Singapore or Kuala Lumpur. I asked the Chinese woman if he'd left any effects. Considering the destitution in which they'd lived it seemed a rather absurd question, but she went to a shabby suit-case that lay in a corner, opened it and showed me a square parcel about the size of two novels put together wrapped in an old newspaper. I had a look at the suit-case. It contained nothing of any value. I took the parcel."

Low's cheroot had gone out and he leaned over to relight it from one of the candles on the table.

"I opened it. Inside was another wrapping, and on this, in a neat, well-educated writing: To the District Officer, me as it happened, and then the words: please deliver personally to the Viscountess Kastellan, 53 Carlton House Terrace, London, S.W. That was a bit of a surprise. Of course I had to examine the contents. I cut the string and the first thing I found was a gold and platinum cigarette case. As you can imagine I was mystified. From all I'd heard the pair of them, the dead man and the Chinese woman, had scarcely enough to eat, and the cigarette-case looked as if it had cost a packet. Besides the cigarette-case there was nothing but a bundle of letters. There were no envelopes. They were in the same neat writing as the directions and they were signed with the initial J. There were forty or fifty of them. I couldn't read them all there, but a rapid glance showed me that they were a man's love letters to a woman. I sent for the Chinese woman to ask her the name of the dead man. Either she didn't know or wouldn't tell me. I gave orders that he should be buried and got back into the launch to go home. I told Bee."

He gave her his sweet little smile.

"I had to be rather firm with Arthur," she said. "At first he wouldn't let me read the letters, but of course I wasn't going to put up with any nonsense like that."

"It was none of our business."

"You had to find out the name if you could."

"And where exactly did you come in?"

"Oh, don't be so silly," she laughed. "I should have gone mad if you hadn't let me read them."

"And did you find out his name?" I asked.

"No."

"Was there no address?"

"Yes, there was, and a very unexpected one. Most of the letters were written on Foreign Office paper."

"That was funny."

"I didn't quite know what to do. I had half a mind to write to the Viscountess Kastellan and explain the circumstances, but I didn't know what trouble I might be starting; the directions were to deliver the parcel to her personally, so I wrapped everything up again and put it in the safe. We were going home on leave in the spring and I thought the best thing was to leave everything over till then. The letters were by way of being rather compromising."

"To put it mildly," giggled Mrs. Low. "The truth is they gave the whole show away."

"I don't think we need go into that," said Low.

A slight altercation ensued; but I think on his part it was more for form's sake, since he must have known that his desire to preserve an official discretion stood small chance against his wife's determination to tell me everything. She had a down on Lady Kastellan and didn't care what she said about her. Her sympathies were with the man. Low did his best to tone down her rash assertions. He corrected her exaggerations. He told her that she'd let her imagination run away with her and had read into the letters more than was there. She would have none of it. They'd evidently made a deep impression on her, and from her vivid account and Low's interruptions I gained a fairly coherent impression of them. It was plain for one thing that they were very moving.

"I can't tell you how it revolted me, the way Bee gloated over them," said Low.

"They were the most wonderful letters I've ever read. You never wrote letters like that to me."

"What a damned fool you would have thought me if I had," he grinned.

She gave him a charming, affectionate smile.

"I suppose I should, and yet, God knows I was crazy about you, and I'm damned if I know why."

The story emerged clearly enough. The writer, the mysterious J, presumably a clerk in the Foreign Office, had fallen in love with Lady Kastellan and she with him. They had become lovers and the early letters were passionately lyrical. They were happy. They expected their love to last for ever. He wrote to her immediately after he had left her and told her how much he adored her and how much she meant to him. She was never for a moment absent from his thoughts. It looked as though her infatuation was equal to his, for in one letter he justified himself because she had reproached him for not coming to some place where he knew she would be. He told her what agony it had been to him that a sudden job had prevented him from being with her when he'd so eagerly looked forward to it.

Then came the catastrophe. How it came or why one could only guess. Lord Kastellan learnt the truth. He not merely suspected his wife's infidelity, he had proofs of it. There was a fearful scene between them, she left him and went to her father's. Lord Kastellan announced his intention of divorcing her. The letters changed in character. J. wrote at once asking to see Lady Kastellan, but she begged him not to come. Her father insisted that they shouldn't meet. J. was distressed at her unhappiness and dismayed by the trouble he had brought upon her, and he was deeply sympathetic because of what she was enduring at home, for her father and mother were furious; but at the same time it was plain that he was relieved that the crisis had come. Nothing mattered except that they loved one another. He said he hated Kastellan. Let him bring his action. The sooner they could get married the better. The correspondence was one-sided, there were no letters from her, and one had to guess from his replies what she said in them. She was obviously frightened out of her wits and nothing that he could say helped. Of course he would have to leave the Foreign Office. He assured her that this meant nothing to him. He could get a job somewhere, in the colonies, where he would earn much more money. He was sure he could make her happy. Naturally there would be a scandal, but it would be forgotten, and away from England people would not bother. He besought her to have courage. Then it looked as though she had written somewhat peevishly. She hated being divorced, Kastellan refused to take the blame on himself and be made respondent, she did not want to leave London, it was her whole life, and bury herself in some God-forsaken place on the other side of nowhere. He answered unhappily. He said he would do anything she wanted. He implored her not to love him less and he was tortured by the thought that this disaster had changed her feelings for him. She reproached him for the mess they had got into; he did not try to defend himself; he was prepared to admit that he alone was to blame. Then it appeared that pressure was being brought to bear on Kastellan from some high quarter and there was even yet a chance that something might be arranged. Whatever she wrote made J., the unknown J., desperate. His letter was almost incoherent. He

152

begged her again to see him, he implored her to have strength, he repeated that she meant everything in the world to him, he was frightened that she would let people influence her, he asked her to burn her boats behind her and bolt with him to Paris. He was frantic. Then it seemed that for some days she did not write to him. He could not understand. He did not know if she was receiving his letters. He was in an agony. The blow fell. She must have written to say that if he would resign from the Foreign Office and leave England her husband was prepared to take her back. His answer was broken-hearted.

"He never saw through her for a moment," said Mrs. Low.

"What was there to see through?" I asked.

"Don't you know what she wrote to him? I do."

"Don't be such an ass, Bee. You can't possibly know."

"Ass yourself. Of course I do. She put it up to him. She threw herself on his mercy. She dragged in her father and mother. She brought in her children; I bet that was the first thought she'd given them since they were born. She knew that he loved her so much that he was willing to do everything in the world for her, even lose her. She knew that he was prepared to accept the sacrifice of his love, his life, his career, everything for her sake, and she let him make it. She let the offer come from him. She let him persuade her to accept it."

I listened to Mrs. Low with a smile, but with attention. She was a woman and she felt instinctively how a woman in those circumstances would act. She thought it hateful, but she felt in her bones that in just that way would she herself have acted. Of course it was pure invention, with nothing but J.'s letter as a foundation, but I had an impression that it was very likely.

That was the last letter in the bundle.

I was astonished. I had known Lady Kastellan for a good many years, but only casually; and I knew her husband even less. He was immersed in politics, he was Under-Secretary at the Home Office at the time of the great do to which the Lows and I had been invited; and I never saw him but in his own house. Lady Kastellan had the reputation of being a beauty; she was tall and her figure was good in a massive way. She had a lovely skin. Her blue eyes were large, set rather wide apart and her face was broad. It gave her a slightly cow-like look. She had pretty pale brown hair and she held herself superbly. She was a woman of great self-possession, and it amazed me to learn that she had ever surrendered to such passion as the letters suggested. She was ambitious and there was no doubt that she was very useful to Kastellan in his political life. I should have thought her incapable of indiscretion. Searching my memory I seemed to remember hearing years before that the Kastellans were not getting on very well, but I had never heard any details, and whenever I saw them it looked as though they were on very good terms with one another. Kastellan was a big, red-faced fellow with sleek black hair, jovial and loud-voiced, but with little shrewd eyes that watched and noted. He was industrious, an effective speaker, but a trifle pompous. He was a little too conscious of his own importance. He did not let you forget that he had rank and wealth. He was inclined to be patronising with people of less consequence than himself.

I could well believe that when he discovered that his wife was having an affair with a junior clerk in the Foreign Office there was a devil of a row. Lady Kastellan's father had been for many years permanent Under-Secretary for Foreign Affairs and it would have been more than usually embarrassing for his daughter to be divorced on account of one of his subordinates. For all I knew Kastellan was in love with his wife and he may have been teased by a very natural jealousy. But he was a proud man, deficient in humour. He feared ridicule. The rôle of the deceived husband is difficult to play with dignity. I do not suppose he wanted a scandal that might well jeopardise his political future. It may be that Lady Kastellan's advisers threatened to defend the case and the prospect of washing dirty linen in public horrified him. It is likely enough that pressure was brought to bear on him and the solution to forgive and take his wife back if her lover were definitely eliminated may

A CASUAL AFFAIR

have seemed the best to adopt. I have no doubt Lady Kastellan promised everything she was asked.

She must have had a bad fright. I didn't take such a severe view of her conduct as Mrs. Low. She was very young; she was not more than thirty-five now. Who could tell by what accident she had become J.'s mistress? I suspect that love had caught her unawares and that she was in the middle of an affair almost before she knew what she was about. She must always have been a cold, self-possessed woman, but it is just with people like that that nature at times plays strange tricks. I am prepared to believe that she lost her head completely. There is no means of knowing how Kastellan discovered what was going on, but the fact that she kept her lover's letters shows that she was too much in love to be prudent. Arthur Low had mentioned that it was strange to find in the dead man's possessions his letters and not hers; but that seemed to me easily explainable. At the time of the catastrophe they were doubtless given back to him in exchange for hers. He very naturally kept them. Reading them again he could relive the love that meant everything in the world to him.

I didn't suppose that Lady Kastellan, devoured by passion, could ever have considered what would happen if she were found out. When the blow fell it is not strange that she was scared out of her wits. She may not have had more to do with her children than most women who live the sort of life she lived, but she may for all that not have wanted to lose them. I did not even know whether she had ever cared for her husband, but from what I knew of her I guessed that she was not indifferent to his name and wealth. The future must have looked pretty grim. She was losing everything, the grand house in Carlton House Terrace, the position, the security; her father could give her no money and her lover had still to find a job. It may not have been heroic that she should yield to the entreaties of her family, but it was comprehensible.

While I was thinking all this Arthur Low went on with his story.

155

"I didn't quite know how to set about getting in touch with Lady Kastellan," he said. "It was awkward not knowing the chap's name. However, when we got home I wrote to her. I explained who I was and said that I'd been asked to give her some letters and a gold and platinum cigarette-case by a man who'd recently died in my district. I said I'd been asked to deliver them to her in person. I thought perhaps she wouldn't answer at all or else communicate with me through a solicitor. But she answered all right. She made an appointment for me to come to Carlton House Terrace at twelve one morning. Of course it was stupid of me, but when finally I stood on the doorstep and rang the bell I was quite nervous. The door was opened by a butler. I said I had an appointment with Lady Kastellan. A footman took my hat and coat. I was led upstairs to an enormous drawing-room.

" 'I'll tell her ladyship you're here,' the butler said.

"He left me and I sat on the edge of a chair and looked round. There were huge pictures on the walls, portraits you know, I don't know who they were by, Reynolds I should think and Romney, and there was a lot of Oriental china, and gilded consoles and mirrors. It was all terribly grand and it made me feel very shabby and insignificant. My suit smelt of camphor and it was baggy at the knees. My tie felt a bit loud. The butler came in again and asked me to go with him. He opened another door from the one I'd come in by and I found myself in a further room, not so large as the drawing-room, but large all the same and very grand too. A lady was standing by the fireplace. She looked at me as I came in and bowed slightly. I felt frightfully awkward as I walked along the whole length of the room and I was afraid of stumbling over the furniture. I can only hope I didn't look such a fool as I felt. She didn't ask me to sit down.

" 'I understand you have some things that you wish to deliver to me personally,' she said. 'It's very good of you to bother.'

"She didn't smile. She seemed perfectly self-possessed, but I had a notion that she was sizing me up. To tell you the truth it put my back up. I didn't much fancy being treated as if I were a chauffeur applying for a situation.

" 'Please don't mention it,' I said, rather stiffly. 'It's all in the day's work.'

" 'Have you got the things with you?' she asked.

"I didn't answer, but I opened the dispatch-case I'd brought with me and took out the letters. I handed them to her. She accepted them without a word. She gave them a glance. She was very much made up, but I swear she went white underneath. The expression of her face didn't change. I looked at her hands. They were trembling a little. Then she seemed to pull herself together.

" 'Oh, I'm so sorry,' she said. 'Won't you sit down?'

"I took a chair. For a moment she didn't seem to know quite what to do. She held the letters in her hand. I, knowing what they were, wondered what she felt. She didn't give much away. There was a desk beside the chimney-piece and she opened a drawer and put them in. Then she sat down opposite me and asked me to have a cigarette. I handed her the cigarette-case. I'd had it in my breast pocket.

" 'I was asked to give you this too,' I said.

"She took it and looked at it. For a moment she didn't speak and I waited. I didn't quite know if I ought to get up and go.

" 'Did you know Jack well?' she asked suddenly.

" 'I didn't know him at all,' I answered. 'I never saw him until after his death.'

" 'I had no idea he was dead till I got your note,' she said. 'I'd lost sight of him for a long time. Of course he was a very old friend of mine.'

"I wondered if she thought I hadn't read the letters or if she'd forgotten what sort of letters they were. If the sight of them had given her a shock she had quite got over it by then. She spoke almost casually.

" 'What did he die of in point of fact?' she asked.

" 'Tuberculosis, opium and starvation,' I answered.

" 'How dreadful,' she said.

"But she said it quite conventionally. Whatever she felt, she wasn't going to let me see. She was as cool as a cucumber, but I fancied, though it may have been only my fancy, that she was watching me, with all her wits about her, and wondering how much I knew. I think she'd have given a good deal to be certain of that.

" 'How did you happen to get hold of these things?' she asked me.

" 'I took possession of his effects after his death,' I explained. 'They were done up in a parcel and I was directed to give them to you.'

" 'Was there any need to undo the parcel?'

"I wish I could tell you what frigid insolence she managed to get into the question. It made me go white and I hadn't any make-up on to hide it. I answered that I thought it my duty to find out if I could who the dead man was. I should have liked to be able to communicate with his relations.

" 'I see,' she said.

"She looked at me as though that were the end of the interview and she expected me to get up and take myself off. But I didn't. I thought I'd like to get a bit of my own back. I told her how I'd been sent for and how I'd found him. I described the whole thing and I told her how, as far as I knew, there'd been no one at the end to take pity on him but a Chinese woman. Suddenly the door was opened and we both looked round. A big, middle-aged man came in and stopped when he saw me.

" 'I beg your pardon,' he said, 'I didn't know you were busy.'

" 'Come in,' she said, and when he had approached, 'This is Mr. Low. My husband.'

"Lord Kastellan gave me a nod.

" 'I just wanted to ask you,' he began, and then he stopped.

"His eyes had caught the cigarette-case that was still resting on Lady Kastellan's open hand. I don't know if she saw the look of inquiry in his eyes. She gave him a friendly little smile. She was quite amazingly mistress of herself.

" 'Mr. Low comes from the Federated Malay States. Poor Jack Almond's dead and he's left me his cigarette-case.'

" 'Really?' said Lord Kastellan. 'When did he die?'

" 'About six months ago,' I said.

"Lady Kastellan got up.

" 'Well, I won't keep you any longer. I dare say you're busy. Thank you so much for carrying out Jack's request.'

" 'Things are pretty bad just now in the F.M.S. if all I hear is true,' said Lord Kastellan.

"I shook hands with them both and Lady Kastellan rang a bell.

" 'Are you staying in London?' she asked, as I was going. 'I wonder if you'd like to come to a little party I'm giving next week?'

" 'I have my wife with me,' I said.

" 'Oh, how very nice. I'll send you a card.'

"A couple of minutes later I found myself in the street. I was glad to be alone. I'd had a bad shock. As soon as Lady Kastellan mentioned the name I remembered. It was Jack Almond, the wretched bum I'd found dead in the Chinese house, dead of starvation. I'd known him quite well. It never struck me for a moment that it was he. Why, I'd dined and played cards with him, and we'd played tennis together. It was awful to think of him dying quite near me and me never knowing. He must have known he only had to send me a message and I'd have done something. I made my way into St. James's Park and sat down. I wanted to have a good think."

I could understand that it was a shock to Arthur Low to discover who the dead wastrel had been, for it was a shock to me too. Oddly enough I also had known him. Not intimately, but as a man I met at parties and now and then at a house in the country where we were both passing the week-end. Except that it was years since I had even thought of him it would have been stupid of me not to put two and two together. With

159

his name there flashed back into my memory all my recollections of him. So that was why he had suddenly thrown up a career he liked so much! At that time, it was just after the war, I happened to know several people in the Foreign Office; Jack Almond was thought the cleverest of all the young men attached to it, and the highest posts the Diplomatic Service had to offer were within his reach. Of course it meant waiting. But it did seem absurd for him to fling away his chances in order to go into business in the Far East. His friends did all they could to dissuade him. He said he had had losses and found it impossible to live on his salary. One would have thought he could scrape along till things grew better. I remembered very well what he looked like. He was tall and well-made, a trifle dressy, but he was young enough to carry off his faultless clothes with a dash, with dark brown hair, very neat and sleek, blue eyes with very long lashes, and a fresh brilliant colour. He looked the picture of health. He was amusing, gay and quick-witted. I never knew anyone who had more charm. It is a dangerous quality and those who have it trade on it. Often they think it enough to get them through life without any further effort. It is well to be on one's guard against it. But with Jack Almond it was the expression of a sweet and generous nature. He delighted because he was delightful. He was entirely without conceit. He had a gift for languages, he spoke French and German without a trace of accent, and his manners were admirable. You felt that when the time came he would play the part of an ambassador to a foreign power in the grand style. No one could fail to like him. It was not strange that Lady Kastellan should have fallen madly in love with him. My fancy ran away with me. What is there more moving than young love? The walks together of that handsome pair in one of the parks in the warm evenings of early summer, the dances they went to where he held her in his arms, the enchantment of the secret they shared when they exchanged glances across a dinner-table, and the passionate encounters, hurried and dangerous, but worth a thousand risks, when a

160

some clandestine meeting-place they could give themselves to the fulfilment of their desire. They drank the milk of Paradise.

How frightful that the end of it all should have been so tragic!

"How did you know him?" I now asked Low.

"He was with Dexter and Farmilow. You know, the shipping people. He had quite a good job. He'd brought letters to the Governor and people like that. I was in Singapore at the time. I think I met him first at the club. He was damned good at games and all that sort of thing. Played polo. He was a fine tennis player. You couldn't help liking him."

"Did he drink, or what?"

"No." Arthur Low was quite emphatic. "He was one of the best. The women were crazy about him, and you couldn't blame them. He was one of the most decent fellows I've ever met."

I turned to Mrs. Low.

"Did you know him?"

"Only just. When Arthur and I were married we went to Perak. He was sweet, I remember that. He had the longest eyelashes I've ever seen on a man."

"He was out quite a long time without going home. Five years, I think. I don't want to use hackneyed phrases, but the fact is I can't say it in any other way, he'd won golden opinions. There were a certain number of fellows who'd been rather sick at his being shoved into a damned good job by influence, but they couldn't deny that he'd made good. We knew about his having been in the F.O. and all that, but he never put on any frills."

"I think what took me," Mrs. Low interrupted, "was that he was so tremendously alive. It bucked you up just to talk to him."

"He had a wonderful send-off when he sailed. I happened to have run up to Singapore for a couple of days and I went to the dinner at the Europe the night before. We all got rather tight. It was a grand lark. There was quite a crowd to see

161

him off. He was only going for six months. I think everybody looked forward to his coming back. It would have been better for him if he never had."

"Why, what happened then?"

"I don't know exactly. I'd been moved again, and I was right away north."

How exasperating! It is really much easier to invent a story out of your own head than to tell one about real people, of whom you not only must guess the motives, but whose behaviour even at crucial moments you are ignorant of.

"He was a very good chap, but he was never an intimate friend of ours, you know how cliquey Singapore is, and he moved in rather more exalted circles than we did; when we went north I forgot about him. But one day at the club I heard a couple of fellows talking. Walton and Kenning. Walton had just come up from Singapore. There'd been a big polo match.

" 'Did Almond play?' asked Kenning.

" 'You bet your life he didn't,' said Walton. 'They kicked him out of the team last season.'

"I interrupted.

" 'What *are* you talking about?' I said.

" 'Don't you know?' said Walton. 'He's gone all to pot, poor devil.'

" 'How?' I asked.

" 'Drink.'

" 'They say he dopes too,' said Kenning.

" 'Yes, I've heard that,' said Walton. 'He won't last long at that rate. Opium, isn't it,'

" 'If he doesn't look out he'll lose his job,' said Kenning.

"I couldn't make it out," Low went on. "He was the last man I should ever have expected to go that way. He was so typically English and he was a gentleman and all that. It appeared that Walton had travelled out with him on the same ship when Jack came back from leave. He joined the ship at Marseilles. He was rather low, but there was nothing funny about that; a lot of people don't feel any too good when they're

162

leaving home and have to get back to the mill. He drank a good deal. Fellows do that sometimes too. But Walton said rather a curious thing about him. He said it looked as if the life had gone out of him. You couldn't help noticing it because he'd always had such high spirits. There'd been a general sort of idea that he was engaged to some girl in England and on the ship they jumped to the conclusion that she'd thrown him over."

"That's what I said when Arthur told me," said Mrs. Low. "After all, five years is a long time to leave a girl."

"Anyhow they thought he'd get over it when he got back to work. But he didn't, unfortunately. He went from bad to worse. A lot of people liked him and they did all they could to persuade him to pull himself together. But there was nothing doing. He just told them to mind their own business. He was snappy and rude, which was funny because he'd always been so nice to everybody. Walton said you could hardly believe it was the same man. Government House dropped him and a lot of others followed suit. Lady Ormonde, the Governor's wife, was a snob, she knew he was well-connected and all that, and she wouldn't have given him the cold shoulder unless things had got pretty bad. He was a nice chap, Jack Almond, it seemed a pity that he should make such a mess of things. I was sorry, you know, but of course it didn't impair my appetite or disturb my night's sleep. A few months later I happened to be in Singapore myself, and when I went to the club I asked about him. He'd lost his job all right, it appeared that he often didn't go to the office for two or three days at a time; and I was told that someone had made him manager of a rubber estate in Sumatra in the hope that away from the temptations of Singapore he might pull himself together. You see, everyone had liked him so much, they couldn't bear the thought of his going under without some sort of a struggle. But it was no good. The opium had got him. He didn't keep the job in Sumatra long and he was back again in Singapore. I heard afterwards that you would hardly have recognised him. He'd always been so spruce and smart; he was shabby and unwashed and wild-eyed. A number of fellows at the club got together and arranged something. They felt they had to give him one more chance and they sent him out to Sarawak. But it wasn' any use. The fact is, I think, he didn't want to be helped. I think he just wanted to go to hell in his own way and be a quick as he could about it. Then he disappeared; someone said he'd gone home; anyhow he was forgotten. You know how people drop out in the F.M.S. I suppose that's why when found a dead man in a sarong, with a beard, lying in a little smelly room in a Chinese house thirty miles from anywhere, i never occurred to me for a moment that it might be Jack Almond. I hadn't heard his name for years."

"Just think what he must have gone through in that time," said Mrs. Low, and her eyes were bright with tears, for she had a good and tender heart.

"The whole thing's inexplicable," said Low.

"Why?" I asked.

"Well, if he was going to pieces, why didn't he do it when he first came out? His first five years he was all right. One o the best. If this affair of his had broken him you'd have ex pected him to break when it was all fresh. All that time h was as gay as a bird. You'd have said he hadn't a care in th world. From all I heard it was a different man who came bac from leave."

"Something happened during those six months in London, said Mrs. Low. "That's obvious."

"We shall never know," sighed Low.

"But we can guess," I smiled. "That's where the novelis comes in. Shall I tell you what I think happened?"

"Fire away."

"Well, I think that during those first five years he was buoye up by the sacrifice he'd made. He had a chivalrous soul. H had given up everything that made life worth living to hir to save the woman he loved better than anything in the worl I think he had an exaltation of spirit that never left him. H

loved her still, with all his heart; most of us fall in and out of love; some men can only love once, and I think he was one of them. And in a strange way he was happy because he'd been able to sacrifice his happiness for the sake of someone who was worthy of the sacrifice. I think she was always in his thoughts. Then he went home. I think he loved her as much as ever and I don't suppose he ever doubted that her love was as strong and enduring as his. I don't know what he expected. He may have thought she'd see it was no good fighting her inclination any more and would run away with him. It may have been that he'd have been satisfied to realise that she loved him still. It was inevitable that they should meet; they lived in the same world. He saw that she didn't care a row of pins for him any longer. He saw that the passionate girl had become a prudent, experienced woman of the world, he saw that she'd never loved him as he thought she loved him, and he may have suspected that she'd lured him coldly into making the sacrifice that was to save her. He saw her at parties, self-possessed and triumphant. He knew that the lovely qualities he'd ascribed to her were of his own imagining and she was just an ordinary woman who had been carried away by a momentary infatuation and having got over it had returned to her true life. A great name, wealth, social distinction, worldly success: those were the things that mattered to her. He'd sacrificed everything, his friends, his familiar surroundings, his profession, his usefulness in the world, all that gives value to existence— for nothing. He'd been cheated, and it broke him. Your friend Walton said the true thing, you noticed it yourself, he said it looked as if the life had gone out of him. It had. After that he didn't care any more, and perhaps the worst thing was that even with it all, though he knew Lady Kastellan for what she was, he loved her still. I know nothing more shattering than to love with all your heart, than not to be able however hard you try to break yourself of it, someone who you know is worthless. Perhaps that is why he took to opium. To forget and to remember."

It was a long speech I had made, and now I stopped.

"All that's only fancy," said Low.

"I know it is," I answered, "but it seems to fit the circumstances."

"There must have been a weak strain in him. Otherwise he could have fought and conquered."

"Perhaps. Perhaps there is always a certain weakness attached to such great charm as he possessed. Perhaps few people love as wholeheartedly and as devotedly as he loved. Perhaps he didn't want to fight and conquer. I can't bring myself to blame him."

I didn't add, because I was afraid they would think it cynical, that maybe if only Jack Almond hadn't had those wonderfully long eyelashes he might now have been alive and well, minister to some foreign power and on the high road to the Embassy in Paris.

"Let's go into the drawing-room," said Mrs. Low. "The boy wants to clear the table."

And that was the end of Jack Almond.

THE
POINT OF HONOUR

SOME years ago, being engaged on writing a book about Spain in the Golden Age, I had occasion to read again the plays of Calderon. Among others I read one called *El Medico de su Honra*, which means the Physician of his Honour. It is a cruel play and you can hardly read it without a shudder. But re-reading it, I was reminded of an encounter I had had many years before which has always remained in my memory as one of the strangest I have ever known. I was quite young then and I had gone to Seville on a short visit to see the celebration of the Feast of Corpus Christi. It was the height of summer and the heat was terrific. Great sail-cloths were drawn across the narrow streets, giving a grateful shade, but in the squares the sun beat down mercilessly. In the morning I watched the procession. It was splendid and impressive. The crowd knelt down as the Host was solemnly carried past, and the Civil Guards in full uniform stood at salute to do homage to the heavenly King. And in the afternoon I joined the dense throng which was making its way to the bull-ring. The cigarette girls and the sewing girls wore carnations in their dark hair and their young men were dressed in all their best. It was just after the Spanish American war, and the short, embroidered jacket, the skin-tight trousers and the broad-brimmed, low-crowned hat were still worn. Sometimes the crowd was scattered by a picador on the wretched hack that would never survive the afternoon, and the rider, with conscious pride in his picturesque costume, exchanged pleasantries with the facetious. A long line of carriages, dilapidated and shabby, overfilled with *aficionados,* drove noisily along.

I went early, for it amused me to see the people gradually filling the vast arena. The cheaper seats in the sun were

167

already packed, and it was a curious effect that the countless fans made, like the fluttering of a host of butterflies, as men and women restlessly fanned themselves. In the shade, where I was sitting, the places were taken more slowly, but even there, an hour before the fight began, one had to look rather carefully for a seat. Presently a man stopped in front of me and with a pleasant smile asked if I could make room for him. When he had settled down, I took a sidelong glance at him and noticed that he was well-dressed, in English clothes, and looked like a gentleman. He had beautiful hands, small but resolute, with thin, long fingers. Wanting a cigarette, I took out my case and thought it would be polite to offer him one. He accepted. He had evidently seen that I was a foreigner, for he thanked me in French.

"You are English?" he went on.

"Yes."

"How is it that you haven't run away from the heat?"

I explained that I had come on purpose to see the Feast of Corpus Christi.

"After all, it's something you must come to Seville for."

Then I made some casual remark about the vast concourse of people.

"No one would imagine that Spain was bleeding from the loss of all that remained of her Empire and that her ancient glory is now nothing but a name."

"There's a great deal left."

"The sunshine, the blue sky, and the future."

He spoke dispassionately, as though the misfortunes of his fallen country were no concern of his. Not knowing what to reply, I remained silent. We waited. The boxes began to fill up. Ladies in their mantillas of black or white lace entered them and spread their Manila shawls over the balustrade so as to form a gay and many-coloured drapery. Now and then, when one of them was of particular beauty, a round of applause would greet her appearance and she would smile and bow without embarrassment. At last the president of the bull-figh made his entry, the band struck up, and the fighters, all glittering in their satin and gold and silver, marched swaggering across the ring. A minute later a great black bull charged in. Carried away by the horrible excitement of the contest, I noticed, notwithstanding, that my neighbour remained cool. When a man fell and only escaped by a miracle the horns of the furious beast, and with a gasp thousands sprang to their feet, he remained motionless. The bull was killed and the mules dragged out the huge carcass. I sank back exhausted.

"Do you like bull-fighting?" he asked me. "Most English do, though I have noticed that in their own country they say hard enough things about it."

"Can one like something that fills one with horror and loathing? Each time I come to a fight I swear I will never go to another. And yet I do."

"It's a curious passion that leads us to delight in the peril of others. Perhaps it's natural to the human race. The Romans had their gladiators and the moderns have their melodramas. It may be that it is an instinct in man to find pleasure in bloodshed and torture."

I did not answer directly.

"Don't you think that the bull-fight is the reason why human life is of so little account in Spain?"

"And do you think human life is of any great account?" he asked.

I gave him a quick look, for there was an ironical tone in his voice that no one could have missed, and I saw that his eyes were full of mockery. I flushed a little, for he made me on a sudden feel very young. I was surprised at the change of his expression. He had seemed rather an amiable man, with his large soft friendly eyes, but now his face bore a look of sardonic hauteur which was a trifle disquieting. I shrank back into my shell. We said little to one another during the rest of the afternoon, but when the last bull was killed and we all rose to our feet he shook hands with me and expressed the hope that we might meet again. It was a mere politeness and neither of us,

169

I imagine, thought that there was even a remote possibility of it.
But quite by chance, two or three days later, we did. I was
in a quarter of Seville that I did not know very well. I had
been that afternoon to the palace of the Duke of Alba, which I
knew had a fine garden and in one of the rooms a magnificent
ceiling reputed to have been made by Moorish captives before
the fall of Granada. It was not easy to gain admittance, but
I wanted very much to see it and thought that now, in the
height of summer when there were no tourists, with two or
three pesetas I might be allowed in. I was disappointed. The
man in charge told me that the house was under repair and no
stranger could visit it without a written permission from the
Duke's agent. So, having nothing else to do, I went to the
royal garden of the Alcazar, the old palace of Don Pedro the
Cruel, whose memory lives still among the people of Seville.
It was very pleasant among the orange trees and cypresses.
I had a book with me, a volume of Calderon, and I sat there
for a while and read. Then I went for a stroll. In the older
parts of Seville the streets are narrow and tortuous. It is
delicious to wander along them under the awnings that stretch
above, but not easy to find one's way. I lost mine. When I had
just made up my mind that I had no notion in which direction
to turn I saw a man walking towards me and recognised my
acquaintance of the bull-ring. I stopped him and asked whether
he could direct me. He remembered me.

"You'll never find your way," he smiled, turning round. "I'll
walk a little with you until you can't mistake it."

I protested, but he would not listen. He assured me it was
no trouble.

"You haven't gone away then?" he said.

"I'm leaving tomorrow. I've just been to the Duke of Alba's
house. I wanted to see that Moorish ceiling of his, but they
wouldn't let me in."

"Are you interested in Arabic art?"

"Well, yes. I've heard that that ceiling is one of the finest
things in Seville."

"I think I could show you one as good."

"Where?"

He looked at me for a moment reflectively as though wondering what sort of a person I was. If he was, he evidently came to a satisfactory decision.

"If you have ten minutes to spare I will take you to it."

I thanked him warmly and we turned back and retraced our steps. We chatted of indifferent things till we came to a large house, washed in pale green, with the Arabic look of a prison, the windows on the street heavily barred, which so many houses in Seville have. My guide clapped his hands at the gateway and a servant looked out from a window into the patio, and pulled a cord.

"Whose house is this?"

"Mine."

I was surprised, for I knew how jealously Spaniards guarded their privacy and how little inclined they were to admit strangers into their houses. The heavy iron gate swung open and we walked into the court-yard; we crossed it and went through a narrow passage. Then I found myself suddenly in an enchanted garden. It was walled on three sides, with walls as high as houses; and their old red brick, softened by time, was covered with roses. They clad every inch in wanton, scented luxuriance. In the garden, growing wildly, as if the gardeners had striven in vain to curb the exuberance of nature, were palm-trees rising high into the air in their passionate desire for the sun, dark orange-trees and trees in flower whose names I did not know, and among them roses and more roses. The fourth wall was a Moorish loggia, with horseshoe arches heavily decorated with tracery, and when we entered this I saw the magnificent ceiling. It was like a little bit of the Alcazar, but it had not suffered the restorations that have taken all the charm from that palace, and the colours were exquisitely tender. It was a gem.

"Believe me, you need not regret that you have not been able to see the duke's house. Further, you can say that you have seen something that no other foreigner has seen within living memory."

"It's very kind of you to have shown it to me. I'm infinitely grateful."

He looked about him with a pride with which I could sympathise.

"It was built by one of my ancestors in the time of Don Pedro the Cruel. It is very likely that the King himself more than once caroused under this ceiling with my ancestor."

I held out the book I was carrying.

"I've just been reading a play in which Don Pedro is one of the important characters."

"What is the book?"

I handed it to him and he glanced at the title. I looked about me.

"Of course, what adds to the beauty is that wonderful garden," I said. "The whole impression is awfully romantic."

The Spaniard was evidently pleased with my enthusiasm. He smiled. I had already noticed how grave his smile was. It hardly dispelled the habitual melancholy of his expression.

"Would you like to sit down for a few minutes and smoke a cigarette?"

"I should love to."

We walked out into the garden and came upon a lady sitting on a bench of Moorish tiles like those in the gardens of the Alcazar. She was working at some embroidery. She looked up quickly, evidently taken aback to see a stranger, and gave my companion an enquiring stare.

"Allow me to present you to my wife," he said.

The lady gravely bowed. She was very beautiful, with magnificent eyes, a straight nose with delicate nostrils, and a pale smooth skin. In her black hair, abundant as with most Spanish women, there was a broad white streak. Her face was quite unlined and she could not have been more than thirty.

"You have a very lovely garden, Señora." I said because I had to say something.

172

She gave it an indifferent glance.

"Yes, it is pretty."

I felt suddenly embarrassed. I did not expect her to show me any cordiality, and I could not blame her if she thought my intrusion merely a nuisance. There was something about her that I could not quite make out. It was not an active hostility. Absurd as it seemed, since she was a young woman and beautiful, I felt that there was something dead in her.

"Are you going to sit here?" she asked her husband.

"With your permission. Only for a few minutes."

"I won't disturb you."

She gathered her silks and the canvas on which she had been working and rose to her feet. When she stood up I saw that she was taller than Spanish women generally are. She gave me an unsmiling bow. She carried herself with a sort of royal composure and her gait was stately. I was flippant in those days, and I remember saying to myself that she was not the sort of girl you could very well think of being silly with. We sat down on the multi-coloured bench and I gave my host a cigarette. I held a match to it. He still had my volume of Calderon in his hands, and now he idly turned the pages.

"Which of the plays have you been reading?"

"El Medico de su Honra."

He gave me a look, and I thought I discerned in his large eyes a sardonic glint.

"And what do you think of it?"

"I think it's revolting. The fact is, of course, that the idea is so foreign to our modern notions."

"What idea?"

"The point of honour and all that sort of thing."

I should explain that the point of honour is the mainspring of much of the Spanish drama. It is the nobleman's code that impels a man to kill his wife, in cold blood, not only if she has been unfaithful to him, but even if, however little she was to blame, her conduct has given rise to scandal. In this particular play there is an example of this more deliberate than

173

any I have ever read: the physician of his honour takes vengeance on his wife, though aware that she is innocent, simply as a matter of decorum.

"It's in the Spanish blood," said my friend. "The foreigner must just take it or leave it."

"Oh, come, a lot of water has flowed down the Guadalquivir since Calderon's day. You're not going to pretend that any man would behave like that now."

"On the contrary I pretend that even now a husband who finds himself in such a humiliating and ridiculous position can only regain his self-respect by the offender's death."

I did not answer. It seemed to me that he was pulling a romantic gesture, and within me I murmured, Bosh. He gave me an ironic smile.

"Have you ever heard of Don Pedro Aguria?"

"Never."

"The name is not unknown in Spanish history. An ancestor was Admiral of Spain under Philip II and another was bosom friend to Philip IV. By royal command he sat for his portrait to Velasquez."

My host hesitated a moment. He gave me a long, reflective stare before he went on.

"Under the Philips the Agurias were rich, but by the time my friend Don Pedro succeeded his father their circumstances were much reduced. But still he was not poor, he had estates between Cordova and Aguilar, and in Seville his house retained at least traces of its ancient splendour. The little world of Seville was astonished when he announced his engagement to Soledad, the daughter of the ruined Count of Acaba, for though her family was distinguished her father was an old scamp. He was crippled with debts, and the shifts he resorted to in order to keep his head above water were none too nice. But Soledad was beautiful and Don Pedro in love with her. They were married. He adored her with the vehement passion of which perhaps only a Spaniard is capable. But he discovered to his dismay that she did not love him. She was kind and

174

gentle. She was a good wife and a good housekeeper. She was grateful to him. But that was all. He thought that when she had a child she would change, but the child came, and it made no difference. The barrier between them that he had felt from the beginning was still there. He suffered. At last he told himself that she had a character too noble, a spirit too delicate, to descend to earthly passion, and he resigned himself. She was too high above him for mortal love."

I moved a little uneasily in my seat. I thought the Spaniard was unduly rhetorical. He went on:

"You know that here in Seville the Opera House is open only for the six weeks after Easter, and since the Sevillans don't care very much for European music we go more to meet our friends than to listen to the singers. The Agurias had a box, like everybody else, and they went on the opening night of the season. *Tannhaüser* was being given. Don Pedro and his wife, like typical Spaniards, with nothing to do all day but always late, did not arrive till nearly the end of the first act. In the interval the Count of Acaba, Soledad's father, came into the box accompanied by a young officer of artillery whom Don Pedro had never seen before. But Soledad seemed to know him well.

" 'Here is Pepe Alvarez,' said the Count. 'He's just come back from Cuba and I insisted on bringing him to see you.'

"Soledad smiled and held out her hand, then introduced the newcomer to her husband.

" 'Pepe is the son of the attorney at Carmona. We used to play together when we were children.'

"Carmona is a small town near Seville, and it was here that the Count had retired when his creditors in the city grew too troublesome. The house he owned there was almost all that was left him of the fortune he had squandered. He lived in Seville now through Don Pedro's generosity. But Don Pedro did not like him and he bowed stiffly to the young officer. He guessed that his father the attorney and the count had been concerned together in transactions that were none too reputable. In a minute he left the box to talk with his cousin, the Duchess of Santaguador, whose box was opposite his own. A few days later he met Pepe Alvarez at his club in the Sierpes and had a chat with him. To his surprise he found him a very pleasant young fellow. He was full of his exploits in Cuba and he related them with humour.

"The six weeks about Easter and the great Fair are the gayest in Seville, and the world meets to exchange gossip and laughter, at one festivity after another. Pepe Alvarez with his good nature and high spirits was in great request and the Agurias met him constantly. Don Pedro saw that he amused Soledad. She was more vivacious when he was there, and her laughter, which he had so seldom heard, was a delight to him. Like other members of the aristocracy he took a booth for the Fair, where they danced, supped and drank champagne till dawn. Pepe Alvarez was always the life and soul of the parties.

"One night Don Pedro was dancing with the Duchess of Santaguador and they passed Soledad with Pepe Alvarez.

" 'Soledad is looking very beautiful this evening,' she remarked.

" 'And happy,' he replied.

" 'Is it true that once she was engaged to be married to Pepe Alvarez?'

" 'Of course not.'

"But the question startled him. He had known that Soledad and Pepe had known one another when they were children, but it had never crossed his mind that there could have been anything between them. The Count of Acaba, though a rogue, was a gentleman by birth, and it was inconceivable that he could have thought of marrying his daughter to the son of a provincial attorney. When they got home Don Pedro told his wife what the duchess had said and what he had replied.

" 'But I was engaged to Pepe,' she said.

" 'Why did you never tell me?'

" 'It was finished and done with. He was in Cuba. I never expected to see him again.'

" 'There must be people who know you were engaged to him.'

" 'I dare say. Does it matter?'

" 'Very much. You shouldn't have renewed your acquaintance with him when he returned.'

" 'Does that mean that you have no confidence in me?'

" 'Of course not. I have every confidence in you. All the same I wish you to discontinue it now.'

" 'And if I refuse??'

" 'I shall kill him.'

"They looked long into one another's eyes. Then she gave him a little bow and went to her room. Don Pedro sighed. He wondered whether she still loved Pepe Alvarez and whether it was on account of this that she had never loved him. But he would not allow himself to give way to the unworthy emotion of jealousy. He looked into his heart and was sure that it harboured no feeling of hatred for the young artilleryman. On the contrary, he liked him. This was not an affair of love or hate, but of honour. On a sudden he remembered that a few days before when he went to his club he noticed that the conversation suddenly failed, and, looking back, he seemed to remember that several of the group who were sitting there and chatting eyed him curiously. Was it possible that he had been the subject of their conversation? He shivered a little at the thought.

"The Fair was drawing to its end, and when it was over the Agurias had arranged to go to Cordova, where Don Pedro had an estate which it was necessary for him to visit from time to time. He looked forward to the peace of a country life after the turmoil of Seville. The day after this conversation Soledad, saying she was not well, stayed in the house, and she did the same the day following. Don Pedro visited her in her room morning and evening and they talked of indifferent things. But on the third day his cousin Conchita de Santaguador was giving a ball. It was the last of the season and everyone in her exclusive set would be there. Soledad, saying she was still indisposed, announced that she would stay at home.

" 'Are you refusing to go because of our conversation of the other night?' Don Pedro asked.

" 'I have been thinking over what you said. I think your demand unreasonable, but I shall accede to it. The only way I can cease my friendship with Pepe is by not going to places where I am likely to meet him.' A tremor of pain passed over her lovely face. 'Perhaps it is best.'

" 'Do you love him still?'

" 'Yes.'

"Don Pedro felt himself go cold with anguish.

" 'Then why did you marry me?'

" 'Pepe was away, in Cuba, no one knew when he would come back. Perhaps never. My father said that I must marry you.'

" 'To save him from ruin?'

" 'From worse than ruin.'

" 'I am very sorry for you.'

" 'You have been kind to me. I have done everything in my power to prove to you that I am grateful.'

" 'And does Pepe love you?'

"She shook her head and smiled sadly.

" 'Men are different. He's young. He's too gay to love anyone very long. No, to him I'm just the friend whom he used to play with when he was a child and flirt with when he was a boy. He can make jokes about the love he once had for me.'

"He took her hand and pressed it, then kissed it and left her. He went to the ball by himself. His friends were sorry to hear of Soledad's indisposition, but after expressing a proper sympathy devoted themselves to the evening's amusement. Don Pedro drifted into the card-room. There was room at a table, and he sat down to play *chemin de fer*. He played with extraordinary luck and made a good deal of money. One of the players laughingly asked where Soledad was that evening. Don Pedro saw another give him a startled glance, but he laughed and answered that she was safely in bed and asleep. Then an unlucky incident occurred. Some young man came into the

178

room, and addressing an artillery officer who was playing asked where Pepe Alvarez was.

" 'Isn't he here?' said the officer.

" 'No.'

"An odd silence fell upon the party. Don Pedro exercised all his self-control to prevent his face from showing what he suddenly felt. The thought flashed through his mind that those men at the table suspected that Pepe was with Soledad, his wife. Oh, the shame! The indignity! He forced himself to go on playing for another hour and still he won. He could not go wrong. The game broke up and he returned to the ballroom. He went up to his cousin.

" 'I've hardly had a word with you,' he said. 'Come into another room and let us sit down for a little.'

" 'If you like.'

"The room, Conchita's boudoir, was empty.

" 'Where is Pepe Alvarez tonight?' he asked casually.

" 'I can't think.'

" 'You were expecting him?'

" 'Of course.'

"She was smiling as he was, but he noticed that she looked at him sharply. He dropped his mask of casualness and, though they were alone, lowered his voice.

" 'Conchita, I beseech you to tell me the truth. Are they saying that he is Soledad's lover?'

" 'Pedrito, what a monstrous question to put to me!'

"But he had seen the terror in her eyes and the sudden instinctive movement of her hand to her face.

" 'You've answered it.'

"He got up and left her. He went home and looking up from the patio saw a light in his wife's room. He went upstairs and knocked at the door. There was no answer, but he went in. To his surprise, for it was late, she was sitting up working at the embroidery upon which much of her time was spent.

" 'Why are you working at this hour?'

179

" 'I couldn't sleep, I couldn't read. I thought it would distract my mind if I worked.'

"He did not sit down.

" 'Soledad, I have something to tell you that must cause you pain. I must ask you to be brave. Pepe Alvarez was not at Conchita's tonight.'

" 'What is that to me?'

" 'It is unfortunate that you were not there either. Everyone at the ball thought that you were together.'

" 'That's preposterous.'

" 'I know, but that doesn't help matters. You could have opened the gate for him yourself and let him out, or you could have slipped out yourself without anyone seeing you go or come.'

" 'But do you believe it?'

" 'No. I agreed with you that the thing was preposterous. Where was Pepe Alvarez?'

" 'How do I know? How should I know?'

" 'It is very strange that he should not have come to the most brilliant party, the last party, of the season.'

"She was silent for a minute.

" 'The night after you spoke to me about him I wrote and told him that in view of the circumstances I thought it would be better if in future we saw no more of one another than could be helped. It may be that he did not go to the ball for the same reason that I did not.'

"They were silent for a while. He looked down at the ground, but he felt that her eyes were fixed on him. I should have told you before that Don Pedro possessed one accomplishment which raised him above his fellows, but at the same time was a drawback. He was the best shot in Andalusia. Everyone knew this and it would have been a brave man who ventured to offend him. A few days earlier there had been pigeon-shooting at Tablada, the wide common outside Seville along the Guadalquivir, and Don Pedro had carried all before him. Pepe Alvarez on the other hand had shown himself so in-

180

different a marksman that everyone had laughed at him. The young artilleryman had borne the chaff with good-humour. Cannon were his weapon, he said.

" 'What are you going to do?' Soledad asked him.

" 'You know there is only one thing I can do.'

"She understood. But she tried to treat what he said as a pleasantry.

" 'You're childish. We're not living any more in the sixteenth century.'

'I know. That is why I am talking to you now. If I have to challenge Pepe I shall kill him. I don't want to do that. If he will resign his commission and leave Spain I will do nothing.'

" 'How can he? Where is he to go?'

" 'He can go to South America. He may make his fortune.'

" 'Do you expect me to tell him that?'

" 'If you love him.'

" 'I love him too much to ask him to run away like a coward. How could he face life without honour?'

"Don Pedro laughed.

" 'What has Pepe Alvarez, the son of an attorney at Carmona, to do with honour?'

"She did not answer, but in her eyes he saw the fierce hatred she bore him. That look stabbed his heart, for he loved her, he loved her as passionately as ever.

"Next day he went to his club and joined a group who were sitting at the window looking out at the crowd passing up and down the Sierpes. Pepe Alvarez was in it. They were talking of last night's party.

" 'Where were you, Pepe?' someone asked.

" 'My mother was ill. I had to go to Carmona,' he answered. 'I was dreadfully disappointed, but perhaps it was all for the best.' He turned laughingly to Don Pedro. 'I hear you were in luck and won everybody's money.'

" 'When are you going to give us our revenge, Pedrito?' asked another.

" 'I'm afraid you'll have to wait for that,' he answered. 'I have to go to Cordova. I find that my attorney has been robbing me. I know that all attorneys are thieves, but I stupidly thought this one was honest.'

"He seemed to speak quite lightly, and it was as lightly that Pepe Alvarez put in his word.

" 'I think you exaggerate, Pedrito. Don't forget that my father is an attorney and he at least is honest.'

" 'I don't believe it for a minute,' laughed Don Pedro. 'I have no doubt that your father is as big a thief as any.'

"The insult was so unexpected and so unprovoked that for a moment Pepe Alvarez was staggered. The others were startled into sudden seriousness.

" 'What do you mean, Pedrito?'

" 'Exactly what I say.'

" 'It's a lie and you know it's a lie. You must withdraw that at once.'

"Don Pedro laughed.

" 'Of course I shall not withdraw. Your father is a thief and a rascal.'

"Pepe did the only thing he could do. He sprang from his chair and with his open hand hit Don Pedro in the face. The outcome was inevitable. Next day the two men met on the frontier of Portugal. Pepe Alvarez, the attorney's son, died like a gentleman with a bullet in his heart."

The Spaniard ended his story on such a casual note that for the first moment I hardly took it in. But when I did I was profoundly shocked.

"Barbarous," I said. "It was just cold-blooded murder."

My host got up.

"You're talking nonsense, my young friend. Don Pedro did the only thing he could do in the circumstances."

I left Seville next day, and from then till now have never been able to discover the name of the man who told me this strange story. I have often wondered whether the lady I saw the lady with the pale face and the lock of white hair was the unhappy Soledad.

WINTER
CRUISE

Captain Erdmann knew Miss Reid very little till the *Friedrich Weber* reached Haiti. She came on board at Plymouth, but by then he had taken on a number of passengers, French, Belgian and Haitian, many of whom had travelled with him before, and she was placed at the chief engineer's table. The *Friedrich Weber* was a freighter sailing regularly from Hamburg to Cartagena on the Colombian coast and on the way touching at a number of islands in the West Indies. She carried phosphates and cement from Germany and took back coffee and timber; but her owners, the Brothers Weber, were always willing to send her out of her route if a cargo of any sort made it worth their while. The *Friedrich Weber* was prepared to take cattle, mules, potatoes or anything else that offered the chance of earning an honest penny. She carried passengers. There were six cabins on the upper deck and six below. The accommodation was not luxurious, but the food was good, plain and abundant, and the fares were cheap. The round trip took nine weeks and was not costing Miss Reid more than forty-five pounds. She looked forward not only to seeing many interesting places, with historical associations, but also to acquiring a great deal of information that would enrich her mind.

The agent had warned her that till the ship reached Port au Prince in Haiti she would have to share a cabin with another woman. Miss Reid did not mind that, she liked company, and when the steward told her that her companion was Madame Bollin she thought at once that it would be a very good opportunity to rub up her French. She was only very slightly disconcerted when she found that Madame Bollin was coal-black. She told herself that one had to accept the rough with the smooth and that it takes all sorts to make a world. Miss

Reid was a good sailor, as indeed was only to be expected since her grandfather had been a naval officer, but after a couple of roughish days the weather was fine and in a very short while she knew all her fellow-passengers. She was a good mixer. That was one of the reasons why she had made a success of her business; she owned a tea-room at a celebrated beauty spot in the west of England and she always had a smile and a pleasant word for every customer who came in; she closed down in the winter and for the last four years had taken a cruise. You met such interesting people, she said, and you always learnt something. It was true that the passengers on the *Friedrich Weber* weren't of quite so good a class as those she had met the year before on her Mediterranean cruise, but Miss Reid was not a snob, and though the table manners of some of them shocked her somewhat, determined to look upon the bright side of things she decided to make the best of them. She was a great reader and she was glad, on looking at the ship's library, to find that there were a lot of books by Phillips Oppenheim, Edgar Wallace and Agatha Christie; but with so many people to talk to she had no time for reading and she made up her mind to leave them till the ship emptied itself at Haiti.

"After all," she said, "human nature is more important than literature."

Miss Reid had always had the reputation of being a good talker and she flattered herself that not once during the many days they were at sea had she allowed the conversation at table to languish. She knew how to draw people out, and whenever a topic seemed to be exhausted she had a remark ready to revive it or another topic waiting on the tip of her tongue to set the conversation off again. Her friend Miss Prince, daughter of the late Vicar of Campden, who had come to see her off at Plymouth, for she lived there, had often said to her:

"You know, Venetia, you have a mind like a man. You're never at a loss for something to say."

"Well, I think if you're interested in everyone, everyone will be interested in you," Miss Reid answered modestly. "Practice makes perfect, and I have the infinite capacity for taking pains which Dickens said was genius."

Miss Reid was not really called Venetia, her name was Alice, but disliking it she had, when still a girl, adopted the poetic name which she felt so much better suited to her personality.

Miss Reid had a great many interesting talks with her fellow-passengers and she was really sorry when the ship at length reached Port au Prince and the last of them disembarked. The *Friedrich Weber* stopped two days there, during which she visited the town and the neighbourhood. When they sailed she was the only passenger. The ship was skirting the coast of the island stopping at a variety of ports to discharge or to take on cargo.

"I hope you will not feel embarrassed alone with so many men, Miss Reid," said the captain heartily as they sat down to midday dinner.

She was placed on his right hand and at table besides sat the first mate, the chief engineer and the doctor.

"I'm a woman of the world, Captain. I always think if a lady is a lady gentlemen will be gentlemen."

"We're only rough sailor men, madam, you mustn't expect too much."

"Kind hearts are more than coronets and simple faith than Norman blood, Captain," answered Miss Reid.

He was a short, thick-set man, with a clean-shaven head and a red, clean-shaven face. He wore a white stengah-shifter, but except at meal-times unbuttoned at the neck and showing his hairy chest. He was a jovial fellow. He could not speak without bellowing. Miss Reid thought him quite an eccentric, but she had a keen sense of humour and was prepared to make allowances for that. She took the conversation in hand. She had learnt a great deal about Haiti on the voyage out and more during the two days she had spent there, but she knew that men liked to talk rather than to listen, so she put them a number of questions to which she already knew the answers; oddly enough they didn't. In the end she found herself obliged to

185

give quite a little lecture, and before dinner was over, *Mittag Essen* they called it in their funny way, she had imparted to them a great deal of interesting information about the history and economic situation of the Republic, the problems that confronted it and its prospects for the future. She talked rather slowly, in a refined voice, and her vocabulary was extensive.

At nightfall they put in at a small port where they were to load three hundred bags of coffee, and the agent came on board. The captain asked him to stay to supper and ordered cocktails. As the steward brought them Miss Reid swam into the saloon. Her movements were deliberate, elegant and self-assured. She always said that you could tell at once by the way she walked if a woman was a lady. The captain introduced the agent to her and she sat down.

"What is that you men are drinking?" she asked.

"A cocktail. Will you have one, Miss Reid?"

"I don't mind if I do."

She drank it and the captain somewhat doubtfully asked her if she would have another.

"Another? Well, just to be matey."

The agent, much whiter than some, but a good deal darker than many, was the son of a former minister of Haiti to the German court, and having lived for many years in Berlin spoke good German. It was indeed on this account that he had got a job with a German shipping firm. On the strength of this Miss Reid, during supper, told them all about a trip down the Rhine that she had once taken. Afterwards she and the agent, the skipper, the doctor and the mate sat round a table and drank beer. Miss Reid made it her business to draw the agent out. The fact that they were loading coffee suggested to her that he would be interested in learning how they grew tea in Ceylon, yes, she had been to Ceylon on a cruise, and the fact that his father was a diplomat made it certain that he would be interested in the royal family of England. She had a very pleasant evening. When she at last retired to rest, for she would

186

never have thought of saying she was going to bed, she said
to herself:

"There's no doubt that travel is a great education."

It was really an experience to find herself alone with all
those men. How they would laugh when she told them all
about it when she got home! They would say that things like
that only happened to Venetia. She smiled when she heard the
captain on deck singing with that great booming voice of his.
Germans were so musical. He had a funny way of strutting up
and down on his short legs singing Wagner tunes to words
of his own invention. It was *Tannhäuser* he was singing now
(that lovely thing about the evening star) but knowing no
German Miss Reid could only wonder what absurd words he
was putting to it. It was as well.

"Oh, what a bore that woman is, I shall certainly kill her
if she goes on much longer." Then he broke into Siegfried's
martial strain. "She's a bore, she's a bore, she's a bore. I shall
throw her into the sea."

And that of course is what Miss Reid was. She was a crashing, she was a stupendous, she was an excruciating bore. She
talked in a steady monotone, and it was no use to interrupt her
because then she started again from the beginning. She had an
insatiable thirst for information and no casual remark could be
thrown across the table without her asking innumerable
questions about it. She was a great dreamer and she narrated
her dreams at intolerable length. There was no subject upon
which she had not something prosy to say. She had a truism
for every occasion. She hit on the commonplace like a hammer
driving a nail into the wall. She plunged into the obvious like
a clown in a circus jumping through a hoop. Silence did not
abash her. Those poor men far away from their homes and
the patter of little feet, and with Christmas coming on, no
wonder they felt low; she redoubled her efforts to interest and
amuse them. She was determined to bring a little gaiety into
their dull lives. For that was the awful part of it: Miss Reid
meant well. She was not only having a good time herself, but

she was trying to give all of them a good time. She was convinced that they liked her as much as she liked them. She felt that she was doing her bit to make the party a success and she was naïvely happy to think that she was succeeding. She told them all about her friend Miss Price and how often she had said to her: Venetia, no one ever has a dull moment in your company. It was the captain's duty to be polite to a passenger, and however much he would have liked to tell her to hold her silly tongue he could not, but even if he had been free to say what he liked, he knew that he could not have brought himself to hurt her feelings. Nothing stemmed the torrent of her loquacity. It was as irresistible as a force of nature. Once in desperation they began talking German, but Miss Reid stopped this at once.

"Now I won't have you saying things I don't understand. You ought all to make the most of your good luck in having me all to yourselves and practise your English."

"We were talking of technical matters that would only bore you, Miss Reid," said the captain.

"I'm never bored. That's why, if you won't think me a wee bit conceited to say so, I'm never boring. You see, I like to know things. Everything interests me and you never know when a bit of information won't come in useful."

The doctor smiled drily.

"The captain was only saying that because he was embarrassed. In point of fact he was telling a story that was not fit for the ears of a maiden lady."

"I may be a maiden lady but I'm also a woman of the world, I don't expect sailors to be saints. You need never be afraid of what you say before me, Captain, I shan't be shocked. I should love to hear your story."

The doctor was a man of sixty with thin grey hair, a grey moustache and small bright blue eyes. He was a silent, bitter man, and however hard Miss Reid tried to bring him into the conversation it was almost impossible to get a word out of him. But she wasn't a woman who would give in without a struggle, and one morning when they were at sea and she saw him sitting on deck with a book, she brought her chair next to his and sat down beside him.

"Are you fond of reading, Doctor?" she said brightly.

"Yes."

"So am I. And I suppose like all Germans you're musical."

"I'm fond of music."

"So am I. The moment I saw you I thought you looked clever."

He gave her a brief look and pursing his lips went on reading. Miss Reid was not disconcerted.

"But of course one can always read. I always prefer a good talk to a good book. Don't you?"

"No."

"How very interesting. Now do tell me why?"

"I can't give you a reason."

"That's very strange, isn't it? But then I always think human nature is strange. I'm terribly interested in people, you know. I always like doctors, they know so much about human nature, but I could tell you some things that would surprise even you. You learn a great deal about people if you run a tea-shop like I do, that's to say if you keep your eyes open."

The doctor got up.

"I must ask you to excuse me, Miss Reid. I have to go and see a patient."

"Anyhow I've broken the ice now," she thought, as he walked away. "I think he was only shy."

But a day or two later the doctor was not feeling at all well. He had an internal malady that troubled him now and then, but he was used to it and disinclined to talk about it. When he had one of his attacks he only wanted to be left alone. His cabin was small and stuffy, so he settled himself on a long chair on deck and lay with his eyes closed. Miss Reid was walking up and down to get the half-hour's exercise she took morning and evening. He thought that if he pretended to be asleep she would not disturb him. But when she had passed him half a

189

dozen times she stopped in front of him and stood quite still. Though he kept his eyes closed he knew that she was looking at him.

"Is there anything I can do, Doctor?" she said.

He started.

"Why, what should there be?"

He gave her a glance and saw that her eyes were deeply troubled.

"You look dreadfully ill," she said.

"I'm in great pain."

"I know. I can see that. Can't something be done?"

"No, it'll pass off presently."

She hesitated for a moment then went away. Presently she returned.

"You look so uncomfortable with no cushions or anything. I've brought you my own pillow that I always travel with. Do let me put it behind your head."

He felt at that moment too ill to remonstrate. She lifted his head gently and put the soft pillow behind it. It really did make him feel more comfortable. She passed her hand across his forehead and it was cool and soft.

"Poor dear," she said. "I know what doctors are. They haven't the first idea how to take care of themselves."

She left him, but in a minute or two returned with a chair and a bag. The doctor when he saw her gave a twitch of anguish.

"Now I'm not going to let you talk, I'm just going to sit beside you and knit. I always think it's a comfort when one isn't feeling very well to have someone near."

She sat down and taking an unfinished muffler out of her bag began busily to ply her needles. She never said a word. And strangely enough the doctor found her company a solace. No one else on board had even noticed that he was ill, he had felt lonely, and the sympathy of that crashing bore was grateful to him. It soothed him to see her silently working and presently he fell asleep. When he awoke she was still working. She gave

190

him a little smile, but did not speak. His pain had left him and he felt much better.

He did not go into the saloon till late in the afternoon. He found the captain and Hans Krause, the mate, having a glass of beer together.

"Sit down, Doctor," said the captain. "We're holding a council of war. You know that the day after tomorrow is Sylvester Abend."

"Of course."

Sylvester Abend, New Year's Eve, is an occasion that means a great deal to a German and they had all been looking forward to it. They had brought a Christmas tree all the way from Germany with them.

"At dinner today Miss Reid was more talkative than ever. Hans and I have decided that something must be done about it."

"She sat with me for two hours this morning in silence. I suppose she was making up for lost time."

"It's bad enough being away from one's home and family just now anyway and all we can do is to make the best of a bad job. We want to enjoy our Sylvester Abend, and unless something is done about Miss Reid we haven't a chance."

"We can't have a good time if she's with us," said the mate. "She'll spoil it as sure as eggs is eggs."

"How do you propose to get rid of her, short of throwing her overboard?" smiled the doctor. "She's not a bad old soul; all she wants is a lover."

"At her age?" cried Hans Krause.

"Especially at her age. That inordinate loquacity, that passion for information, the innumerable questions she asks, her prosiness, the way she goes on and on—it is all a sign of her clamouring virginity. A lover would bring her peace. Those jangled nerves of hers would relax. At least for an hour she would have lived. The deep satisfaction which her being demands would travel through those exacerbated centres of speech, and we should have quiet."

191

It was always a little difficult to know how much the doctor meant what he said and when he was having a joke at your expense. The captain's blue eyes, however, twinkled mischievously.

"Well, Doctor, I have great confidence in your powers of diagnosis. The remedy you suggest is evidently worth trying and since you are a bachelor it is clear that it is up to you to apply it."

"Pardon me, Captain, it is my professional duty to prescribe remedies for the patients under my charge in this ship, but not to administer them personally. Besides, I am sixty."

"I am a married man with grown-up children," said the captain. "I am old and fat and asthmatic, it is obvious that I cannot be expected to undertake a task of this kind. Nature cut me out for the rôle of husband and father, not for that of a lover."

"Youth in these matters is essential and good looks are advantageous," said the doctor gravely.

The captain gave a great bang on the table with his fist.

"You are thinking of Hans. You're quite right. Hans must do it."

The mate sprang to his feet.

"Me? Never."

"Hans, you are tall, handsome, strong as a lion, brave and young. We have twenty-three days more at sea before we reach Hamburg, you wouldn't desert your trusted old captain in an emergency or let down your good friend the doctor?"

"No, Captain, it's asking too much of me. I have been married less than a year and I love my wife. I can hardly wait to get back to Hamburg. She is yearning for me as I am yearning for her. I will not be unfaithful to her, especially with Miss Reid."

"Miss Reid's not so bad," said the doctor.

"Some people might call her even nice-looking," said the captain.

And indeed when you took Miss Reid feature by feature she

192

was not in fact a plain woman. True, she had a long, stupid face, but her brown eyes were large and she had very thick lashes; her brown hair was cut short and curled rather prettily over her neck; she hadn't a bad skin, and she was neither too fat nor too thin. She was not old as people go nowadays, and if she had told you that she was forty you would have been quite willing to believe it. The only thing against her was that she was drab and dull.

"Must I then for twenty-three mortal days endure the prolixity of that tedious woman? Must I for twenty-three mortal days answer her inane questions and listen to her fatuous remarks? Must I, an old man, have my Sylvester Abend, the olly evening I was looking forward to, ruined by the unwelcome company of that intolerable virgin? And all because o one can be found to show a little gallantry, a little human kindness, a mark of charity to a lonely woman. I shall wreck the ship."

"There's always the radio-operator," said Hans.

The captain gave a loud shout.

"Hans, let the ten thousand virgins of Cologne arise and call you blessed. Steward," he bellowed, "tell the radio-operator hat I want him."

The radio-operator came into the saloon and smartly clicked his heels together. The three men looked at him in silence. He wondered uneasily whether he had done something for which he was to be hauled over the coals. He was above the middle height, with square shoulders and narrow hips, erect and slender, his tanned, smooth skin looked as though a razor had never touched it, he had large eyes of a startling blue and a mane of curling golden hair. He was a perfect specimen of young Teutonic manhood. He was so healthy, so vigorous, so much alive that even when he stood some way from you, you felt the glow of his vitality.

"Aryan, all right," said the captain. "No doubt about that. How old are you, my boy?"

"Twenty-one, sir."

193

"Married?"

"No, sir."

"Engaged?"

The radio-operator chuckled. There was an engaging boyishness in his laugh.

"No, sir."

"You know that we have a female passenger on board?"

"Yes, sir."

"Do you know her?"

"I've said good morning to her when I've seen her on deck."

The captain assumed his most official manner. His eyes, which generally twinkled with fun, were stern and he got a sort of bark into his rich, fruity voice.

"Although this is a cargo-boat and we carry valuable freight we also take such passengers as we can get, and this is a branch of our business that the company is anxious to encourage. My instructions are to do everything possible to promote the happines and comfort of the passengers. Miss Reid needs a lover. The doctor and I have come to the conclusion that you are well suited to satisfy Miss Reid's requirements."

"Me, sir?"

The radio-operator blushed scarlet and then began to giggle, but quickly composed himself when he saw the set faces of the three men who confronted him.

"But she's old enough to be my mother."

"That at your age is a matter of no consequence. She is a woman of the highest distinction and allied to all the great families of England. If she were German she would be at least a countess. That you should have been chosen for this responsible position is an honour that you should greatly appreciate. Furthermore, your English is halting and this will give you an excellent opportunity to improve it."

"That of course is something to be thought of," said the radio-operator. "I know that I want practice."

"It is not often in this life that it is possible to combine pleasure with intellectual improvement, and you must congratulate yourself on your good fortune."

"But if I may be allowed to put the question, sir, why does Miss Reid want a lover?"

"It appears to be an old English custom for unmarried women of exalted rank to submit themselves to the embraces of a lover at this time of year. The company is anxious that Miss Reid should be treated exactly as she would be on an English ship, and we trust that if she is satisfied, with her aristocratic connections she will be able to persuade many of her friends to take cruises in the line's ships."

"Sir, I must ask to be excused."

"It is not a request that I am making, it is an order. You will present yourself to Miss Reid, in her cabin, at eleven o'clock tonight."

"What shall I do when I get there?"

"Do?" thundered the captain. "Do? Act naturally."

With a wave of the hand he dismissed him. The radio-operator clicked his heels, saluted and went out.

"Now let us have another glass of beer," said the captain.

At supper that evening Miss Reid was at her best. She was verbose. She was playful. She was refined. There was not a truism that she failed to utter. There was not a commonplace that she forebore to express. She bombarded them with foolish questions. The captain's face grew redder and redder as he sought to contain his fury; he felt that he could not go on being polite to her any longer and if the doctor's remedy did not help, one day he would forget himself and give her, not a piece, but the whole of his mind.

"I shall lose my job," he thought, "but I'm not sure that it wouldn't be worth it."

Next day they were already sitting at table when she came in to dinner.

"Sylvester Abend tomorrow," she said, brightly. That was the sort of thing she would say. She went on: "Well, what have you all been up to this morning?"

Since they did exactly the same thing every day, and she knew very well what that was, the question was enraging. The captain's heart sank. He briefly told the doctor what he thought of him.

"Now, no German, please," said Miss Reid archly. "You know I don't allow that, and why, Captain, did you give the poor doctor that sour look? It's Christmas time, you know; peace and good-will to all men. I'm so excited about tomorrow evening, and will there be candles on the Christmas tree?"

"Naturally."

"How thrilling! I always think a Christmas tree without candles isn't a Christmas tree. Oh, d'you know, I had such a funny experience last night. I can't understand it at all."

A startled pause. They all looked intently at Miss Reid. For once they hung on her lips.

"Yes," she went on in that monotonous, rather finicking way of hers, "I was just getting into bed last night when there was a knock at my door. 'Who is it?' I said. 'It's the radio-operator,' was the answer. 'What is it?' I said. 'Can I speak to you?' he said."

They listened with rapt attention.

" 'Well, I'll just pop on a dressing-gown,' I said, 'and open the door.' So I popped on a dressing-gown and opened the door. The radio-operator said: 'Excuse me, miss, but do you want to send a radio?' Well, I did think it was funny his coming at that hour to ask me if I wanted to send a radio, I just laughed in his face, it appealed to my sense of humour if you understand what I mean, but I didn't want to hurt his feelings so I said: 'Thank you so much, but I don't think I want to send a radio.' He stood there, looking so funny, as if he was quite embarrassed, so I said: 'Thank you all the same for asking me,' and then I said 'Good night, pleasant dreams' and shut the door."

"The damned fool," cried the captain.

"He's young, Miss Reid," the doctor put in. "It was excess of zeal. I suppose he thought you would want to send a New

196

P Gleason

Year's greeting to your friends and he wished you to get the advantage of the special rate."

"Oh, I didn't mind at all. I like these queer little things that happen to one when one's travelling. I just get a good laugh out of them."

As soon as dinner was over and Miss Reid had left them the captain sent for the radio-operator.

"You idiot, what in heaven's name made you ask Miss Reid last night whether she wanted to send a radio?"

"Sir, you told me to act naturally. I am a radio-operator. I thought it natural to ask her if she wanted to send a radio. I didn't know what else to say."

"God in heaven," shouted the captain, "when Siegfried saw Brünhilde lying on her rock and cried: *Das ist kein Mann,*" (the captain sang the words, and being pleased with the sound of his voice, repeated the phrase two or three times before he continued), "did Siegfried when she awoke ask her if she wished to send a radio, to announce to her papa, I suppose, that she was sitting up after her long sleep and taking notice?"

"I beg most respectfully to draw your attention to the fact that Brünhilde was Siegfried's aunt. Miss Reid is a total stranger to me."

"He did not reflect that she was his aunt. He knew only that she was a beautiful and defenceless woman of obviously good family and he acted as any gentleman would have done. You are young, handsome, Aryan to the tips of your fingers, the honour of Germany is in your hands."

"Very good, sir. I will do my best."

That night there was another knock on Miss Reid's door

"Who is it?"

"The radio-operator. I have a radio for you, Miss Reid."

"For me?" She was surprised, but it at once occurred to her that one of her fellow-passengers who had got off at Haiti had sent her New Year's greetings. "How very kind people are," she thought. "I'm in bed. Leave it outside the door."

"It needs an answer. Ten words prepaid."

197

Then it couldn't be a New Year's greeting. Her heart stopped beating. It could only mean one thing; her shop had been burned to the ground. She jumped out of bed.

"Slip it under the door and I'll write the answer and slip it back to you."

The envelope was pushed under the door and as it appeared on the carpet it had really a sinister look. Miss Reid snatched it up and tore the envelope open. The words swam before her eyes and she couldn't for a moment find her spectacles. This is what she read:

"Happy New Year. Stop. Peace and goodwill to all men. Stop. You are very beautiful. Stop. I love you. Stop. I must speak to you. Stop. Signed: Radio Operator."

Miss Reid read this through twice. Then she slowly took off her spectacles and hid them under a scarf. She opened the door.

"Come in," she said.

Next day was New Year's Eve. The officers were cheerful and a little sentimental when they sat down to dinner. The stewards had decorated the saloon with tropical creepers to make up for holly and mistletoe, and the Christmas tree stood on a table with the candles ready to be lit at supper time. Miss Reid did not come in till the officers were seated, and when they bade her good morning she did not speak but merely bowed. They looked at her curiously. She ate a good dinner, but uttered never a word. Her silence was uncanny. At last the captain could stand it no longer, and he said:

"You're very quiet today, Miss Reid."

"I'm thinking," she remarked.

"And will you not tell us your thoughts, Miss Reid?" the doctor asked playfully.

She gave him a cool, you might almost have called it a supercilious, look.

"I prefer to keep them to myself, Doctor. I will have a little more of that hash, I've got a very good appetite."

They finished the meal in a blessed silence. The captain heaved a sigh of relief. That was what meal-time was for, to

198

eat, not chatter. When they had finished he went up to the doctor and wrung his hand.

"Something has happened, Doctor."

"It has happened. She's a changed woman."

"But will it last?"

"One can only hope for the best."

Miss Reid put on an evening dress for the evening's celebration, a very quiet black dress, with artificial roses at her bosom and a long string of imitation jade round her neck. The lights were dimmed and the candles on the Christmas tree were lit. It felt a little like being in church. The junior officers were supping in the saloon that evening and they looked very smart in their white uniforms. Champagne was served at the company's expense and after supper they had a *Maibowle*. They pulled crackers. They sang songs to the gramophone, *Deutschland, Deutschland über Alles, Alt Heidelberg* and *Auld Lang Syne*. They shouted out the tunes lustily, the captain's voice rising loud above the others, and Miss Reid joining in with a pleasing contralto. The doctor noticed that Miss Reid's eyes from time to time rested on the radio-operator, and in them he read an expression of some bewilderment.

"He's a good-looking fellow, isn't he?" said the doctor.

Miss Reid turned round and looked at the doctor coolly.

"Who?"

"The radio-operator. I thought you were looking at him."

"Which is he?"

"The duplicity of women," the doctor muttered, but with a smile he answered: "He's sitting next to the chief engineer."

"Oh, of course, I recognise him now. You know, I never think it matters what a man looks like. I'm so much more interested in a man's brains than in his looks."

"Ah," said the doctor.

They all got a little tight, including Miss Reid, but she did not lose her dignity and when she bade them good-night it was in her best manner.

"I've had a very delightful evening. I shall never forget my New Year's Eve on a German boat. It's been very interesting. Quite an experience."

She walked steadily to the door, and this was something of a triumph, for she had drunk drink for drink with the rest of them through the evening.

They were all somewhat jaded next day. When the captain, the mate, the doctor and the chief engineer came down to dinner they found Miss Reid already seated. Before each place was a small parcel tied up in pink ribbon. On each was written: Happy New Year. They gave Miss Reid a questioning glance.

"You've all been so very kind to me I thought I'd like to give each of you a little present. There wasn't much choice at Port au Prince, so you mustn't expect too much."

There was a pair of briar pipes for the captain, half a dozen silk handkerchiefs for the doctor, a cigar-case for the mate and a couple of ties for the chief engineer. They had dinner and Miss Reid retired to her cabin to rest. The officers looked at one another uncomfortably. The mate fiddled with the cigar-case she had given him.

"I'm a little ashamed of myself," he said at last.

The captain was pensive and it was plain that he too was a trifle uneasy.

"I wonder if we ought to have played that trick on Miss Reid," he said. "She's a good old soul and she's not rich; she's a woman who earns her own living. She must have spent the best part of a hundred marks on these presents. I almost wish we'd left her alone."

The doctor shrugged his shoulders.

"You wanted her silenced and I've silenced her."

"When all's said and done, it wouldn't have hurt us to listen to her chatter for three weeks more," said the mate.

"I'm not happy about her," added the captain. "I feel there's something ominous in her quietness."

She had spoken hardly a word during the meal they had just shared with her. She seemed hardly to listen to what they said.

"Don't you think you ought to ask her if she's feeling quite well, doctor?" suggested the captain.

"Of course she's feeling quite well. She's eating like a wolf. If you want inquiries made you'd much better make them of the radio-operator."

"You may not be aware of it, Doctor, but I am a man of great delicacy."

"I am a man of heart myself," said the doctor.

For the rest of the journey those men spoilt Miss Reid outrageously. They treated her with the consideration they would have shown to someone who was convalescent after a long and dangerous illness. Though her appetite was excellent they sought to tempt her with new dishes. The doctor ordered wine and insisted on her sharing his bottle with him. They played dominoes with her. They played chess with her. They played bridge with her. They engaged her in conversation. But there was no doubt about it, though she responded to their advances with politeness, she kept herself to herself. She seemed to regard them with something very like disdain; you might almost have thought that she looked upon those men and their efforts to be amiable as pleasantly ridiculous. She seldom spoke unless spoken to. She read detective stories and at night sat on deck looking at the stars. She lived a life of her own.

At last the journey drew to its close. They sailed up the English Channel on a still grey day; they sighted land. Miss Reid packed her trunk. At two o'clock in the afternoon they docked at Plymouth. The captain, the mate and the doctor came along to say good-bye to her.

"Well, Miss Reid," said the captain in his jovial way, "we're sorry to lose you, but I suppose you're glad to be getting home."

"You've been very kind to me, you've all been very kind to me, I don't know what I've done to deserve it. I've been very happy with you. I shall never forget you."

She spoke rather shakily, she tried to smile, but her lips quivered, and tears ran down her cheeks. The captain got very red. He smiled awkwardly.

201

CREATURES OF CIRCUMSTANCE

"May I kiss you, Miss Reid?"

She was taller than he by half a head. She bent down and he planted a fat kiss on one wet cheek and a fat kiss on the other. She turned to the mate and the doctor. They both kissed her.

"What an old fool I am," she said. "Everybody's so good."

She dried her eyes and slowly, in her graceful, rather absurd way, walked down the companion. The captain's eyes were wet. When she reached the quay she looked up and waved to someone on the boat deck.

"Who's she waving to?" asked the captain.

"The radio-operator."

Miss Price was waiting on the quay to welcome her. When they had passed the customs and got rid of Miss Reid's heavy luggage they went to Miss Price's house and had an early cup of tea. Miss Reid's train did not start till five. Miss Price had much to tell Miss Reid.

"But it's too bad of me to go on like this when you've just come home. I've been looking forward to hearing all about your journey."

"I'm afraid there's not very much to tell."

"I can't believe that. Your trip was a success, wasn't it?"

"A distinct success. It was very nice."

"And you didn't mind being with all those Germans?"

"Of course they're not like English people. One has to get used to their ways. They sometimes do things—well, that English people wouldn't do, you know. But I always think that one has to take things as they come."

"What sort of things do you mean?"

Miss Reid looked at her friend calmly. Her long, stupid face had a placid look, and Miss Price never noticed that in the eyes was a strangely mischievous twinkle.

"Things of no importance really. Just funny, unexpected, rather nice things. There's no doubt that travel is a wonderful education."

THE
HAPPY COUPLE

I DON'T know that I very much liked Landon. He was a member of a club I belonged to, and I had often sat next to him at lunch. He was a judge at the Old Bailey, and it was through him I was able to get a privileged seat in court when there was an interesting trial that I wanted to attend. He was an imposing figure on the bench in his great full-bottomed wig, his red robes and his ermine tippet; and with his long, white face, thin lips and pale blue eyes, a somewhat terrifying one. He was just, but harsh; and sometimes it made me uncomfortable to hear the bitter scolding he gave a convicted prisoner whom he was about to sentence to a long term of imprisonment. But his acid humour at the lunch-table and his willingness to discuss the cases he had tried made him sufficiently good company for me to disregard the slight malaise I felt in his presence. I asked him once whether he did not feel a certain uneasiness of mind after he had sent a man to the gallows. He smiled as he sipped his glass of port.

"Not at all. The man's had a fair trial; I've summed up as fairly as I could, and the jury has found him guilty. When I condemn him to death, I sentence him to a punishment he richly deserves; and when the court rises, I put the case out of my head. Nobody but a sentimental fool would do anything else."

I knew he liked to talk to me, but I never thought he looked upon me as anything but a club acquaintance, so I was not a little surprised when one day I received a telegram from him saying that he was spending his vacation on the Riviera, and would like to stay with me for two or three days on his way to Italy. I wired that I should be glad to see him. But it was with a certain trepidation that I met him at the station.

203

CREATURES OF CIRCUMSTANCE

On the day of his arrival, to help me out, I asked Miss Gray, a neighbour and an old friend of mine, to dinner. She was of mature age, but charming, and she had a flow of lively conversation which I knew nothing could discourage. I gave them a very good dinner, and though I had no port to offer the judge, I was able to provide him with a good bottle of Montrachet and an even better bottle of Mouton Rothschild. He enjoyed them both; and I was glad of that, because when I had offered him a cocktail, he had refused with indignation.

"I have never understood," he said, "how people presumably civilised can indulge in a habit that is not only barbarous but disgusting."

I may state that this did not deter Miss Gray and me from having a couple of dry Martinis, though it was with impatience and distaste that he watched us drink them.

But the dinner was a success. The good wine and Miss Gray's sprightly chatter combined to give Landon a geniality I had never before seen in him. It was plain to me that notwithstanding his austere appearance he liked feminine society; and Miss Gray in a becoming dress, with her neat head only just touched with grey and her delicate features, her sparkling eyes, was still alluring. After dinner the judge, with some old brandy still further to mellow him, let himself go, and for a couple of hours held us entranced while he told us of celebrated trials in which he had been concerned. I was not surprised therefore that when Miss Gray asked us to lunch with her next day, Landon, even before I could answer, accepted with alacrity.

"A very nice woman," he said when she had left us. "And a head on her shoulders. She must have been very pretty as a girl. She's not bad now. Why isn't she married?"

"She always says nobody asked her."

"Stuff and nonsense! Women ought to marry. Too many of these women about who want their independence. I have no patience with them."

Miss Gray lived in a little house facing the sea at St. Jean, which is a couple of miles from my own house at Cap Ferrat.

204

We drove down next day at one and were shown into her sitting-room.

"I have a surprise for you," she said to me, as we shook hands. "The Craigs are coming."

"You've got to know them at last."

"Well, I thought it was too absurd that we should live next door to one another, and bathe from the same beach every day and not speak. So I forced myself on them, and they've promised to come to lunch today. I wanted you to meet them, to see what you make of them." She turned to Landon. "I hope you don't mind."

But he was on his best behaviour.

"I'm sure I shall be delighted to meet any friends of yours, Miss Gray," he said.

"But they're not friends of mine. I've seen a lot of them, but I never spoke to them till yesterday. It'll be a treat for them to meet an author and a celebrated judge."

I had heard a good deal of the Craigs from Miss Gray during the previous three weeks. They had taken the cottage next to hers, and at first she feared they would be a nuisance. She liked her own company and did not want to be bothered with the trivialities of social intercourse. But she very quickly discovered that the Craigs were as plainly disinclined to strike up an acquaintance with her as she with them. Though in that little place they could not but meet two or three times a day, the Craigs never by so much a glance gave an indication that they had ever seen her before. Miss Gray told me she thought it very tactful of them to make no attempt to intrude upon her privacy, but I had an idea that she was not affronted, a little puzzled rather, that they apparently wanted to know her as little as she wanted to know them. I had guessed some time before that she would not be able to resist making the first advance. On one occasion, while we were walking, we passed them, and I was able to have a good look at them. Craig was a handsome man, with a red, honest face, a grey moustache and thick strong grey hair. He held himself well, and there

205

was a bluff heartiness of manner about him that suggested a broker who had retired on a handsome fortune. His wife was a woman hard of visage, tall and of masculine appearance, with dull, fair hair too elaborately dressed, a large nose, a large mouth and a weather-beaten skin. She was not only plain but grim. Her clothes, pretty, flimsy and graceful, sat oddly upon her, for they would better have suited a girl of eighteen, and Mrs. Craig was certainly forty. Miss Gray told me they were well cut and expensive. I thought he looked commonplace and she looked disagreeable, and I told Miss Gray she was lucky that they were obviously disposed to keep themselves to themselves.

"There's something rather sweet about them," she answered.

"What?"

"They love one another. And they adore the baby."

For they had a child that was not more than a year old; and from this Miss Gray had concluded that they had not long been married. She liked to watch them with their baby. A nurse took it out every morning in a pram, but before this, father and mother spent an ecstatic quarter of an hour teaching it to walk. They stood a few yards apart and urged the child to flounder from one to the other; and each time it tumbled into the parental arms it was lifted up and rapturously embraced. And when finally it was tucked up in the smart pram, they hung over it with charming baby talk and watched it out of sight as though they couldn't bear to let it go.

Miss Gray used often to see them walking up and down the lawn of their garden arm in arm; they did not talk, as though they were so happy to be together that conversation was unnecessary; and it warmed her heart to observe the affection which that dour, unsympathetic woman so obviously felt for her tall, handsome husband. It was a pretty sight to see Mrs. Craig brush an invisible speck of dust off his coat, and Miss Gray was convinced that she purposely made holes in his socks in order to have the pleasure of darning them. And it looked as though he loved her as much as she loved him. Every now and then he would give her a glance, and she would look up at him and smile, and he gave her cheek a little pat. Because they were no longer young, their mutual devotion was peculiarly touching.

I never knew why Miss Gray had never married; I felt as certain as the judge that she had had plenty of chances; and I asked myself, when she talked to me about the Craigs, whether the sight of this matrimonial felicity didn't give her a slight pang. I suppose complete happiness is very rare in this world, but these two people seemed to enjoy it, and it may be that Miss Gray was so strangely interested in them only because she could not quite suppress the feeling in her heart that by remaining single she had missed something.

Because she didn't know what their first names were, she called them Edwin and Angelina. She made up a story about them. She told it to me one day; and when I ridiculed it, she was quite short with me. This, as far as I can remember, is how it went: They had fallen in love with one another years before—perhaps twenty years—when Angelina, a young girl then, had the fresh grace of her teens and Edwin was a brave youth setting out joyously on the journey of life. And since the gods, who are said to look upon young love with kindliness, nevertheless do not bother their heads with practical matters, neither Edwin nor Angelina had a penny. It was impossible for them to marry, but they had courage, hope and confidence. Edwin made up his mind to go out to South America or Malaya or where you like, make his fortune and return to marry the girl who had patiently waited for him. It couldn't take more than two or three years, five at the utmost; and what is that, when you're twenty and the whole of life is before you? Meanwhile of course Angelina would live with her widowed mother.

But things didn't pan out according to schedule. Edwin found it more difficult than he had expected to make a fortune; in fact, he found it hard to earn enough money to keep body and soul together, and only Angelina's love and her tender

207

letters gave him the heart to continue the struggle. At the end of five years he was not much better off than when he started. Angelina would willingly have joined him and shared his poverty, but it was impossible for her to leave her mother, bedridden as she was, poor thing, and there was nothing for them to do but have patience. And so the years passed slowly, and Edwin's hair grew grey, and Angelina became grim and haggard. Hers was the harder lot, for she could do nothing but wait. The cruel glass showed such charms as she had possessed slipping away from her one by one; and at last she discovered that youth, with a mocking laugh and a pirouette, had left her for good. Her sweetness turned sour from long tending of a querulous invalid; her mind was narrowed by the society of the small town in which she lived. Her friends married and had children, but she remained a prisoner to duty.

She wondered if Edwin still loved her. She wondered if he would ever come back. She often despaired. Ten years went by, and fifteen, and twenty. Then Edwin wrote to say that his affairs were settled, he had made enough money for them to live upon in comfort, and if she were still willing to marry him, he would return at once. By a merciful interposition of providence, Angelina's mother chose that very moment to abandon a world in which she had made herself a thorough nuisance. But when after so long a separation they met, Angelina saw with dismay that Edwin was as young as ever. It's true his hair was grey, but it infinitely became him. He had always been good-looking, but now he was a very handsome man in the flower of his age. She felt as old as the hills. She was conscious of her narrowness, her terrible provincialism, compared with the breadth he had acquired by his long sojourn in foreign countries. He was gay and breezy as of old, but her spirit was crushed. The bitterness of life had warped her soul. It seemed monstrous to bind that alert and active man to her by a promise twenty years old, and she offered him his release. He went deathly pale.

"Don't you care for me any more?" he cried brokenly.

And she realised on a sudden—oh, the rapture, oh, the relief!
—that to him too she was just the same as she had ever been.
He had thought of her always as she was; her portrait had
been, as it were, stamped on his heart, so that now, when the
real woman stood before him, she was, to him, still eighteen.

So they were married.

"I don't believe a word of it," I said when Miss Gray had
brought her story to its happy ending.

"I insist on you believing it," she said. "I'm convinced
it's true, and I haven't the smallest doubt that they'll live
happily together to a ripe old age." Then she made a remark
that I thought rather shrewd. "Their love is founded on an
illusion, perhaps; but since it has to them all the appearance
of reality, what does it matter?"

While I have told you this idyllic story of Miss Gray's invention, the three of us, our hostess, Landon and myself, waited
for the Craigs to come.

"Have you ever noticed that if people live next door to you,
they're invariably late?" Miss Gray asked the judge.

"No, I haven't," he answered acidly. "I'm always punctual
myself, and I expect other people to be punctual."

"I suppose it's no good offering you a cocktail?"

"None whatever, madam."

"But I have some sherry that they tell me isn't bad."

The judge took the bottle out of her hands and looked at the
label. A faint smile broke on his thin lips.

"This is a civilised drink, Miss Gray. With your permission
I will help myself. I never knew a woman yet who knew how
to pour out a glass of wine. One should hold a woman by the
waist, but a bottle by the neck."

While he was sipping the old sherry with every sign of satisfaction, Miss Gray glanced out of the window.

"Oh, that's why the Craigs are late. They were waiting for
the baby to come back."

I followed her eyes and saw that the nurse had just pushed
the pram past Miss Gray's house on her way home. Craig took

the baby out of the pram and lifted it high in the air. The baby, trying to tug at his moustache, crowed gleefully. Mrs. Craig stood by, watching, and the smile on her face made her harsh features almost pleasant. The window was open, and we heard her speak.

"Come along, darling," she said, "we're late."

He put the baby back in the pram, and they came up to the door of Miss Gray's house and rang the bell. The maid showed them in. They shook hands with Miss Gray, and because I was standing near, she introduced me to them. Then she turned to the judge.

"And this is Sir Edward Landon—Mr. and Mrs. Craig."

One would have expected the judge to move forward with an outstretched hand, but he remained stock-still. He put his eyeglass up to his eye, that eyeglass that I had on more than one occasion seen him use with devastating effect in court, and stared at the newcomers.

"Gosh, what a dirty customer," I said to myself.

He let the glass drop from his eye.

"How do you do," he said. "Am I mistaken in thinking that we've met before?"

The question turned my eyes to the Craigs. They stood side by side close to one another, as though they had drawn together for mutual protection. They did not speak. Mrs. Craig looked terrified. Craig's red face was darkened by a purple flush, and his eyes appeared almost to start out of his head. But that only lasted a second.

"I don't think so," he said in a rich, deep voice. "Of course I've heard of you, Sir Edward."

"More people know Tom Fool than Tom Fool knows," said he.

Miss Gray meanwhile had been giving the cocktail-shaker a shake, and now she handed cocktails to her two guests. She had noticed nothing. I didn't know what it all meant; in fact, I wasn't sure it meant anything. The incident, if incident there was, passed so quickly that I was half inclined to think that I

210

had read into the strangers' momentary embarrassment on being introduced to a celebrated man something for which there was no foundation. I set about making myself pleasant. I asked them how they liked the Riviera and if they were comfortable in their house. Miss Gray joined in, and we chatted, as one does with strangers, of commonplace things. They talked easily and pleasantly. Mrs. Craig said how much they enjoyed the bathing and complained of the difficulty of getting fish at the seaside. I was aware that the judge did not join in the conversation, but looked down at his feet as though he were unconscious of the company.

Lunch was announced. We went into the dining-room. We were only five, and it was a small round table, so the conversation could not be anything but general. I must confess that it was carried on chiefly by Miss Gray and myself. The judge was silent, but he often was, for he was a moody creature, and I paid no attention. I noticed that he ate the omelette with good appetite, and when it was passed round again took a second helping. The Craigs struck me as a little shy, but that didn't surprise me, and as the second course was produced they began to talk more freely. It didn't strike me that they were very amusing people; they didn't seem interested in very much besides their baby, the vagaries of the two Italian maids they had, and an occasional flutter at Monte Carlo; and I couldn't help thinking that Miss Gray had erred in making their acquaintance. Then suddenly something happened: Craig rose abruptly from his chair and fell headlong to the floor. We jumped up. Mrs. Craig threw herself down, over her husband, and took his head in her hands.

"It's all right, George," she cried in an agonised tone. "It's all right!"

"Put his head down," I said. "He's only fainted."

I felt his pulse and could feel nothing. I said he had fainted, but I wasn't sure it wasn't a stroke. He was the sort of heavy, plethoric man who might easily have one. Miss Gray dipped her napkin into water and dabbed his forehead. Mrs. Craig

211

seemed distraught. Then I noticed that Landon had remained quietly sitting in his chair.

"If he's fainted, you're not helping him to recover by crowding round him," he said acidly.

Mrs. Craig turned her head and gave him a look of bitter hatred.

"I'll ring up the doctor," said Miss Gray.

"No, I don't think that's necessary," I said. "He's coming to."

I could feel his pulse growing stronger, and in a minute or two he opened his eyes. He gasped when he realised what had happened, and tried to struggle to his feet.

"Don't move," I said. "Lie still a little longer."

I got him to drink a glass of brandy, and the colour came back to his face.

"I feel all right now," he said.

"We'll get you into the next room, and you can lie on the sofa for a bit."

"No, I'd sooner go home. It's only a step."

He got up from the floor.

"Yes, let's go back," said Mrs. Craig. She turned to Miss Gray. "I'm so sorry; he's never done anything like this before."

They were determined to go, and I thought myself it was the best thing for them to do.

"Put him to bed and keep him there, and he'll be as right as rain tomorrow."

Mrs. Craig took one of his arms and I took the other; Miss Gray opened the door, and though still a bit shaky, he was able to walk. When we arrived at the Craigs' home, I offered to go in and help undress him; but they would neither of them hear of it. I went back to Miss Gray's and found them at dessert.

"I wonder why he fainted," Miss Gray was saying. "All the windows are open, and it's not particularly hot today."

"I wonder," said the judge.

I noticed that his thin pale face bore an expression of some complacency. We had our coffee; and then, since the judge

212

and I were going to play golf, we got into the car and drove up the hill to my house.

"How did Miss Gray get to know those people?" Landon asked me. "They struck me as rather second-rate. I shouldn't have thought they were very much her mark."

"You know women. She likes her privacy, and when they settled in next door, she was quite decided that she wouldn't have anything to do with them; but when she discovered that they didn't want to have anything to do with her, she couldn't rest till she'd made their acquaintance."

I told him the story she had invented about her neighbours. He listened with an expressionless face.

"I'm afraid your friend Miss Gray is a sentimental donkey, my dear fellow," he said when I had come to an end. "I tell you, women ought to marry. She'd soon have had all that nonsense knocked out of her if she'd had half a dozen brats."

"What do you know about the Craigs?" I asked.

He gave me a frigid glance.

"I? Why should I know anything about them? I thought they were very ordinary people."

I wish I knew how to describe the strong impression he gave me, both by the glacial austerity of his look and by the rasping finality of his tone, that he was not prepared to say anything more. We finished the drive in silence.

Landon was well on in his sixties, and he was the kind of golfer who never hits a long ball but is never off the straight, and he was a deadly putter, so, though he gave me strokes, he beat me handsomely. After dinner I took him in to Monte Carlo, where he finished the evening by winning a couple of thousand francs at the roulette table. These successive events put him into a remarkably good humour.

"A very pleasant day," he said when we parted for the night. "I've thoroughly enjoyed it."

I spent the next morning at work, and we did not meet till lunch. We were just finishing when I was called to the telephone.

When I came back, my guest was drinking a second cup of coffee.

"That was Miss Gray," I said.

"Oh? What had she to say?"

"The Craigs have done a bolt. They disappeared last night. The maids live in the village; and when they came this morning, they found the house empty. They'd skipped—the Craigs, the nurse and the baby—and taken their luggage with them. They left money on the table for the maids' wages, the rent to the end of their tenancy and the tradesmen's bills."

The judge said nothing. He took a cigar from the box, examined it carefully and then lit it with deliberation.

"What have you got to say about that?" I asked.

"My dear fellow, are you obliged to use these American phrases? Isn't English good enough for you?"

"Is that an American phrase? It expresses exactly what I mean. You can't imagine I'm such a fool as not to have noticed that you and the Craigs had met before; and if they've vanished into thin air like figments of the imagination, it's a fairly reasonable conclusion that the circumstances under which you met were not altogether pleasant."

The judge gave a little chuckle, and there was a twinkle in his cold blue eyes.

"That was a very good brandy you gave me last night," he said. "It's against my principles to drink liqueurs after lunch, but it's a very dull man who allows his principles to enslave him, and for once I think I should enjoy one."

I sent for the brandy and watched the judge while he poured himself out a generous measure. He took a sip with obvious satisfaction.

"Do you remember the Wingford murder?" he asked me.

"No."

"Perhaps you weren't in England at the time. Pity—you might have come to the trial. You'd have enjoyed it. It caused a lot of excitement; the papers were full of it.

"Miss Wingford was a rich spinster of mature age who lived

214

in the country with a companion. She was a healthy woman for her age; and when she died rather suddenly, her friends were surprised. Her physician, a fellow called Brandon, signed the certificate and she was duly buried. The will was read, and it appeared that she had left everything she had, something between sixty and seventy thousand pounds, to her companion. The relations were very sore, but there was nothing they could do about it. The will had been drawn up by her lawyer and witnessed by his clerk and Dr. Brandon.

"But Miss Wingford had a maid who had been with her for thirty years and had always understood that she would be remembered in the will; she claimed that Miss Wingford had promised to leave her well provided for, and when she found that she wasn't even mentioned, she flew into a passion. She told the nephew and the two nieces who had come down for the funeral that she was sure Miss Wingford had been poisoned, and she said that if they didn't go to the police, she'd go herself. Well, they didn't do that, but they went to see Dr. Brandon. He laughed. He said that Miss Wingford had had a weak heart and he'd been treating her for years. She died just as he had always expected her to die, peacefully in her sleep; and he advised them not to pay any attention to what the maid said. She had always hated the companion, a Miss Starling, and been jealous of her. Dr. Brandon was highly respected; he had been Miss Wingford's doctor for a long time, and the two nieces, who'd stayed with her often, knew him well. He was not profiting by the will, and there seemed no reason to doubt his word, so the family thought there was nothing to do but make the best of a bad job and went back to London.

"But the maid went on talking; she talked so much that at last the police, much against their will, I must admit, were obliged to take notice, and an order to exhume the body was made. There was an inquest, and it was found that Miss Wingford had died from an overdose of veronal. The coroner's jury found that it had been administered by Miss Starling, and she was arrested. A detective was sent down from Scotland

Yard, and he got together some unexpected evidence. It appeared that there'd been a good deal of gossip about Miss Starling and Dr. Brandon. They'd been seen a lot together in places in which there was no reason for them to be except that they wanted to be together, and the general impression in the village was that they were only waiting for Miss Wingford to die to get married. That put a very different complexion on the case. To make a long story short, the police got enough evidence i_ their opinion to justify them in arresting the doctor and charging him and Miss Starling with the murder of the old lady."

The judge took another sip of brandy.

"The case came up for trial before me. The case for the prosecution was that the accused were madly in love with one another and had done the poor old lady to death so that they could marry on the fortune Miss Starling had wheedled her employer into leaving her. Miss Wingford always had a cup of cocoa when she went to bed, which Miss Starling prepared for her; and the counsel for the prosecution claimed that it was in this that Miss Starling had dissolved the tablets that caused Miss Wingford's death. The accused elected to give evidence on their own behalf, and they made a miserable showing in the witness-box. They lied their heads off. Though witnesses testified they had seen them walking together at night with their arms round one another's waists, though Brandon's maid testified she had seen them kissing one another in the doctor's house they swore they were no more than friends. And oddly enough medical evidence proved that Miss Starling was *virgo intacta*

"Brandon admitted that he had given Miss Wingford a bottle of veronal tablets because she complained of sleeplessness, but declared he had warned her never to take more than one, and then only when absolutely necessary. The defence sought to prove that she had taken the tablets either by accident or because she wanted to commit suicide. That didn't hold water for a moment. Miss Wingford was a jolly, normal old lady who thoroughly enjoyed life; and her death occurred two days before the expected arrival of an old friend for a week's visit. She hadn't complained to the maid of sleeping badly—in fact, her maid had always thought her a very good sleeper. It was impossible to believe that she had accidentally taken a sufficient number of tablets to kill herself. Personally, I had no doubt that it was a put-up job between the doctor and the companion. The motive was obvious and sufficient. I summed up and I hope summed up fairly; but it was my duty to put the facts before the jury, and to my mind the facts were damning. The jury filed out. I don't suppose you know that when you are sitting on the bench, you somehow get the feeling of the court. You have to be on your guard against it, to be sure it doesn't influence you. I never had it more strongly than on that day that there wasn't a soul in court who wasn't convinced that those two people had committed the crime with which they were charged. I hadn't the shadow of a doubt that the jury would bring in a verdict of guilty. Juries are incalculable. They were out for three hours, and when they came back I knew at once that I was mistaken. In a murder case, when a jury is going to bring in a verdict of guilty they won't look at the prisoner; they look away. I noticed that three or four of the jurymen glanced at the two prisoners in the dock. They brought in a verdict of not guilty. The real names of Mr. and Mrs. Craig are Dr. and Mrs. Brandon. I'm just as certain as I am that I'm sitting here that they committed between them a cruel and heartless murder and richly deserved to be hanged."

"What do you think made the jury find them not guilty?"

"I've asked myself that; and do you know the only explanation I can give? The fact that it was conclusively proved that they had never been lovers. And if you come to think of it, that's one of the most curious features of the whole case. That woman was prepared to commit murder to get the man she loved, but she wasn't prepared to have an illicit love-affair with him."

"Human nature is very odd, isn't it?"

"Very," said Landon, helping himself to another glass of brandy.

A MAN
FROM GLASGOW

It is not often that anyone entering a great city for the first time has the luck to witness such an incident as engaged Shelley's attention when he drove into Naples. A youth ran out of a shop pursued by a man armed with a knife. The man overtook him and with one blow in the neck laid him dead on the road. Shelley had a tender heart. He didn't look upon it as a bit of local colour; he was seized with horror and indignation. But when he expressed his emotions to a Calabrian priest who was travelling with him, a fellow of gigantic strength and stature, the priest laughed heartily and attempted to quiz him. Shelley says he never felt such an inclination to beat anyone.

I have never seen anything so exciting as that, but the first time I went to Algeciras I had an experience that seemed to me far from ordinary. Algeciras was then an untidy, neglected town. I arrived somewhat late at night and went to an inn on the quay. It was rather shabby, but it had a fine view of Gibraltar, solid and matter-of-fact, across the bay. The moon was full. The office was on the first floor, and a slatternly maid, when I asked for a room, took me upstairs. The landlord was playing cards. He seemed little pleased to see me. He looked me up and down, curtly gave me a number, and then, taking no further notice of me, went on with his game.

When the maid had shown me to my room I asked her what I could have to eat.

"What you like," she answered.

I knew well enough the unreality of the seeming profusion.

"What have you got in the house?"

"You can have eggs and ham."

The look of the hotel had led me to guess that I should get

little else. The maid led me to a narrow room with white-washed walls and a low ceiling in which was a long table laid already for the next day's luncheon. With his back to the door sat a tall man, huddled over a *brasero,* the round brass dish of hot ashes which is erroneously supposed to give sufficient warmth for the temperate winter of Andalusia. I sat down at the table and waited for my scanty meal. I gave the stranger an idle glance. He was looking at me, but meeting my eyes he quickly turned away. I waited for my eggs. When at last the maid brought them he looked up again.

"I want you to wake me in time for the first boat," he said.

"Sí, señor."

His accent told me that English was his native tongue, and the breadth of his build, his strongly marked features, led me to suppose him a northerner. The hardy Scot is far more often found in Spain than the Englishman. Whether you go to the rich mines of Rio Tinto, or to the bodegas of Jerez, to Seville or to Cadiz, it is the leisurely speech of beyond the Tweed that you hear. You will meet Scotsmen in the olive groves of Carmona, on the railway between Algeciras and Bobadilla, and even in the remote cork woods of Merida.

I finished eating and went over to the dish of burning ashes. It was midwinter and the windy passage across the bay had chilled my blood. The man pushed his chair away as I drew mine forwards.

"Don't move," I said. "There's heaps of room for two."

I lit a cigar and offered one to him. In Spain the Havana from Gib is never unwelcome.

"I don't mind if I do," he said, stretching out his hand.

I recognised the singing speech of Glasgow. But the stranger was not talkative, and my efforts at conversation broke down before his monosyllables. We smoked in silence. He was even bigger than I had thought, with great broad shoulders and ungainly limbs; his face was sunburned, his hair short and grizzled. His features were hard; mouth, ears and nose were large and heavy and his skin much wrinkled. His blue eyes were pale. He was constantly pulling his ragged, grey moustache. It was a nervous gesture that I found faintly irritating. Presently I felt that he was looking at me, and the intensity of his stare grew so irksome that I glanced up expecting him, as before, to drop his eyes. He did, indeed, for a moment, but then raised them again. He inspected me from under his long, bushy eyebrows.

"Just come from Gib?" he asked suddenly.

"Yes."

"I'm going tomorrow—on my way home. Thank God."

He said the last two words so fiercely that I smiled.

"Don't you like Spain?"

"Oh, Spain's all right."

"Have you been here long?"

"Too long. Too long."

He spoke with a kind of gasp. I was surprised at the emotion my casual inquiry seemed to excite in him. He sprang to his feet and walked backwards and forwards. He stamped to and fro like a caged beast, pushing aside a chair that stood in his way, and now and again repeated the words in a groan. "Too long. Too long." I sat still. I was embarrassed. To give myself countenance I stirred the *brasero* to bring the hotter ashes to the top, and he stood suddenly still, towering over me, as though my movement had brought back my existence to his notice. Then he sat down heavily in his chair.

"D'you think I'm queer?" he asked.

"Not more than most people," I smiled.

"You don't see anything strange in me?"

He leant forward as he spoke so that I might see him well.

"No."

"You'd say so if you did, wouldn't you?"

"I would."

I couldn't quite understand what all this meant. I wondered if he was drunk. For two or three minutes he didn't say anything and I had no wish to interrupt the silence.

220

A MAN FROM GLASGOW

"What's your name?" he asked suddenly. I told him.

"Mine's Robert Morrison."

"Scotch?"

"Glasgow. I've been in this blasted country for years. Got any baccy?"

I gave him my pouch and he filled his pipe. He lit it from a piece of burning charcoal.

"I can't stay any longer. I've stayed too long. Too long."

He had an impulse to jump up again and walk up an down, but he resisted it, clinging to his chair. I saw on his face the effort he was making. I judged that his restlessness was due to chronic alcoholism. I find drunks very boring, and I made up my mind to take an early opportunity of slipping off to bed.

"I've been managing some olive groves," he went on. "I'm here working for the Glasgow and South of Spain Olive Oil Company, Limited."

"Oh, yes."

"We've got a new process for refining oil, you know. Properly treated, Spanish oil is every bit as good as Lucca. And we can sell it cheaper."

He spoke in a dry, matter-of-fact, business-like way. He chose is words with Scotch precision. He seemed perfectly sober.

"You know Ecija is more or less the centre of the olive trade, and we had a Spaniard there to look after the business. But I found he was robbing us right and left, so I had to turn him out. I used to live in Seville; it was more convenient for shipping the oil. However, I found I couldn't get a trustworthy man to be at Ecija, so last year I went there myself. D'you know it?"

"No."

"The firm has got a big estate two miles from the town, just outside the village of San Lorenzo, and it's got a fine house on it. It's on the crest of a hill, rather pretty to look at, all white, you know, and straggling, with a couple of storks perched on the roof. No one lived there, and I thought it would save the rent of a place in town if I did."

"It must have been a bit lonely," I remarked.

"It was."

Robert Morrison smoked on for a minute or two in silence. I wondered whether there was any point in what he was telling me.

I looked at my watch.

"In a hurry?" he asked sharply.

"Not particularly. It's getting late."

"Well, what of it?"

"I suppose you didn't see many people?" I said, going back.

"Not many. I lived there with an old man and his wife who looked after me, and sometimes I used to go down to the village and play *tresillo* with Fernandez, the chemist, and one or two men who met at his shop. I used to shoot a bit and ride."

"It doesn't sound such a bad life to me."

"I'd been there two years last spring. By God, I've never known such heat as we had in May. No one could do a thing. The labourers just lay about in the shade and slept. Sheep died and some of the animals went mad. Even the oxen couldn't work. They stood around with their backs all humped up and gasped for breath. That blasted sun beat down and the glare was so awful, you felt your eyes would shoot out of your head. The earth cracked and crumbled, and the crops frizzled. The olives went to rack and ruin. It was simply hell. One couldn't get a wink of sleep. I went from room to room, trying to get a breath of air. Of course I kept the windows shut and had the floors watered, but that didn't do any good. The nights were just as hot as the days. It was like living in an oven.

"At last I thought I'd have a bed made up for me downstairs on the north side of the house in a room that was never used because in ordinary weather it was damp. I had an idea that I might get a few hours' sleep there at all events. Anyhow it was worth trying. But it was no damned good; it was a wash-out. I turned and tossed and my bed was so hot that I couldn't stand it. I got up and opened the doors that led to the veranda and walked out. It was a glorious night. The moon was so

222

right that I swear you could read a book by it. Did I tell you the house was on the crest of a hill? I leant against the parapet and looked at the olive-trees. It was like the sea. I suppose that's what made me think of home. I thought of the cool breeze in the fir-trees and the racket of the streets in Glasgow. Believe it or not, I could smell them, and I could smell the sea. By God, I'd have given every bob I had in the world for an hour of that air. They say it's a foul climate in Glasgow. Don't you believe it. I like the rain and the grey sky and that yellow sea and the waves. I forgot that I was in Spain, in the middle of the olive country, and I opened my mouth and took a long breath as though I were breathing-in the sea-fog.

"And then all of a sudden I heard a sound. It was a man's voice. Not loud, you know, low. It seemed to creep through the silence like—well, I don't know what it was like. It surprised me. I couldn't think who could be down there in the olives at this hour. It was past midnight. It was a chap laughing. A funny sort of laugh. I suppose you'd call it a chuckle. It seemed to crawl up the hill—disjointedly."

Morrison looked at me to see how I took the odd word he used to express a sensation that he didn't know how to describe.

"I mean, it seemed to shoot up in little jerks, something like shooting stones out of a pail. I leant forward and stared. With the full moon it was almost as light as day, but I'm dashed if I could see a thing. The sound stopped, but I kept on looking at where it had come from in case somebody moved. And in a minute it started off again, but louder. You couldn't have called it a chuckle any more, it was a real belly laugh. It just rang through the night. I wondered it didn't wake my servants. It sounded like someone who was roaring drunk.

" 'Who's there?' I shouted.

"The only answer I got was a roar of laughter. I don't mind telling you I was getting a bit annoyed. I had half a mind to go down and see what it was all about. I wasn't going to let some drunken swine kick up a row like that on my place in the middle of the night. And then suddenly there was a yell. By God, I was startled. Then cries. The man had laughed with a deep bass voice, but his cries were—shrill, like a pig having his throat cut.

" 'My God,' I cried.

"I jumped over the parapet and ran down towards the sound. I thought somebody was being killed. There was silence and then one piercing shriek. After that sobbing and moaning. I'll tell you what it sounded like, it sounded like someone at the point of death. There was a long groan and then nothing. Silence. I ran from place to place. I couldn't find anyone. At last I climbed the hill again and went back to my room.

"You can imagine how much sleep I got that night. As soon as it was light, I looked out of the window in the direction from which the row had come and I was surprised to see a little white house in a sort of dale among the olives. The ground on that side didn't belong to us and I'd never been through it. hardly ever went to that part of the house and so I'd never seen the house before. I asked José who lived there. He told me that a madman had inhabited it, with his brother and a servant."

"Oh, was that the explanation?" I said. "Not a very nice neighbour."

The Scot bent over quickly and seized my wrist. He thrust his face into mine and his eyes were starting out of his head with terror.

"The madman has been dead for twenty years," he whispered.

He let go my wrist and leant back in his chair panting.

"I went down to the house and walked all round it. The windows were barred and shuttered and the door was locked. I knocked. I shook the handle and rang the bell. I heard it tinkle, but no one came. It was a two-storey house and I looked up. The shutters were tight closed, and there wasn't a sign of life anywhere."

"Well, what sort of condition was the house in?" I asked.

"Oh, rotten. The whitewash had worn off the walls and there

224

was practically no paint left on the door or the shutters. Some of the tiles off the roof were lying on the ground. They looked as though they'd been blown away in a gale."

"Queer," I said.

"I went to my friend Fernandez, the chemist, and he told me the same story as José. I asked about the madman and Fernandez said that no one ever saw him. He was more or less comatose ordinarily, but now and then he had an attack of acute mania and then he could be heard from ever so far laughing his head off and then crying. It used to scare people. He died in one of his attacks and his keepers cleared out at once. No one had ever dared to live in the house since.

"I didn't tell Fernandez what I'd heard. I thought he'd only laugh at me. I stayed up that night and kept watch. But nothing happened. There wasn't a sound. I waited about till dawn and then I went to bed."

"And you never heard anything more?"

"Not for a month. The drought continued and I went on sleeping in the lumber-room at the back. One night I was fast asleep, when something seemed to happen to me; I don't exactly know how to describe it, it was a funny feeling as though some-one had given me a little nudge, to warn me, and suddenly I was wide awake. I lay there in my bed and then in the same way as before I heard a long, low gurgle, like a man enjoying an old joke. It came from away down in the valley and it got louder. It was a great bellow of laughter. I jumped out of bed and went to the window. My legs began to tremble. It was horrible to stand there and listen to the shouts of laughter that rang through the night. Then there was the pause, and after that a shriek of pain and that ghastly sobbing. It didn't sound human. I mean, you might have thought it was an animal being tortured. I don't mind telling you I was scared stiff. I couldn't have moved if I'd wanted to. After a time the sounds stopped, not suddenly, but dying away little by little. I strained my ears, but I couldn't hear a thing. I crept back to bed and hid my face.

"I remembered then that Fernandez had told me that th
madman's attacks only came at intervals. The rest of the tim
he was quite quiet. Apathetic, Fernandez said. I wondered
the fits of mania came regularly. I reckoned out how long
had been between the two attacks I'd heard. Twenty-eight day
It didn't take me long to put two and two together; it wa
quite obvious that it was the full moon that set him off. I'ı
not a nervous man really and I made up my mind to get to th
bottom of it, so I looked out in the calendar which day th
moon would be full next and that night I didn't go to bec
I cleaned my revolver and loaded it. I prepared a lantern an
sat down on the parapet of my house to wait. I felt perfectl
cool. To tell you the truth, I was rather pleased with myse
because I didn't feel scared. There was a bit of a wind, an
it whistled about the roof. It rustled over the leaves of th
olive trees like waves swishing on the pebbles of the beach. Th
moon shone on the white walls of the house in the hollov
I felt particularly cheery.

"At last I heard a little sound, the sound I knew, and I almos
laughed. I was right; it was the full moon and the attack
came as regular as clockwork. That was all to the good.
threw myself over the wall into the olive grove and ran straigh
to the house. The chuckling grew louder as I came near. I gc
to the house and looked up. There was no light anywhere.
put my ears to the door and listened. I heard the madma
simply laughing his bloody head off. I beat on the door witl
my fist and I pulled the bell. The sound of it seemed to amus
him. He roared with laughter. I knocked again, louder an
louder, and the more I knocked the more he laughed. The
I shouted at the top of my voice.

" 'Open the blasted door, or I'll break it down.'

"I stepped back and kicked the latch with all my might
I flung myself at the door with the whole weight of my body
It cracked. Then I put all my strength into it and the damnec
thing smashed open.

"I took the revolver out of my pocket and held my lantern

226

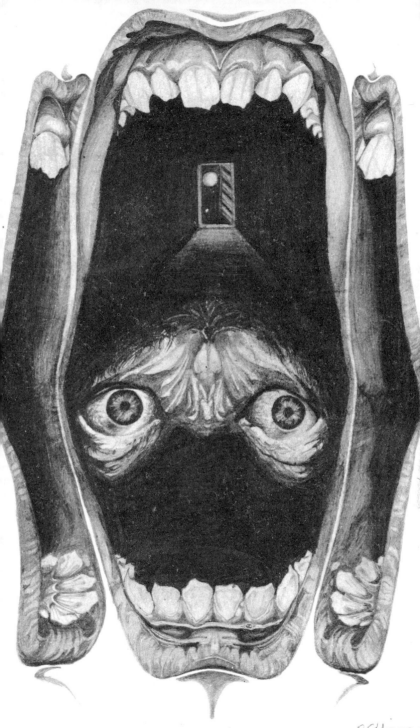

P Ellison

n the other hand. The laughter sounded louder now that the
door was opened. I stepped in. The stink nearly knocked me
down. I mean, just think, the windows hadn't been opened
for twenty years. The row was enough to raise the dead, but for
moment I didn't know where it was coming from. The walls
seemed to throw the sound backwards and forwards. I pushed
open a door by my side and went into a room. It was bare
and white and there wasn't a stick of furniture in it. The
sound was louder and I followed it. I went into another room,
but there was nothing there. I opened a door and found myself
at the foot of a staircase. The madman was laughing just over
my head. I walked up, cautiously, you know, I wasn't taking
any risks, and at the top of the stairs there was a passage.
walked along it, throwing my light ahead of me, and I came
o a room at the end. I stopped. He was in there. I was only
separated from the sound by a thin door.

"It was awful to hear it. A shiver passed through me and I
cursed myself because I began to tremble. It wasn't like a
human being at all. By Jove, I very nearly took to my heels
and ran. I had to clench my teeth to force myself to stay.
But I simply couldn't bring myself to turn the handle. And
then the laughter was cut, cut with a knife you'd have said,
and I heard a hiss of pain. I hadn't heard that before, it was
so low to carry to my place, and then a gasp.

" 'Ay!' I heard the man speak in Spanish. 'You're killing
me. Take it away. O God, help me!'

"He screamed. The brutes were torturing him. I flung open
the door and burst in. The draught blew a shutter back and
the moon streamed in so bright that it dimmed my lantern.
In my ears, as clearly as I hear you speak and as close, I heard
the wretched chap's groans. It was awful, moaning and sobbing,
and frightful gasps. No one could survive that. He was at the
point of death. I tell you I heard his broken, choking cries right
in my ears. And the room was empty."

Robert Morrison sank back in his chair. That huge solid
man had strangely the look of a lay figure in a studio. You

felt that if you pushed him he would fall over in a heap on to the floor.

"And then?" I asked.

He took a rather dirty handkerchief out of his pocket and wiped his forehead.

"I felt I didn't much want to sleep in that room on the north side, so, heat or no heat, I moved back to my own quarters. Well, exactly four weeks later, about two in the morning, I was waked up by the madman's chuckle. It was almost at my elbow. I don't mind telling you that my nerve was a bit shaken by then, so next time the blighter was due to have an attack, next time the moon was full, I mean, I got Fernandez to come and spend the night with me. I didn't tell him anything. I kept him up playing cards till two in the morning and then I heard it again. I asked him if he heard anything. 'Nothing,' he said. 'There's somebody laughing,' I said. 'You're drunk, man,' he said, and he began laughing too. That was too much. 'Shut up, you fool,' I said. The laughter grew louder and louder. I cried out. I tried to shut it out by putting my hands to my ears, but it wasn't a damned bit of good. I heard it and I heard the scream of pain. Fernandez thought I was mad. He didn't dare say so, because he knew I'd have killed him. He said he'd go to bed, and in the morning I found he'd slunk away. His bed hadn't been slept in. He'd taken himself off when he left me.

"After that I couldn't stop in Ecija. I put a factor there and went back to Seville. I felt myself pretty safe there, but as the time came near I began to get scared. Of course I told myself not to be a damned fool, but, you know, I damned well couldn't help myself. The fact is, I was afraid the sounds had followed me, and I knew if I heard them in Seville I'd go on hearing them all my life. I've got as much courage as any man, but damn it all, there are limits to everything. Flesh and blood couldn't stand it. I knew I'd go stark staring mad. I got in such a state that I began drinking, the suspense was so awful, and I used to lie awake counting the days. And at last I knew it'd come. And it came. I heard those sounds in Seville—sixty miles away from Ecija."

I didn't know what to say. I was silent for a while.

"When did you hear the sounds last?" I asked.

"Four weeks ago."

I looked up quickly. I was startled.

"What d'you mean by that? It's not full moon tonight?"

He gave me a dark, angry look. He opened his mouth to speak and then stopped as though he couldn't. You would have said his vocal cords were paralysed, and it was with a strange croak that at last he answered.

"Yes, it is."

He stared at me and his pale blue eyes seemed to shine red. I have never seen in a man's face a look of such terror. He got up quickly and stalked out of the room, slamming the door behind him.

I must admit that I didn't sleep any too well that night myself.

THE

UNCONQUERED

He came back into the kitchen. The man was still on the floor
lying where he had hit him, and his face was bloody. He wa
moaning. The woman had backed against the wall and wa
staring with terrified eyes at Willi, his friend, and when h
came in she gave a gasp and broke into loud sobbing. Will
was sitting at the table, his revolver in his hand, with a hal
empty glass of wine beside him. Hans went up to the table
filled his glass and emptied it at a gulp.

"You look as though you'd had trouble, young fellow," sai
Willi with a grin.

Hans's face was blood-stained and you could see the gashe
of five sharp finger-nails. He put his hand gingerly to hi
cheek.

"She'd have scratched my eyes out if she could, the bitch
I shall have to put some iodine on. But she's all right now
You go along."

"I don't know. Shall I? It's getting late."

"Don't be a fool. You're a man, aren't you? What if i
is getting late? We lost our way."

It was still light and the westering sun streamed into th
kitchen windows of the farm-house. Willi hesitated a momen
He was a little fellow, dark and thin-faced, a dress designer i
civil life, and he didn't want Hans to think him a cissy. H
got up and went towards the door through which Hans ha
come. When the woman saw what he was going to do s
gave a shriek and sprang forwards.

"*Non, Non,*" she cried.

With one step Hans was in front of her. He seized her b
the shoulders and flung her violently back. She tottered an
fell. He took Willi's revolver.

THE UNCONQUERED

"Stop still, both of you," he rasped in French, but with his guttural German accent. He nodded his head towards the door. "Go on. I'll look after them."

Willi went out, but in a moment was back again.

"She's unconscious."

"Well, what of it?"

"I can't. It's no good."

"Stupid, that's what you are. *Ein Weibchen*. A woman."

Willi flushed.

"We'd better be getting on our way."

Hans shrugged a scornful shoulder.

"I'll just finish the bottle of wine and then we'll go."

He was feeling at ease and it would have been pleasant to linger. He had been on the job since morning and after so many hours on his motor-cycle his limbs ached. Luckily they hadn't far to go, only to Soissons—ten or fifteen kilometres. He wondered if he'd have the luck to get a bed to sleep in. Of course all this wouldn't have happened if the girl hadn't been a fool. They had lost their way, he and Willi, they had stopped a peasant working in a field and he had deliberately misled them, and they found themselves on a side road. When they came to the farm they stopped to ask for a direction. They'd asked very politely, for orders were to treat the French population well as long as they behaved themselves. The door was opened for them by the girl and she said she didn't know the way to Soissons, so they pushed in; then the woman, her mother, Hans guessed, told them. The three of them, the farmer, his wife and daughter, had just finished supper and there was a bottle of wine on the table. It reminded Hans that he was as thirsty as the devil. The day had been sweltering and he hadn't had a drink since noon. He asked them for a bottle of wine and Willi had added that they would pay them well for it. Willi was a good little chap, but soft. After all, they were the victors. Where was the French army? In headlong flight. And the English, leaving everything behind, had scuttled like rabbits back to their island. The conquerors took

231

what they wanted, didn't they? But Willi had worked at a
Paris dressmaker's for two years. It's true he spoke French well
that's why he had his present job, but it had done something to
him. A decadent people. It did a German no good to live
among them.

The farmer's wife put a couple of bottles of wine on the
table and Willi took twenty francs out of his pocket and gave
it to her. She didn't even say thank you. Hans's French wasn'
as good as Willi's, but he could make himself understood, and
he and Willi spoke it together all the time. Willi corrected
his mistakes. It was because Willi was so useful to him in this
way that he had made him his friend, and he knew that Will
admired him. He admired him because he was so tall, slim and
broad-shouldered, because his curly hair was so fair and his
eyes so blue. He never lost an opportunity to practise his
French, and he tried to talk now, but those three French people
wouldn't meet him half-way. He told them that he was a
farmer's son himself and when the war was over was going
back to the farm. He had been sent to school in Munich because
his mother wanted him to go into business, but his heart wasn't
in it, and so after matriculating he had gone to an agricultural
college.

"You came here to ask your way and now you know it,"
said the girl. "Drink up your wine and go."

He had hardly looked at her before. She wasn't pretty, but
she had fine dark eyes and a straight nose. Her face was very
pale. She was plainly dressed, but somehow she didn't look
quite like what she evidently was. There was a sort of distinction about her. Ever since the war started he'd heard fellows
talk about the French girls. They had something the German
girls hadn't. Chic, Willi said it was, but when he asked him
just what he meant by that Willi could only say that you had to
see it to understand. Of course he'd heard others say that they
were mercenary and hard as nails. Well, they'd be in Paris in a
week and he'd find out for himself. They said the High Command had already arranged for houses for the men to go to.

"Finish your wine and let's go," said Willi.

But Hans was feeling comfortable and didn't want to be hurried.

"You don't look like a farmer's daughter," he said to the girl.

"And so what?" she answered.

"She's a teacher," said her mother.

"Then you've had a good education." She shrugged her shoulders, but he went on good-humouredly in his bad French. "You ought to understand that this is the best thing that has ever happened to the French people. We didn't declare war. You declared war. And now we're going to make France a decent country. We're going to put order into it. We're going to teach you to work. You'll learn obedience and discipline."

She clenched her fists and looked at him, her eyes black with hatred. But she did not speak.

"You're drunk, Hans," said Willi.

"I'm as sober as a judge. I'm only telling them the truth and they may just as well know it at once."

"He's right," she cried out, unable any longer to contain herself. "You're drunk. Now go. Go."

"Oh, you understand German, do you? All right, I'll go. But you must give me a kiss first."

She took a step back to avoid him, but he seized her wrist.

"Father," she cried. "Father."

The farmer flung himself on the German. Hans let go of her and with all his might hit him in the face. He crumpled up on the floor. Then, before she could escape him, he caught the girl in his arms. She gave him a swinging blow on the cheek. . . . He chuckled grimly.

"Is that how you take it when a German soldier wants to kiss you? You'll pay for this."

With his great strength he pinioned her arms and was dragging her out of the door, but her mother rushed at him and catching him by the clothes tried to pull him away. With one arm holding the girl close to him, with the flat of his other hand he gave the woman a great push and she staggered back to the wall.

"Hans, Hans," cried Willi.

"Shut up, damn you."

He put his hands over the girl's mouth to stop her shrieking and carried her out of the room. That was how it had happened and you had to admit that she'd brought it on herself. She shouldn't have slapped him. If she'd given him the kiss he'd asked for he'd have gone away. He gave a glance at the farmer still lying where he had fallen and he could hardly help laughing at his funny face. There was a smile in his eyes when he looked at the woman cowering against the wall. Was she afraid it was her turn next? Not likely. He remembered a French proverb.

"*C'est le premier pas qui coûte.* There's nothing to cry about, old woman. It had to come sooner or later." He put his hand to his hip pocket and pulled out a wallet. "Look, here's a hundred francs so that mademoiselle can buy herself a new dress. There's not much left of that one." He placed the note on the table and put his helmet back on his head. "Let's go."

They slammed the door behind them and got on their motor-cycles. The woman went into the parlour. Her daughter was lying on the divan. She was lying as he had left her and she was weeping bitterly.

Three months later Hans found himself in Soissons again. He had been in Paris with the conquering army and had ridden through the Arc de Triomphe on his motor-cycle. He had advanced with the army first to Tours and then to Bordeaux. He'd seen very little fighting. The only French soldiers he'd seen were prisoners. The campaign had been the greatest spree he could ever have imagined. After the armistice he had spent a month in Paris. He'd sent picture postcards to his family in Bavaria and bought them all presents. Willi, because he knew the city like the palm of his hand, had stayed on, but he and the rest of his unit were sent to Soissons to join the force that was holding it. It was a nice little town and he was comfortably billeted. Plenty to eat and champagne for less than a mark a bottle in German money. When he was ordered to proceed there it had occurred to him that it would be fun to go and have a look at the girl he'd had. He'd take her a pair of silk stockings to show there was no ill-feeling. He had a good bump of locality and he thought he would be able to find the farm without difficulty. So one afternoon, when he had nothing to do, he put the silk stockings in his pocket and got on his machine. It was a lovely autumn day, with hardly a cloud in the sky, and it was pretty, undulating country that he rode through. It had been fine and dry for so long that, though it was September, not even the restless poplars gave sign that the summer was drawing to an end. He took one wrong turning, which delayed him, but for all that he got to the place he sought in less than half an hour. A mongrel dog barked at him as he walked up to the door. He did not knock, but turned the handle and stepped in. The girl was sitting at the table peeling potatoes. She sprang to her feet when she saw the uniformed man.

"What d'you want?" Then she recognised him. She backed to the wall, clutching the knife in her hands. "It's you. *Cochon.*"

"Don't get excited. I'm not going to hurt you. Look, I've brought you some silk stockings."

"Take them away and take yourself off with them."

"Don't be silly. Drop that knife. You'll only get hurt if you try to be nasty. You needn't be afraid of me."

"I'm not afraid of you," she said.

She let the knife fall to the floor. He took off his helmet and sat down. He reached out with his foot and drew the knife towards him.

"Shall I peel some of your potatoes for you?" She did not answer. He bent down for the knife and then took a potato out of the bowl and went to work on it. Her face hard, her eyes hostile, she stood against the wall and watched him. He smiled at her disarmingly. "Why do you look so cross? I didn't do you much harm, you know. I was excited, we all were, they'd talked of the invincible French army and the Maginot line . . ." he finished the sentence with a chuckle. "And the wine went to my head. You might have fared worse. Women have told me that I'm not a bad-looking fellow."

She looked him up and down scornfully.

"Get out of here."

"Not until I choose."

"If you don't go my father will go to Soissons and complain to the general."

"Much he'll care. Our orders are to make friends with the population. What's your name?"

"That's not your business."

There was a flush in her cheeks now and her angry eyes were blazing. She was prettier than he remembered her. He hadn't done so badly. She had a refinement that suggested the city-dweller rather than the peasant. He remembered her mother saying she was a teacher. Because she was almost a lady it amused him to torment her. He felt strong and healthy. He passed his hand through his curly blond hair, and giggled when he thought that many girls would have jumped at the chance she had had. His face was so deeply tanned by the summer that his eyes were startlingly blue.

"Where are your father and mother?"

"Working in the fields."

"I'm hungry. Give me a bit of bread and cheese and a glass of wine. I'll pay."

She gave a harsh laugh.

"We haven't seen cheese for three months. We haven't enough bread to stay our hunger. The French took our horses a year ago and now the Boches have taken our cows, our pigs, our chickens, everything."

"Well, they paid you for them."

"Can we eat the worthless paper they gave us?"

She began to cry.

"Are you hungry?"

236

THE UNCONQUERED

"Oh, no," she answered bitterly, "we can eat like kings on potatoes and bread and turnips and lettuce. Tomorrow my father's going to Soissons to see if he can buy some horse meat."

"Listen, Miss. I'm not a bad fellow. I'll bring you a cheese, and I think I can get hold of a bit of ham."

"I don't want your presents. I'll starve before I touch the food you swine have stolen from us."

"We'll see," he said good-humouredly.

He put on his hat, got up, and with an *Au revoir, mademoiselle,* walked out.

He wasn't supposed to go joy-riding round the country and he had to wait to be sent on an errand before he was able to get to the farm again. It was ten days later. He walked in as unceremoniously as before and this time he found the farmer and his wife in the kitchen. It was round about noon and the woman was stirring a pot on the stove. The man was seated at table. They gave him a glance when he came in, but there was no surprise in it. Their daughter had evidently told them of his visit. They did not speak. The woman went·on with her cooking, and the man, a surly look on his face, stared at the oil-cloth on the table. But it required more than this to disconcert the good-humoured Hans.

"Bonjour, la compagnie," he said cheerfully. "I've brought you a present."

He undid the package he had with him and set out a sizable piece of gruyère cheese, a piece of pork and a couple of tins of sardines. The woman turned round and he smiled when he saw the light of greed in her eyes. The man looked at the foodstuff sullenly. Hans gave him his sunny grin.

"I'm sorry we had a misunderstanding the first time I came here. But you shouldn't have interfered."

At that moment the girl came in.

"What are you doing here?" she cried harshly. Then her eyes fell on the things he had brought. She swept them together and flung them at him. "Take them away. Take them."

But her mother sprang forward.

"Annette, you're crazy."

"I won't take his presents."

"It's our own food that they've stolen from us. Look at the sardines. They're Bordeaux sardines."

She picked the things up. Hans looked at the girl with a mocking smile in his light blue eyes.

"Annette's your name, is it? A pretty name. Do you grudge your parents a little food? You said you hadn't had cheese for three months. I couldn't get any ham; I did the best I could."

The farmer's wife took the lump of meat in her hands and pressed it to her bosom. You felt that she could have kissed it. Tears ran down Annette's cheeks.

"The shame of it," she groaned.

"Oh, come now, there's no shame in a bit of gruyère and a piece of pork."

Hans sat down and lit a cigarette. Then he passed the packet over to the old man. The farmer hesitated for a moment, but the temptation was too strong for him; he took one and handed back the packet.

"Keep it," said Hans. "I can get plenty more." He inhaled the smoke and blew a cloud of it from his nostrils. "Why can't we be friends? What's done can't be undone. War is war, and, well, you know what I mean. I know Annette's an educated girl and I want her to think well of me. I expect we shall be in Soissons for quite a while and I can bring you something now and then to help out. You know, we do all we can to make friends with the townspeople, but they won't let us. They won't even look at us when we pass them in the street. After all, it was an accident, what happened that time I came here with Willi. You needn't be afraid of me. I'll respect Annette as if she was my own sister."

"Why do you want to come here? Why can't you leave us alone?" asked Annette.

He really didn't know. He didn't like to say that he wanted a little human friendship. The silent hostility that surrounded them all at Soissons got on his nerves so that sometimes he wanted to go up to a Frenchman who looked at him as if he wasn't there and knock him down, and sometimes it affected him so that he was almost inclined to cry. It would be nice if he had some place to go where he was welcome. He spoke the truth when he said he had no desire for Annette. She wasn't the sort of woman he fancied. He liked women to be tall and full-breasted, blue-eyed and fair-haired like himself; he liked them to be strong and hefty and well-covered. That refinement which he couldn't account for, that thin fine nose and those dark eyes, the long pale face—there was something intimidating about the girl, so that if he hadn't been excited by the great victories of the German armies, if he hadn't been so tired and yet so elated, if he hadn't drunk all that wine on an empty stomach, it would never have crossed his mind that he could have anything to do with her.

For a fortnight after that Hans couldn't get away. He'd left the food at the farm and he had no doubt that the old people had wolfed it. He wondered if Annette had eaten it too; he wouldn't have been surprised to discover that the moment his back was turned she had set to with the others. These French people, they couldn't resist getting something for nothing. They were weak and decadent. She hated him, yes, God, how she hated him, but pork was pork and cheese was cheese. He thought of her quite a lot. It tantalised him that she should have such a loathing for him. He was used to being liked by women. It would be funny if one of these days she fell in love with him. He'd been her first lover and he'd heard the students at Munich over their beer saying that it was her first lover a woman loved, after that it was love. When he'd set his mind on getting a girl he'd never failed yet. Hans laughed to himself and a sly look came into his eyes.

At last he got his chance to go to the farm. He got hold of cheese and butter, sugar, a tin of sausages, and some coffee, and set off on his motor-cycle. But that time he didn't see Annette. She and her father were at work in the fields. The

239

old woman was in the yard and her face lit up when she saw the parcel he was bringing. She led him into the kitchen. Her hands trembled a little as she untied the string and when she saw what he had brought her eyes filled with tears.

"You're very good," she said.

"May I sit down?" he asked politely.

"Of course." She looked out of the window and Hans guessed that she wanted to make sure that Annette was not coming. "Can I offer you a glass of wine?"

"I'd be glad of it."

He was sharp enough to see that her greed for food had made her, if not friendly to him, at least willing to come to terms with him. That look out of the window made them almost fellow conspirators."

"Did you like the pork?" he asked.

"It was a treat."

"I'll try to bring you some more next time I come. Did Annette like it?"

"She wouldn't touch a thing you'd left. She said she'd rather starve."

"Silly."

"That's what I said to her. As long as the food is there, I said, there's nothing to be gained by not eating it."

They chatted quite amicably while Hans sipped his wine. He discovered that she was called Madame Périer. He asked her whether there were any other members of the family. She sighed. No, they'd had a son, but he'd been mobilised at the beginning of the war and he'd died. He hadn't been killed, he'd got pneumonia and died in the hospital at Nancy.

"I'm sorry," said Hans.

"Perhaps he's better off than if he'd lived. He was like Annette in many ways. He could never have borne the shame of defeat." She sighed again. "Oh, my poor friend, we've been betrayed."

"Why did you want to fight for the Poles? What were they to you?"

"You're right. If we had let your Hitler take Poland he would have left us alone."

When Hans got up to go he said he would come again soon. "I shan't forget the pork."

Then Hans had a lucky break; he was given a job that took him twice a week to a town in the vicinity so that he was able to get to the farm much oftener. He took care never to come without bringing something. But he made no headway with Annette. Seeking to ingratiate himself with her, he used the simple wiles that he had discovered went down with women; but they only excited her derision. Thin-lipped and hard, she looked at him as though he were dirt. On more than one occasion she made him so angry that he would have liked to take her by the shoulders and shake the life out of her. Once he found her alone, and when she got up to go he barred her passage.

"Stop where you are. I want to talk to you."

"Talk. I am a woman and defenceless."

"What I want to say is this: for all I know I may be here for a long time. Things aren't going to get easier for you French, they're going to get harder. I can be useful to you. Why don't you be reasonable like your father and mother?"

It was true that old Périer had come round. You couldn't say that he was cordial, he was indeed cold and gruff, but he was civil. He had even asked Hans to bring him some tobacco, and when he wouldn't accept payment for it had thanked him. He was pleased to hear the news of Soissons and grabbed the paper that Hans brought him. Hans, a farmer's son, could talk about the farm as one who knew. It was a good farm, not too big and not too small, well watered, for a sizable brook ran through it, and well wooded, with arable land and pasture. Hans listened with understanding sympathy when the old man bewailed himself because without labour, without fertilisers, his stock taken from him, it was all going to rack and ruin.

"You ask me why I can't be reasonable like my father and mother," said Annette.

She pulled her dress tight and showed herself to him. He couldn't believe his eyes. What he saw caused such a convulsion in his soul as he had never known. The blood rushed to his cheeks.

"You're pregnant."

She sank back on her chair and leaning her head on her hands began to weep as though her heart would break.

"The shame of it. The shame."

He sprang towards her to take her in his arms.

"My sweet," he cried.

But she sprang to her feet and pushed him away.

"Don't touch me. Go away. Go away. Haven't you done me enough harm already?"

She flung out of the room. He waited by himself for a few minutes. He was bewildered. His thoughts in a whirl, he rode slowly back to Soissons, and when he went to bed he couldn't get to sleep for hours. He could think of nothing but Annette and her swollen body. She had been unbearably pathetic as she sat there at the table crying her eyes out. It was his child she bore in her womb. He began to feel drowsy, and then with a start he was once more wide awake, for suddenly it came to him, it came to him with the shattering suddenness of gun-fire: he was in love with her. It was such a surprise, such a shock that he couldn't cope with it. Of course he'd thought of her a lot, but never in that way, he'd thought it would be a great joke if he made her fall in love with him, it would be a triumph if the time came when she offered what he had taken by force; but not for a moment had it occurred to him that she was anything to him but a woman like another. She wasn't his type. She wasn't very pretty. There was nothing to her. Why should he have all of a sudden this funny feeling for her? It wasn't a pleasant feeling either, it was a pain. But he knew what it was all right; it was love, and it made him feel happier than he had ever felt in his life. He wanted to take her in his arms, he wanted to pet her, he wanted to kiss those tear-stained eyes of hers. He didn't desire her, he thought, as a man desires a woman, he wanted to comfort her, he wanted her to smile at him—strange, he had never seen her smile, he wanted to see her eyes—fine eyes they were, beautiful eyes—soft with tenderness.

For three days he could not leave Soissons and for three days, three days and three nights, he thought of Annette and the child she would bear. Then he was able to go to the farm. He wanted to see Madame Périer by herself, and luck was with him, for he met her on the road some way from the house. She had been gathering sticks in the wood and was going home with a great bundle on her back. He stopped his motor-cycle. He knew that the friendliness she showed him was due only to the provisions he brought with him, but he didn't care; it was enough that she was mannerly, and that she was prepared to be so as long as she could get something out of him. He told her he wanted to talk to her and asked her to put her bundle down. She did as he bade. It was a grey, cloudy day, but not cold.

"I know about Annette," he said.

She started.

"How did you find out? She was set on your not knowing.'

"She told me."

"That was a pretty job of work you did that evening."

"I didn't know. Why didn't you tell me sooner?"

She began to talk, not bitterly, not blaming him even, but as though it were a misfortune of nature, like a cow dying in giving birth to a calf or a sharp spring frost nipping the fruit trees and ruining the crop, a misfortune that human kind must accept with resignation and humility. After that dreadful night Annette had been in bed for days with a high fever. They thought she was going out of her mind. She would scream for hours on end. There were no doctors to be got. The village doctor had been called to the colours. Even in Soissons there were only two doctors left, old men both of them, and how could they get to the farm even if it had been possible to send for them? They weren't allowed to leave the town. Even when the fever went down Annette was too ill to leave her bed, and when she got up she was so weak, so pale, it was pitiful. The shock had been terrible, and when a month went by, and another month, without her being unwell she paid no attention. She had always been irregular. It was Madame Périer who first suspected that something was wrong. She questioned Annette. They were terrified, both of them, but they weren't certain and they said nothing to Périer. When the third month came it was impossible to doubt any longer. Annette was pregnant.

They had an old Citroën in which before the war Madame Périer had taken the farm produce into the market at Soissons two mornings a week, but since the German occupation they had had nothing to sell that made the journey worth while. Petrol was almost unobtainable. But now they got it out and drove into town. The only cars to be seen were the military cars of the Germans. German soldiers lounged about. There were German signs in the streets, and on public buildings proclamations in French signed by the Officer Commanding. Many shops were closed. They went to the old doctor they knew, and he confirmed their suspicions. But he was a devout Catholic and would not help them. When they wept he shrugged his shoulders.

"You're not the only one," he said. *"Il faut souffrir."*

They knew about the other doctor too and went to see him. They rang the bell and for a long time no one answered. At last the door was opened by a sad-faced woman in black, but when they asked to see the doctor she began to cry. He had been arrested by the Germans because he was a freemason, and was held as a hostage. A bomb had exploded in a café frequented by German officers and two had been killed and several wounded. If the guilty were not handed over before a certain date he was to be shot. The woman seemed kindly and Madame Périer told her of their trouble.

"The brutes," she said. She looked at Annette with compassion. "My poor child."

She gave them the address of a midwife in the town and

told them to say that they had come from her. The midwife gave them some medicine. It made Annette so ill that she thought she was going to die, but it had no further effect. Annette was still pregnant.

That was the story that Madame Périer told Hans. For a while he was silent.

"It's Sunday tomorrow," he said then. "I shall have nothing to do. I'll come and we'll talk. I'll bring something nice."

"We have no needles. Can you bring some?"

"I'll try."

She hoisted the bundle of sticks on her back and trudged down the road. Hans went back to Soissons. He dared not use his motor-cycle, so next day he hired a push-bike. He tied his parcel of food on the carrier. It was a larger parcel than usual because he had put a bottle of champagne into it. He got to the farm when the gathering darkness made it certain that they would all be home from work. It was warm and cosy in the kitchen when he walked in. Madame Périer was cooking and her husband was reading a *Paris-Soir*. Annette was darning stockings.

"Look, I've brought you some needles," he said, as he undid his parcel. "And here's some material for you, Annette."

"I don't want it."

"Don't you?" he grinned. "You'll have to begin making things for the baby."

"That's true, Annette," said her mother, "and we have nothing." Annette did not look up from her sewing. Madame Périer's greedy eyes ran over the contents of the parcel. "A bottle of champagne."

Hans chuckled.

"I'll tell you what that's for presently. I've had an idea." He hesitated for a moment, then drew up a chair and sat down facing Annette. "I don't know quite how to begin. I'm sorry for what I did that night, Annette. It wasn't my fault, it was the circumstances. Can't you forgive me?"

She threw him a look of hatred.

245

"Never. Why don't you leave me alone? Isn't it enough that you've ruined my life?"

"Well, that's just it. Perhaps I haven't. When I knew you were going to have a baby it had a funny effect on me. It's all different now. It's made me so proud."

"Proud?" she flung at him viciously.

"I want you to have the baby, Annette. I'm glad you couldn't get rid of it."

"How dare you say that?"

"But listen to me. I've been thinking of nothing else since I knew. The war will be over in six months. We shall bring the English to their knees in the spring. They haven't got a chance. And then I shall be demobilised and I'll marry you."

"You? Why?"

He blushed under his tan. He could not bring himself to say it in French, so he said it in German. He knew she understood it.

"Ich liebe dich."

"What does he say?" asked Madame Périer.

"He says he loves me."

Annette threw back her head and broke into a peal of harsh laughter. She laughed louder and louder and she couldn't stop and tears streamed from her eyes. Madame Périer slapped her sharply on both cheeks.

"Don't pay any attention," she said to Hans. "It's hysteria. Her condition, you know."

Annette gasped. She gained control over herself.

"I brought the bottle of champagne to celebrate our engagement," said Hans.

"That's the bitterest thing of all," said Annette, "that we were beaten by fools, by such fools."

Hans went on speaking in German.

"I didn't know I loved you till that day when I found out that you were going to have a baby. It came like a clap of thunder, but I think I've loved you all the time."

"What does he say?" asked Madame Périer.

246

"Nothing of importance."

He fell back into French. He wanted Annette's parents to hear what he had to say.

"I'd marry you now, only they wouldn't let me. And don't think I'm nothing at all. My father's well-to-do and we're well thought of in our commune. I'm the eldest son and you'd want for nothing."

"Are you a Catholic?" asked Madame Périer.

"Yes, I'm a Catholic."

"That's something."

"It's pretty, the country where we live and the soil's good. There's not better farming land between Munich and Innsbrück, and it's our own. My grandfather bought it after the war of '70. And we've got a car and a radio, and we're on the telephone."

Annette turned to her father.

"He has all the tact in the world, this gentleman," she cried ironically. She eyed Hans. "It would be a nice position for me, the foreigner from the conquered country with a child born out of wedlock. It offers me a chance of happiness, doesn't it? A fine chance."

Périer, a man of few words, spoke for the first time.

"No. I don't deny that it's a fine gesture you're making. I went through the last war and we all did things we wouldn't have done in peace time. Human nature is human nature. But now that our son is dead, Annette is all we have. We can't let her go."

"I thought you might feel that way," said Hans, "and I've got my answer to that. I'll stay here."

Annette gave him a quick look.

"What do you mean?" asked Madame Périer.

"I've got another brother. He can stay and help my father. I like this country. With energy and initiative a man could make a good thing of your farm. When the war's over a lot of Germans will be settling here. It's well known that you haven't got enough men in France to work the land you've got. A fellow gave us a lecture the other day at Soissons. He said that a third of the farms were left uncultivated because there aren't the men to work them."

Périer and his wife exchanged glances and Annette saw that they were wavering. That was what they'd wanted since their son had died, a son-in-law who was strong and hefty and could take over when they grew too old to do more than potter about.

"That changes the case," said Madame Périer. "It's a proposition to consider."

"Hold your tongue," cried Annette roughly. She leant forward and fixed her burning eyes on the German. "I'm engaged to a teacher who worked in the boys' school in the town where I taught, we were to be married after the war. He's not strong and big like you, or handsome; he's small and frail. His only beauty is the intelligence that shines in his face, his only strength is the greatness of his soul. He's not a barbarian, he's civilised; he has a thousand years of civilisation behind him. I love him. I love him with all my heart and soul."

Hans's face grew sullen. It had never occurred to him that Annette might care for anyone else.

"Where is he now?"

"Where do you suppose he is? In Germany. A prisoner and starving. While you eat the fat of our land. How many times have I got to tell you that I hate you? You ask me to forgive you. Never. You want to make reparation. You fool." She threw her head back and there was a look of intolerable anguish on her face. "Ruined. Oh, he'll forgive me. He's tender. But I'm tortured by the thought that one day the suspicion may come to him that perhaps I hadn't been forced—that perhaps I'd given myself to you for butter and cheese and silk stockings. I shouldn't be the only one. And what would our life be with that child between us, your child, a German child? Big like you, and blond like you, and blue-eyed like you. Oh, my God, why do I have to suffer this?"

She got up and went swiftly out of the kitchen. For a minute

248

the three were left in silence. Hans looked ruefully at his bottle of champagne. He sighed and rose to his feet. When he went out Madame Périer accompanied him.

"Did you mean it when you said you would marry her?" she asked him, speaking in a low voice.

"Yes. Every word. I love her."

"And you wouldn't take her away? You'd stay here and work on the farm?"

"I promise you."

"Evidently my old man can't last for ever. At home you'd have to share with your brother. Here you'd share with nobody."

"There's that too."

"We never were in favour of Annette marrying that teacher, but our son was alive then and he said, if she wants to marry him, why shouldn't she? Annette was crazy about him. But now that our son's dead, poor boy, it's different. Even if she wanted to, how could she work the farm alone?"

"It would be a shame if it was sold. I know how one feels about one's own land."

They had reached the road. She took his hand and gave it a little squeeze.

"Come again soon."

Hans knew that she was on his side. It was a comfort to him to think that as he rode back to Soissons. It was a bother that Annette was in love with somebody else. Fortunately he was a prisoner; long before he was likely to be released the baby would be born. That might change her: you could never tell with a woman. Why, in his village there'd been a woman who was so much in love with her husband that it had been a joke, and then she had a baby and after that she couldn't bear the sight of him. Well, why shouldn't the contrary happen too? And now that he'd offered to marry her she must see that he was a decent sort of fellow. God, how pathetic she'd looked with her head flung back, and how well she'd spoken! What language! An actress on the stage couldn't have expressed herself better, and yet it had all sounded so natural. You had to admit that, these French people knew how to talk. Oh, she was clever. Even when she lashed him with that bitter tongue it was a joy to listen to her. He hadn't had a bad education himself, but he couldn't hold a candle to her. Culture, that's what she had.

"I'm a donkey," he said out loud as he rode along. She'd said he was big and strong and handsome. Would she have said that if it hadn't meant something to her? And she'd talked of the baby having fair hair and blue eyes like his own. If that didn't mean that his colouring had made an impression on her he was a Dutchman. He chuckled. "Give me time. Patience, and let nature go to work."

The weeks went by. The C.O. at Soissons was an elderly, easy-going fellow and in view of what the spring had in store for them he was content not to drive his men too hard. The German papers told them that England was being wrecked by the Luftwaffe and the people were in a panic. Submarines were sinking British ships by the score and the country was starving. Revolution was imminent. Before summer it would be all over and the Germans would be masters of the world. Hans wrote home and told his parents that he was going to marry a French girl and with her a fine farm. He proposed that his brother should borrow money to buy him out of his share of the family property so that he could increase the size of his own holding while land, owing to the war and the exchange, could still be bought for a song. He went over the farm with Périer. The old man listened quietly when Hans told him his ideas: the farm would have to be restocked and as a German he would have a pull; the motor tractor was old, he would get a fine new one from Germany, and a motor plough. To make a farm pay you had to take advantage of modern inventions. Madame Périer told him afterwards that her husband had said he wasn't a bad lad and seemed to know a lot. She was very friendly with him now and insisted that he should share their midday meal with them on Sundays.

She translated his name into French and called him Jean. He was always ready to give a hand, and as time went on and Annette could do less and less it was useful to have a man about who didn't mind doing a job of work.

Annette remained fiercely hostile. She never spoke to him except to answer his direct questions and as soon as it was possible went to her own room. When it was so cold that she couldn't stay there she sat by the side of the kitchen stove, sewing or reading, and took no more notice of him than if he hadn't been there. She was in radiant health. There was colour in her cheeks and in Hans's eyes she was beautiful. Her approaching maternity had given her a strange dignity and he was filled with exultation when he gazed upon her. Then one day when he was on his way to the farm he saw Madame Périer in the road waving to him to stop. He put his brakes on hard.

"I've been waiting for an hour. I thought you'd never come. You must go back. Pierre is dead."

"Who's Pierre?"

"Pierre Gavin. The teacher Annette was going to marry."

Hans's heart leapt. What luck! Now he'd have his chance. "Is she upset?"

"She's not crying. When I tried to say something she bit my head off. If she saw you today she's capable of sticking a knife into you."

"It's not my fault he died. How did you hear?"

"A prisoner, a friend of his, escaped through Switzerland and he wrote to Annette. We got the letter this morning. There was a mutiny in the camp because they weren't given enough to eat, and the ringleaders were shot. Pierre was one of them."

Hans was silent. He could only think it served the man right. What did they think that a prison camp was—the Ritz?

"Give her time to get over the shock," said Madame Périer. "When she's calmer I'll talk to her. I'll write you a letter when you can come again."

"All right. You will help me, won't you?"

251

"You can be sure of that. My husband and I, we're agreed. We talked it over and we came to the conclusion that the only thing to do was to accept the situation. He's no fool, my husband, and he says the best chance for France now is to collaborate. And take it all in all I don't dislike you. I shouldn't wonder if you didn't make Annette a better husband than that teacher. And with the baby coming and all."

"I want it to be a boy," said Hans.

"It's going to be a boy. I know for certain. I've seen it in the coffee grounds and I've put out the cards. The answer is a boy every time."

"I almost forgot, here are some papers for you," said Hans, as he turned his cycle and prepared to mount.

He handed her three numbers of *Paris-Soir*. Old Périer read every evening. He read that the French must be realistic and accept the new order that Hitler was going to create in Europe. He read that the German submarines were sweeping the sea. He read that the General Staff had organised to the last detail the campaign that would bring England to her knees and that the Americans were too unprepared, too soft and too divided to come to her help. He read that France must take the heaven-sent opportunity and by loyal collaboration with the Reich regain her honoured position in the new Europe. And it wasn't Germans who wrote it all; it was Frenchmen. He nodded his head with approval when he read that the plutocrats and the Jews would be destroyed and the poor man in France would at last come into his own. They were quite right, the clever fellows who said that France was essentially an agricultural country and its backbone was its industrious farmers. Good sense, that was.

One evening, when they were finishing their supper, ten days after the news had come of Pierre Gavin's death, Madame Périer, by arrangement with her husband, said to Annette:

"I wrote a letter to Hans a few days ago telling him to come here tomorrow."

"Thank you for the warning. I shall stay in my room."

252

"Oh, come, daughter, the time has passed for foolishness. You must be realistic. Pierre is dead. Hans loves you and wants to marry you. He's a fine-looking fellow. Any girl would be proud of him as a husband. How can we restock the farm without his help? He's going to buy a tractor and a plough with his own money. You must let bygones be bygones."

"You're wasting your breath, Mother. I earned my living before, I can earn my living again. I hate him. I hate his vanity and his arrogance. I could kill him: his death wouldn't satisfy me. I should like to torture him as he's tortured me. I think I should die happy if I could find a way to wound him as he's wounded me."

"You're being very silly, my poor child."

"Your mother's right, my girl," said Périer. "We've been defeated and we must accept the consequences. We've got to make the best arrangement we can with the conquerors. We're cleverer than they are and if we play our cards well we shall come out on top. France was rotten. It's the Jews and the plutocrats who ruined the country. Read the papers and you'll see for yourself!"

"Do you think I believe a word in that paper? Why do you think he brings it to you except that it's sold to the Germans? The men who write in it—traitors, traitors. Oh God, may I live to see them torn to pieces by the mob. Bought, bought every one of them—bought with German money. The swine."

Madame Périer was getting exasperated.

"What have you got against the boy? He took you by force—yes, he was drunk at the time. It's not the first time that's happened to a woman and it won't be the last time. He hit your father and he bled like a pig, but does your father bear him malice?"

"It was an unpleasant incident, but I've forgotten it," said Périer.

Annette burst into harsh laughter.

"You should have been a priest. You forgive injuries with a spirit truly Christian."

253

"And what is there wrong about that?" asked Madame Périe angrily. "Hasn't he done everything he could to make amends. Where would your father have got his tobacco all these month if it hadn't been for him. If we haven't gone hungry it's owing to him."

"If you'd had any pride, if you'd had any sense of decency you'd have thrown his presents in his face."

"You've profited by them, haven't you?"

"Never. Never."

"It's a lie and you know it. You've refused to eat the cheese he brought and the butter and the sardines. But the soup you've eaten, you know I put the meat in it that he brought; and the salad you ate tonight, if you didn't have to eat it dry, it's because he brought me oil."

Annette sighed deeply. She passed her hand over her eyes.

"I know. I tried not to, I couldn't help myself, I was so hungry. Yes, I knew his meat went into the soup and I ate it. I knew the salad was made with his oil. I wanted to refuse it; I had such a longing for it, it wasn't I that ate it, it was a ravenous beast within me."

"That's neither here nor there. You ate it."

"With shame. With despair. They broke our strength firs with their tanks and their planes, and now when we're defence less they're breaking our spirit by starving us."

"You get nowhere by being theatrical, my girl. For an educated woman you have really no sense. Forget the pas and give a father to your child, to say nothing of a good work man for the farm who'll be worth two hired men. That is sense."

Annette shrugged her shoulders wearily and they lapsed into silence. Next day Hans came. Annette gave him a sullen look but neither spoke nor moved. Hans smiled.

"Thank you for not running away," he said.

"My parents asked you to come and they've gone down to the village. It suits me because I want to have a definitive talk with you. Sit down."

254

He took off his coat and helmet and drew a chair to the table.

"My parents want me to marry you. You've been clever; with your presents, with your promises, you've got round them. They believe all they read in the papers you bring them. I want to tell you that I will never marry you. I wouldn't have thought it possible that I could hate a human being as I hate you."

"Let me speak in German. You understand enough to know what I'm saying."

"I ought to. I taught it. For two years I was governess to two little girls in Stuttgart."

He broke into German, but she went on speaking French.

"It's not only that I love you, I admire you. I admire your distinction and your grace. There's something about you I don't understand. I respect you. Oh, I can see that you don't want to marry me now even if it were possible. But Pierre is dead."

"Don't speak of him," she cried violently. "That would be the last straw."

"I only want to tell you that for your sake I'm sorry he died."

"Shot in cold blood by his German jailers."

"Perhaps in time you'll grieve for him less. You know, when someone you love dies, you think you'll never get over it, but you do. Won't it be better then to have a father for your child?"

"Even if there were nothing else do you think I could ever forget that you are a German and I'm a Frenchwoman? If you weren't as stupid as only a German can be you'd see that that child must be a reproach to me as long as I live. Do you think I have no friends? How could I ever look them in the face with the child I had with a German soldier? There's only one thing I ask you: leave me alone with my disgrace. Go, go—for God's sake go and never come back again."

"But he's my child too. I want him."

"You?" she cried in astonishment. "What can a by-blow that you got in a moment of savage drunkenness mean to you?"

"You don't understand. I'm so proud and so happy. It was

255

when I knew you were going to have a baby that I knew I loved you. At first I couldn't believe it; it was such a surprise to me. Don't you see what I mean? That child that's going to be born means everything in the world to me. Oh, I don't know how to put it; it's put feelings in my heart that I don't understand myself."

She looked at him intently and there was a strange gleam in her eyes. You would have said it was a look of triumph. She gave a short laugh.

"I don't know whether I more loathe the brutality of you Germans or despise your sentimentality."

He seemed not to have heard what she said.

"I think of him all the time."

"You've made up your mind it'll be a boy?"

"I know it'll be a boy. I want to hold him in my arms and I want to teach him to walk. And then when he grows older I'll teach him all I know. I'll teach him to ride and I'll teach him to shoot. Are there fish in your brook? I'll teach him to fish. I'm going to be the proudest father in the world."

She stared at him with hard, hard eyes. Her face was set and stern. An idea, a terrible idea was forming itself in her mind. He gave her a disarming smile.

"Perhaps when you see how much I love our boy, you'll come to love me too. I'll make you a good husband, my pretty."

She said nothing. She merely kept on gazing at him sullenly.

"Haven't you one kind word for me?" he said.

She flushed. She clasped her hands tightly together.

"Others may despise me. I will never do anything that can make me despise myself. You are my enemy and you will always be my enemy. I only live to see the deliverance of France. It'll come, perhaps not next year or the year after, perhaps not for thirty years, but it'll come. The rest of them can do what they like, I will never come to terms with the invaders of my country. I hate you and I hate this child that you've given me. Yes, we've been defeated. Before the end comes you'll see that we haven't been conquered. Now go. My mind's made up and nothing on God's earth can change it."

He was silent for a minute or two.

"Have you made arrangements for a doctor? I'll pay all the expenses."

"Do you suppose we want to spread our shame through the whole countryside? My mother will do all that's necessary."

"But supposing there's an accident?"

"And supposing you mind your own business!"

He sighed and rose to his feet. When he closed the door behind him she watched him walk down the pathway that led to the road. She realised with rage that some of the things he said had aroused in her heart a feeling that she had never felt for him before.

"O God, give me strength," she cried.

Then, as he walked along, the dog, an old dog they'd had for years, ran up to him barking angrily. He had tried for months to make friends with the dog, but it had never responded to his advances; when he tried to pat it, it backed away growling and showing its teeth. And now as the dog ran towards him, irritably giving way to his feeling of frustration, Hans gave it a savage, brutal kick and the dog was flung into the bushes and limped yelping away.

"The beast," she cried. "Lies, lies, lies. And I was weak enough to be almost sorry for him."

There was a looking-glass hanging by the side of the door and she looked at herself in it. She drew herself up and smiled at her reflection. But rather than a smile it was a fiendish grimace.

It was now March. There was a bustle of activity in the garrison at Soissons. There were inspections and there was intensive training. Rumour was rife. There was no doubt they were going somewhere, but the rank and file could only guess where. Some thought they were being got ready at last for the invasion of England, others were of opinion that they would be sent to the Balkans, and others again talked of the

Ukraine. Hans was kept busy. It was not till the second Sunday afternoon that he was able to get out to the farm. It was a cold grey day, with sleet that looked as though it might turn to snow falling in sudden windy flurries. The country was grim and cheerless.

"You!" cried Madame Périer when he went in. "We thought you were dead."

"I couldn't come before. We're off any day now. We don't know when."

"The baby was born this morning. It's a boy."

Hans's heart gave a great leap in his breast. He flung his arms round the old woman and kissed her on both cheeks.

"A Sunday child, he ought to be lucky. Let's open the bottle of champagne. How's Annette?"

"She's as well as can be expected. She had a very easy time. She began to have pains last night and by five o'clock this morning it was all over."

Old Périer was smoking his pipe sitting as near the stove as he could get. He smiled quietly at the boy's enthusiasm.

"One's first child, it has an effect on one," he said.

"He has quite a lot of hair and it's as fair as yours; and blue eyes just like you said he'd have," said Madame Périer. "I've never seen a lovelier baby. He'll be just like his papa."

"Oh, my God, I'm so happy," cried Hans. "How beautiful the world is! I want to see Annette."

"I don't know if she'll see you. I don't want to upset her on account of the milk."

"No, no, don't upset her on my account. If she doesn't want to see me it doesn't matter. But let me see the baby just for a minute."

"I'll see what I can do. I'll try to bring it down."

Madame Périer went out and they heard her heavy tread clumping up the stairs. But in a moment they heard her clattering down again. She burst into the kitchen.

"They're not there. She isn't in her room. The baby's gone."

Périer and Hans cried out and without thinking what they

258

were doing all three of them scampered upstairs. The harsh light of the winter afternoon cast over the shabby furniture, the iron bed, the cheap wardrobe, the chest of drawers, a dismal squalor. There was no one in the room.

"Where is she?" screamed Madame Périer. She ran into the narrow passage, opening doors, and called the girl's name. "Annette, Annette. Oh, what madness!"

"Perhaps in the sitting-room."

They ran downstairs to the unused parlour. An icy air met them as they opened the door. They opened the door of a store-room.

"She's gone out. Something awful has happened."

"How could she have got out?" asked Hans sick with anxiety.

"Through the front door, you fool."

Périer went up to it and looked.

"That's right. The bolt's drawn back."

"Oh, my God, my God, what madness," cried Madame Périer. "It'll kill her."

"We must look for her," said Hans. Instinctively, because that was the way he always went in and out, he ran back into the kitchen and the others followed him. "Which way?"

"The brook," the old woman gasped.

He stopped as though turned to stone with horror. He stared at the old woman aghast.

"I'm frightened," she cried. "I'm frightened."

Hans flung open the door, and as he did so Annette walked in. She had nothing on but her nightdress and a flimsy rayon dressing-gown. It was pink, with pale blue flowers. She was soaked, and her hair, dishevelled, clung damply to her head and hung down her shoulders in bedraggled wisps. She was deathly white. Madame Périer sprang towards her and took her in her arms.

"Where have you been? Oh, my poor child, you're wet through. What madness!"

But Annette pushed her away. She looked at Hans.

"You've come at the right moment, you."

"Where's the baby?" cried Madame Périer.

"I had to do it at once. I was afraid if I waited I shouldn't have the courage."

"Annette, what have you done?"

"I've done what I had to do. I took it down to the brook and held it under water till it was dead."

Hans gave a great cry, the cry of an animal wounded to death; he covered his face with his hands, and staggering like a drunken man flung out of the door. Annette sank into a chair, and leaning her forehead on her two fists burst into passionate weeping.

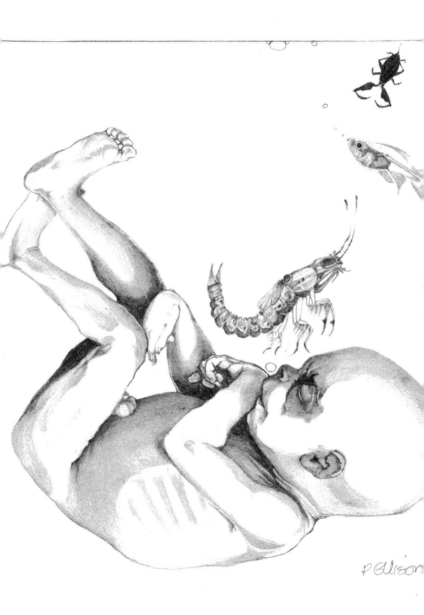

P Ellison

EPISODE

It was quite a small party, because our hostess liked general conversation; we never sat down to dinner more than eight, and generally only six, and after dinner when we went up to the drawing-room the chairs were so arranged that it was impossible for two persons to go into a huddle in a corner and so break things up. I was glad on arriving to find that I knew everyone. There were two nice clever women besides our hostess and two men besides myself. One was my friend Ned Preston. Our hostess made it a point never to ask wives with their husbands, because she said each cramped the other's style and if they didn't like to come separately they needn't come at all. But since her food and her wine were good and the talk almost always entertaining they generally came. People sometimes accused her of asking husbands more often than wives, but she defended herself by saying that she couldn't possibly help it because more men were husbands than women were wives.

Ned Preston was a Scot, a good-humoured, merry soul, with a gift for telling a story, sometimes too lengthily, for he was uncommonly loquacious, but with dramatic intensity. He was a bachelor with a small income which sufficed for his modest needs, and in this he was lucky since he suffered from that form of chronic tuberculosis which may last for years without killing you, but which prevents you from working for your living. Now and then he would be ill enough to stay in bed for two or three weeks, but then he would get better and be as gay, cheerful, and talkative as ever. I doubt whether he had enough money to live in an expensive sanatorium and he certainly hadn't the temperament to suit himself to its life. He was worldly. When he was well he liked to go out, out to lunch, out to dinner, and he liked to sit up late into the night smoking his pipe and drinking a good deal of whisky. If he had been content to live the life of an invalid he might have been alive now, but he wasn't; and who can blame him? He died at the age of fifty-five of a hæmorrhage which he had one night after coming home from some house where, he may well have flattered himself, he was the success of the party.

He had that febrile vitality that some consumptives have, and was always looking for an occupation to satisfy his desire for activity. I don't know how he heard that at Wormwood Scrubs they were in want of prison visitors, but the idea took his fancy, so he went to the Home Office and saw the official in charge of prisons to offer his services. The job is unpaid, and though a number of persons are willing to undertake it, either from compassion or curiosity, they are apt to grow tired of it, or find it takes up too much time, and the prisoners whose problems, interests and future they have been concerned with are left somewhat in the lurch. The Home Office people consequently are wary of taking on anyone who does not look as if he would persevere, and they make careful inquiries into the applicant's antecedents, character and general suitability. Then he is given a trial, is discreetly watched, and if the impression is unfavourable is politely thanked and told that his services are no longer required. But Ned Preston satisfied the dour and shrewd official who interviewed him that he was in every way reliable, and from the beginning he got on well with the governor, the warders and the prisoners. He was entirely lacking in class-consciousness, so prisoners, whatever their station in life, felt at ease with him. He neither preached nor moralised. He had never done a criminal, or even a mean, thing in his life, but he treated the crime of the prisoners he had to deal with as though it were an illness like his own tuberculosis which was a nuisance you had to put up with, but which it did no good to talk about.

Wormwood Scrubs is a first offenders' prison and it is a building, grim and cold, of forbidding appearance. Ned took me over it once and I had goose-flesh as the gates were unlocked for us and we went in. We passed through the halls in which the men were working.

"If you see any pals of yours take no notice' of them," Ned said to me. "They don't like it."

"Am I likely to see any pals of mine?" I asked drily.

"You never can tell. I shouldn't be surprised if you had had friends who'd passed bad cheques once too often or were caught in a compromising situation in one of the parks. You'd be surprised how often I run across chaps I've met out at dinner."

One of Ned's duties was to see prisoners through the first difficult days of their confinement. They were often badly shaken by their trial and sentence; and when, after the preliminary proceedings they had to go through on entering the gaol, the stripping, the bath, the medical examination and the questioning, the getting into prison clothes, they were led into a cell and locked up, they were apt to break down. Sometimes they cried hysterically; sometimes they could neither eat nor sleep. Ned's business then was to cheer them, and his breezy manner, his natural kindliness, often worked wonders. If they were anxious about their wives and children he would go to see them and if they were destitute provide them with money. He brought them news so that they might get over the awful feeling that they were shut away from the common interests of their fellow-men. He read the sporting papers to be able to tell them what horse had won an important race or whether the champion had won his fight. He would advise them about their future, and when the time approached for their release see what jobs they were fitted for and then persuade employers to give them a chance to make good.

Since everyone is interested in crime it was inevitable that sooner or later, with Ned there, the conversation should turn upon it. It was after dinner and we were sitting comfortably in the drawing-room with drinks in our hands.

"Had any interesting cases at the Scrubs lately, Ned?" I asked him.

"No, nothing much."

263

He had a high, rasping voice and his laugh was a raucous cackle. He broke into it now.

"I went to see an old girl today who was a packet of fun. Her husband's a burglar. The police have known about him for years, but they've never been able to get him till just now. Before he did a job he and his wife concocted an alibi, and though he's been arrested three or four times and sent up for trial, the police have never been able to break it and he's always got off. Well, he was arrested again a little while ago, but he wasn't upset, the alibi he and his wife had made up was perfect and he expected to be acquitted as he'd been before. His wife went into the witness-box and to his utter amazement she didn't give the alibi and he was convicted. I went to see him. He wasn't so much worried at being in gaol as puzzled by his wife not having spoken up, and he asked me to go and see her and ask what the game was. Well, I went, and d'you know what she said to me? She said: 'Well, sir, it's like this; it was such a beautiful alibi I just couldn't bear to waste it.'"

Of course we all laughed. The story-teller likes an appreciative audience, and Ned Preston was never disinclined to hold the floor. He narrated two or three more anecdotes. They tended to prove a point he was fond of making, that in what till we all got democratic in England were called the lower orders there was more passion, more romance, more disregard of consequences than could ever be found in the well-to-do and presumably educated classes, whom prudence has made timid and convention inhibited.

"Because the working man doesn't read much," he said, "because he has no great gift for expressing himself, you think he has no imagination. You're wrong. He's extravagantly imaginative. Because he's a great husky brute you think he has no nerves. You're wrong again. He's a bundle of nerves."

Then he told us a story which I shall tell as best I can in my own words.

264

EPISODE

Fred Manson was a good-looking fellow, tall, well-made, with blue eyes, good features and a friendly, agreeable smile, but what made him remarkable so that people turned round in the streets to stare at him was that he had a thick head of hair, with a great wave in it, of a deep rich red. It was really a great beauty. Perhaps it was this that gave him so sensual a look. His maleness was like a heady perfume. His eyebrows were thick, only a little lighter than his hair, and he was lucky enough not to have the ugly skin that so often disfigures redheads. His was a smooth olive. His eyes were bold, and when he smiled or laughed, which in the healthy vitality of his youth he did constantly, his expression was wonderfully alluring. He was twenty-two and he gave you the rather pleasant impression of just loving to be alive. It was inevitable that with such looks and above all with that troubling sexuality he should have success with women. He was charming, tender and passionate, but immensely promiscuous. He was not exactly callous or brazen, he had a kindly nature, but somehow or other he made it quite clear to the objects of his passing fancy that all he wanted was a little bit of fun and that it was impossible for him to remain faithful to anyone.

Fred was a postman. He worked in Brixton. It is a densely populated part of London, and has the curious reputation of harbouring more criminals than any other suburb because trams run to it from across the river all night long, so that when a man has done a job of housebreaking in the West End he can be sure of getting home without difficulty. Fred liked his job. Brixton is a district of innumerable streets lined with little houses inhabited by the people who work in the neighbourhood and also by clerks, shop-assistants, skilled workers of one sort or another whose jobs take them every day across the river. He was strong and healthy and it was a pleasure to him to walk from street to street delivering the letters. Sometimes there would be a postal packet to hand in or a registered letter that had to be signed for, and then he would have the opportunity of seeing people. He was a sociable creature. It was never long before he was well known on whatever round he was assigned to. After a time his job was changed. His duty then was to go to the red pillar-boxes into which the letters were put, empty them, and take the contents to the main post-office of the district. His bag would be pretty heavy sometimes by the time he was through, but he was proud of his strength and the weight only made him laugh.

One day he was emptying a box in one of the better streets, a street of semi-detached houses, and had just closed his bag when a girl came running along.

"Postman," she cried, "take this letter, will you. I want it to go by this post most particularly."

He gave her his good-natured smile.

"I never mind obliging a lady," he said, putting down his bag and opening it.

"I wouldn't trouble you, only it's urgent," she said as she handed him the letter she had in her hand.

"Who is it to—a feller?" he grinned.

"None of your business."

"All right, be haughty. But I tell you this, he's no good. Don't you trust him."

"You've got a nerve," she said.

"So they tell me."

He took off his cap and ran his hand through his mop of curling red hair. The sight of it made her gasp.

"Where'd you get your perm?" she asked with a giggle.

"I'll show you one of these days if you like."

He was looking down at her with his amused eyes, and there was something about him that gave her a funny little feeling in the pit of her stomach.

"Well, I must be on my way," he said. "If I don't get on with the job pretty damn quick I don't know what'll happen to the country."

"I'm not detaining you," she said coolly.

"That's where you make a mistake," he answered.

He gave her a look that made her heart beat nineteen to the

266

dozen and she felt herself blushing all over. She turned away and ran back to the house. Fred noticed it was four doors away from the pillar-box. He had to pass it and as he did so he looked up. He saw the net curtains twitch and he knew she was watching. He felt pleased with himself. During the next few days he looked at the house whenever he passed it, but never caught a glimpse of the girl. One afternoon he ran across her by chance just as he was entering the street in which she lived.

"Hulloa," he said, stopping.

"Hulloa."

She blushed scarlet.

"Haven't seen you about lately."

"You haven't missed much."

"That's what you think."

She was prettier than he remembered, dark-haired, dark-eyed, rather tall, slight, with a good figure, a pale skin and very white teeth.

"What about coming to the pictures with me one evening?"

"Taking a lot for granted, aren't you?"

"It pays," he said with his impudent, charming grin.

She couldn't help laughing.

"Not with me, it doesn't."

"Oh, come on. One's only young once."

There was something so attractive in him that she couldn't bring herself to give him a saucy answer.

"I couldn't really. My people wouldn't like me going out with a fellow I don't know. You see, I'm the only one they have and they think a rare lot of me. Why, I don't even know your name."

"Well, I can tell you, can't I? Fred. Fred Manson. Can't you say you're going to the pictures with a girl friend?"

She had never felt before what she was feeling then. She didn't know if it was pain or pleasure. She was strangely breathless.

"I suppose I could do that."

They fixed the night, the time and the place. Fred was waiting for her and they went in, but when the picture started and he put his arm round her waist, without a word, her eyes fixed on the screen, she quietly took it away. He took hold of her hand, but she withdrew it. He was surprised. That wasn't the way girls usually behaved. He didn't know what one went to the pictures for if it wasn't to have a bit of a cuddle. He walked home with her after the show. She told him her name. Grace Carter. Her father had a shop of his own in the Brixton Road, he was a draper and he had four assistants.

"He must be doing well," said Fred.

"He doesn't complain."

Gracie was a student at London University. When she got her degree she was going to be a school teacher.

"What d'you want to do that for when there's a good business waiting for you?"

"Pa doesn't want me to have anything to do with the shop—not after the education he's given me. He wants me to better myself, if you know what I mean."

Her father had started life as an errand boy, then become a draper's assistant and because he was hard-working, honest and intelligent was now owner of a prosperous little business. Success had given him grand ideas for his only child. He didn't want her to have anything to do with trade. He hoped she'd marry a professional man perhaps, or at least someone in the City. Then he'd sell the business and retire, and Gracie would be quite the lady.

When they reached the corner of her street Gracie held out her hand.

"You'd better not come to the door," she said.

"Aren't you going to kiss me good-night?"

"I am not."

"Why?"

"Because I don't want to."

"You'll come to the pictures again, won't you?"

"I think I'd better not."

"Oh, come on."

EPISODE

There was such a warm urgency in his voice that she felt as though her knees would give way.

"Will you behave if I do?" He nodded. "Promise?"

"Swop me bob."

He scratched his head when he left her. Funny girl. He'd never met anyone quite like her. Superior, there was no doubt about that. There was something in her voice that got you. It was warm and soft. He tried to think what it was like. It was like as if the words kissed you. Sounded silly, that did, but that's just what it was like.

From then on they went to the pictures once or twice a week. After a while she allowed him to put his arm round her waist and to hold her hand, but she never let him go farther than that.

"Have you ever been kissed by a fellow?" he asked her once.

"No, I haven't," she said simply. "My ma's funny, she says you've got to keep a man's respect."

"I'd give anything in the world just to kiss you, Gracie."

"Don't be so silly."

"Won't you let me just once?" She shook her head. "Why not?"

"Because I like you too much," she said hoarsely, and then walked quickly away from him.

It gave him quite a turn. He wanted her as he'd never wanted a woman before. What she'd said finished him. He'd been thinking of her a lot, and he'd looked forward to the evenings they spent together as he'd never looked forward to anything in his life. For the first time he was uncertain of himself. She was above him in every way, what with her father making money hand over fist and her education and everything, and him only a postman. They had made a date for the following Friday night and he was in a fever of anxiety lest she shouldn't come. He repeated to himself over and over again what she'd said: perhaps it meant that she'd made up her mind to drop him. When at last he saw her walking along the street he almost sobbed with relief. That evening he neither

269

put his arm round her nor took her hand and when he walked her home he never said a word.

"You're very quiet tonight, Fred," she said at last. "What's the matter with you?"

He walked a few steps before he answered.

"I don't like to tell you."

She stopped suddenly and looked up at him. There was terror on her face.

"Tell me whatever it is," she said unsteadily.

"I'm gone, I can't help myself, I'm so stuck on you I can't see straight. I didn't know what it was to love like I love you."

"Oh, is that all? You gave me such a fright. I thought you were going to say you were going to be married."

"Me? Who d'you take me for? It's you I want to marry."

"Well, what's to prevent you, silly?"

"Gracie! D'you mean it?"

He flung his arms round her and kissed her full on the mouth. She didn't resist. She returned his kiss and he felt in her a passion as eager as his own.

They arranged that Gracie should tell her parents that she was engaged to him and that on the Sunday he should come and be introduced to them. Since the shop stayed open late on Saturday and by the time Mr. Carter got home he was tired out, it was not till after dinner on Sunday that Gracie broke her news. George Carter was a brisk, not very tall man, but sturdy, with a high colour, who with increasing prosperity had put on weight. He was more than rather bald and he had a bristle of grey moustache. Like many another employer who has risen from the working class he was a slave-driver and he got as much work out of his assistants for as little money as was possible. He had an eye for everything and he wouldn't put up with any nonsense, but he was reasonable and even kindly, so that they did not dislike him. Mrs. Carter was a quiet, nice woman, with a pleasant face and the remains of good looks. They were both in the early fifties, for they had married late after "walking out" for nearly ten years.

EPISODE

They were very much surprised when Gracie told them what she had to tell, but not displeased.

"You are a sly one," said her father. "Why, I never suspected for a minute you'd taken up with anyone. Well, I suppose it had to come sooner or later. What's his name?"

"Fred Manson."

"A fellow you met at college?"

"No. You must have seen him about. He clears our pillarbox. He's a postman."

"Oh, Gracie," cried Mrs. Carter, "you can't mean it. You can't marry a common postman, not after all the education we've given you."

For an instant Mr. Carter was speechless. He got redder in the face than ever.

"Your ma's right, my girl," he burst out now. "You can't throw yourself away like that. Why, it's ridiculous."

"I'm not throwing myself away. You wait till you see him."

Mrs. Carter began to cry.

"It's such a come-down. It's such a humiliation. I shall never be able to hold up my head again."

"Oh, Ma, don't talk like that. He's a nice fellow and he's got a good job."

"You don't understand," she moaned.

"How d'you get to know him?" Mr. Carter interrupted. "What sort of a family's he got?"

"His pa drives one of the post-office vans," Gracie answered defiantly.

"Working-class people."

"Well, what of it? His pa's worked twenty-four years for the post-office and they think a lot of him."

Mrs. Carter was biting the corner of her handkerchief.

"Gracie, I want to tell you something. Before your pa and me got married I was in domestic service. He wouldn't ever let me tell you because he didn't want you to be ashamed of me. That's why we was engaged all those years. The lady I

271

was with said she'd leave me something in her will if I staye_
with her till she passed away."

"It was that money that gave me my start," Mr. Carter broke
in. "Except for that I'd never have been where I am today.
And I don't mind telling you your ma's the best wife a man
ever had."

"I never had a proper education," Mrs. Carter went on, "but
I always was ambitious. The proudest moment of my life was
when your pa said we could afford a girl to help me and he
said then: 'The time'll come when you have a cook *and* a house-
maid,' and he's been as good as his word, and now you're going
back to what I come from. I'd set my heart on your marrying
a gentleman."

She began crying again. Gracie loved her parents and
couldn't bear to see them so distressed.

"I'm sorry, Ma, I knew it would be a disappointment to you,
but I can't help it, I can't really. I love him so, I love him
so terribly. I'm sure you'll like him when you see him. We're
going for a walk on the Common this afternoon. Can't I bring
him back to supper?"

Mrs. Carter gave her husband a harassed look. He sighed.

"I don't like it and it's no good pretending I do, but I
suppose we'd better have a look at him."

Supper passed off better than might have been expected. Fred
wasn't shy, and he talked to Gracie's parents as though he had
known them all his life. If to be waited on by a maid, if to
sup in a dining-room furnished in solid mahogany and afterwards to sit in a drawing-room that had a grand piano in it was
new to him, he showed no embarrassment. After he had gone
and they were alone in their bedroom Mr. and Mrs. Carter
talked him over.

"He is handsome, you can't deny that," she said.

"Handsome is as handsome does. D'you think he's after her
money?"

"Well, he must know that you've got a tidy little bit tucked
away somewhere, but he's in love with her all right."

"Oh, what makes you think that?"

"Why, you've only got to see the way he looks at her."

"Well, that's something at all events."

In the end the Carters withdrew their opposition on the condition that the young things shouldn't marry until Gracie had taken her degree. That would give them a year, and at the back of their minds was the hope that by then she would have changed her mind. They saw a good deal of Fred after that. He spent every Sunday with them. Little by little they began quite to like him. He was so easy, so gay, so full of high spirits, and above all so obviously head over ears in love with Gracie, that Mrs. Carter soon succumbed to his charm, and after a while even Mr. Carter was prepared to admit that he didn't seem a bad fellow. Fred and Gracie were happy. She went to London every day to attend lectures and worked hard. They spent blissful evenings together. He gave her a very nice engagement ring and often took her out to dinner in the West End and to a play. On fine Sundays he drove her out into the country in a car that he said a friend had lent him. When she asked him if he could afford all the money he spent on her he laughed, and said a chap had given him a tip on an outsider and he'd made a packet. They talked interminably of the little flat they would have when they were married and the fun it would be to furnish it. They were more in love with one another than ever.

Then the blow fell. Fred was arrested for stealing money from the letters he collected. Many people, to save themselves the trouble of buying postal orders, put notes in their envelopes, and it wasn't difficult to tell that they were there. Fred went up for trial, pleaded guilty, and was sentenced to two years' hard labour. Gracie went to the trial. Up to the last moment she had hoped that he would be able to prove his innocence. It was a dreadful shock to her when he pleaded guilty. She was not allowed to see him. He went straight from the dock to the prison van. She went home and, locking herself up in her bedroom, threw herself on the bed and wept. When Mr. Carter came back from the shop Gracie's mother went up to her room.

"Gracie, you're to come downstairs," she said. "Your father wants to speak to you."

Gracie got up and went down. She did not trouble to dry her eyes.

"Seen the paper?" he said, holding out to her the *Evening News*.

She didn't answer.

"Well, that's the end of that young man," he went on harshly.

They too, Gracie's parents, had been shocked when Fred was arrested, but she was so distressed, she was so convinced that everything could be explained, that they hadn't had the heart to tell her that she must have nothing more to do with him. But now they felt it time to have things out with her.

"So that's where the money came from for those dinners and theatres. And the car. I thought it funny he should have a friend who'd lend him a car on Sundays when he'd be wanting it himself. He hired it, didn't he?"

"I suppose so," she answered miserably. "I just believed what he told me."

"You've had a lucky escape, my girl, that's all I can say."

"He only did it because he wanted to give me a good time. He didn't want me to think I couldn't have everything as nice when I was with him as what I've been used to at home."

"You're not going to make excuses for him, I hope. He's a thief, that's what he is."

"I don't care," she said sullenly.

"You don't care? What d'you mean by that?"

"Exactly what I say. I'm going to wait for him and the moment he comes out I'm going to marry him."

Mrs. Carter gave a gasp of horror.

"Gracie, you can't do a thing like that," she cried. "Think of the disgrace. And what about us? We've always held our heads high. He's a thief, and once a thief always a thief."

"Don't go on calling him a thief," Gracie shrieked, stamping

274

her foot with rage. "What he did he did just because he loved me. I don't care if he is a thief. I love him more than ever I loved him. You don't know what love is. You waited ten years to marry Pa just so as an old woman should leave you some money. D'you call that love?"

"You leave your ma out of this," Mr. Carter shouted. Then an idea occurred to him and he gave her a piercing glance. "Have you *got* to marry the feller?"

Gracie blushed furiously.

"No. There's never been anything of that sort. And not through any fault of mine either. He loved me too much. He didn't want to do anything perhaps he'd regret afterwards."

Often on summer evenings in the country when they'd been lying in a field in one another's arms, mouth to mouth, her desire had been as intense as his. She knew how much he wanted her and she was ready to give him what he asked. But when things got too desperate he'd suddenly jump up and say:

"Come on, let's walk."

He'd drag her to her feet. She knew what was in his mind. He wanted to wait till they were married. His love had given him a delicacy of sentiment that he'd never known before. He couldn't make it out himself, but he had a funny sort of feeling about her, he felt that if he had her before marriage it would spoil things. Because she guessed what was in his heart she loved him all the more.

"I don't know what's come over you," moaned Mrs. Carter. "You was always such a good girl. You've never given me a day's uneasiness."

"Stop it, Ma," said Mr. Carter violently. "We've got to get this straight once and for all. You've got to give up this man, see? I've got me own position to think of and if you think I'm going to have a gaol-bird for a son-in-law you'd better think again. I've had enough of this nonsense. You've got to promise me that you'll have nothing more to do with the feller ever."

"D'you think I'm going to give him up now? How often d'you want me to tell you I'm going to marry him the moment he gets out?"

"All right, then you can get out of my house and get out pretty damn quick. And stay out."

"Pa!" cried Mrs. Carter.

"Shut up."

"I'll be glad to go," said Gracie.

"Oh, will you? And how d'you think you're going to live?"

"I can work, can't I? I can get a job at Payne & Perkins. They'll be glad to have me."

"Oh, Gracie, you couldn't go and work in a shop. You can't demean yourself like that,' said Mrs. Carter.

"Will you shut up, Ma," shouted Mr. Carter, beside himself now with rage. "Work, will you? You that's never done a stroke of work in your life except that tomfoolery at the college. Bright idea it was of your ma's to give you an education. Fat lot of good it'll be to you when you've got to stand on your feet for hours and got to be civil and pleasant to a lot of old trouts who just try and give you all the trouble they can just to show how superior they are. I bet you'll like it when you're bawled out by the manageress because you're not bright and snappy. All right, marry your gaol-bird. I suppose you know you'll have to keep him too. You don't think anyone's going to give him a job, do you, not with his record. Get out, get out, get out."

He had worked himself up to such a pitch of fury that he sank panting into a chair. Mrs. Carter, frightened, poured out a glass of water and gave him some to drink. Gracie slipped out of the room.

Next day, when her father had gone to work and her mother was out shopping, she left the house with such effects as she could get into a suit-case. Payne & Perkins was a large department store in the Brixton Road, and with her good appearance and pleasant manner she found no difficulty in getting taken on. She was put in the ladies' lingerie. For a few days she stayed at the Y.W.C.A. and then arranged to share a room with one of the girls who worked with her.

Ned Preston saw Fred in the evening of the day he went to gaol. He found him shattered, but only because of Gracie. He took his thieving very lightly.

"I had to do the right thing by her, didn't I? Her people, they didn't think I was good enough for her; I wanted to show them I was just as good as they were. When we went up to the West End I couldn't give her a sandwich and half of bitter in a pub, why, she's never been in a pub in her life, I *had* to take her to a restaurant. If people are such fools as to put money in letters, well, they're just asking for it."

But he was frightened. He wasn't sure that Gracie would see it like that.

"I've got to know what she's going to do. If she chucks me now—well, it's the end of everything for me, see? I'll find some way of doing meself in, I swear to God I will."

He told Ned the whole story of his love for Gracie.

"I could have had her over and over again if I'd wanted to. And I did want to and so did she. I knew that. But I respected her, see? She's not like other girls. She's one in a thousand, I tell you."

He talked and talked. He stormed, he wept. From that confused torrent of words emerged one thing very clearly. A passionate, a frenzied love. Ned promised that he would see the girl.

"Tell her I love her, tell her that what I did I just did because I wanted her to have the best of everything, and tell her I just can't live without her."

As soon as he could find time Ned Preston went to the Carters' house, but when he asked for Gracie the maid who opened the door told him that she didn't live there any more. Then he asked to see her mother.

"I'll go and see if she's in."

He gave the maid his card, thinking the name of his club engraved in the corner would impress Mrs. Carter enough to make her willing to see him. The maid left him at the door but in a minute or two asked him to come in. He was shown into the stiff and little-used sitting-room. Mrs. Carter kept him waiting for some time and when she came in, holding his card in the tips of her fingers, he guessed it was because she had thought fit to change her dress. The black silk she wore was evidently a dress for occasions. He told her his connection with Wormwood Scrubs and said that he had to do with a man named Frederick Manson. The moment he mentioned the name Mrs. Carter assumed a hostile attitude.

"Don't speak to me of that man," she cried. "A thief, that's what he is. The trouble he's caused us. They ought to have given him five years, they ought."

"I'm sorry he's caused you trouble," said Ned mildly. "Perhaps if you'd give me a few facts I might help to straighten things out."

Ned Preston certainly had a way with him. Perhaps Mrs. Carter was impressed because he was a gentleman. "Class he is," she probably said to herself. Anyhow it was not long before she was telling him the whole story. She grew upset as she told it and began to cry.

"And now she's gone and left us. Run away. I don't know how she could bring herself to do a thing like that. God knows, we love her. She's all we've got and we done everything in the world for her. Her pa never meant it when he told her to get out of the house. Only she was so obstinate. He got in a temper, he always was a quick-tempered man, he was just as upset as I was when we found she'd gone. And d'you know what she's been and gone and done? Got herself a job at Payne & Perkins. Mr. Carter can't abide them. Cutting prices all the time they are. Unfair competition, he calls it. And to think of our Gracie working with a lot of shop-girls—oh, it's so humiliating."

Ned made a mental note of the store's name. He hadn't been at all sure of getting Gracie's address out of Mrs. Carter.

"Have you seen her since she left you?" he asked.

278

EPISODE

"Of course I have. I knew they'd jump at her at Payne & Perkins, a superior girl like that, and I went there, and there she was, sure enough—in the ladies' lingerie. I waited outside till closing time and then I spoke to her. I asked her to come home. I said her pa was willing to let bygones be bygones. And d'you know what she said? She said she'd come home if we never said a word against Fred and if we was prepared to have her marry him as soon as ever he got out. Of course I had to tell her pa. I never saw him in such a state, I thought he was going to have a fit, he said he'd rather see her dead at his feet than married to that gaol-bird."

Mrs. Carter again burst into tears and as soon as he could Ned Preston left her. He went to the department store, up to the ladies' lingerie, and asked for Grace Carter. She was pointed out to him and he went up to her.

"Can I speak to you for a minute? I've come from Fred Manson."

She went deathly white. For a moment it seemed that she could not utter a word.

"Follow me, please."

She took him into a passage smelling of disinfectants which seemed to lead to the lavatories. They were alone. She stared at him anxiously.

"He sends you his love. He's worried about you. He's afraid you're awfully unhappy. What he wants to know really is if you're going to chuck him?"

"Me?" Her eyes filled with tears, but on her face was a look of ecstasy. "Tell him that nothing matters to me as long as he loves me. Tell him I'd wait twenty years for him if I had to. Tell him I'm counting the days till he gets out so as we can get married."

For fear of the manageress she couldn't stay away from her work for more than a minute or two. She gave Ned all the loving messages she could get into the time to give Fred Manson. Ned didn't get to the Scrubs till nearly six. The prisoners are allowed to put down their tools at five-thirty and

Fred had just put his down. When Ned entered the cell he turned pale and sank on to the bed as though his anxiety was such that he didn't trust his legs. But when Ned told him his news he gave a gasp of relief. For a while he couldn't trust himself to speak.

"I knew you'd seen her the moment you came in. I smelt her."

He sniffed as though the smell of her body were strong in his nostrils, and his face was as it were a mask of desire. His features on a sudden seemed strangely blurred.

"You know, it made me feel quite uncomfortable so that I had to look the other way," said Ned Preston when he told us this, with a cackle of his shrill laughter. "It was sex in its nakedness all right."

Fred was an exemplary prisoner. He worked well, he gave no trouble. Ned suggested books for him to read and he took them out of the library, but that was about as far as he got.

"I can't get on well with them somehow," he said. "I start reading and then I begin thinking of Gracie. You know, when she kisses you ordinary-like—oh, it's so sweet, but when she kisses you really, my God, it's lovely."

Fred was allowed to see Gracie once a month, but their meetings, with a glass screen between, under the eyes of a warder, were so painful that after several visits they agreed it would be better if she didn't come any more. A year passed. Owing to his good behaviour he could count on a remittance of his sentence and so would be free in another six months. Gracie had saved every penny she could out of her wages and now as the time approached for Fred's release she set about getting a home ready for him. She took two rooms in a house and furnished them on the hire purchase system. One room of course was to be their bedroom and the other the living-room and kitchen. There was an old-fashioned range in it and this she had taken out and replaced by a gas-stove. She wanted everything to be nice and new and clean and comfortable. She took pains to make the two little rooms bright and pretty.

EPISODE

To do all this she had to go without all but the barest necessities of existence and she grew thin and pale. Ned suspected that she was starving herself and when he went to see her took a box of chocolates or a cake so that she should have at least something to eat. He brought the prisoner news of what Gracie was doing and she made him promise to give him accurate accounts of every article she bought. He took fond, more than fond, passionate messages from one to the other. He was convinced that Fred would go straight in future and he got him a job as commissionaire from a firm that had a chain of restaurants in London. The wages were good and by calling taxis or fetching cars he would be able to make money on the side. He was to start work as soon as he came out of gaol. Gracie took the necessary steps so that they could get married at once. The eighteen months of Fred's imprisonment were drawing to an end. Gracie was in a fever of excitement.

It happened then that Ned Preston had one of his periodical bouts of illness and was unable to go to the prison for three weeks. It bothered him, for he didn't like to abandon his prisoners, so as soon as he could get out of bed he went to the Scrubs. The chief warder told him that Manson had been asking for him.

"I think you'd better go and see him. I don't know what's the matter with him. He's been acting rather funny since you've been away."

It was just a fortnight before Fred was due to be released. Ned Preston went to his cell.

"Well, Fred, how are you?" he asked. "Sorry I haven't been able to come and see you. I've been ill, and I haven't been able to see Gracie either. She must be all of a dither by now."

"Well, I want you to go and see her."

His manner was so surly that Ned was taken aback. It was unlike him to be anything but pleasant and civil.

"Of course I will."

"I want you to tell her that I'm not going to marry her."

Ned was so astounded that for a minute he could only stare blankly at Fred Manson.

"What on earth d'you mean?"

"Exactly what I say."

"You can't let her down now. Her people have thrown her out. She's been working all this time to get a home ready for you. She's got the licence and everything."

"I don't care. I'm not going to marry her."

"But why, why, why?"

Ned was flabbergasted. Fred Manson was silent for a bit. His face was dark and sullen.

"I'll tell you. I've thought about her night and day for eighteen months and now I'm sick to death of her."

When Ned Preston reached this point of his story our hostess and our fellow guests broke into loud laughter. He was plainly taken aback. There was some little talk after that and the party broke up. Ned and I, having to go in the same direction, walked along Piccadilly together. For a time we walked in silence.

"I noticed you didn't laugh with the others," he said abruptly.

"I didn't think it funny."

"What d'you make of it?"

"Well, I can see his point, you know. Imagination's an odd thing, it dries up; I suppose, thinking of her incessantly all that time he'd exhausted every emotion she'd could give him, and I think it was quite literally true, he'd just got sick to death of her. He'd squeezed the lemon dry and there was nothing to do but throw away the rind."

"I didn't think it funny either. That's why I didn't tell them the rest of the story. I wouldn't accept it at first. I thought it was just hysteria or something. I went to see him two or three days running. I argued with him. I really did my damnedest. I thought if he'd only see her it would be all right, but he wouldn't even do that. He said he hated the sight of her. I couldn't move him. At last I had to go and tell her."

We walked on a little longer in silence.

EPISODE

"I saw her in that beastly, stinking corridor. She saw at once
there was something the matter and she went awfully white.
She wasn't a girl to show much emotion. There was something gracious and rather noble about her face. Tranquil. Her
lips quivered a bit when I told her and she didn't say anything
for a minute. When she spoke it was quite calmly, as though—
well, as though she'd just missed a bus and would have to wait
for another. As though it was a nuisance, you know, but
nothing to make a song and dance about. 'There's nothing for
me to do now but put my head in the gas-oven,' she said.

"And she did."

THE KITE

I KNOW this is an odd story. I don't understand it myself and if I set it down in black and white it is only with a faint hope that when I have written it I may get a clearer view of it, or rather with the hope that some reader, better acquainted with the complications of human nature than I am, may offer me an explanation that will make it comprehensible to me. Of course the first thing that occurs to me is that there is something Freudian about it. Now, I have read a good deal of Freud, and some books by his followers, and intending to write this story I have recently flipped through again the volume published by the Modern Library which contains his basic writings. It was something of a task, for he is a dull and verbose writer, and the acrimony with which he claims to have originated such and such a theory shows a vanity and a jealousy of others working in the same field which somewhat ill become a man of science. I believe, however, that he was a kindly and benign old party. As we know, there is often a great difference between the man and the writer. The writer may be bitter, harsh and brutal while the man may be so meek and mild that he wouldn't say boo to a goose. But that is neither here nor there. I found nothing in my re-reading of Freud's works that cast any light on the subject I had in mind. I can only relate the facts and leave it at that.

First of all I must make it plain that it is not my story and that I knew none of the persons with whom it is concerned. It was told me one evening by my friend Ned Preston, and he told it me because he didn't know how to deal with the circumstances and he thought, quite wrongly as it happened, that I might be able to give him some advice that would help him. In a previous story I have related what I thought the reader should know about Ned Preston, and so now I need only remind him that my friend was a prison visitor at Wormwood

284

THE KITE

Scrubs. He took his duties very seriously and made the prisoners' troubles his own. We had been dining together at the Café Royal in that long, low room with its absurd and charming decoration which is all that remains of the old Café Royal that painters have loved to paint; and we were sitting over our coffee and liqueurs and, so far as Ned was concerned against his doctors' orders, smoking very long and very good Havanas.

"I've got a funny chap to deal with at the Scrubs just now," he said, after a pause, "and I'm blowed if I know how to deal with him."

"What's he in for?" I asked.

"He left his wife and the court ordered him to pay so much a week in alimony and he's absolutely refused to pay it. I've argued with him till I was blue in the face. I've told him he's only cutting off his nose to spite his face. He says he'll stay in gaol all his life rather than pay her a penny. I tell him he can't let her starve, and all he says is: 'Why not?' He's perfectly well behaved, he's no trouble, he works well, he seems quite happy, he's just getting a lot of fun out of thinking what a devil of a time his wife is having."

"What's he got against her?"

"She smashed his kite."

"She did what?" I cried.

"Exactly that. She smashed his kite. He says he'll never forgive her for that till his dying day."

"He must be crazy."

"No, he isn't, he's a perfectly reasonable, quite intelligent, decent fellow."

Herbert Sunbury was his name, and his mother, who was very refined, never allowed him to be called Herb or Bertie, but always Herbert, just as she never called her husband Sam but only Samuel. Mrs. Sunbury's first name was Beatrice, and when she got engaged to Mr. Sunbury and he ventured to call her Bea she put her foot down firmly.

"Beatrice I was christened," she said, "and Beatrice I always have been and always shall be, to you and to my nearest and dearest."

She was a little woman, but strong, active and wiry, with a sallow skin, sharp, regular features and small, beady eyes. Her hair, suspiciously black for her age, was always very neat, and she wore it in the style of Queen Victoria's daughters, which she had adopted as soon as she was old enough to put it up and had never thought fit to change. The possibility that she did something to keep her hair its original colour was, if such was the case, her only concession to frivolity, for, far from using rouge or lipstick, she had never in her life so much as passed a powder-puff over her nose. She never wore anything but black dresses of good material, but made (by a little woman round the corner) regardless of fashion after a pattern that was both serviceable and decorous. Her only ornament was a thin gold chain from which hung a small gold cross.

Samuel Sunbury was a little man too. He was as thin and spare as his wife, but he had sandy hair, gone very thin now so that he had to wear it very long on one side and brush it carefully over the large bald patch. He had pale blue eyes and his complexion was pasty. He was a clerk in a lawyer's office and had worked his way up from office boy to a respectable position. His employer called him Mr. Sunbury and sometimes asked him to see an unimportant client. Every morning for twenty-four years Samuel Sunbury had taken the same train to the City, except of course on Sundays and during his fortnight's holiday at the seaside, and every evening he had taken the same train back to the suburb in which he lived. He was neat in his dress; he went to work in quiet grey trousers, a black coat and a bowler hat, and when he came home he put on his slippers and a black coat which was too old and shiny to wear at the office; but on Sundays when he went to the chapel he and Mrs. Sunbury attended he wore a morning coat with his bowler. Thus he showed his respect for the day of rest and at the same time registered a protest against the

286

ungodly who went bicycling or lounged about the streets until the pubs opened. On principle the Sunburys were total abstainers, but on Sundays, when to make up for the frugal lunch, consisting of a scone and butter with a glass of milk, which Samuel had during the week, Beatrice gave him a good dinner of roast beef and Yorkshire pudding, for his health's sake she liked him to have a glass of beer. Since she wouldn't for the world have kept liquor in the house, he sneaked out with a jug after morning service and got a quart from the pub round the corner; but nothing would induce him to drink alone, so, just to be sociable-like, she had a glass too.

Herbert was the only child the Lord had vouchsafed to them, and this certainly through no precaution on their part. It just happened that way. They doted on him. He was a pretty baby and then a good-looking child. Mrs. Sunbury brought him up carefully. She taught him to sit up at table and not put his elbows on it, and she taught him how to use his knife and fork like a little gentleman. She taught him to stretch out his little finger when he took his tea-cup to drink out of it and when he asked why, she said:

"Never you mind. That's how it's done. It shows you know what's what."

In due course Herbert grew old enough to go to school. Mrs. Sunbury was anxious because she had never let him play with the children in the street.

"Evil communications corrupt good manners," she said. "I always have kept myself to myself and I always shall keep myself to myself."

Although they had lived in the same house ever since they were married she had taken care to keep her neighbours at a distance.

"You never know who people are in London," she said. "One thing leads to another, and before you know where you are you're mixed up with a lot of riff-raff and you can't get rid of them."

She didn't like the idea of Herbert being thrown into contact with a lot of rough boys at the County Council school and she said to him:

"Now, Herbert, do what I do; keep yourself to yourself and don't have anything more to do with them than you can help."

But Herbert got on very well at school. He was a good worker and far from stupid. His reports were excellent. It turned out he had a good head for figures.

"If that's a fact," said Samuel Sunbury, "he'd better be an accountant. There's always a good job waiting for a good accountant."

So it was settled there and then that this was what Herbert was to be. He grew tall.

"Why, Herbert," said his mother, "soon you'll be as tall as your dad."

By the time he left school he was two inches taller, and by the time he stopped growing he was five feet ten.

"Just the right height," said his mother. "Not too tall and not too short."

He was a nice-looking boy, with his mother's regular features and dark hair, but he had inherited his father's blue eyes, and though he was rather pale his skin was smooth and clear. Samuel Sunbury had got him into the office of the accountant who came twice a year to do the accounts of his own firm and by the time he was twenty-one he was able to bring back to his mother every week quite a nice little sum. She gave him back three half-crowns for his lunches and ten shillings for pocket money, and the rest she put in the Savings Bank for him against a rainy day.

When Mr. and Mrs. Sunbury went to bed on the night of Herbert's twenty-first birthday, and in passing I may say that Mrs. Sunbury never went to bed, she retired, but Mr. Sunbury who was not quite so refined as his wife, always said: "Me for Bedford,"—when then Mr. and Mrs. Sunbury went to bed Mrs. Sunbury said:

"Some people don't know how lucky they are; thank the Lord, I do. No one's ever had a better son than our Herbert

THE KITE

Hardly a day's illness in his life and he's never given me a moment's worry. It just shows if you bring up somebody right they'll be a credit to you. Fancy him being twenty-one, I can hardly believe it."

"Yes, I suppose before we know where we are he'll be marrying and leaving us."

"What should he want to do that for?" asked Mrs. Sunbury with asperity. "He's got a good home here, hasn't he? Don't you go putting silly ideas into his head, Samuel, or you and me'll have words and you know that's the last thing I want. Marry indeed! He's got more sense than that. He knows when he's well off. He's got sense, Herbert has."

Mr. Sunbury was silent. He had long ago learnt that it didn't get him anywhere with Beatrice to answer back.

"I don't hold with a man marrying till he knows his own mind," she went on. "And a man doesn't know his own mind till he's thirty or thirty-five."

"He was pleased with his presents," said Mr. Sunbury to change the conversation.

"And so he ought to be," said Mrs. Sunbury still upset.

They had in fact been handsome. Mr. Sunbury had given him a silver wrist-watch, with hands that you could see in the dark, and Mrs. Sunbury had given him a kite. It wasn't by any means the first one she had given him. That was when he was seven years old, and it happened this way. There was a large common near where they lived and on Saturday afternoons when it was fine Mrs. Sunbury took her husband and son for a walk there. She said it was good for Samuel to get a breath of fresh air after being cooped up in a stuffy office all the week. There were always a lot of people on the common, but Mrs. Sunbury who liked to keep herself to herself kept out of their way as much as possible.

"Look at them kites, Mum," said Herbert suddenly one day.

There was a fresh breeze blowing and a number of kites, small and large, were sailing through the air.

"*Those*, Herbert, not them," said Mrs. Sunbury.

"Would you like to go and see where they start, Herbert?" asked his father.

"Oh, yes, Dad."

There was a slight elevation in the middle of the commons and as they approached it they saw boys and girls and some men racing down it to give their kites a start and catch the wind. Sometimes they didn't and fell to the ground, but when they did they would rise, and as the owner unravelled his string go higher and higher. Herbert looked with ravishment.

"Mum, can I have a kite?" he cried.

He had already learnt that when he wanted anything it was better to ask his mother first.

"Whatever for?" she said.

"To fly it, Mum."

"If you're so sharp you'll cut yourself," she said.

Mr. and Mrs. Sunbury exchanged a glance over the little boy's head. Fancy him wanting a kite. Growing quite a little man he was.

"If you're a good boy and wash your teeth regular every morning without me telling you I shouldn't be surprised if Santa Claus didn't bring you a kite on Christmas Day."

Christmas wasn't far off and Santa Claus brought Herbert his first kite. At the beginning he wasn't very clever at managing it, and Mr. Sunbury had to run down the hill himself and start it for him. It was a very small kite, but when Herbert saw it swim through the air and felt the little tug it gave his hand he was thrilled; and then every Saturday afternoon, when his father got back from the City, he would pester his parents to hurry over to the common. He quickly learnt how to fly it, and Mr. and Mrs. Sunbury, their hearts swelling with pride, would watch him from the top of the knoll while he ran down and as the kite caught the breeze lengthened the cord in his hand.

It became a passion with Herbert, and as he grew older and bigger his mother bought him larger and larger kites. He grew very clever at gauging the winds and could do things with his

THE KITE

kite you wouldn't have thought possible. There were other kite-flyers on the common, not only children, but men, and since nothing brings people together so naturally as a hobby they share it was not long before Mrs. Sunbury, notwithstanding her exclusiveness, found that she, her Samuel and her son were on speaking terms with all and sundry. They would compare their respective kites and boast of their accomplishments. Sometimes Herbert, a big boy of sixteen now, would challenge another kite-flyer. Then he would manœuvre his kite to windward of the other fellow's, allow his cord to drift against his, and by a sudden jerk bring the enemy kite down. But long before this Mr. Sunbury had succumbed to his son's enthusiasm and he would often ask to have a go himself. It must have been a funny sight to see him running down the hill in his striped trousers, black coat and bowler hat. Mrs. Sunbury would trot sedately behind him and when the kite was sailing free would take the cord from him and watch it as it soared. Saturday afternoon became the great day of the week for them, and when Mr. Sunbury and Herbert left the house in the morning to catch their train to the City the first thing they did was to look up at the sky to see if it was flying weather. They liked best of all a gusty day, with uncertain winds, for that gave them the best chance to exercise their skill. All through the week, in the evenings, they talked about it. They were contemptuous of smaller kites than theirs and envious of bigger ones. They discussed the performances of other flyers as hotly, and as scornfully, as boxers or football-players discuss their rivals. Their ambition was to have a bigger kite than anyone else and a kite that would go higher. They had long given up a cord, for the kite they gave Herbert on his twenty-first birthday was seven feet high, and they used piano wire wound round a drum. But that did not satisfy Herbert. Somehow or other he had heard of a box-kite which had been invented by somebody, and the idea appealed to him at once. He thought he could devise something of the sort himself and since he could draw a little he set about making designs of it. He got a small model

291

made and tried it out one afternoon, but it wasn't a success. He was a stubborn boy and he wasn't going to be beaten. Something was wrong, and it was up to him to put it right.

Then an unfortunate thing happened. Herbert began to go out after supper. Mrs. Sunbury didn't like it much, but Mr. Sunbury reasoned with her. After all, the boy was twenty-two, and it must be dull for him to stay at home all the time. If he wanted to go for a walk or see a movie there was no great harm. Herbert had fallen in love. One Saturday evening, after they'd had a wonderful time on the common, while they were at supper, out of a clear sky he said suddenly:

"Mum, I've asked a young lady to come in to tea tomorrow. Is that all right?"

"You done what?" said Mrs. Sunbury, for a moment forgetting her grammar.

"You heard, Mum."

"And may I ask who she is and how you got to know her?"

"Her name's Bevan, Betty Bevan, and I met her first at the pictures one Saturday afternoon when it was raining. It was an accident-like. She was sitting next me and she dropped her bag and I picked it up and she said thank you and so naturally we got talking."

"And d'you mean to tell me you fell for an old trick like that? Dropped her bag indeed!"

"You're making a mistake, Mum, she's a nice girl, she is really, and well educated too."

"And when did all this happen?"

"About three months ago."

"Oh, you met her three months ago and you've asked her to come to tea tomorrow?"

"Well, I've seen her since of course. That first day, after the show, I asked her if she'd come to the pictures with me on the Tuesday evening, and she said she didn't know, perhaps she would and perhaps she wouldn't. But she came all right."

"She would. I could have told you that."

"And we've been going to the pictures about twice a week ever since."

"So that's why you've taken to going out so often?"

"That's right. But, look, I don't want to force her on you, if you don't want her to come to tea I'll say you've got a headache and take her out."

"Your mum will have her to tea all right," said Mr. Sunbury. "Won't you, dear? It's only that your mum can't abide strangers. She never has liked them."

"I keep myself to myself," said Mrs. Sunbury gloomily. "What does she do?"

"She works in a typewriting office in the City and she lives at home, if you call it home; you see, her mum died and her dad married again, and they've got three kids and she doesn't get on with her step-ma. Nag, nag, nag all the time, she says."

Mrs. Sunbury arranged the tea very stylishly. She took the knick-knacks off a little table in the sitting-room, which they never used, and put a tea-cloth on it. She got out the tea service and the plated tea-kettle which they never used either, and she made scones, baked a cake, and cut thin bread-and-butter.

"I want her to see that we're not just nobody," she told her Samuel.

Herbert went to fetch Miss Bevan, and Mr. Sunbury intercepted them at the door in case Herbert should take her into the dining-room where normally they ate and sat. Herbert gave the tea-table a glance of surprise as he ushered the young woman into the sitting-room.

"This is Betty, Mum," he said.

"Miss Bevan, I presume," said Mrs. Sunbury.

"That's right, but call me Betty, won't you?"

"Perhaps the acquaintance is a bit short for that," said Mrs. Sunbury with a gracious smile. "Won't you sit down, Miss Bevan?"

Strangely enough, or perhaps not strangely at all, Betty Bevan looked very much as Mrs. Sunbury must have looked at her age. She had the same sharp features and the same rather

293

small beady eyes, but her lips were scarlet with paint, her cheeks lightly rouged and her short black hair permanently waved. Mrs. Sunbury took in all this at a glance, and she reckoned to a penny how much her smart rayon dress had cost, her extravagantly high-heeled shoes and the saucy hat on her head. Her frock was very short and she showed a good deal of flesh-coloured stocking. Mrs. Sunbury, disapproving of her make-up and of her apparel, took an instant dislike to her, but she had made up her mind to behave like a lady, and if she didn't know how to behave like a lady nobody did, so that at first things went well. She poured out tea and asked Herbert to give a cup to his lady friend.

"Ask Miss Bevan if she'll have some bread-and-butter or a scone, Samuel, my dear."

"Have both," said Samuel, handing round the two plates, in his coarse way. "I like to see people eat hearty."

Betty insecurely perched a piece of bread-and-butter and a scone on her saucer and Mrs. Sunbury talked affably about the weather. She had the satisfaction of seeing that Betty was getting more and more ill-at-ease. Then she cut the cake and pressed a large piece on her guest. Betty took a bite at it and when she put it in her saucer it fell to the ground.

"Oh, I am sorry," said the girl, as she picked it up.

"It doesn't matter at all, I'll cut you another piece," said Mrs. Sunbury.

"Oh, don't bother, I'm not particular. The floor's clean."

"I hope so," said Mrs. Sunbury with an acid smile, "but I wouldn't dream of letting you eat a piece of cake that's been on the floor. Bring it here, Herbert, and I'll give Miss Bevan some more."

"I don't want any more, Mrs. Sunbury, I don't really."

"I'm sorry you don't like my cake. I made it specially for you." She took a bit. "It tastes all right to me."

"It's not that, Mrs. Sunbury, it's a beautiful cake, it's only that I'm not hungry."

She refused to have more tea and Mrs. Sunbury saw she was

glad to get rid of the cup. "I expect they have their meals in the kitchen," she said to herself. Then Herbert lit a cigarette.

"Give us a fag, Herb," said Betty. "I'm simply dying for a smoke."

Mrs. Sunbury didn't approve of women smoking, but she only raised her eyebrows slightly.

"We prefer to call him Herbert, Miss Bevan," she said.

Betty wasn't such a fool as not to see that Mrs. Sunbury had been doing all she could to make her uncomfortable, and now she saw a chance to get back at her.

"I know," she said. "When he told me his name was Herbert I nearly burst out laughing. Fancy calling anyone Herbert. A scream, I call it."

"I'm sorry you don't like the name my son was given at his baptism. I think it's a very nice name. But I suppose it all depends on what sort of class of people one is."

Herbert stepped in to the rescue.

"At the office they call me Bertie, Mum."

"Then all I can say is, they're a lot of very common men."

Mrs. Sunbury lapsed into a dignified silence and the conversation, such as it was, was maintained by Mr. Sunbury and Herbert. It was not without satisfaction that Mrs. Sunbury perceived that Betty was offended. She also perceived that the girl wanted to go, but didn't quite know how to manage it. She was determined not to help her. Finally Herbert took the matter into his own hands.

"Well, Betty, I think it's about time we were getting along," he said. "I'll walk back with you."

"Must you go already?" said Mrs. Sunbury, rising to her feet. "It's been a pleasure, I'm sure."

"Pretty little thing," said Mr. Sunbury tentatively after the young things had left.

"Pretty my foot. All that paint and powder. You take my word for it, she'd look very different with her face washed and without a perm. Common, that's what she is, common as dirt."

An hour later Herbert came back. He was angry.

"Look here, Mum, what d'you mean by treating the poor girl like that? I was simply ashamed of you."

"Don't talk to your mother like that, Herbert," she flared up. "You didn't ought to have brought a woman like that into my house. Common, she is, common as dirt."

When Mrs. Sunbury got angry not only did her grammar grow shaky, but she wasn't quite safe on her aitches. Herbert took no notice of what she said.

"She said she'd never been so insulted in her life. I had a rare job pacifying her."

"Well, she's never coming here again, I tell you that straight."

"That's what you think. I'm engaged to her, so put that in your pipe and smoke it."

Mrs. Sunbury gasped.

"You're not?"

"Yes, I am. I've been thinking about it for a long time, and then she was so upset tonight I felt sorry for her, so I popped the question and I had a rare job persuading her, I can tell you."

"You fool," screamed Mrs. Sunbury. "You fool."

There was quite a scene then. Mrs. Sunbury and her son went at it hammer and tongs, and when poor Samuel tried to intervene they both told him roughly to shut up. At last Herbert flung out of the room and out of the house and Mrs. Sunbury burst into angry tears.

No reference was made next day to what had passed. Mrs. Sunbury was frigidly polite to Herbert and he was sullen and silent. After supper he went out. On Saturday he told his father and mother that he was engaged that afternoon and wouldn't be able to come to the common with them.

"I dare say we shall be able to do without you," said Mrs. Sunbury grimly.

It was getting on to the time for their usual fortnight at the seaside. They always went to Herne Bay, because Mrs. Sunbury said you had a nice class of people there, and for years they had taken the same lodgings. One evening, in as casual a way as he could, Herbert said:

"By the way, Mum, you'd better write and tell them I shan't be wanting my room this year. Betty and me are getting married and we're going to Southend for the honeymoon."

For a moment there was dead silence in the room.

"Bit sudden-like, isn't it, Herbert?' said Mr. Sunbury uneasily.

"Well, they're cutting down at Betty's office and she's out of a job, so we thought we'd better get married at once. We've taken two rooms in Dabney Street and we're furnishing out of my Savings Bank money."

Mrs. Sunbury didn't say a word. She went deathly pale and tears rolled down her thin cheeks.

"Oh, come on, Mum, don't take it so hard," said Herbert. "A fellow has to marry sometime. If Dad hadn't married you, I shouldn't be here now, should I?"

Mrs. Sunbury brushed her tears away with an impatient hand.

"Your dad didn't marry me; I married 'im. I knew he was steady and respectable. I knew he'd make a good 'usband and father. I've never 'ad cause to regret it and no more 'as your dad. That's right, Samuel, isn't it?"

"Right as rain, Beatrice," he said quickly.

"You know, you'll like Betty when you get to know her. She's a nice girl, she is really. I believe you'd find you had a lot in common. You must give her a chance, Mum."

"She's never going to set foot in this house only over my dead body."

"That's absurd, Mum. Why, everything'll be just the same if you'll only be reasonable. I mean, we can go on flying on Saturday afternoons same as we always did. Just this time I've been engaged it's been difficult. You see, she can't see what there is in kite-flying, but she'll come round to it, and after I'm married it'll be different, I mean I can come and fly with you and Dad; that stands to reason."

"That's what you think. Well, let me tell you that if you marry that woman you're not going to fly my kite. I never gave it you, I bought it out of the housekeeping money, and it's mine, see."

"All right then, have it your own way. Betty says it's a kid's game anyway and I ought to be ashamed of myself, flying a kite at my age."

He got up and once more stalked angrily out of the house. A fortnight later he was married. Mrs. Sunbury refused to go to the wedding and wouldn't let Samuel go either. They went for their holiday and came back. They resumed their usual round. On Saturday afternoons they went to the common by themselves and flew their enormous kite. Mrs. Sunbury never mentioned her son. She was determined not to forgive him. But Mr. Sunbury used to meet him on the morning train they both took and they chatted a little when they managed to get into the same carriage. One morning Mr. Sunbury looked up at the sky.

"Good flying weather today," he said.

"D'you and Mum still fly?"

"What do you think? She's getting as clever as I am. You should see her with her skirts pinned up running down the hill. I give you my word, I never knew she had it in her. Run? Why, she can run better than what I can."

"Don't make me laugh, Dad!"

"I wonder you don't buy a kite of your own, Herbert. You've been always so keen on it."

"I know I was. I did suggest it once, but you know what women are, Betty said: 'Be your age,' and oh, I don't know what all. I don't want a kid's kite, of course, and them big kites cost money. When we started to furnish Betty said it was cheaper in the long run to buy the best and so we went to one of them hire purchase places and what with paying them every month and the rent, well, I haven't got any more money than just what we can manage on. They say it doesn't cost any more to keep two than one, well, that's not my experience so far."

"Isn't she working?"

"Well, no, she says after working for donkeys' years as you might say, now she's married she's going to take it easy, and of course someone's got to keep the place clean and do the cooking."

So it went on for six months, and then one Saturday afternoon when the Sunburys were as usual on the common Mrs. Sunbury said to her husband:

"Did you see what I saw, Samuel?"

"I saw Herbert, if that's what you mean. I didn't mention it because I thought it would only upset you."

"Don't speak to him. Pretend you haven't seen him."

Herbert was standing among the idle lookers-on. He made no attempt to speak to his parents, but it did not escape Mrs. Sunbury that he followed with all his eyes the flight of the big kite he had flown so often. It began to grow chilly and the Sunburys went home. Mrs. Sunbury's face was brisk with malice.

"I wonder if he'll come next Saturday," said Samuel.

"If I didn't think betting wrong I'd bet you sixpence he will, Samuel. I've been waiting for this all along."

"You have?"

"I knew from the beginning he wouldn't be able to keep away from it."

She was right. On the following Saturday and on every Saturday after that when the weather was fine Herbert turned up on the common. No intercourse passed. He just stood there for a while looking on and then strolled away. But after things had been going on like this for several weeks, the Sunburys had a surprise for him. They weren't flying the big kite which he was used to, but a new one, a box-kite, a small one, on the model for which he had made the designs himself. He saw it was creating a lot of interest among the other kite-flyers; they were standing round it and Mrs. Sunbury was talking volubly. The first time Samuel ran down the hill with it the thing didn't rise, but flopped miserably on the ground, and Herbert clenched his hands and ground his teeth. He couldn't bear to see it fail. Mr. Sunbury climbed up the little hill again, and the second time the box-kite took the air. There was a cheer among the bystanders. After a while Mr. Sunbury pulled it down and walked back with it to the hill. Mrs. Sunbury went up to her son.

"Like to have a try, Herbert?"

He caught his breath.

"Yes, Mum, I should."

"It's just a small one because they say you have to get the knack of it. It's not like the old-fashioned sort. But we've got specifications for a big one, and they say when you get to know about it and the wind's right you can go up to two miles with it."

Mr. Sunbury joined them.

"Samuel, Herbert wants to try the kite."

Mr. Sunbury handed it to him, a pleased smile on his face, and Herbert gave his mother his hat to hold. Then he raced down the hill, the kite took the air beautifully, and as he watched it rise his heart was filled with exultation. It was grand to see that little black thing soaring so sweetly, but even as he watched it he thought of the great big one they were having made. They'd never be able to manage that. Two miles in the air, mum had said. Whew!

"Why don't you come back and have a cup of tea, Herbert," said Mrs. Sunbury, "and we'll show you the designs for the new one they want to build for us. Perhaps you could make some suggestions."

He hesitated. He'd told Betty he was just going for a walk to stretch his legs, she didn't know he'd been coming to the common every week, and she'd be waiting for him. But the temptation was irresistible.

"I don't mind if I do," he said.

After tea they looked at the specifications. The kite was huge, with gadgets he had never seen before, and it would cost a lot of money.

300

"You'll never be able to fly it by yourselves," he said.

"We can try."

"I suppose you wouldn't like me to help you just at first?" he asked uncertainly.

"Mightn't be a bad idea," said Mrs. Sunbury.

It was late when he got home, much later than he thought, and Betty was vexed.

"Wherever have you been, Herb? I thought you were dead. Supper's waiting and everything."

"I met some fellows and got talking."

She gave him a sharp look, but didn't answer. She sulked.

After supper he suggested they should go to a movie, but she refused.

"You go if you want to," she said. "I don't care to."

On the following Saturday he went again to the common and again his mother let him fly the kite. They had ordered the new one and expected to get it in three weeks. Presently his mother said to him:

"Elizabeth is here."

"Betty?"

"Spying on you."

It gave him a nasty turn, but he put on a bold front.

"Let her spy. I don't care."

But he was nervous and wouldn't go back to tea with his parents. He went straight home. Betty was waiting for him.

"So that's the fellows you got talking to. I've been suspicious for some time, you going for a walk on Saturday afternoons, and all of a sudden I tumbled to it. Flying a kite, you, a grown man. Contemptible I call it."

"I don't care what you call it. I like it, and if you don't like it you can lump it."

"I won't have it and I tell you that straight. I'm not going to have you make a fool of yourself."

"I've flown a kite every Saturday afternoon ever since I was a kid, and I'm going to fly a kite as long as ever I want to."

CREATURES OF CIRCUMSTANCE

"It's that old bitch, she's just trying to get you away from me. I know her. If you were a man you'd never speak to her again, not after the way she's treated me."

"I won't have you call her that. She's my mother and I've got the right to see her as often as ever I want to."

The quarrel went on hour after hour. Betty screamed at him and Herbert shouted at her. They had had trifling disagreements before, because they were both obstinate, but this was the first serious row they had had. They didn't speak to one another on the Sunday, and during the rest of the week, though outwardly there was peace between them, their ill-feeling rankled. It happened that the next two Saturdays it poured with rain. Betty smiled to herself when she saw the downpour, but if Herbert was disappointed he gave no sign of it. The recollection of their quarrel grew dim. Living in two rooms as they did, sleeping in the same bed, it was inevitable that they should agree to forget their differences. Betty went out of her way to be nice to her Herb, and she thought that now she had given him a taste of her tongue and he knew she wasn't going to be put upon by anyone, he'd be reasonable. He was a good husband in his way, generous with his money and steady. Give her time and she'd manage him all right.

But after a fortnight of bad weather it cleared.

"Looks as if we're going to have good flying weather tomorrow," said Mr. Sunbury as they met on the platform to await their morning train. "The new kite's come."

"It has?"

"Your mum says of course we'd like you to come and help us with it, but no one's got the right to come between a man and his wife, and if you're afraid of Betty, her kicking up a rumpus, I mean, you'd better not come. There's a young fellow we've got to know on the common who's just mad about it, and he says he'll get it to fly if anybody can."

Herbert was seized with a pang of jealousy.

"Don't you let any strangers touch our kite. I'll be there all right."

302

"Well, you think it over, Herbert, and if you don't come we shall quite understand."

"I'll come," said Herbert.

So next day when he got back from the City he changed from his business clothes into slacks and an old coat. Betty came into the bedroom.

"What are you doing?"

"Changing," he answered gaily. He was so excited, he couldn't keep the secret to himself. "Their new kite's come and I'm going to fly it."

"Oh no, you're not," she said. "I won't have it."

"Don't be a fool, Betty. I'm going, I tell you, and if you don't like it you can do the other thing."

"I'm not going to let you, so that's that."

She shut the door and stood in front of it. Her eyes flashed and her jaw was set. She was a little thing and he was a tall strong man. He took hold of her two arms to push her out of the way, but she kicked him violently on the shin.

"D'you want me to give you a sock on the jaw?"

"If you go you don't come back," she shouted.

He caught her up, though she struggled and kicked, threw her on to the bed and went out.

If the small box-kite had caused an excitement on the common it was nothing to what the new one caused. But it was difficult to manage, and though they ran and panted and other enthusiastic flyers helped them Herbert couldn't get it up.

"Never mind," he said, "we'll get the knack of it presently. The wind's not right today, that's all."

He went back to tea with his father and mother and they talked it over just as they had talked in the old days. He delayed going because he didn't fancy the scene Betty would make him, but when Mrs. Sunbury went into the kitchen to get supper ready he had to go home. Betty was reading the paper. She looked up.

"Your bag's packed," she said.

"My what?"

"You heard what I said. I said if you went you needn't come back. I forgot about your things. Everything's packed. It's in the bedroom."

He looked at her for a moment with surprise. She pretended to be reading again. He would have liked to give her a good hiding.

"All right, have it your own way," he said.

He went into the bedroom. His clothes were packed in a suitcase, and there was a brown-paper parcel in which Betty had put whatever was left over. He took the bag in one hand, the parcel in the other, walked through the sitting-room without a word and out of the house. He walked to his mother's and rang the bell. She opened the door.

"I've come home, Mum," he said.

"Have you, Herbert? Your room's ready for you. Put your things down and come in. We were just sitting down to supper." They went into the dining-room. "Samuel, Herbert's come home. Run out and get a quart of beer."

Over supper and during the rest of the evening he told them the trouble he had had with Betty.

"Well, you're well out of it, Herbert," said Mrs. Sunbury when he had finished. "I told you she was no wife for you. Common she is, common as dirt, and you who's always been brought up so nice."

He found it good to sleep in his own bed, the bed he'd been used to all his life, and to come down to breakfast on the Sunday morning, unshaved and unwashed, and read the *News of the World*.

"We won't go to chapel this morning," said Mrs. Sunbury. "It's been an upset to you, Herbert; we'll take it easy today."

During the week they talked a lot about the kite, but they also talked a lot about Betty. They discussed what she would do next.

"She'll try and get you back," said Mrs. Sunbury.

"A fat chance she's got of doing that," said Herbert.

"You'll have to provide for her," said his father.

304

THE KITE

"Why should he do that?" cried Mrs. Sunbury. "She trapped him into marrying her and now she's turned him out of the home he made for her."

"I'll give her what's right as long as she leaves me alone."

He was feeling more comfortable every day, in fact he was beginning to feel as if he'd never been away, he settled in like a dog in its own particular basket; it was nice having his mother to brush his clothes and mend his socks; she gave him the sort of things he'd always eaten and liked best; Betty was a scrappy sort of cook, it had been fun just at first, like picnicking, but it wasn't the sort of eating a man could get his teeth into, and he could never get over his mother's idea that fresh food was better than the stuff you bought in tins. He got sick of the sight of tinned salmon. Then it was nice to have space to move about in rather than be cooped up in two small rooms, one of which had to serve as kitchen as well.

"I never made a bigger mistake in my life than when I left home, Mum," he said to her once.

"I know that, Herbert, but you're back now and you've got no cause ever to leave it again."

His salary was paid on Friday and in the evening when they had just finished supper the bell rang.

"That's her," they said with one voice.

Herbert went pale. His mother gave him a glance.

"You leave it to me," she said. "I'll see her."

She opened the door. Betty was standing on the threshold. She tried to push her way in, but Mrs. Sunbury prevented her.

"I want to see Herb."

"You can't. He's out."

"No, he isn't. I watched him go in with his dad and he hasn't come out again."

"Well, he doesn't want to see you, and if you start making a disturbance I'll call the police."

"I want my week's money."

"That's all you've ever wanted of him." She took out her purse. "There's thirty-five shillings for you."

305

CREATURES OF CIRCUMSTANCE

"Thirty-five shillings? The rent's twelve shillings a week."

"That's all you're going to get. He's got to pay his board here, hasn't he?"

"And then there's the instalments on the furniture."

"We'll see about that when the time comes. D'you want the money or don't you?"

Confused, unhappy, browbeaten, Betty stood irresolutely. Mrs. Sunbury thrust the money in her hand and slammed the door in her face. She went back to the dining-room.

"I've settled her hash all right," she said.

The bell rang again, it rang repeatedly, but they did not answer it, and presently it stopped. They guessed that Betty had gone away.

It was fine next day, with just the right velocity in the wind, and Herbert, after failing two or three times, found he had got the knack of flying the big box-kite. It soared into the air and up and up as he unreeled the wire.

"Why, it's a mile up if it's a yard," he told his mother excitedly.

He had never had such a thrill in his life.

Several weeks passed by. They concocted a letter for Herbert to write in which he told Betty that so long as she didn't molest him or members of his family she would receive a postal order for thirty-five shillings every Saturday morning and he would pay the instalments on the furniture as they came due. Mrs. Sunbury had been much against this, but Mr. Sunbury, for once at variance with her, and Herbert agreed that it was the right thing to do. Herbert by then had learnt the ways of the new kite and was able to do great things with it. He no longer bothered to have contests with the other kite-flyers. He was out of their class. Saturday afternoons were his moments of glory. He revelled in the admiration he aroused in the bystanders and enjoyed the envy he knew he excited in the less fortunate flyers. Then one evening when he was walking back from the station with his father Betty waylaid him.

"Hulloa, Herb," she said.

306

"Hulloa."

"I want to talk to my husband alone, Mr. Sunbury."

"There's nothing you've got to say to me that my dad can't hear," said Herbert sullenly.

She hesitated. Mr. Sunbury fidgeted. He didn't know whether to stay or go.

"All right, then," she said. "I want you to come back home, Herb. I didn't mean it that night when I packed your bag. I only did it to frighten you. I was in a temper. I'm sorry for what I did. It's all so silly, quarrelling about a kite."

"Well, I'm not coming back, see. When you turned me out you did me the best turn you ever did me."

Tears began to trickle down Betty's cheeks.

"But I love you, Herb. If you want to fly your silly old kite, you fly it, I don't care so long as you come back."

"Thank you very much, but it's not good enough. I know when I'm well off and I've had enough of married life to last me a lifetime. Come on, Dad."

They walked on quickly and Betty made no attempt to follow them. On the following Sunday they went to chapel and after dinner Herbert went to the coal-shed where they kept the kite to have a look at it. He just couldn't keep away from it. He doted on it. In a minute he rushed back, his face white, with a hatchet in his hand.

"She's smashed it up. She did it with this."

The Sunburys gave a cry of consternation and hurried to the coal-shed. What Herbert had said was true. The kite, the new, expensive kite, was in fragments. It had been savagely attacked with the hatchet, the woodwork was all in pieces, the reel was hacked to bits.

"She must have done it while we were at chapel. Watched us go out, that's what she did."

"But how did she get in?" asked Mr. Sunbury.

"I had two keys. When I came home I noticed one was missing, but I didn't think anything about it."

"You can't be sure she did it, some of them fellows on the

307

common have been very snooty, I wouldn't put it past them to have done this."

"Well, we'll soon find out," said Herbert. "I'll go and ask her, and if she did it I'll kill her."

His rage was so terrible that Mrs. Sunbury was frightened.

"And get yourself hung for murder? No, Herbert, I won't let you go. Let your dad go, and when he comes back we'll decide what to do."

"That's right, Herbert, let me go."

They had a job to persuade him, but in the end Mr. Sunbury went. In half an hour he came back.

"She did it all right. She told me straight out. She's proud of it. I won't repeat her language, it fair startled me, but the long and short of it was she was jealous of the kite. She said Herbert loved the kite more than he loved her and so she smashed it up and if she had to do it again she'd do it again."

"Lucky she didn't tell me that. I'd have wrung her neck even if I'd had to swing for it. Well, she never gets another penny out of me, that's all."

"She'll sue you," said his father.

"Let her."

"The instalment on the furniture is due next week, Herbert," said Mrs. Sunbury quietly. "In your place I wouldn't pay it."

"Then they'll just take it away," said Samuel, "and all the money he's paid on it so far will be wasted."

"Well, what of it?" she answered. "He can afford it. He's rid of her for good and all and we've got him back and that's the chief thing."

"I don't care twopence about the money," said Herbert. "I can see her face when they come and take the furniture away. It meant a lot to her, it did, and the piano, she set a rare store on that piano."

So on the following Friday he did not send Betty her weekly money, and when she sent him on a letter from the furniture people to say that if he didn't pay the instalment due by such and such a date they would remove it, he wrote back and said

308

he wasn't in a position to continue the payments and they could remove the furniture at their convenience. Betty took to waiting for him at the station, and when he wouldn't speak to her followed him down the street screaming curses at him. In the evenings she would come to the house and ring the bell till they thought they would go mad, and Mr. and Mrs. Sunbury had the greatest difficulty in preventing Herbert from going out and giving her a sound thrashing. Once she threw a stone and broke the sitting-room window. She wrote obscene and abusive postcards to him at his office. At last she went to the magistrate's court and complained that her husband had left her and wasn't providing for her support. Herbert received a summons. They both told their story and if the magistrate thought it a strange one he didn't say so. He tried to effect a reconciliation between them, but Herbert resolutely refused to go back to his wife. The magistrate ordered him to pay Betty twenty-five shillings a week. He said he wouldn't pay it.

"Then you'll go to prison," said the magistrate. "Next case."

But Herbert meant what he said. On Betty's complaint he was brought once more before the magistrate, who asked him what reason he had for not obeying the order.

"I said I wouldn't pay her and I won't, not after she smashed my kite. And if you send me to prison I'll go to prison."

The magistrate was very stern with him this time.

"You're a very foolish young man," he said. "I'll give you a week to pay the arrears, and if I have any more nonsense from you you'll go to prison till you come to your senses."

Herbert didn't pay, and that is how my friend Ned Preston came to know him and I heard the story.

"What d'you make of it?" asked Ned as he finished. "You know, Betty isn't a bad girl. I've seen her several times, there's nothing wrong with her except her insane jealousy of Herbert's kite; and he isn't a fool by any means. In fact he's smarter than the average. What d'you suppose there is in kite-flying that makes the damned fool so mad about it?"

"I don't know," I answered. I took my time to think. "You

see, I don't know a thing about flying a kite. Perhaps it gives him a sense of power as he watches it soaring towards the clouds and of mastery over the elements as he seems to bend the winds of heaven to his will. It may be that in some queer way he identifies himself with the kite flying so free and so high above him, and it's as it were an escape from the monotony of life. It may be that in some dim, confused way it represents an ideal of freedom and adventure. And you know, when a man once gets bitten with the virus of the ideal not all the King's doctors and not all the King's surgeons can rid him of it. But all this is very fanciful and I dare say it's just stuff and nonsense. I think you'd better put your problem before someone who knows a lot more about the psychology of the human animal than I do."

*This book was designed
by William B. Taylor
for Heron Books, London*

Printed in Switzerland